Tuscan Shadows

Tuscan Shadows

Maureen Donegan

ROBERT HALE · LONDON

© Maureen Donegan 2001
First published in Great Britain 2001

ISBN 0 7090 6961 8

Robert Hale Limited
Clerkenwell House
Clerkenwell Green
London EC1R 0HT

The right of Maureen Donegan to be identified as
author of this work has been asserted by her
in accordance with the Copyright, Designs and
Patents Act 1988.

2 4 6 8 10 9 7 5 3 1

Typeset by
Derek Doyle & Associates, Liverpool.
Printed in Great Britain by
St Edmundsbury Press Ltd, Bury St Edmunds, Suffolk.
Bound by Woolnough Bookbinding Limited.

For Bonita

I would like to acknowledge the valuable suggestions made by Bonita Brindley, Evelyn Clancy, Paul Mitchell and Tom Hazekamp.

My grateful thanks are also due to Massimo and Roberto who patiently answered questions about *carabinieri* procedures. Any errors and omissions are, of course, entirely my own.

Maureen Donegan

CHAPTER 1

Rose rang the doorbell of an elegant house in London and for one dismaying moment wondered how many times she had done this, how many interviews she had been to and how many temporary, Arthur would say unsuitable, jobs she had taken in the past few years.

She didn't often think like this, at least she tried not to. A couple of days before Arthur had asked her what she could possibly be getting out of this chaotic lifestyle of hers.

She could hear his voice again. 'You can't go on like this forever, Rose, you're thirty-six.' He'd hesitated and then said, 'Is it because you want to get away from me?'

'No,' she said, 'no, of course not.' And put her arms around him so that he couldn't see her face. When she was with Arthur she always felt either grateful or guilty.

But the question had disturbed her. What was she getting out of these jobs? Was it simply that she preferred it to what Arthur called, 'putting her life in order'?

The door was opened by a small grey-haired woman in a well cut but severe navy suit. 'You must be Ms. . . ?'

'Rose Childs.'

'I'm Mrs Venables-Brown. Please come in.'

Coffee in large mugs was brought by a blonde *au pair*. Mrs Venables-Brown looked at the girl over her gold rimmed half-glasses.

8   *Maureen Donegan*

'I thought the blue cups, Ilse . . .' she said faintly. The girl ignored her and flounced out.

'I'm sorry,' Mrs Venables-Brown said, 'but nowadays . . .' She sighed expressively then tapped Rose's letter of application which was lying on the table. 'You do realize that you are totally over-qualified, Ms Childs . . . a degree in history and then the Royal College of Art. . . .' She sighed again. Her eyes travelled slowly downwards over Rose's calf-length, blue cotton skirt and jacket and fixed a startled glance somewhere near Rose's feet. Rose wondered if her Birkenstock sandals had been a mistake. Or perhaps it was her bag. It was too bright, too ethnic, too. . . .

Mrs Venables-Brown coughed and seemed to collect herself. 'Um . . . what we need . . . what my sister had in mind was . . . someone to act as a go-between. The Italian couple haven't a word of English and this year my sister has let the villa to an Englishwoman, a Mrs Tenby. Indeed I think most of the houseparty will be English speaking. Your Italian. . . ?'

'Slightly rusty, but some years ago I spent a term teaching in Turin. I don't anticipate any difficulty.'

'I see you also speak French and German.'

'Some. And restaurant Chinese,' Rose said. She grinned and Mrs Venables-Brown laughed.

'Well, you're certainly a refreshing change from some of the other people I've seen. Most of them, of course, were far too young.'

Ouch, Rose thought. Perhaps Arthur was right after all and she'd done enough of this sort of thing.

Since she'd given up regular teaching, her life had teetered precariously on the edge of an alternative existence. In the last few years she had been companion to a seventeen year old pyromaniac, driven an elderly Rolls-Royce for its owner, an equally ancient duchess, taught English to immigrant Asian children and accompanied an Australian businessman through Europe as girl-Friday-cum-interpreter. The latter job had almost resulted in a permanent break with Arthur.

Out loud she said, 'Tell me about your sister – about the villa. How many staff exactly? How are the housekeeping accounts arranged? Who would I contact if anything serious should go wrong?'

TUSCAN SHADOWS

'I don't anticipate any serious problems,' Mrs Venables-Brown said, in a bemused kind of way. She began to describe the villa and its day-to-day running.

'My sister will be visiting her son in Australia for a few months and, of course, you must have a contact address. In any case, you can always get in touch with me. I'll be here until mid-July and then in France for a couple of weeks. Last year we had a Greek girl, the daughter of some friends. It seemed to work, there were no big crises. The important thing is to be able to get on well with Maria-Grazia, she's the cook-housekeeper. She and her husband Giulio are the mainstay of Villa Antonia.' She smiled. 'Maria-Grazia is a bit special, but she has a heart of gold.'

Rose nodded. She had become an expert at reading between the lines at interviews and she knew that she would find out soon enough in what particular way Maria-Grazia was special. Nevertheless her heart sank slightly. 'Um, where exactly is the villa? You said Tuscany?'

'Capulana. It's on the coast, was a busy fishing village once but it's got very smart now.' Mrs Venables-Brown made a face. 'Full of "the beautiful people", but we still love it. It has a lot of charm.' She produced a hand drawn map. 'It's about two hours from Rome by train.'

Rose took the piece of paper but didn't look at it immediately. 'I think I know where it is. I was at school with a girl whose people had a house there.'

'What was the name?'

'Grenbelli. Do you know them?'

'Of course.' The older woman's face lit up. 'In fact Maria-Grazia and Giulio came to us from the Grenbellis. Let's see, your friend must have been Laura.'

'Yes, she's in Peru now, but we still write. She gave me this bag as a matter of fact.'

'Ah, it's very um . . . colourful.' But Mrs Venables-Brown had relaxed visibly and a look of comprehension passed over her face. 'I think that more or less settles it. I'm sure you're going to enjoy Villa Antonia, Ms Childs.'

Rose cancelled her subscription to the *Guardian* and arranged to let her flat to one of Arthur's former students. Arthur was being helpful but predictably pessimistic.

'I haven't forgotten the time you barely escaped with your life in that fire,' he said.

'Oh Arthur, don't exaggerate. The girl was disturbed; I knew that from the beginning. And it was only a little fire.'

'It wasn't only a little fire. You ended up in hospital.'

'Only overni—'

'Because,' Arthur went on inexorably, 'you thought you could put it out yourself.'

'But I did.'

A picture of the girl dancing in the gazebo flashed into her mind. There were crackling yellow tongues around her and the roof groaned and swayed against the night sky. Rose shuddered at the memory and hoped that Arthur wouldn't notice.

'I made a considered decision,' she said, as calmly as she could. She'd grabbed the girl and thrown her own dressing-gown over her and they'd escaped just before the roof fell. With its collapse the fire had been contained and the danger to the surrounding trees averted. She'd worked it out, in a split second, and had been proved right. 'As I've told you a hundred times,' she said, irritated.

The girl, still high on the elation of the shooting flames and sparks, had danced her way down to the stream and carried buckets of water under Rose's orders and together they'd reduced the fire to a heap of smoking ashes.

'You had to have your hair cut off,' Arthur said, 'and that was the least of—'

'It grew again.' She ran her fingers through her springy dark curls. 'Are we having a row, Arthur?'

'No, but I'm concerned about you. You think you can handle everything yourself. A one-woman SAS.'

'No, I don't. In any case this is quite different. It's a perfectly normal holiday let and the tenant is English.'

'And there was the time you were arrested for carrying hash from Morocco.'

'Nearly arrested. And it wasn't hash; it was camomile for the duchess.'

TUSCAN SHADOWS

'What I'm saying is that your life, the way you conduct it, leads to . . . to well, misunderstandings at the very least and downright danger more often than not.'

'You could come out to Italy later on,' she said, quickly. Too quickly. Damn, why do I always end up placating him? But she knew why. When Arthur expressed concern about her she was always reminded of how much she owed him, how his calm, loving presence had entered her life at a time when she most needed constancy. She'd had one very destructive relationship and was beginning to be afraid that she might always choose men who would cause her pain. Arthur had replaced uncertainty with safety. She remembered their first night together, the flowers, the dinner, the cautious invitation to come up for a last drink, the clean sheets, the whole evening so carefully organized that it had been a relief not to mention a pleasure to let him take over. She remembered too the warm and satisfied awakening the next morning to a smell of fresh coffee and croissants brought to her by a freshly showered and shaved Arthur.

Arthur was a stimulating companion, someone she could say anything to, someone who organized his life well and had the gift of making his surroundings enviously warm and welcoming. Arthur was also a skilled cook. A bit pretentious though. She had a momentary stab of guilt as she remembered Stefan and the night of the nettle soup. But it was the home-loving qualities in Arthur, so unexpected in such a physical man, that had first broken down her defences.

Certainly she had never felt an edge-of-the-precipice longing for him. It was something she wondered about in the dead hours of the night. Instead, she had accepted him the way one would slip into a warm and soothing bath. But since the incident of the nettle soup, which had in turn led to the incident of Stefan, a reluctant fondness and perhaps a desire to make amends had taken the place of what she had thought of as love.

Arthur had forgiven her, but she had never really forgiven herself.

'You know nothing about these people,' he said now. 'They could be Mafia, or ex-train robbers. Did you ask for references?'

'It's usually the employer who does that,' Rose said, mixing a salad. 'I gave your name in fact.'

12   *Maureen Donegan*

'I don't remember you asking my permission.'

'You gave it years ago. Before I went to Turin.'

'That was for a specific job.'

'And so is this. Oh, do stop looking so cross, Arthur, and open the wine.'

'I could tell them you were a kleptomaniac,' he said.

'You could.' She gave him the grin that had disarmed Mrs Venables-Brown. 'If you never wanted to see me again.'

He came over and put his arms around her. 'When are you going to . . .'

'. . . get a proper job?'

'That wasn't what I was going to say.'

She knew it wasn't. 'I think you're just jealous,' she said, lightly, to head him off. 'You'd like to be flying off to Italy, too, following your beloved Dante.'

'But you're going to be a kind of servant!'

'No, I won't. I'll be drinking *chianti* in its natural habitat and eating apricots straight from the tree.'

But she knew, and so did he, that it wouldn't really be like that.

'You're an incurable romantic,' he said gloomily, 'and there'll be all those passionate Mediterranean types.'

'Good,' she said. She patted his hand affectionately.' But you know I love you.'

'As a friend,' he said. His face crumpled into a look of dismay. 'Rose, I know you don't find me very romantic. . . .'

She leaned over and touched his face. 'Oh, Arthur, come on. You know I'll write.'

CHAPTER 2

Gillian Tenby, packing in her recently inherited house in Berkshire, was also defending her position.

'All those Chiantishire types sitting around drinking their heads off,' her son Dom said. 'It's just not my kind of thing.'

'But you will try to come for a couple of weeks, darling. You might be pleasantly surprised.'

'And why did you ask Frankie and Johnny?'

'Peter and Johnny.' Gillian Tenby gave him a wary smile. 'I thought you liked Peter.'

'I don't know what makes you think that. I reckon he's a remittance man. Honestly Mum you're an absolute sucker for—'

'He's very amusing.'

'And you hardly know Johnny.'

'It's his yacht.'

'Yes, I know, but how does Johnny's girlfriend fit in?'

'She doesn't like sailing,' Gillian said, 'and I can certainly sympathize with that. So, she'd prefer to stay at the villa. And Peter said Johnny wouldn't come without her. I think it's quite natural they'd want to be together.'

Dom laughed. 'Natural, Mum?'

'Well, you know what I mean. Anyway they say the rich are different.'

'But are they? Rich, I mean?'

'Elizabeth Halliwell is. You could do worse than cultivate her.'

'You're joking.'

She looked at him thoughtfully. 'Yes, I suppose I am.'

Dom was very like her, although as fair as she was dark and lean and rangy where she was, to her intense annoyance, short and rather stocky, but she dealt with this by rigorous dieting and exercise. She ran her hand down the curve of her hip. She would have to eat nothing, absolutely nothing, before she went to Italy. It was more important than ever to make herself as perfect as possible. Even though, she thought wryly, she'd been given only moderately good material to work with.

But that made the challenge all the greater and Gillian liked challenges. In fact, she'd always known that life had something special in store for her and finally she was going to realize that promise. She imagined the villa covered with bougainvillaea, a sunlit terrace, wine and . . . excitement. Dom might sneer at Chiantishire, but the Sunday-supplement life was exactly what she wanted, at least for a while.

But another part of Gillian had always craved security which was why she had married Donald. Now that he was dead she didn't have to plead for the use of the car, to cajole him for his reluctant agreement to open their house to the drama group, or to let her off the leash for a few precious days in London. In spite of Donald's hostility, she had always managed to gather offbeat and sensitive people around her. Being boring was the worst of all possible crimes in Gillian's book.

Neither mother nor son had conventional good looks but both had a louche air. Gillian also had the kind of charisma which made her appear to share completely the concerns of whoever she was with. People were drawn to her. Peter Kinaid had been drawn to her at that party last winter.

'Susie's going, isn't that enough family?' Dom knew better than to criticize his mother's new enthusiasms too much.

'Oh darling, you know how fond I am of her, but she's not half as much fun as you.'

He eyed her cases. 'All this holiday business doesn't mean you won't be able to help me, does it? I mean, what is it all going to cost?'

'Please don't talk about money, Dom. Not now. I've told you, we'll deal with your overdraft when we get back.'

*

Susie, her stepdaughter, was also packing and thinking about how unfair it all was. At first, she'd decided to stay behind, but Gillian had let the house for the summer, the house where she, Susie, had spent her early childhood with her father and her own mother. She'd lost her mother and inherited Gillian and then . . . but she didn't want to think about her father. And now she was being virtually kicked out of her own home.

Susie pushed a heavy sweater into her case. For once she would make her own plans. She was going to Denmark first and Gillian could say what she liked. She would stay there as long as it suited her, or as long as her friend made her welcome, and then go on to Italy, and she was only doing that because Mike wanted to go. He could meet her there if he was so keen to see the famous villa.

Alison and Keith Drinkwater, who lived near the Tenbys, had suggested Susie go in the car with them, but that would tie her down too much. And Alison had become very . . . unfocused, lately. She felt bad even thinking this. Alison had always been very good to her.

She went to the wardrobe and took out a rolled-up plaid shirt which she'd borrowed from her father after she'd put on so much weight. She held it to her face and imagined that she could still smell his pipe tobacco. She felt tears welling behind her eyes and rubbed them fiercely with the cloth.

Daddy, she thought, would have hated all this. She wished he was there now, whistling for the dogs. They had had a favourite walk past the old saw mill with its redolent smell of resin, along the bank of the stream and into Boden's wood. A sharp pain knifed through her. She still hadn't taken it in.

She put the shirt into the case and slammed down the lid. Fortunately, Mike had to work the first week and that had made it easy for her to get out of travelling in a foursome with Dom and Gillian. And after the holiday the flat would be ready, and she would have Mike all to herself.

The Hon. Johnny Langdon Smythe was already in Italy. His boat, *L'Alba*, was moored in a small island harbour south of Sardinia. Access to the small pier was by a steep rough track and the surrounding hills had a fortress-like appearance. The local population was no more friendly than the terrain but the paid hand, Pino, was a Sard and had contacts in the village. He organized

16   *Maureen Donegan*

their supplies and spent long hours drinking beer and playing scopone in the only bar.

Johnny lay on the deck in the brilliant sunshine squinting occasionally at the gap in the hills. He spread his fingers to ensure an even tan between them and his companion dug him in the ribs and giggled.

'You're like a stranded starfish.'

'I feel like one.'

'Go on,' Peter Kinaid said. 'Thousands would give their eye teeth to be in a spot like this. Imagine tourist coaches on the pass.'

'Mmm,' Johnny brightened. 'Going over the edge.'

'It could happen. I saw a beach umbrella in the bar yesterday. Still in its plastic wrapper. And they were washing down the table.'

Johnny sighed and rolled over on his back. 'It's not the place, it's the waiting. It's like sitting on a bomb. Why haven't we heard from Nardi? He was in enough of a hurry to get the stuff here.'

'He'll get in touch.'

'He'd better. It would have been a lot easier to deliver on the mainland.'

'Suppose so.'

'Maybe Nardi was a mistake.'

'I dunno.'

'He's too big. Safer with Pulcini.'

'Pulcini was small fry.'

'Not that small.'

'You were the one who wanted to play with the big boys.'

'And now they're playing with us.'

'Ah, for God's sake.'

'And there's another thing. Why do we have to go to that wretched woman's villa?'

'I promised. And she did say Elizabeth could come.'

Johnny was silent for a few moments. 'I suppose it might be all right. Elizabeth likes that sort of thing.' He said this without much conviction. Elizabeth wouldn't know anyone there and that meant he would have to make a bigger effort. But Villa Antonia would be a good cover.

'We'll be able to move in a few days.' Peter gave the older man a look from under his lashes. 'When you've worked up a tan.'

'When I've worked up a tan,' Johnny repeated. He sometimes felt that life would be so much simpler without Peter. It would certainly be simpler without Franco Nardi. He didn't want to admit to Peter that he had been flattered when one of Nardi's people approached him. He'd thought working with an organization like that meant you got protection. So long as you toed the line. But now it was Nardi who wasn't coming up to scratch. And going back to Pulcini would be difficult once he'd been involved with another more distant branch of the Family.

At least Peter was a great crew, he told himself. He supplied other needs, too, but Johnny had learned long ago not to believe in happy ever after. For a brief moment he imagined spending the whole summer like this, sailing to remote coves, just the two of them, fishing for sardines, cooking potatoes in sea water and washing it all down with local wine. Pipe dreams.

Instead, there were packets of smoked salmon and pre-prepared gourmet meals in the freezer and Johnny wasn't sure whether they were there to please Peter, or to reinforce the paid hand's notion of what an English Honourable should eat.

He pushed these thoughts away and murmured, 'Rub some oil on my back.'

Later, he lay awake in the relative coolness of their cabin. He touched Peter's shoulder length hair, bleached almost white by the sun and remembered the hot brilliance of his blue eyes only a short time before. Easy for him to sleep, he thought.

But it had been a good day, made all the better by Pino's absence. It had been a mistake to take on someone with the Sard's predilection. Peter liked Pino. Too much.

Johnny felt he was losing control of the situation. This Tenby woman, for instance. Peter was uncharacteristically keen to go to the Villa Antonia and Johnny didn't know why. Surely there wasn't a boy there that Peter wanted? He struggled to remember where Peter had met the owner. Some dinner in London with a man in advertising?

The back of his neck was wet and little rivers of sweat ran down his chest. He stroked Peter's face, then eased his body away and went to have a shower.

18   *Maureen Donegan*

He was sitting on the deck smoking a cigarette when the soft sound of oars heralded Pino's return. He caught the painter and tied on the dinghy.

'Nothing,' the Sard said in reply to his questioning look. 'I'll go back again tomorrow.'

Johnny gave him a hand up on to the deck. 'Open a bottle of wine,' he said abruptly, 'and we'll talk about it in the morning.'

At the Villa Antonia, Maria-Grazia Muletti and her husband Giulio were also contemplating the summer.

'An English *professoressa* to look after the guests,' Maria-Grazia said loudly. 'She'll just want to boss us around.'

'She might be better than Melina.'

Maria-Grazia grunted and shifted her ample arms on the kitchen table. 'She couldn't be much worse.'

'English people will be all right,' Giulio said.

'Spanish, German, Italian, they're all the same.' She laughed suddenly. 'But the worst was that old French viper, the *marchesa*, sliding in and out of the kitchen, spreading poison everywhere.'

Giulio smiled at his wife affectionately. He enjoyed her sharp tongue so long as it wasn't directed at himself.

'English people are *molto per bene*,' he said. 'They behave well. And they do not demand dinner at eleven at night.'

'Do you remember the year of the Spanish?' Maria-Grazia said. Giulio gave a reminiscent smile. He was thinking not of the Spanish, who had turned night into day, but of the Italians of the previous year, swimming topless and occasionally dispensing with the other half of their bikinis too.

'The English will drink whisky and soda and the men will smoke pipes,' he said authoritatively. 'And they will burn their skin and get sunstroke. But there will be no orgies.' He added regretfully, 'They are very cold people.'

Maria-Grazia grunted.

'You will see,' Giulio said. 'Meals will be on time and everything will go smoothly.'

'I hope so.' Maria-Grazia let out her breath in a long whistling sigh and then began to tick off items on her fingers. 'Have you had the car serviced?'

'*Si, cara.*'

'And collected a spare gas bombola?'

'*Si, cara.*'

'And rung the technician for the ice machine?'

'*Si, cara.*'

Franco Nardi put down the telephone and stared out of the open french windows at the calm lake below. Beyond was Switzerland, and that was where he had been advised to go. At least for a while until Rossi, his accountant, had resolved a number of problems. But that would mean putting too much power into his hands. He needed to stay in the country, at the centre of things, to stay in control. He tapped the receiver with his thick fingers. There was a well-established route to settle such matters, but what Rossi had said made him uneasy about just how secure it was. Not everyone, he thought bitterly, had a price these days.

He heard the dogs barking and a car drawing up outside and a few moments later his younger daughter, Francesca, came around the corner, smiling. The rest of the family had already gone to Tuscany but she had stayed behind to travel with him.

'*Papi.*' They embraced and he ruffled her long blonde hair. 'You're ready?'

'Not quite. Some business things. . . .'

She pouted. 'But we can go today?'

'Maybe.'

'Oh, *Papi!*' When she looked at him like that he could see her mother's face, not as it was when she lay ill and dying, but in the full freshness of youth. Francesca was his favourite child and he had never been able to say 'no' to her, nor did he want her to see how worried he was.

'Let me make a couple of calls, then,' he said, smiling.

She hugged him again. 'Don't be too long.'

He didn't pick up the phone until she was out of the room. Better settle with the Englishmen. They'd delivered, but a couple of things were broken. Or so they said. Fucking amateurs. He'd seen them pottering around in their boat the year before, had thought their cover was good, but he'd come to realize they were both loose cannons. He barked an order down the phone, listened for a moment then cut the call and began to punch in his accountant's number again.

Rose peered through the window of the car as it slowed to pass through a rose-covered arch and drew up with a scatter of gravel. She knew from Mrs Venables-Brown that the villa was only about twenty years old but, somehow, the building looked as though it had nestled there comfortably for centuries. In the courtyard, geraniums, marguerites and lavender bloomed in earthenware pots and opposite was a two-storey annex partly covered with honeysuckle and bougainvillaea.

From a side door, a plump, white-aproned woman looked towards the car without expression. Rose took a deep breath and went over, her hand outstretched.

'You must be Maria-Grazia,' she said. 'I'm Rose. Rosa in Italian.'

'*Benvenuta*,' Maria-Grazia said. Her mouth twitched slightly. 'Come in, come in.' She bustled Rose into a large kitchen with a red *cotto* floor and Giulio was despatched to another part of the house with the luggage.

'You are an artist?' Maria-Grazia asked, giving Rose's painting equipment a hard stare.

Rose smiled. 'Only for fun. To relax.'

Maria-Grazia nodded uncomprehendingly. 'When I need to relax I lie down.'

'Much more sensible,' Rose said.

Maria-Grazia made some coffee and explained that she was putting Rose in one of the guest rooms for the time being. Her hands gripped together on the table. 'Tonight I make *gnocchi*.' She waved towards a marble table where rows of potato pasta were arranged. 'You like Italian food?' she asked anxiously.

'I love it. And I've heard you're a wonderful cook.'

Maria-Grazia smiled, finally. 'Food is important.'

Rose followed her into the main hall and took in an impression of pale walls and dark beams and then Maria-Grazia opened large double doors and drew back full-length, fine, white lawn curtains from the windows which filled the opposite wall. The room was furnished with big comfortable chairs in the English style, an eighteenth century bureau and a marble topped console. A large Hariz rug partly covered the polished floor and at the far end of the room sat a long, dark refectory table.

A stone fireplace was full of flowers and above it perched a seventeenth century Venetian mirror. Some scenes of Tuscany, several Piranesi prints of Rome and a portrait of a woman who looked very much like Mrs Venables-Brown decorated the other walls.

'*La signora*,' Maria-Grazia said, waving at the picture. She opened the doors to a long veranda. Far below, an olive grove spread green and grey shadows over dry, golden grass. In the distance, a medieval hill town shimmered in the heat and between was the vast plain Rose had passed through in the car with Giulio.

'It's wonderful,' she said.

Maria-Grazia sniffed. '*E molto lavoro.*'

She led the way down some shallow stone steps to another flower filled terrace and Rose realized that her impression of a single-storey farmhouse had been an illusion and that there was another floor below the main part of the house.

'*La signora* said it was built like this because of the hill,' Maria-Grazia said. 'They had a famous architect from Rome, but me, I think it was stupid.' She pushed back one of the slatted outer doors revealing a bedroom with more dark beams and white walls. A bowl of fresh lavender on a table by the bed helped to disperse a slightly shut-in smell. 'You will be all right here?' she asked.

'Yes, of course. It's lovely. You have gone to a lot of trouble.'

'It is what I always do. Do you need *acqua minerale* for your teeth? The water is good here but I thought as you were English. . . ?'

Rose shook her head.

'Then after you have rested I will show you the other rooms and the annexe.'

'Thank you very much,' Rose said. Maria-Grazia responded with the vestige of an anachronistic bob of the head.

She's nervous, she thought, as Maria-Grazia went out into a corridor, closing the door gently behind her. I wonder what sort of ogre she expected?

Or does she think I have to be waited on? It would be as well to dispel that idea as quickly as possible.

She had a shower and then put on a cotton dress and made her way back up to the main part of the house via the inner corridor and a flight of tiled steps. There was no one in the kitchen or in any part of the house that she could see. She went out into the courtyard and then through a low iron gate. The fall of the land was held by cultivated terraces, one green with staked vines, the others with herbs and vegetables. The path petered out into a flight of stone steps leading to a mushroom-shaped swimming pool. From where she stood, the pool seemed to be cantilevered along an outcrop of rock hanging precariously above a sheer drop on to the plain below. As she got nearer she saw that the red-tiled surround of the pool was flanked by flower beds and a low wall guarded the far end where the land sheered off into a landscape which could have changed little for centuries. A good place to paint, she thought.

Later, she toured the house with Maria-Grazia, praised the extreme cleanliness of everything and admired the numerous gadgets in the kitchen.

'But most of them are *stupidi*,' Maria-Grazia said.

She gave Rose a typed list of house rules, in English and Italian. 'This is for the guests. Read it so that you can tell them if they are not doing the right things.'

'Um . . . such as?'

'Not having meals on time. That is the worst thing of all because if breakfast is late, then so is lunch. We get no *siesta* and then they play tennis when it is cooler and want dinner at ten. Or eleven.'

'We'll try to keep them up to scratch.' Rose was beginning to see what her role was to be. She could hear Arthur's voice saying, 'Neither fish nor fowl.'

She smiled as reassuringly as she could. 'And now you must tell me where I can best help out. I can wait on table and sweep and dust.'

Maria-Grazia gave her a look of pleased surprise. '*Beh*, there are plenty of all those things. And you can help us with the shopping list. It is always difficult and they will want strange things.'

Later they sat down to the *gnocchi* rich with fresh tomato sauce and parmisan cheese. It melted in the mouth and Rose said, truthfully, 'I've never tasted better.' She raised her glass. 'To a good summer!'

'*Beh*,' Maria-Grazia said, but she smiled.

Rose jumped up to help clear the table.

'Sit down, sit down, it's your first day,' Maria-Grazia said. 'And tomorrow you can swim in the pool if you wish, enjoy the peace.' She glared balefully at the door to the dining-room. 'It will not last long.'

L'Alba cut through the calm sea, a straight line creaming the dark water behind them. A three-quarter moon lit the sea and the air was warm but much fresher than during the day. Peter was at the helm. The wind was light but steady and the sky was so clear that the stars seemed almost within reach. Pino was asleep below and Johnny sat beside Peter in the cockpit smoking.

'Ten minutes on this tack,' Johnny said.

'I'm watching it. Why don't you put your head down?'

'Not yet.' The cigarette glowed as he drew on it before throwing it into the water. 'We could be the only people in the world,' he said.

'Yes.'

'Did Pino clean up the hold?' The hold was a rather grand name for a locker hidden behind the head.

'Yes, I think so.'

'You only think so? I saw bits of packing straw in there. Check it tomorrow yourself.'

'OK, OK.'

Johnny put his hand briefly on Peter's bare knee and the younger man smiled in the half darkness. 'You know what, Peterkins?'

'What?'

'We're in the wrong time warp. Should have been born in the eighteenth century, we could be challenging privateers and dodging the excise men.'

Peter laughed. 'You mean we're not?'

'Steering by the stars,' Johnny went on, dreamily, 'no engine, no radar.'

'You're feeling better.'

'Much. But I wish I knew what went wrong. Three days like sitting ducks . . .' He paused. 'Elizabeth talked about an autumn wedding.'

Peter didn't answer. He knew this mood, knew it would pass, but it still frightened him.

'Perhaps spring would be a better time,' Johnny said, after a while.

'And next summer?'

Johnny laughed. 'Another Mediterranean cruise. Elizabeth could take her own villa, invite her father and his widow-woman for company.'

Peter felt his tension draining away. Johnny was trailing his coat, that was all. Taking it out on him because the courier's lateness had terrified the life out of him. It had terrified Peter, too, but the adrenalin gave him a charge. He needed it, needed the fear and the wash of relief that followed it. It was better than sex, almost.

'You know,' Johnny said in a slow voice, 'the first time I went on a boat was on the lake at Herrin. I must have been about three or four. I remember holding my hand under the water, how cold it was and the splash of the oars. My father was teaching my brother to row. He always got to do things first did Alun, but he wasn't much good.'

'Not like you.'

'Not like me, no.'

It was a story Peter had heard dozens of times, but he didn't mind how often it was repeated. When Johnny talked about Herrin Park it meant he was relaxed. And its existence didn't worry Peter too much. Alun, Lord Stennington, might live for years despite his heart condition and Johnny's inheritance would be postponed indefinitely. Or Lady Stennington might have a child after all. Didn't infertile women sometimes have a rush of hormones in middle age? Sometimes he even teased Johnny about becoming an uncle but only when he was in a particularly good mood. Tonight he decided not to risk it.

The wind slackened slightly and Peter trimmed the sails. 'Engine?' he asked.

'We're not in a hurry, are we?' Johnny asked, lazily.

He caught the gleam of Johnny's smile in the silver light. 'Not in the slightest.'

Maria-Grazia sat at the kitchen table sucking a stub of pencil, a frown between her eyes. Giulio sat opposite.

'Flour,' she said. 'Bread, *acqua minerale*.'

Giulio wrote obediently and then Rose saw that Maria-Grazia's paper had a few irregular letters on it, such as a child might make.

'*Prosciutto crudo*, butter, eggs and sugar,' Maria-Grazia said. 'That's all.'

She can't write, Rose realized with a shocked stab of pity. No wonder she found the shopping lists difficult. She picked up her cup and plate and moved away discreetly to rinse them. Maria-Grazia would hardly want her illiteracy commented on, although she must be aware that she couldn't hide it for very long. Rose stood at the window and gazed out at the brilliant flowers in the courtyard while Giulio repeated his list and Maria-Grazia gazed uncertainly at her own.

It was difficult, Rose thought, to reconcile Maria-Grazia, the bustling, efficient cook, with this anxious woman labouring over a scrap of paper.

Later she wrote to Arthur and tried to describe her impressions. It was clear that the Mulettis were very fond of their *signora* but very much disliked the idea of strangers coming. She wondered what they thought about her and felt a sudden wave of loneliness. Stop it, she told herself, and wondered, not for the first time, why she felt closer to Arthur when he was physically far away than when they were together.

Keith Drinkwater drove off the car ferry and rather gingerly followed the signs for the *autoroute* to the south. His wife, Alison, who had been leaning back sleepily, opened her eyes and peered out.

'I thought we were going to Paris,' she said.

'We don't have time, love. I promised Gillian we'd be at the villa by Tuesday.'

'You promised me a night in Paris.'

Keith glanced at her uneasily, then quickly back at the road where French cars were passing him with angry Gallic hoots.

'Just let me get used to the driving, Alison.'

'You promised me,' she repeated. She reached into her large leather shoulder bag on the floor by her feet and took out a small glass phial and a bottle of water.

He watched her out of the corner of his eye. 'Please don't . . . I need you

26   *Maureen Donegan*

to navigate.' But it was too late. Alison was already washing down some more Valium. Or maybe it was something else. He didn't know how she managed to get the prescriptions, it certainly wasn't from their own doctor because he'd checked with him. He tried to remember how many times he'd seen pills in her hand.

'We could go to Paris on the way back.'

'We could,' Alison agreed. She closed her eyes again. 'But we won't. Gillian will have some scheme. A last meal in a "super restaurant".' She drew out the words in a fair imitation of Gillian's voice. 'Or to see a one-legged Italian dancer, or a manic-depressive's "wonderful paintings". We all know how artistic she is.'

Keith gripped the steering wheel hard. 'It's very kind of her to invite us. You are going to make an effort, aren't you, Alison?'

'Oh yes, I'll make an effort.' She smiled faintly to herself.

'Gillian's had a tough year, Donald's death. . . .'

'Poor bugger,' Alison said. Then she was silent.

Giulio took Rose with him on his shopping expedition. Capulana was bigger than she had imagined. The *centro storico* was perched high on a rock and a jumble of narrow streets and alleyways and was crowned by a church with a medieval tower. Below the old part of the town the fishing port was full of activity and, beyond the main harbour, a series of yacht marinas appeared to stretch for miles along a hinterland of pine woods. Rose stood for a few moments at the stone balustrade in the seventeenth-century piazza and looked down at the casually, but elegantly dressed people strolling along the waterfront with its smart boutiques and restaurants. Mrs Venables-Brown had described Capulana well, she thought.

She heard Giulio's voice and turned to see him in conversation with a tall man of around forty with thick dark hair. The man was asking if the visitors had arrived yet. He looked enquiringly at Rose and Giulio hastened to introduce them. 'This is Capitano Tavazzi,' he said.

'Rose Childs.' She held out her hand.

He drew his heels together. 'Sergio Tavazzi. How do you do?' he said in perfect English, and then laughed at her surprised expression. 'I was

brought up in Bedford,' he said. 'I'm an awkward mixture of two cultures.'
He turned back to Giulio. 'So, how many are you expecting this year?'

'Oh, six, eight, I'm not sure. Too many in any case.'

Sergio laughed and clapped him on the shoulder. '*Couraggio*, Giulio.' He
shook hands with Rose again. 'I hope you have a good summer,
Professoressa.'

Rose gazed after him as he took the steps of a large building two at a
time. 'How did he know I was. . . ?'

'He knows everything,' Giulio said proudly.

She grinned. 'I suppose he's a friend of yours and you told him?'

'Perhaps. I can't remember. But he is a friend of the *signora* too. It's not
so mysterious, Rose. He comes from here and it is a small place.'

'I suppose you know everyone,' Rose said.

'Not everyone. I'm from Naples and Maria-Grazia is Sicilian. We came
here to work for the Contessa Grenbelli years ago, but we're still foreigners,
if you like. Then the Grenbellis closed their house and we found a job
together with the Signora Martin.'

Rose hesitated for a moment. 'Yes, Mrs Venables-Brown told me. And
you like it here?'

'It's not so bad,' Giulio said. He gave an expressive shrug.

They made their way towards the market where ceramic pots rubbed
shoulders with imitation Valentino jeans and a profusion of fruit and vegetables were piled on stalls next to crates of live hens. On the way Giulio
saluted a slender, tanned woman with dark greying hair. She was wearing a
simple white linen dress with a heavily decorated brown leather belt; her bag
evidently came from the same designer, but she also carried a well-used
shopping basket full of apricots.

'Giulio! How are you? And how is Maria-Grazia?' She used the familiar *tu*
but Giulio responded with the formal *lei*. And then the woman noticed her.

'Rose!' she exclaimed.

'Lena,' Rose said. They embraced and Giulio looked from one to the
other uncertainly. 'How are you? And Laura?'

'Very well. Still in South America, and I hope to go out there in the
autumn. But what are you doing here? One of your amusing little jobs?'

'Something like that.'

'What heaven. You must come and see me and tell me all about it. We're staying in the Selvas' beach house. We closed the villa years ago you know.' She fumbled for a piece of paper in her bag and scribbled down a number. 'Whenever you can.'

'I'd love to,' Rose said, and they embraced again and then the other woman continued on her way and Rose saw her deliver her apricots to one of the stall holders.

Giulio had also seen this transaction. 'They still have the orchard,' he said, pulling down the corners of his mouth. He hesitated. 'She is a friend of yours, the *contessa*?'

'I was at school with her daughter.'

'Then you have been here before?'

'No. The villa was before my time. I stayed with them in Rome a couple of times.'

'I see,' Giulio said, but it was clear that he did not. He lapsed into a puzzled silence and over lunch it was evident that he had reported the encounter to Maria-Grazia because she barely spoke and then only in mono-syllables and dinner was conducted in the same awkward atmosphere.

It was a pity, because they'd begun to accept her but now it seemed they didn't know what to think. She didn't fit into their known world of masters and servants. Arthur, of course, had pointed this out before she left. All right, she thought firmly, as she went to her room with a book, one step forward and three steps back, but at least the library was all that had been promised.

Gillian had already given more than one sideways glance at the man in the window seat when the pilot announced that they had missed their slot and wouldn't be taking off for at least another twenty minutes.

She groaned and the man smiled sympathetically. 'Flying is supposed to be quicker but it seldom is,' he said.

'Well, we're only going as far as Tuscany,' she said, 'and the last bit's by train, so it doesn't really matter. We've taken a house for the summer.'

'And very nice too,' he said. He glanced over at Dom and acknowledged him with a nod. 'You're very alike. Brother and sister?'

'My son.' Her smile widened and she wriggled her spine pleasurably against the back of the upright seat.

Tom – they were immediately on first name terms – was going to Rome on business. He knew the hotel where she had once stayed with Donald and this fragile link made her confidential.

'Donald didn't want to see the sights. I had to drag him round the Forum and we did St Peter's in twenty minutes.' She paused and gave him a candid glance. 'He is . . . was . . . rather a stay-at-home.'

'What a shame,' Tom said. 'I don't usually have much time for sightseeing either, but I enjoy it when I can. And this trip should be different. I have a few days, maybe even a week before I go on to Addis.'

'Addis, fantastic,' Gillian said.

'Mmm. It used to be.'

Gillian assessed him unobtrusively. Thinning dark hair and rather a leathery, narrow face set in firm lines which relaxed into a surprisingly warm and boyish smile as he talked. He looked fit. Saunas and ski slopes, she decided. She wondered why he didn't tell her any more about himself, why he was going to Ethiopia for instance.

She made another effort to draw him out and got the impression that he lived alone. Certainly if he had a wife or children he was keeping this information to himself. But it was all very enjoyable and she hardly noticed when the cabin crew began to prepare for landing.

They were in the grey marble arrivals hall at Fiumicino airport before she told Dom that she had invited Tom to the villa.

'Mother!' he said.

'He's interesting!' she said defensively. It was what she used to say to Donald when she brought yet another stranger home.

Dom made a face. 'Oh, no doubt.' They moved towards the EU passport control. 'He looks like an arms dealer to me,' he said.

'They're here,' Rose called.

Maria-Grazia emerged from the kitchen, tying the strings of her apron. 'Oh . . . oh . . . oh . . .' she said, letting out her breath. 'I hope. . . .' But she didn't say what it was that she hoped. Instead she told Rose to go and speak to them and gave her a little push. But it wasn't an unfriendly gesture. The coolness engendered by Rose's meeting with Lena Grenbelli had faded during the previous day as Rose had shown herself more than willing to tackle the chores.

Maria-Grazia followed Rose outside to the car, but stood back, eyes down with her hands folded over her stomach as the Tenbys got out of the car.

'Welcome to Villa Antonia,' Rose said.

'Thank you,' Gillian said. She swept a quick glance at Maria-Grazia followed by an all-enveloping smile. 'This looks super,' she said as she shook hands with Rose.

'I think so, too,' Rose said.

Mrs Tenby looked about her own age, Rose thought, but if the tall young man with the thinning hairline was her son, then she must be older. There was a definite resemblance. Both had the same round face and large blue eyes but Gillian's were spectacular. Her eyelashes were thick and dark with firmly defined eyebrows and her skin had warm creamy tones in contrast to Dom's fair, more insipid, colouring.

She was wearing a clear yellow silk shirt and tailored navy shorts. Over her arm was a matching navy jacket. There was a delicate gold necklace in the vee of her shirt and a matching bracelet gleamed on her already tanned arm. She certainly didn't look as though she had been travelling.

Giulio started to take the luggage out of the car and Rose drew Maria-Grazia forward and introduced her, repeating in English everything that was said in Italian.

'Wish I could speak the language like that,' Dom Tenby said. 'I did French at school, but. . . .' He shrugged expressively.

'Yes, I can see we're going to rely on you a great deal,' Mrs Tenby said. 'Now, you must call me Gillian, and this is Dom. I'm sure we're all going to be great friends.'

Rose smiled and said she hoped so. She hoped, too, that Gillian Tenby's expressed egalitarian attitude would extend to the Italian couple, otherwise there were going to be a lot more periods of heavy silence in the kitchen.

*

'You will live as family with us, won't you?' Gillian said that evening on the terrace.

'That's very kind, but I think not,' Rose said, firmly. 'Maria-Grazia may need some moral support. I don't think they've ever had tenants who had no Italian at all.'

'Ah.' Gillian frowned slightly. 'Actually I found her rather surly. Perhaps that's the reason. Are they unhappy about the situation?'

'Not at all,' Rose said, untruthfully. 'They're just anxious that everything goes smoothly.'

'Yes, yes, of course.' Gillian turned up her face to the last rays of the sun. 'And will she want us to tell her what to cook? Or can she decide for herself?'

'Perhaps you could give her a menu in the evening and Giulio will do the shopping the next morning.'

Gillian made a little moue. 'But I'm on holiday!' And then she turned to Rose with a wide smile. 'Perhaps you would do that for me? You know the food and you can talk to them. Yes, I really think that would be the best.'

When this conversation was relayed to Maria-Grazia, Rose heard her laugh out loud for the first time. 'This one is not used to servants, eh?'

'Perhaps not,' Rose said.

'Definitely not,' Maria-Grazia said emphatically.

However, her dinner of home-made *fettuccine* with fried zucchini and *cotolette alla milanese* was evidently entirely successful. Dom came to the kitchen for some brandy afterwards. 'Mummy says we may have some people coming,' he said. He put his arm around Rose and squeezed her.

'Great food,' he said, as she disengaged herself.

'I'm glad you enjoyed it,' she said coolly, 'but it's Maria-Grazia you should thank.'

'*Grazie*, Maria-Grazia,' he said. He crossed the kitchen and she stepped back quickly before he could do the same to her.

She let out her breath when he had gone. 'So that is the English?' she said. 'We have had all kinds, but not one of them was ever familiar before!'

They were sitting in a bar near the marina drinking grappa and coffee. 'We should really have gone up there tonight,' Peter said.

32   *Maureen Donegan*

'Oh, let them settle in first,' Johnny said, impatiently. 'Elizabeth isn't arriving until tomorrow.'

'I did say we'd go and have a drink. . . .'

'Oh, did you? Well, we're having one.'

'You know that's not. . . . Look, we've been cooped up on the boat all day.'

'I thought we were enjoying ourselves. So now you want to be cooped up with this nouveau woman. Is she paying you for services, or something?'

'Oh, sure. Ha ha.'

The harmony of the past two days had definitely gone, Peter thought.

'Go on up there, if you're so keen.' Johnny beckoned the waiter. '*Un'altra grappa, per favore*. Take Pino with you. You've been itching to get him on his own.'

'Don't be ridiculous.' Peter hunched his shoulders. 'And a *grappa* for me,' he called.

'Ah, so you're staying?'

'Not if you're going to be like this.'

'In case you've forgotten, we have an appointment.'

He pushed back his chair as a large man in a sleeveless T-shirt with a heavy gold chain around his neck came up to them.

'Signor Nardi.'

They all shook hands and Johnny signalled the waiter again.

'So,' the Italian said, 'it all went smoothly.'

'I'm glad you think so. We had to wait three days for the contact. Three very long days.'

Franco Nardi spread his large, be-ringed hands. 'But in the end all was well.' It was a statement, rather than a question.

Elizabeth Halliwell watched the lush Tuscan countryside flash past the first-class compartment window of her train. She was hot. Her long fair hair, caught up into a knot, felt heavy and damp against her neck. She hoped that the promise of a swimming pool at the villa was not just a figment of Johnny's imagination. It would not be the first time he had got her into a situation where the facilities were exaggerated and the people were, well, strange.

TUSCAN SHADOWS
33

But the villa sounded pleasant enough. If only Johnny didn't have to drag Peter along. Away from England and from his family, Johnny was a different animal. She sighed. Peter was a nuisance, but at least he was from the right background.

The right background was very important to Elizabeth. Her father had made his money from a chain of fast food restaurants and there was still almost a tangible air of frying fat about him. But Elizabeth had been sent to a very upmarket school where she had concealed her background and tried to blend into the woodwork. Johnny's family went back to the Conqueror and he gave her the impression that this was enough for both of them, but she knew that the particular kind of respectability he needed could only be provided by a wife. It was a bargain, and they both knew it.

'You'll be mistress of Herrin Park one day,' her father had told her. And I'll command respect, she had added silently to herself. There was another bonus: Johnny would never have the power to cause her emotional pain. He wasn't like other men who were mostly beastly and horrible. Even her father had that awful woman in Edinburgh. It was disgusting.

The train drew into the station and she peered out hoping that he would be there to meet her but she couldn't see either Johnny or Peter. The guard helped her off with her cases and she stood for a few moments waiting for the small crowd to disperse. And then a tall, dark-haired woman came over and spoke to her in English.

'Miss Halliwell? I'm Rose Childs. Mrs Tenby asked me to meet you. And this is Giulio. Let him take your bags.'

'Have you heard from Mr Langdon Smythe?' Elizabeth asked anxiously, as she followed them to the car and tried to match Rose's long strides.

'We thought he'd be here last night but he didn't telephone until this morning, some problem with the boat I think. He and Mr Kinaid will be up for dinner this evening.'

'Oh, I see,' Elizabeth said. She got into the back of the car and sat upright as she had been taught to do at finishing school.

'We could have stopped at Pisa,' Alison said, plaintively. 'It's not Paris, but I know we won't get another chance. Not with Gillian in charge of things.'

'When I rang she said she'd keep dinner for us.'

'So we'd have had time to see the tower. And the Baptistry. An hour, an hour and a half.'

'And found our way into the town, and parked, and found our way out again? More like three hours. Anyway dinner is at half past seven and she said she'd wait until eight.'

'Big deal.' She paused for a moment. 'Well, I'm afraid you're going to have to stop, even if it isn't Pisa, because I want to pee.'

'OK, OK.' Keith gave the clock on the dashboard a covert glance then slowed down and after a while drew up on a quiet part of the road near a patch of woodland. Alison took her bag and the water bottle and headed towards it. Oh, God, she was going to take some more pills. He sat quietly, gazing sightlessly at the road and then looked at his reflection in the driving mirror. He'd aged, he thought, even in the short time since they'd left Calais.

CHAPTER 3

Elizabeth had found a quiet corner on the roof terrace where she could enjoy the morning sun and observe both the courtyard and the verandas at the other side of the villa. She intended to keep an eye on Johnny.

He had seemed pleased to see her last night, although that may have been because she was a familiar face in a situation which she felt was not to his liking. She wondered if it was Peter who was Gillian's friend. If friendship was what it was. Why, she wondered, forgetting for a moment her own ambiguous situation, did middle-aged woman flirt with gay men?

Mind you, dinner had not been too bad, except that Johnny had not been sitting next to her. Instead, he was between Gillian and what's-her-name, oh yes, Alison, the one who seemed to have sleeping sickness. Elizabeth suspected that the seating had been carefully thought out in advance and that Gillian's apparently spontaneous, hand-clapping, 'Let's split everyone up so we can all get to know each other,' had been thought out well in advance.

Elizabeth had found herself next to Dom, who made himself agreeable. Well, quite agreeable. He had his mother's eyes and apparently artless expression and many women might well find him attractive but, to Elizabeth, Dom and Gillian were two sides of the same coin.

She had taken a dislike to her hostess from the first moment when Gillian, ignoring her outstretched hand, had embraced her, saying that any friend of Peter's was a friend of hers. This inappropriately gushing reception had dragged up memories of her father acting with the same insensitivity, embarrassing her in front of her schoolfriends, or worse, their parents.

And there was something else: Elizabeth, with her finely attuned antennae for such things, wondered why Gillian Tenby had chosen a housekeeper like Rose, whose voice and comportment served only to underline Gillian's own somewhat uneven social graces.

Nevertheless she had to admit that Gillian had something. She laughed a lot and the people around her, the men in particular, responded. The air around her positively crackled. Why couldn't I have been given that sort of personality? Elizabeth wondered.

Her mind moved back along the evening. She was just thinking about Johnny's goodnight peck when she was distracted by voices in the courtyard.

'I want it back soon!' Gillian said in a loud voice and Rose translated this to Giulio quietly.

'Do you have to do the shopping now? I have to go to the station to meet two more guests.'

She didn't bother to meet me, Elizabeth thought.

Giulio spoke in rapid Italian, waving his hands and pointing to his watch and then Rose said, 'He says he could go directly from the market to the station to save you time. Wouldn't that be easier?'

Gillian ignored Giulio completely. 'No, it would not. Kindly tell him I want him back here at eleven. No later.' She walked away, without waiting for an answer, her heels clicking angrily. The voices continued for a few moments in Italian, Rose's soft and placating and Giulio's loud and protesting. Elizabeth lost interest then because the Sardinian drove up in a hire car and Johnny and Peter stepped out from the shade of the doorway where they had been hidden from view. Doors slammed and both cars drove off, tyres squealing, with Giulio well in the lead.

'La Signora Tenby has a bad temper,' Maria-Grazia remarked. She and Rose were sitting over coffee in the kitchen during a well-earned break.

Rose sighed. 'Yes.'

'Who's she going to meet? *Un amico?*'

'I think it's her daughter's boyfriend.'

'*Allora, non capisco.*'

'And another man.'

'Ah,' Maria-Grazia said.

Giulio arrived back punctually but without the particular kind of cheese that Maria-Grazia wanted and she had also shouted at him. He'd listened sullenly to her complaints and then flung himself off down the garden with an angry face.

'I will cook him snails for dinner,' Maria-Grazia said, 'that will stop him from being nervoso.' The snails were in an enamel bowl and had been gathered that morning by Giulio. At least some of them were in the bowl, others were escaping across the kitchen floor. Rose, who had memories of French snails being hung in a basket for a couple of weeks to be cleaned out, hoped that she wasn't going to have to share Giulio's dinner.

There was a knock at the door and the policeman she and Giulio had met in Capulana put his head in. He glanced hopefully at the table. 'Any chance of a coffee, Maria-Grazia?'

'*Certo,*' she said, with a pleased expression.

He shook hands with Rose. 'How are you settling in?'

'Very well, thank you.'

'Good. Make sure Maria-Grazia looks after you.'

Rose smiled. 'She is doing so already.'

Maria-Grazia handed him a cup. 'Rose is a friend of the Contessa Grenbelli,' she said, with a sudden edge in her voice.

'Oh, really? Then you must know this area.'

'No, it's my first time here. I was at school with Laura Grenbelli, that's all.'

His large brown eyes considered her. 'Ah. In England?'

'Yes.'

'And that is how you came to the villa.'

'No, in fact. . . .' She stopped.

'*Scusi,* it is my job to ask questions and it becomes a bad habit.'

Maria-Grazia poured Rose another coffee, as though in apology for her sharpness, and then gave Sergio Tavazzi a sly look. 'I thought you'd be around,' she said.

'Did you?' he said. He was still looking at Rose, who returned his gaze until he finally dropped his eyes.

'We saw a lot of him last summer,' Maria-Grazia said. She paused for a moment. 'Do you ever hear from Melina?'

'A card at Christmas, I think,' he said easily. 'But I come to see you, Maria-Grazia. And your wonderful food.'

She laughed and went to take the remains of a cherry tart out of the fridge.

'You see what flattery can do,' he said to Rose as Maria-Grazia cut a slice for him. 'How's Giulio?'

'*Nervoso*,' she said.

The inner door opened and Gillian Tenby came in. She was dressed in a black and white linen suit and held the car keys in her hand. Rose got up and went over to her.

'I shouldn't be more than an hour,' Gillian said. 'Mr Kinaid and Mr Langdon Smythe won't be here for lunch, but we shall have two other guests.'

'Fine,' Rose said.

'So you'll tell the cook?' She didn't look at Maria-Grazia.

'I've already done so. You remember we spoke about it last night.'

Captain Tavazzi had stood up when Gillian came into the room and now she caught his eye. He nodded at her.

'And perhaps you'd send Giulio for some more of those mosquito things when I come back.' Gillian put up her hand to where a large red mark was spreading across her neck.

'Certainly. In fact I have something to put on that in my room.'

'I haven't time now,' Gillian said, irritably, 'I'm late already.'

'At least the insects like her,' Maria-Grazia said, when the door closed.

Sergio Tavazzi grinned. 'Do I detect a little atmosphere?'

'*Beh*,' Maria-Grazia said, 'she is not a lady.'

'Maybe one day you will have the perfect tenant,' he said.

'*Mai*,' Maria-Grazia said, pulling down her mouth.

'Never is a long time,' he said, still amused. 'Well, thank you for the coffee. I'll go and say hello to Giulio.' He turned to Rose. 'A *presto*, *Professoressa*. I hope we'll meet again.'

He had a way with him, Rose thought, as they shook hands.

He stood in the doorway for a moment. 'I take it that Mr Kinaid and Mr Landgon Smythe are the Englishmen with the boat?'

'Hmm,' Maria-Grazia said. '*Sono finocchi.*'

He laughed. 'Now what would you know about gays, Maria-Grazia?' He paused. 'But they are not here today?'

'I think they have gone to do some repairs to the boat.'

'And the Sard? Is he also a *finocchio*?' the captain asked, still grinning.

Maria-Grazia shrugged. 'He does not talk. He was here eating with us yesterday, but he didn't say a word, *neanche una parola!*'

'But I imagine he sleeps on the boat?'

'Who knows?' Maria-Grazia said, drily.

'And the English fiancé?'

'Quiet, polite. But she does not speak Italian.'

The captain's curiosity seemed beyond mere gossip, Rose thought. If he was a friend of Mrs Martin, then she might well have asked him to keep an eye on the villa, but even so. . . .

'A nice man,' she said, when he had gone, 'but inquisitive.'

'He is a detective,' Maria-Grazia said, proudly, 'from an ordinary family, but he is very clever.'

'I suppose he's based here?'

'No, no. Here there is only a *maresiallo*. Sergio works in the *Centrale Operativa* of the region.'

'And who is Melina?'

'She was here last year, helping at the villa like you. Only not like you.'

'What do you mean, not like me?'

'She was a *puttana*,' Maria-Grazia said. She wriggled her hips meaningfully, then swept the crumbs from the table with an air of finality.

The train slowed as it reached the coast, but Mike Harding barely registered the view of gleaming turquoise water dotted with small craft. He was both longing for and dreading his journey's end. Would Susie already be there? She was very vague about her plans and he'd vowed to wait until he was sure that she'd arrived but, somehow, he managed to clear his desk and leave earlier than he had planned.

When Keith had introduced him to the Tenbys, the year before, he'd found them entirely delightful: Donald so upright and admirable, Gillian warm and fascinating, Dom amusing. And in Susie he'd felt he'd discovered someone absolutely uncomplicated and straightforward, someone who would help him to create the family he'd never had.

His father had disappeared one day when Mike was young. At first it seemed a relief because all the screaming and hitting stopped. Afterwards his mother struggled to send him to school and there were years of grey and unremitting poverty.

He'd been drawn inexorably into the Tenbys' orbit, refusing to believe Susie's stepmother stories or to recognise that there could be any tension beneath the surface of their lives. He had a small frisson of excitement as he remembered his first meeting with them and the way they seemed to form a circle around Gillian, who was laughing with her head to one side in that way she had. He'd responded like a starving child to the golden amalgam of the two Tenby women in their comfortable and apparently stable family life.

And then his mind swerved like a magnetized compass back to the day of his mother's funeral just a few weeks before he'd got his degree. It was one of the biggest regrets of his life that she hadn't lived to see him graduate. His life had been simpler then. Simpler but empty.

The train drew gently into the small station of Capulana Scala and he looked eagerly for a familiar face on the platform.

Dom came up from the pool and found Keith, Alison and Elizabeth sitting on the terrace. Rose had brought a tray of drinks and Dom slicked back his wet hair and poured himself a glass of wine.

'They're not back yet?'

'No,' Elizabeth said. She glanced at her watch. 'And Gillian said lunch would be at one.'

'I hope she's all right,' Keith said. 'I wanted to take her . . . she doesn't know the roads here.'

'Neither do you,' Alison said. She looked brighter today, but there were

TUSCAN SHADOWS 41

dark shadows under her eyes and her face was puffy with weariness. She had looked so ill the previous night that Dom had wondered how she had made the journey.

Elizabeth also looked unhappy. Dom felt sorry for her. She didn't really know any of them after all and Johnny – what was his surname? – hadn't done much in the way of keeping her company. He went over to sit with her.

'Maybe I should go and look for her,' Keith was saying.

'She didn't want you,' Alison said. She leaned back in her chair and her eyelids drooped. 'Didn't you get the message?'

Keith gave her a cold look. 'Alison,' he began, and then stopped as Rose emerged from the house with Tom Graham in tow.

'Mr Graham has arrived by taxi,' she announced. 'He must have missed your mother at the station.'

'Oh.' Dom felt a twinge of unease as he shook the newcomer's hand. Maybe something had happened to Gillian after all. 'Sorry about the confusion . . .' he began. And then Maria-Grazia appeared and beckoned Rose from the terrace door and spoke to her urgently. A few moments later Mike Harding emerged, blinking in the strong sunlight.

'Didn't you meet Mummy?' Dom said.

Mike shook his head. 'No sign of her. And I didn't realize there was someone else on the same train. My taxi must have followed his on the way here.'

'Surely she'd have seen one of them at the station?' Keith was on his feet. 'I'll go and look for her.'

Dom bit his lip. 'We should organize it properly, not all go rushing off in different directions.'

Despite his anxiety, Dom noticed Rose moving about, giving Mike's bag to Maria-Grazia, getting cold drinks and making soothing remarks to the new arrivals. She looked over at him with a questioning look.

'Should I call anyone? Or should we wait for a while? Lunch will hold, that's not a problem.'

'Maybe we should wait a few minutes,' he said. Gillian would be furious if a fuss was made for no reason. He could imagine her, only too clearly, asking if there had to be a national emergency just because she was late for lunch.

'I don't agree.' Keith had come back with his keys. 'We shouldn't waste any time.'

'But where are you going to look?' Alison asked.

'We could ring the hospitals,' Elizabeth said, and everyone turned to look at her. She flushed. 'Or she may just have lost her way,' she said.

'Perhaps I could show Mr Graham and Mr Harding their rooms,' Rose said, 'and when they've freshened up we can decide what to do.'

Dom looked at her gratefully. 'Yes, good idea.'

Mike was looking around the group. 'Where's Susie?' he said, suddenly. 'Did she go to the station as well?'

'She's in Denmark,' Dom said, 'or on her way down here. I really don't know exactly.'

'But she said . . .' Mike broke off, frowning. Then he went over to the edge of the veranda and stood with his back to them, staring at the view.

Rose reappeared with a tray of cheese biscuits and a large bowl of olives. 'To keep starvation at bay,' she said, smiling.

Dom helped himself to another drink. His feeling of unease was developing into a sharp pain of anxiety and then, suddenly, he heard Gillian's raised voice in the house. A moment later she came through the terrace doors. Her linen suit was crumpled and the narrow skirt torn in two places. There were scratches on her face and a large bump on her forehead.

'Gillian!' Keith said in alarm. He rushed over and put his arms around her. 'What happened?'

'What happened,' she said in a tight voice, which shook slightly, 'was that someone didn't check the car properly. The brakes failed on a sharp bend and I'm lucky to be alive. For God's sake stop staring at me and give me a drink.'

Giulio was sitting in the garden shed. Although he had closed the door, light came through the slatted shutters, casting bars of gold over the shelves of tools, cans of oil and petrol.

He needed time to think and to get away from the strident voice of La Signora Tenby. He didn't understand what she said, but her tone had been unmistakable. And then Maria-Grazia had added her voice to the commotion and his head felt as though it would burst.

TUSCAN SHADOWS

Giulio crouched on the floor and drew up his knees. He could only cope with one thing at a time, unlike Maria-Grazia who kept all kinds of problems simmering together in her head.

He had had the car serviced. And it had been perfectly all right this morning. La Tenby wasn't used to the Italian roads, that was it. She had lost control of the car and now she wanted to blame him.

Perhaps he should have checked the brakes again, but it was only two days since the servicing. What could have gone wrong in that time? They had found the car on the winding road down to the port, its nose in a tree. And when the Englishman checked the brake fluid there wasn't a drop left.

At least it was quiet in the hut. His eye wandered over the bands of light and caught sight of a gap in the ranged tools. *Cristo*, there was a spanner missing. He sighed. It looked as if he would get the blame again.

All he asked of life, Giulio told a silent Christ, was regular work, regular meals and the warm plump body of Maria-Grazia in bed. But Maria-Grazia wasn't going to welcome him with open arms tonight. Even the snails in tomato sauce she had promised wouldn't compensate for the noisy and complicated events of the day.

Giulio heard footsteps on the gravel and he scrambled to his feet in alarm.

'It must be nice and cool in there,' Sergio Tavazzi said. His tall figure filled the doorway, changing the hut from a refuge to a prison.

Gillian lay beside the pool with her eyes half closed. Mike was rubbing oil on her back and shoulders. She wondered if he was disappointed at not finding Susie at the villa. She undid the top of her bikini to avoid a strap mark and felt Mike's fingers slide around and just touch her breast. She moved slightly in response but after a moment he leaned back on his heels and gave her a gentle slap.

'That enough?'

'For the time being,' she said, turning her head to look at him. Mike was a sweet boy, but Tom Graham was. . . . Out of the corner of her eye she could see his long body stretched out on a towel nearby.

She let her eyes slide around the group. Elizabeth was wearing a plain, but expensive white swimsuit and lying on a thick black towel. A black and red straw hat was balanced over her face. Gillian had seen the same combination in a high fashion glossy, but the model had been a deep golden colour. Elizabeth was decidedly not golden, nor would she ever be.

But Gillian wasn't as relaxed as she appeared. Her bruises hurt and her hand shook slightly when she held it up to shade her eyes. That fool of a gardener. He mustn't have checked the car properly. Rose had told her he was a Neapolitan. Weren't they all involved in the Mafia in the south? Kidnappings and extortion and the like? She hadn't liked the way he or his wife looked at her from the very beginning. She shook herself slightly. She was being ridiculous. He didn't look bright enough to be involved in anything organized, much less organized crime.

She lifted her head again and Tom smiled at her.

'I feel I belong here,' she said. 'My husband would never have agreed to a holiday like this. He liked his "abroad" carefully arranged in a package tour.'

'Really?'

'But I'm more of a free spirit.'

'I'm sure you are.' He gave her a warm look.

'I used to try to get him to stop thinking about the business, to have a bit of fun for a change. I told him life's serious enough without brooding about it.'

'You're absolutely right.' She dragged her eyes away reluctantly as he stretched like a sleepy cat.

Yes, it had been an uphill struggle with Donald all those years. And Susie hadn't helped. Obviously she felt abandoned, her mother going off like that, but you had to get over these things. In fact, Gillian often wondered if it had been unremitting boredom that had driven Donald's first wife away.

She looked around again and saw that the sun had made distressing red blotches on Elizabeth's shoulders.

'You're getting pink,' she called. 'Dom, take the factor twenty over to Elizabeth.'

Dom ought to make a bit more effort with Elizabeth. He didn't take after her in that respect, that was for sure. She raised her voice. 'Dom!'

'It's all right,' Elizabeth said. She got up and moved into the shade and Dom sank back into his chair again.

Alison appeared at the top of the steps.

'Keith?' she called.

'He isn't here,' Gillian said. She suspected he'd gone off in a huff when he'd realized Tom was someone she'd met on the plane. But she could deal with Keith.

A few drops of cool water on her legs made her jump.

'Coming in?' Mike said, crouching beside her.

'You're too energetic,' she said, sleepily.

He put out his hand. 'Come on.'

Better fasten her bikini again, she supposed, although it was private enough here. She allowed herself to be pulled to her feet and then stood watching as he climbed up on to the board.

He dived in, his well-muscled body cutting neatly into the water. Gillian sat on the edge of the pool for a moment and reflected that she and she alone had brought all these people here. To a villa in Tuscany. It wasn't mirror mirror on the wall; she wasn't stupid enough to believe that she was irresistible. But you had to make an effort, to keep up with what was going on, to make people like you.

She turned her head to look at Elizabeth. 'What time did Johnny say he'd be here tonight?' she asked.

Elizabeth stared at her, as though she hadn't heard and then after a while said, 'He didn't say, actually.'

Gillian nodded then slipped quietly into the water and swam over to Mike.

CHAPTER 4

'Would you like me to find a doctor?' Rose asked. She had come down in answer to two impatient rings from the master bedroom and found Gillian lying on the bed while Keith examined the bruises on her shoulders.

Gillian turned over and pulled up the sheet, but not before Rose saw that she was naked. 'No, of course not. I just ache, that's all,' she said. 'And I thought I should take it easy today.'

'Very sensible,' Keith said, edging towards the door.

'I wondered if you could bring me up a little breakfast, Rose. Or ask what's-her-name.'

'Maria-Grazia's down at the pool, tidying up,' Rose said, 'but I can do it. What would you like?'

'Tea, toast, perhaps some fruit.'

'I'll bring it,' Keith said, 'save Rose coming up again.'

'Oh, Rose doesn't mind, do you Rose? But it would be lovely if you. . . .' Gillian paused, 'Where's Alison?'

'Fast asleep. She won't surface for hours.'

'Then she won't be needing you, will she? You can come back and talk to me.' She patted the side of the bed and smiled.

Rose and Keith walked along the corridor together.

'She had quite a shock yesterday,' he said, carefully. 'Nasty bruises.'

'Very nasty,' Rose agreed.

He let her go ahead of him up the stairs. 'We're very old friends,' he said, 'all of us. Alison too. Known Gillian since school.'

'Ah.'

He continued uncertainly, 'So we grew up together.'

Rose opened the kitchen door and went to put the kettle on. 'Then you knew her husband?'

Keith pulled out a chair and sat astride it. 'Donald. One of the nicest people you could meet. But a bit, well, set in his ways. Gillian knew how to handle him, though.'

Rose washed two peaches and put them on a plate.

'He wouldn't have agreed to a holiday like this though.'

'Ah,' Rose said, again.

'Well, I suppose she can afford it. Wouldn't be doing it if she couldn't.'

'Certainly not.'

Keith picked up one of the peaches. He took it over to the window and stood for a moment staring out at the courtyard.

'Funny how things turn out,' he said. 'I went to America and when I came back she was married to Donald.' He turned around and bit hard into the peach. Juice spattered over his chin and on to his shirt. 'Shit!' he said, 'um ... sorry, but. . . .'

She took a tea towel, wet it and mopped at his shirt.

'Are you all right, Keith?' Gillian's voice came from the doorway.

'Yes, sure. Just a bit of juice on my. . . .'

'I've changed my mind about breakfast, Rose, please bring it out to the terrace. And perhaps you could have Keith's shirt washed.' Her voice sharpened. 'Oh, do take it off, Keith, and stop messing about.'

A shadow fell across one of the poolside sunbeds and Maria-Grazia turned with a start.

'Oh, it's you,' she said. 'If you want to catch her swimming, you'll have to get up very early in the morning.'

'The delightful English Rose?' Sergio Tavazzi laughed. 'That wasn't my intention, but thank you for the idea. No, I was just passing and I thought I'd say hello to you and Giulio.'

48   *Maureen Donegan*

'He's gone to the market.'

'Then I'll see him another time,' Sergio Tavazzi said easily. 'He's all right, isn't he? He seemed a bit upset yesterday.'

'He loses things and then puts the blame on other people. But it was an accident, wasn't it?'

'So it appears.' He leaned against the bar counter as Maria-Grazia rubbed vigorously at some imagined grease on the surface. 'And I suppose it was just bad luck that Mrs Tenby was the one to use it, and not anyone else.'

'It could have been Giulio in the car,' Maria-Grazia said, sudden tears filling her eyes, 'or that queer pair. They wanted to go down to the port, but then the Sard got a hire car.'

'And I suppose everyone in a house like this knows what everyone else is doing?'

Maria-Grazia laughed. '*Quella bionda*, Signorina Elizabeth, would know. She watches everybody, specially her *fidanzato*. But he's always with his boyfriend. And there's something else that's funny about him. He speaks Italian, I heard him on the phone. But he never speaks it in front of La Tenby or any of the others.'

'You're very observant, Maria-Grazia.'

'Yes,' she agreed, 'and I'm not fooled by all these stupid questions about cars. I know you came to see Rosa. But she's a lady, not like that Melina.'

'When lovely lady stoops to folly,' he said slowly, in English.

'*Cosa dici?*'

'Something I learned in school.'

'Oh, in England,' Maria-Grazia said, dismissively. '*Beh*, I believe the English are *peggio di tutto*.'

'I thought you'd get around to saying that,' he said, laughing.

'It's true,' she said, excitedly. 'La Signora Tenby is not a real lady and La Signora Alison, the one with the straggly hair, she's like a dead person only no one seems to notice, especially her husband, and there's a man who arrived out of nowhere, Tom, he's called. He speaks a bit of Italian too, but he pretends he doesn't. I heard him asking the sailor yesterday where they'd been with the boat.'

'Did he now?'

'You know what she's like, La Tenby?'

'Tell me.'

'A spider. A poisonous one. And anyone who gets near her gets trapped. Especially the men.'

Sergio looked at her with admiration. 'You're very clever, Maria-Grazia,' he said.

She turned away with a flicker of annoyance. 'I wasn't allowed to go to school, that's all.' She shrugged. 'The teacher came once. She offered to teach me for free, in the evenings, but *Mamma* said no.'

'They were hard times,' Sergio said.

'*Mamma* she was always ill or pregnant or both. Eleven babies and only three survived. But God never gave me one of my own.' Maria-Grazia wiped the spotless counter again vigorously then and changed the subject. 'I suppose we'll see you again soon?'

'Oh, you will, Maria-Grazia, you will.'

Tom emerged from the rough scrubland and skirted the top of the headland. From this vantage point there was a magnificent view of the coastline. To his left was the harbour where dark blue fishing boats bobbed beside the white fibreglass of the yachts along the marina. To his right were the ruins of an old fort, its crenellated turrets golden in the sunlight. He lifted his binoculars from around his neck and focused the lens. An old man sat on the roof of the fort holding a cigarette in his gnarled fingers. He seemed so near that Tom felt he could put out a hand to touch him.

It wasn't a bad place, he thought, as he swept the glasses around the bay. He smiled slightly as he found the yacht marina. Ah, there was Johnny Langdon Smythe's boat. Tom picked out the figures of Peter and the Sardinian in the cockpit. He fiddled with the lens again. Well, there was no mistaking the expression on Kinaid's face as he watched the Italian coiling a rope. The English boy leaned over and touched the other and the Sardinian turned and smiled with a look of complicity. Johnny appeared in the hatchway and looked quickly from one to the other. The Sard went on coiling the rope and Peter's hand moved to grasp the tiller and began to push it idly back and forth. A very uneasy partnership, Tom thought, amused.

He wondered how long he would have to stay here, when the phone call would come. Some people, he knew, envied him his apparent freedom to travel and there were some compensations. The world was full of women like Gillian Tenby for instance, bored, afraid of the passing years and with an over-active libido like a flashing neon sign. He didn't trust any woman, but he enjoyed watching the way she manoeuvred the various men around her, not least her son. Touch of the Oedipus there, or Narcissus, or both.

Tom put the binoculars in their case and pushed his way back down through the bushes. It was hot and the flies were a nuisance. A viper slid from under his feet and he stepped back hastily. Not such a safe haven, after all. He would go back to the villa and have a shower and maybe even a swim before lunch. And await events.

'I'm sending Pino to Civitavécchia for a new water pump tomorrow, they didn't have one at the port,' Johnny said. 'And after that I thought he could have a few days off.'

Peter stared at him. They were sitting in their regular bar at the port drinking *caffè corretti*.

'But we'll need him.'

'You may need him,' Johnny said, 'but I can do without him right now.'

'I thought we were going to invite Gillian and her friends out in the boat.'

'Are you saying we can't manage without him?'

'No, of course not,' Peter said quickly. 'I'm not saying that at all. But it would be a lot easier with another pair of hands.'

Johnny stared into Peter's guileless blue eyes.

'I saw you two today,' he said suddenly.

'When?'

'Does it bloody matter when?' Johnny shouted. 'I saw you. Isn't that enough?'

'You imagine things.'

'I didn't imagine your hand on his balls.' Johnny paused, then said more quietly. 'You can't leave him alone.'

'He's playing us off against each other, or trying to, that's all. Thinks he'll get more out of us that way. Don't be an idiot, Johnny.'

TUSCAN SHADOWS 51

'I am not an idiot. I saw you.'

Peter signalled for two more coffees.

'Bring the brandy bottle,' Johnny called, 'we'll correct them ourselves!' His mouth tightened. 'Just remember, Peterkins, that it's my boat and my outfit. And there are plenty of pretty boys bumming around the Med if you don't like the way I run things.'

'Don't threaten me Johnny.'

'I'm not threatening you.' Johnny picked up the bottle and poured a generous measure of brandy into his coffee, but his hand shook as he put the bottle back on the table.

'Get rid of Pino then, if that's what you want,' Peter said, sulkily.

'He's useful.'

'And I'm not?'

'Of course you are.' Johnny's voice softened. 'Look, we can't afford to quarrel.' He paused. 'The trip over was tremendous, wasn't it?'

'Yes, it was, but you're the one who started it. And look what I have to put up with.'

'What?'

'I have to share you with Elizabeth.'

'You know that's not true.'

'The way she follows you around. We have to sneak away when she's not looking.'

Johnny suddenly felt very tired. 'All right then, let's leave. Now. Lift anchor and just go.'

Peter frowned, petulantly. 'I promised Gillian we'd stay.'

'And why did you do that?'

'She's amusing. They're all amusing.'

'Amusing?'

'Anyway,' Peter said, silkily, 'you can't leave. First of all Nardi has another job lined up and you'd have to explain to Elizabeth why we were leaving, maybe even take her with us.'

'I told you, Elizabeth doesn't come into it. And I'm not sure I want to work with Nardi again.' There was something about the Italian, a coldness that his hearty greeting belied. Something had changed and he hoped it wasn't that Nardi no longer trusted them.

'Thought we needed the money.'

'We do.'

'Then don't go on about Pino. Nothing happened with him.' He paused. 'Don't push me too far, Johnny. And don't think you can buy me.' He threw some notes on the table and pushed back his chair.

A tiff, Johnny told himself, but Peter would come around. His kind always did. Peter had trained as an accountant, very much against his own inclinations but he messed up any chance of a career by diverting his very first client's money to his own account. He'd once bragged to Johnny that he'd done it on purpose to get out of the rut. But that was a typical Peter-like boast. His family paid him a small allowance to keep him away for the most part of the year and this would dry up immediately if Peter didn't keep his part of the bargain. Johnny smiled sourly to himself. There was also a limit to what he himself would put up with, he thought, as he watched Peter striding away along the waterfront, his narrow back rigid with anger.

Tom found Gillian stretched out by the pool. She was wearing a red bikini and had pulled a thin red and blue beach wrap around her shoulders.

'Where is everyone?' he asked.

'Here and there.' She waved her hand idly. 'One of the things I like about this place is that we can all do our own thing.'

'And what is your thing?' he asked, pulling a chair near to her.

'Oh, I don't know. Freedom, I suppose.'

'No one is really free,' he said.

'You seem to be.'

'Yes and no.'

'What does that mean?'

'It means,' he said slowly, 'that I have children I hardly ever see.'

'Oh, I'm so sorry. Boys?'

'Two girls.'

Gillian nodded sympathetically.

'I live one kind of life, serving my masters and they . . .'

'. . . are living a different one?'

'Yes, with their mother and a rich stepfather. My job makes it difficult to . . . to know when I'll be free.'

'What do you do, Tom?'

He pretended not to have heard. 'So one has to make the most of these moments of freedom.'

She smiled and returned his look. 'That's true. But you must miss them very much. The children, I mean.'

He was irritated with himself. Normally he didn't reveal even this small nugget of his life.

'I manage,' he said, shortly. 'I just can't compete with ponies for Christmas, that's all.'

'And your work?'

If I kissed her she'd shut up, he thought.

She had let the wrap slip and he saw two or three livid marks on her shoulders. He put out his hand, not quite touching her.

'Yesterday's accident?'

'Mm. I must have hit the steering wheel. My knees too.' She sat up suddenly and guided his hand to her leg. 'Here and here.'

'You had a lucky escape.'

'Yes.' She gave him a long, direct look. 'You're very brown. Are you the same colour all over?'

He laughed. 'More or less.'

'And where did you get it?'

'I was in Muscat last month.'

'On business?'

'Yes.'

'Do you go all over the world?'

'I haven't been to Antarctica.'

'I can see that,' she said. She lay back in her chair and regarded him speculatively. 'Dom thinks you're a white mercenary,' she said.

He laughed again. 'Do you?'

'I think you're a beautifully tanned white mercenary.'

'She's back on form,' Alison said.

54   *Maureen Donegan*

Keith jumped. 'Don't sneak up on me like that.' He was leaning over the parapet of the upper terrace looking down at the scene at the pool.

'Never misses an opportunity, does she?'

'I thought you were asleep.'

'Well, I'm not.'

He looked at her uncertainly. 'Have you eaten? I'm sure Rose would get you something.'

'I've no doubt she would. And that would leave you in peace to watch the little idyll down below.'

'Alison,' he said wearily. He moved back from the edge and sat down. 'Must you?'

'Must I?' she said, mockingly.

There were slack, dark patches under her eyes and her skin had an almost grey tinge. 'We could go for a walk down to the port,' he said, 'look at the shops, have a coffee and watch the world go by.'

Alison turned away. 'No thanks.'

'I was trying to be pleasant, that's all,' he said.

'Then don't bother. Because it's all a pretence, isn't it? All of it.'

Compassion fought with anger.' No,' he said, 'no, Alison.' He took her arm and walked with her towards the steps, but she left him abruptly, without speaking. He returned to the parapet only to discover that Gillian and Tom had disappeared from view.

After lunch Gillian announced that she was going to read and maybe have a nap in the oleander grove she had discovered high up in the garden.

She had only just settled herself when Peter appeared. He looked at her hesitantly for a moment then came and sat on the second rug which she had arranged next to her own.

'You're not expecting anyone?' he said.

She controlled her annoyance. 'Of course not. I'm feeling a bit Garbo-ish, as a matter of fact.'

'So am I.' He was silent for a minute. 'Had a row with Johnny.'

'Oh dear. What about?'

'Oh, this and that. He said he was going to leave at one point.'

Gillian's expression changed as she imagined her carefully organized party disintegrating, but she kept her voice light. 'Oh, come on, I'm sure it was nothing serious.'

'Serious enough.'

'But you made it up with him?'

'Why should I?' Peter burst out. 'He watches me like a hawk, wants to own me.'

Gillian thought fleetingly of Donald. 'I know,' she said, 'but—'

'But nothing! I don't have to put up with it.'

'It would be a pity if he left,' Gillian said, her voice still gentle, 'in fact I would be very very disappointed. I'm sure you understand that.'

Peter was picking at some sunburned skin on his arm.

'You haven't forgotten that little chat we had in London, have you Peter? When you told me how much Johnny needed you in his . . . business?'

Peter shrugged. 'I was high, fantasizing that's all.'

'I don't think so. I still have that lovely bowl you gave me.' She held up her hand. 'Oh, don't worry, it's in the back of a cupboard. No one will see it. Unless I want them to.'

In the ensuing silence, soft footsteps sounded on the grass and Tom appeared with a book in his hand.

'Hi!' Gillian said. 'You've found my hideout.'

'So it seems.' He stood there, regarding them.

'Peter was just looking for Johnny, weren't you?' she said.

Peter stared at her. 'I suppose I was.' He hunched his shoulders. The golden look, the eager-to-please expression he invariably wore had been wiped away leaving someone so ordinary, so withdrawn and colourless that he could have blended into a crowd anywhere and completely disappeared.

Gillian turned to Tom and smiled as Peter stood up and walked away.

CHAPTER 5

'Why don't you and Elizabeth go down to the port if Johnny's going to be busy on the yacht?' Gillian said to Dom, as she cut an apricot into small pieces.

Elizabeth's mouth twitched slightly but she didn't reply.

'There're some wonderful boutiques in Capulana,' Gillian went on. 'I might come down and join you later. Maybe we can all meet on the marina. Johnny's been promising to show me his yacht.'

Eizabeth's mouth twitched again. 'Boat,' she said in a quiet voice.

'What?'

'I believe most people refer to it as a boat.'

After a moment Gillian laughed, but she did not sound amused. 'Boat then. Johnny promised to show me his boat.'

As Rose collected the breakfast plates she heard Johnny say, somewhat ungraciously, that yes, of course he would be delighted to take them all out as soon as he was happy about the pump.

'I think I'll have a walk before it gets too hot,' Tom was saying when Rose returned with more fruit.

'I'll come with you,' Keith said, 'that is if you don't mind.'

'Actually I was planning something a bit strenuous up on the cliffs.'

'No problem.'

'All right,' Tom said, but he sounded reluctant, Rose thought.

'Alison's still in bed,' Keith said. 'Maybe you'd look in on her later, Rose?'

'Yes, of course.' The previous evening Alison had been half carried to bed by Keith.

'That just leaves you and me then, Mike,' Gillian said gaily and Mike's face brightened. 'Do you think you could organize some cold drinks down by the pool, Rose? And perhaps we could have another pot of coffee now?' She turned to Mike. 'I wonder if one could go topless down there? No one can see from the road, can they?'

Rose, passing behind Keith's chair, saw the back of his neck go bright red.

Dom said, 'Why not go naked, Ma, if that's what you want?' and laughed.

Elizabeth got up and went towards the steps at the end of the terrace, her back registering controlled distaste.

'Ten minutes, Elizabeth?' Dom called.

Elizabeth stopped, then made an obvious effort and turned to smile at him. 'Ten minutes,' she agreed. She ignored Johnny.

'Giulio can drive you down,' Gillian said. 'I understand the car has been fixed. Make sure he's ready, will you Rose?'

A reluctant Giulio, placated by Rose and Maria-Grazia, was at the wheel of the car ten minutes later, but there was no sign of his passengers. Then Dom appeared, in white cotton trousers and an Armani T-shirt.

'Girls are never on time,' he said and Giulio, comprehending the sense, but not the words, nodded glumly. There was the sound of an approaching car and a taxi drew into the courtyard.

Dom went to open the car door. 'Susie!' he exclaimed. 'Well, you made it.'

A pale, overweight young woman got out and paid the driver. 'Please give me a hand with my bags,' she said, in a tense voice, 'I've been travelling all night and I'm exhausted.'

Elizabeth stepped out of the house. Behind her, in a pink bikini with a towel over one arm, was Gillian.

'Sweetie!' Gillian pecked Susie's cheek. 'How lovely. Mike will be thrilled.'

'Where is he?' Susie asked.

'I was just going to join him down at the pool. Everyone else is going off somewhere or other.' She looked around, vaguely. 'Why don't you sort yourself out and come down. Rose!'

Rose, who had heard the car, came out of the kitchen.

'My late husband's daughter, Susie,' Gillian said. 'I think we agreed she could have your room when she arrived? I'm sure Maria-Grazia will help you move your things to the annexe. Just make yourself at home, sweetie. Oh, you haven't met Elizabeth, have you?'

She made the introduction and then included Tom who had appeared. Keith who came out a moment later hurried over and gave Susie a hug.

'By train all the way from Denmark?' he said. 'You must be very tired.'

'Poor little Susie, always tired,' Gillian said, in a caressing voice. 'Just look at you sweetie. Don't you know staying up all night doesn't suit you? Remember when you used to do night duty?'

It wasn't said kindly, but certainly Susie looked the worse for her journey. Her clothes were creased and her mousy hair was thin and oily. Rose could not imagine her in a clean, crisp uniform nor did her surly manner suggest someone in a caring profession.

'Where is Mike?' Susie asked in a tight high voice.

'Waiting for me by the pool, I hope,' Gillian said. 'We were going to have a lovely peaceful morning.' She paused. 'But it's lovely to see you so soon. I was under the impression you'd be staying with your friend another week.'

'That was the plan, but it didn't work out,' Susie said.

'Oh well, how nice for us, then,' Gillian said, after another moment of silence. 'Giulio will take your bags – Rose, will you ask him please, and if Maria-Grazia can rustle up some coffee? I'll see you all later.'

She gave them all a brief smile and sped off in the direction of the pool.

Giulio took Susie's case and Rose and Susie followed with the smaller bags.

'I'll get you fresh towels and change the bed straight away,' Rose said, 'and then you can have a rest, if that's what you'd like. I can bring you a tray, or would you prefer to have something to eat on the terrace while I clear the room?'

'I'd like to see Mike,' Susie said. 'Why is he down at the pool with Gillian?'

'Perhaps you'd like something down there instead? It would be no trouble.'

'I'm not hungry,' Susie said, then, more quietly, 'but thank you. Did you say your name was Rose?'

'Rose Childs.'

'Gillian always manages to get someone else to do the work.' She smiled for the first time. Her wide mouth and very white even teeth were her most attractive features.

'That's what I'm here for,' Rose said.

'But surely you aren't a—'

'Maid?'

'Sorry, I'm a bit, well, disorientated this morning.'

'It's the travelling,' Rose said sympathetically. 'I'm sure you'll feel better after a shower and some breakfast. And then I'll come and move my things.'

'I didn't realize I was turning you out of your room. I seem to be causing a lot of trouble. Look, I'll just have some coffee. Nothing to eat. I can take it down to the pool myself.'

Rose was returning with a tray when she met Mike hurrying down the corridor towards Susie's room.

A moment later there was the sound of Susie's raised voice and the placating rumble of Mike's. Rose knocked gently and, as Mike opened the door to take the coffee, she heard Susie sobbing.

They emerged about half an hour later. Rose heard Mike call to Susie that he would tell Gillian she was coming to join them. He headed in the direction of the pool and Susie followed more slowly through the garden.

As Rose began to move her things, she realized that she was relieved to be getting away from the main house. There were two bedrooms in her part of the annexe; Pino occupied the other one when he didn't sleep on the boat. He came to the door of his room as she opened up the shutters to let in some air and light, but he only nodded and didn't offer to help. Later she saw him from the window walking through the copse near the road.

'I thought he'd gone away,' she said to Maria-Grazia.

'Who knows what he's doing?' the Italian woman said. 'He's a strange one, even for a Sard.'

When Rose returned to the house for her painting gear she came upon Alison emerging blearily from her room.

'What time is it?' she asked.

'Almost midday,' Rose said.

'Keith should have woken me,' Alison said more to herself than to Rose. She put out a hand to steady herself on the door frame. 'There seemed to be some commotion earlier on.'

'Mrs Tenby's daughter arrived,' Rose said.

Alison's face lit up. 'Susie, oh good.' She laughed unexpectedly. 'Well, that will set the cat among the pigeons. Maybe she just arrived in time.'

Rose tried to keep her expression blank.

'Don't tell me you hadn't noticed how our leader was making a play for Mike? In between her other interests.' She straightened her back suddenly. 'Where is my husband this morning?'

'I believe he's gone for a walk with Mr Graham along the cliffs.'

'Let's hope they don't push each other over,' Alison said pleasantly. 'Oh, come on, Rose. You'd have to be deaf and blind not to notice. Subtlety has never been Gillian's strong suit.' She gripped Rose's arm. 'She's having it off with friend Tom as well, isn't she?'

Evidently there were even more complications in the house than Rose had realized, but she didn't think it was her place to comment. She waited a moment, half curious, half repelled, but Alison had fallen silent and was staring into space. Rose drew her arm away and said that Maria-Grazia needed her in the kitchen.

'It must be pleasant to be needed,' Alison said, under her breath. She sagged against the door frame.

The telephone was ringing as she returned to the kitchen. Maria-Grazia answered and then held out to the receiver to Rose. 'É uno straniero,' she said.

It was Arthur. 'I haven't heard from you,' he said. 'Are you all right?'

'Yes, fine. The Italian post is slow, you know.'

'I do know, but I thought you might have rung.'

'That's a bit difficult. How are you, anyway? How are the exams going?'

'Not bad. One more lot of orals, then there's summer school, but after that I should be free. What are the people like there? I presume that was half of the Italian couple?'

'Yes. It's OK here.'

'And the English group?'

'Mmm, mixed.'

'Do I take it you can't talk?'

'No, it's not that. It's a bit . . . there's a lot of tension here, that's all.' She looked over her shoulder but there were no English-speaking people within earshot. 'And there's been an accident.'

'An accident? In the house?'

'No, no. A car.'

'What? Are you sure you're all right? They drive like maniacs over there.'

'I wasn't involved . . . Arthur. . . . .' She held the receiver away from her ear. 'Arthur – it was the tenant and there's a policeman sniffing around, but I don't know if it's because of that or what it is.'

'You see,' Arthur said, triumphantly. 'I knew there was something fishy about the job from the start.'

'No, there wasn't, I mean there isn't.' She should have known it was a mistake to even hint to Arthur that Gillian's crash could have been brought about deliberately, but she felt the need to talk to someone outside the confines of the villa. 'It's just that these people, well, they're all supposed to be friends but there seems to be almost. . . .'

'Almost what?'

'There're all these cross-currents. Some of them seem to dislike each other intensely.'

There was a silence from the other end and then Arthur said in a quiet voice, 'It sounds like a potentially dangerous situation. Rose, please come home.'

'You know I can't do that.'

'Yes you can.'

'Arthur, I'm not going to abandon a job after barely a week.'

He sighed, heavily. 'All right, all right. Just promise me you won't go poking your nose into this accident. Let the authorities—'

62   *Maureen Donegan*

'I can't talk now,' Rose said, hastily, 'but I'm glad you rang.' The trouble with Arthur's advice was that it always made her want to do the opposite. There was also an echo on the line which was making the conversation more difficult. 'I'll write again.'

'Send it express this time. Or ring. You know I worry.'

'Yes, I do know.'

'And look after yourself.'

'I will. You do the same.'

'I miss you,' he said. There was a pause. 'Do you miss me?'

'You know I do. Look, I have to go now.'

'You sound so far away,' Arthur said. His voice, distorted by the hollow echo, sounded plaintive. 'You will be careful, won't you?'

'Yes, yes, I will. Goodbye, Arthur.' She put the phone down firmly and stood for a moment gazing at it. Maria-Grazia looked at her inquisitively.

'A friend,' Rose said absently, 'from England.' She shook herself slightly. Talking to Arthur had cemented her already uneasy feeling about the group at the villa.

Down at the port, in one of the fashionable boutiques, Elizabeth was trying on a figure-hugging silk dress. The saleswoman wound a matching scarf around a large straw hat but Dom shook his head.

'Too big,' he said.

Elizabeth put on the hat and regarded herself in a long mirror. 'Mmm, you're right.'

They had been there for some time and the clothes that Elizabeth had rejected covered several bamboo chairs. The sales staff looked harassed, but Elizabeth and Dom were enjoying themselves.

'Johnny hardly ever notices what I wear,' she said. She turned to the girl. 'I'll try those black silk shorts on again, and the striped shirt.'

'They were good on you,' Dom said. 'And you should definitely take the dress.'

The saleswoman who understood enough English to recognize that Elizabeth didn't think much of her stock, gave Dom a grateful look.

Inside the cubicle, Elizabeth wondered if Dom made a habit of choosing clothes for women. He certainly had a good eye. Her father would have said a glad eye. 'Most men hate shops,' she said, pushing open the swing door. 'What do you think of these?'

'Perfect,' he said.

'You're very decisive,' she said, smiling. She twisted around to see her back view.

'It's a skill I developed from years of shopping with Mummy.'

'So you choose her clothes?'

'Oh, God no. I just tell her what she wants to hear. It's much more fun with you. Actually she really started serious shopping since Dad died. He viewed clothes only as a necessary alternative to nakedness.'

'Oh, I see,' Elizabeth said. As she went back into the cubicle, she wondered if Dom knew the extent of his mother's indulgence in other directions.

'Buying clothes is harmless enough,' Dom said, as though reading her mind, 'so long as she doesn't start buying Tuscan castles.'

'Would she do that?'

'She's restless. Life never has enough excitement for her,' he said. 'That's why she took the villa.' There was a silence. 'Elizabeth, are you all right in there?'

'Yes, coming.'

She felt a bit guilty about his confiding in her. She rummaged for her credit cards in her bag as she came out in order to avoid his eye.

'People can do stupid things after a death,' he said.

'Yes,' Elizabeth said. 'Um, have you got a pen?'

He didn't answer and the saleswoman handed her one. Elizabeth glanced sideways at Dom. He suddenly looked very young and she realized that she felt sorry for him. What could it have been like growing up with a mother like that?

'I understand her,' Dom went on, 'but there's enough of my father in me to want to call a halt at a certain point.'

'Your father sounds a bit like mine,' Elizabeth said, as they were ushered solicitously out of the shop. 'He is always right. My mother was . . . a much softer person.'

'Was?'

'She's dead,' Elizabeth said, abruptly.

'I'm sorry.' Dom took her packages from her and gave her a sympathetic look. 'My father was very cautious,' he said after a few moments.

'But you must miss him?'

'I didn't think I would. He always seemed to stop me from doing what I wanted to do.'

'Which was?'

'Oh, art. Design. Said there was no future in it. Then I went off to be a pilot but I don't have twenty-twenty vision. That wasn't his fault, of course. Unless you blame the genes.'

'And that would be unfair.'

'Mmm.'

'So what are you doing?'

'Selling property. His idea.'

'It's not such a good time for that.'

'No,' he agreed, 'but I manage.'

'I work for my father,' Elizabeth said. 'I didn't want to at first.' She hesitated. 'He's a bit like a steamroller. And one gets caught up in the excitement of the business somehow.'

'You're an only child?'

'Yes. He wanted a son, of course. I'm not sure I could ever take over from him but in any case,' she said, thinking of Johnny and Herrin Park, 'I don't see my life like that.'

'How do you see it?'

'I want somewhere safe,' she said. She smiled at him. 'Where are we going now? Do you fancy coffee or a drink?'

'Aren't we supposed to be meeting the others at the boat?'

'There's no rush,' Elizabeth said.

Lunch was very late and as a result Maria-Grazie was in a sullen mood.

'It's always like this,' she complained, not for the first time, 'breakfast goes on all morning, lunch is late, we get no siesta. . . .'

'I can serve. It's all cold. You and Giulio go and have your rest,' Rose said.

TUSCAN SHADOWS

'I couldn't do that.' Maria-Grazia seemed determined to be a martyr.

'Why not? Are you afraid I'll drop the plates?'

'No.' The Italian woman put her hand over Rose's. 'It's just that it wouldn't be fair. Although how anyone can eat in this weather. . . .' They were sitting in their usual position at the kitchen table, the midday heat simmering around them. Outside the air was thick and still; even the bees were silent. Maria-Grazia wiped her face on her apron and resumed fanning herself with a white feather and lace fan. She'd told Rose it was the only thing she'd inherited from her mother.

'It's probably cooler down by the water,' Rose said. 'Didn't they say they were meeting at the boat?'

'Wherever they are they didn't take their watches,' Maria-Grazia said.

Susie came into the kitchen. She had washed her hair and looked much better. Mike followed her in.

'They're not back?' Susie said.

'I don't think they'll be long,' Rose said. 'Did you sleep?'

'Mmm. Sort of.' Susie shot Mike a mischievous glance. 'Until he woke me up.'

They seemed to have sorted out their problems, Rose thought.

Keith drove into the courtyard. With him were Alison, Gillian and Johnny. The hire car followed and disgorged Tom, Peter, Elizabeth and Dom.

'Lunch,' Rose said, thankfully.

But there was a further delay while Gillian went to her room. She returned a few moments later, evidently furious. 'Someone has been at my things,' she said.

'Sorry?'

'I'm not accusing you, Rose, although I know you do the beds.' Gillian looked meaningfully at Maria-Grazia then spoke to Rose again. 'May I have a word?'

Rose followed her out.

'There's some money missing from my room. Quite a lot, in fact. And he's a Neapolitan and she's a Sicilian. . . .'

'I'm afraid you're quite mistaken if you think that Maria-Grazia or Giulio . . .' Rose began heatedly.

66   *Maureen Donegan*

'Then who else could it be?' Gillian's eyes glittered. 'It couldn't have been anyone else. Everyone here is a friend of mine.'

Except for me, Rose thought. 'But are you quite sure?'

'Of course I'm sure,' Gillian snapped. 'I put the money in a shoe bag and it isn't there now.' She took a deep, rather trembling breath. 'I want you to call the police.'

'Perhaps we should have another look for the money?' Rose said, her heart sinking. It was just this kind of problem that Arthur had warned her about: the classic impossible situation.

'It could have been gypsies,' she said instead. 'Giulio told me there were some break-ins down at the port.'

'Well, he would say that – setting up an alibi in advance.'

'Mrs Tenby, Giulio and Maria-Grazia are the two most honest people I've ever met in my life.'

'Then you can't have met many,' Gillian said. She clamped her lips together angrily.

'But they've been here for years. They're part of the family, almost.'

'There isn't anyone else it could have been,' Gillian said, obstinately. 'Unless the sailor . . . but he's gone.'

'I'm not sure about that,' Rose said. 'He was around the garden this morning.'

Dom came out of the dining-room and looked from one to the other. 'What's up? I thought we were going to eat.'

'There's a thief in the house,' Gillian said, dramatically, 'and Rose refuses to call the police.'

'I just think that we should try less drastic means first.'

'What's been stolen?' Dom asked.

'A couple of thousand pounds,' Gillian said, reluctantly.

'What?'

'Look, my credit card was out of date and there wasn't time. . . .'

'You could have got travellers' cheques.'

'Don't look at me like that,' Gillian said, 'it wasn't my fault.' She glared at Dom and he glared back. Rose thought they were more like two children, fighting, than mother and son. 'You'd better talk to them, Rose, if you don't want to call the police. I don't speak the language and maybe if you can frighten them enough they might give the money back.'

The villa was not unlike a smouldering volcano, Rose thought, sending out hot, unexpected sparks. Arthur might not have put it so picturesquely, but he hadn't been far out when he'd said it was a potentially dangerous set-up. Just as well he didn't know about the robbery.

'It must have been the Sard,' Maria-Grazia said, when Rose related the story to her as tactfully as possible. 'Didn't you say he was hanging about this morning? He could have gone into the house without anyone seeing him.'

Rose sighed. 'But I was in and out of the bedroom area all morning.'

'Then if it wasn't him, who could it have been?' There was a silence and then Maria-Grazia turned white. 'Surely she doesn't think that I . . . that we. . . ?'

'No, no of course not. But she thinks that maybe if we all allowed our rooms to be searched. . . .'

'Giulio!' Maria-Grazia shouted. He came running in from the courtyard. 'We've been accused of stealing. Money. A lot of money. Oh . . . oh.' She threw her apron over her head and began to cry in great gulping sobs. Giulio put his thin arm across her ample shoulders and looked at Rose helplessly.

'Is it true?' he asked.

'I'm sure,' Rose said, although she was sure of nothing of the sort, 'that there's been some kind of misunderstanding.'

'No misunderstanding,' Maria-Grazia said, from below the folds of her apron. 'She is a wicked woman, wicked, wicked. Giulio, go and ring Sergio Tavazzi and get him to tell her what kind of people we are.'

'I think we should stay calm,' Rose said. 'I don't think we should call the police. Not yet. Mrs Tenby thinks that . . . perhaps whoever took the money will put it back, if they realize that the police would have to be called eventually.'

'You mean she thinks we will put it back.' Giulio's gentle, rather henpecked manner had been replaced by an icy dignity. He helped Maria-Grazia to her feet and they walked together silently across the kitchen. 'La Signora Tenby will regret this,' he said.

Rose watched them cross the courtyard from the window and heard Maria-Grazia begin her litany about the French and the Spanish and the Italians, and that never, never in all these years had anyone accused them of. . . .

'This is not like other years,' Giulio said. 'She will find out that I am a man of honour.'

Rose sighed and picked up the dish of mozzarella and tomato salad which Maria-Grazia had prepared and went into the dining room. An awkward silence greeted her entry.

Gillian had two bright red spots on her cheeks. 'Did you tell them?' she demanded.

'Yes,' Rose said. She made her way around the table but no one seemed to have much of an appetite.

'Then I'll give them until this evening.' Gillian gave herself a large help-ing and clattered the serving spoons on to the platter. 'Did you hear me?'

'Yes,' Rose said.

'And I suggest we all eat out this evening. It will give the Mulettis time to consider their situation.'

In any case, Rose thought, as she went to get the fish mousse, it was hardly likely that Maria-Grazia would be willing to cook again today. Or any other day, if things didn't improve.

In the late afternoon, Rose escaped thankfully to have tea with Lena Grenbelli.

'They do sound a rather rum lot, my dear,' she said, as Rose recounted the events of the past few days, 'brakes failing in a car and now a robbery. Poor Maria-Grazia and Giulio, they must be quite bewildered by it all.'

'Not just bewildered. Very upset.'

'It really is too bad of this woman. Do you think I should ring and say that I would trust them with my life.'

'It wouldn't hurt,' Rose said. 'They wanted to call Capitano Tavazzi. He's an old friend, apparently.'

'Ah, yes. Sergio. Nice man. But surely it's better not to involve the *cara-binieri*? The money will turn up. Mrs Tenby sounds like just the kind of tiresome woman who would mislay things and blame others.'

'I hope it's only that,' Rose said, 'but there's a terrible atmosphere in the house, quite apart from the missing money.'

'Sexual tension,' Lena Grenbelli said briskly, 'if what you've been telling me is anything to go by.'

Rose laughed and put down her cup. 'Oh, I'm so glad I came over.'

The older woman gave her a sharp look. 'Good. You should have come before.'

'It's not always easy to get away,' Rose said.

'And what about yourself, my dear? All you've talked about is the villa and these peculiar people.'

'I'm fine,' Rose said. 'Busy. Enjoying life.'

'I was sorry about your divorce,' Lena said.

'It was a long time ago.' She was silent for a moment. 'I hardly ever think about it now.'

Lena passed a plate of tiny spinach savouries. 'Do eat them up or Carmina will be offended.' She paused. 'I hope you've found someone else who's interesting?'

Rose thought about Arthur. 'Yes, and no.'

Lena's bright brown eyes gleamed with amusement. 'And what does that mean?'

'I have a friend who—'

'When a woman of my age says "a friend" it implies a certain relationship.'

'Well, we do have a—'

'But perhaps he's not the right one for you?'

Rose tried to remember if Lena had always been so inquisitive and then realized that since the death of her husband, and with Laura so far away, she must be very lonely.

'He would be the right person for someone. He's very decent, has a good mind, cares about me.'

'But there's something missing?'

'Yes,' Rose said. 'There's something missing.'

'And your painting?'

'I still do a bit.' Arthur had made her start again. It was something she should remember when she found herself unbearably irritated by him. She turned the conversation as deftly as she could, by asking about Laura and soon Lena was producing photographs of her grandchildren and talking about her plans to visit them in the autumn.

'I do miss Giorgio terribly, especially when it comes to travelling. He was always so organized.' Her hand fluttered. 'But he did manage to see his first grandson, thank God.'

'How long has it been?'

'Five years now, but never a day passes that. . . .'

'I know. I know. He was a wonderful man.' Rose remembered Conte Grenbelli's dignified bearing and his warm, contrasting sense of fun.

'Yes. I have to tell myself we were lucky to have had the years we had. It's the only way to look at it, my dear.'

Rose leaned over and touched one of the thin, liver-spotted hands which were Lena Grenbelli's only real sign of age. She thought sadly that she herself would probably never be able to say anything like that. For a moment, she envied Lena's memory-filled widowhood.

Just before Rose left, Lena said, 'If things get too difficult at the villa, my dear, come and stay here. You know I'd love to have your company.'

'That's very kind of you,' Rose said, meaning it, 'but I don't give up easily.'

'I don't imagine that you do,' Lena said, smiling. 'But there's always a bed here. Remember that.'

At least Lena's offer was presented with gentle tact, Rose thought, unlike Arthur's, but both had precisely the same effect in that it made her more determined than ever to stick it out.

CHAPTER 6

In the evening the Mulettis kept to their own quarters and Rose watched thankfully as everyone left for a restaurant in the port.

She took some bread and cheese and carried it across the courtyard to her room. She could hear the shrill cadences of Maria-Grazia's voice from their balcony and the lower, intermittent murmur of Giulio's ineffectual efforts to console her. The sounds continued long into the night. Eventually she heard two cars return and the slamming of doors, cheerful shouts and laughter. The Mulettis had by then fallen silent, perhaps from sheer exhaustion. Somehow this seemed more ominous than their earlier complaining.

Rose fell into an uneasy sleep, her last thoughts of food and how she would cope should Maria-Grazia refuse to work.

She woke suddenly, aware of some noise and wondered if Pino had returned. Had he, in fact, taken the money and was even now packing in preparation for flight? But that was ridiculous. He would have gone already if that was the case. She heard the noise again, a heavy footstep followed by a dull thumping sound. She steeled herself to get out of bed and creep quietly to the window. Through the slats of the shutter she could see a dark shape and the thumping noise was replaced by rustling and shuffling. Outside in the grey dawn, a large black pig and two of her young were snuffling along the terrace rooting among the fallen pine cones for nuts. A small laugh escaped her. But nevertheless her hand slid down the door to make sure that it was locked. She had no wish to share her quarters with a family of wild boar. Black monsters, the real stuff of nightmares, she thought wryly, and then went back to bed and slept soundly until her alarm went.

Much to her surprise, the morning routine seemed unchanged. Giulio went to fetch fresh bread and *cornetti* as usual but, after he had gone, a somewhat red-eyed Maria-Grazia announced that they were leaving the villa. They would stay with friends in the port until they found another job.

'Let me ring Mrs Venables-Brown,' Rose said urgently. 'She'll be very upset if you go. And this money business will be sorted out, I'm sure of it.'

'But we have been accused,' Maria-Grazia said. 'Nothing can take that away. I shall never forget it, nor will Giulio. Never.'

'But what about La Signora Martin? Are you going to let her down, ruin all her arrangements for the summer?'

'That cannot be helped,' Maria-Grazia said.

'Think of all the years you've been here, your comfortable apartment.'

'*Beh!* it is our honour we are talking about, not four walls and a roof.'

Dom came into the kitchen. He looked from one to the other, smiling. 'Good news,' he said.

'What?' Rose demanded.

'The money was down the side of a chair on the terrace. We had a big search of my mother's room last night before we went out but we didn't find anything and then when we came back we had a drink outside and Tom felt something against the cushion of his chair.'

Rose translated quickly for Maria-Grazia.

'Down the side of the chair?' Maria-Grazia repeated incredulously. 'But I tidied the terrace yesterday. I would have seen it.'

'The main thing is that it was found,' Rose said.

'That isn't the important thing,' the other woman said. 'We have been slighted.'

'When something like this happens,' Rose said, with a certain amount of desperation, 'everyone feels bad. No one has been accused, but there is always a feeling of suspicion. And it's not just you and Giulio.'

'I think it is,' Maria-Grazia said.

Out of the corner of her eye Rose saw Dom sliding out of the kitchen. He gave her an encouraging wave and closed the door behind him. She sighed and set about the uphill task of talking Maria-Grazia round.

TUSCAN SHADOWS

*

'I expect Gillian put it there herself,' Alison said. She yawned.

'Don't be ridiculous,' Keith said. He had come down to give her the news. 'Why should she take money out of her room and put it down the side of a chair out on the terrace?'

'She had it in her hand and forgot it. Probably distracted by something . . . or someone. Tom probably,'

'Tom?'

'She's mad for him. You haven't noticed?'

'No.'

'You could have fooled me.' She smiled, ironically, but Keith didn't react. 'So – any chance of a cup of tea in bed?'

'I think there's something of a crisis in the kitchen.'

'That doesn't surprise me either. Gillian more or less accused the couple of taking the money.'

'No, she didn't,' Keith said patiently. 'She was very objective about it all.'

'Impartial as a judge, in fact.' Alison yawned again and pulled the sheet up over her head.

'I'm going down to the boat,' Johnny said abruptly to Peter. 'See if Pino is there.'

'I thought he'd gone away,' Elizabeth said. 'Dom do you think you could go and ask for more coffee.'

He pulled a face and nodded towards the kitchen where Maria-Grazia's raised voice could still be heard. 'Doubt it.'

'What do you want to see him for, anyway?' Peter asked.

'I reckon he knows something about the money.'

'He wasn't even here!' Peter said, angrily.

'When? We don't know when the money was taken.'

'Or if it was taken,' Dom said, in a placatory voice. 'Mum could have mislaid it.'

'You're looking for an excuse to get rid of him,' Peter said.

'No, I'm not.'

74   *Maureen Donegan*

'If you accuse him, he'll go.' Peter also nodded meaningfully at the kitchen door. 'It doesn't take Einstein to work that out.'

'So?'

'Oh, go down to the boat yourself then!' Peter shouted. 'I'm going for a swim.' He lurched out of his chair and half stumbled down the steps at the end of the terrace.

Dom suppressed a grin. 'The coffee's cold,' he said, as Tom and Gillian appeared, 'but I'd advise you not to ask for any more. Not for a while.'

Gillian opened her eyes wide. 'Why not?'

He shrugged. 'Problems in the kitchen.'

'Oh dear. Should I go and—'

'No!' he said emphatically.

'Surely they're not still upset? The money's been found.' She paused. 'Or was put back. And that's the most important thing.'

'Found, surely?' Tom said into the ensuing silence. He poured himself some fruit juice.

'Yes, well, found.' Gillian gave her tinkling laugh. 'That's what I meant. What shall we all do today?' she asked brightly. 'Anyone any ideas?'

Giulio stacked the shopping carefully into the boot of the car and then looked at his watch. It was still early, he would treat himself to a coffee. He felt he deserved a brief respite. The events of the past twenty four hours had taken a great deal out of him. He retraced his footsteps through the market, mentally ticking off the items he had bought. In the distance he saw the Contessa Grenbelli and he made a detour to avoid her. Last night, Maria-Grazia had told him to go and see her to tell her they were looking for a job but he thought it would be foolish to do that. The story of the missing money might go around, damaging their reputation. And La Rosa had said that the summer would pass and these horrible English would go. She hadn't called them horrible, any more than she had said outright that their prospects of another job, if La Tenby spread malicious gossip, were not wonderful, but Maria-Grazia had understood that was what she meant. La Rosa, he reflected, was very wise and so, most of the time, was Maria-Grazia. But he could not forget how they had been insulted.

He went into a bar in the old part of the port and joined a group of fishermen at the counter.

'Maria-Grazia's coffee not good enough for you?' an amused voice said.

'Eh, Sergio,' Giulio said, looking around. 'I needed a few moments to myself, that's all.'

'Things are no better?'

'They are worse.' He plunged into the story of the missing money.

Sergio Tavazzi did not seem particularly impressed by its gravity. 'These things happen,' he said, 'people are careless, then they blame others.'

Giulio nodded. 'That is what La Rosa says.'

'She is a sensible woman. And you say the Sard has gone?'

'And not before time,' Giulio grunted.

But his companion had turned to watch Johnny Langdon Smythe in the company of a powerfully built man walking along the waterfront in the direction of the marina. It was Franco Nardi, he recognized him from photographs both on file and in the newspapers. A link, a definite link.

'Have you seen that man before?' he asked.

Giulio sniggered. 'Nah, he does not look the *inglese*'s type.'

'I don't think it's a social meeting.' Sergio watched until the two were out of sight. He pulled a coin from his pocket and passed it quickly from one hand to the other, then held out his empty hands.

Giulio looked at him blankly. 'What's that?'

'Nothing is what it seems, that's all.' Sergio was silent for a moment, then said, 'So tell me, what else had been happening? Where is the blond boyfriend this morning?'

'Probably gone looking for the Sard,' Giulio said. 'They were,' he placed one finger over another, 'like that. I saw him going into Pino's room a couple of times. You know, even if I was *finocchio*, I would not fancy him.'

'The *inglese*?'

Giulio laughed. 'No, the Sard.'

'Well, at least you've managed to smile.'

'*Beh*,' Giulio said, 'it is not easy.'

76   *Maureen Donegan*

*

Susie lay with her face up to the sun. For a change, Mike was by her side. Tom, Peter and Gillian were in the pool indulging in horseplay. Susie thought Gillian was making a fool of herself.

'Come on,' Peter shouted, 'you're not trying.'

The trio had sorted themselves out into a line and Gillian's voice floated up to her, 'Oh, is it a race?'

Susie raised her head to watch. Tom had let Gillian go ahead and was now pursuing her with a powerful crawl and Peter had pulled himself out of the water and was cheering them both on. It must have been obvious to him, as it was to Susie, that at the last moment Tom slowed down and let Gillian reach the far end ahead of him.

'She's a good swimmer,' Mike said. He had sat up just in time to see the finish.

And Tom was very clever, Susie thought. What was a man like that doing at the villa? Unless he genuinely had time on his hands. There had been some talk of waiting for a phone call but he was impervious to questioning. He had the knack of half smiling instead of answering, his head cocked to one side as though he were the one who needed an answer. She'd seen him going to Gillian's room, and that was fine, but unfortunately he would probably leave in a few days and then, she glanced at Mike, it would be open season again.

'Shall we go again?' she heard Tom say.

'Uh, uh,' Gillian said, 'that was a fluke. I'm not going to risk it again.'

Some fluke. Pathetic really, although there was minor satisfaction in watching Tom outmanoeuvring Gillian.

'What's pathetic?' Mike asked.

God, she must have spoken out loud. Susie jumped up, employing Tom's tactics. 'I'm going to change,' she said. 'Coming?'

'Why are you so restless?' Mike asked, making no attempt to move.

'I'm not restless,' she said, 'I've had enough sun for today, that's all.'

Mike stretched and then turned over on his stomach. 'If you'd come out with Gillian and Dom instead of going off to Denmark, you'd be acclimatized by now.'

TUSCAN SHADOWS

'Jenny's an old friend, I told you.'

'You never talked about her much before.'

'We were at school together. She's asked me dozens of times to go over there.' She paused. 'OK, it was an excuse not to travel with . . . them.' She nodded vaguely towards Gillian. 'But in any case I wanted to go. And I enjoyed it,' she added defiantly.

'Mmm.' Mike rested his head on his outstretched arms. 'If it was so enjoyable, why did you leave a week early?'

'Her sister was coming and it's only a small place.'

'Oh.'

Out of the corner of her eye Susie saw that Gillian had removed the top of her bikini and was arranging herself on one of the sunbeds. She felt renewed resentment against her father for marrying again and then dying and leaving her alone with Gillian and Dom.

'You're staying down here then?' she asked Mike.

He grunted, without opening his eyes.

'Maybe you'll have a sleep,' she said, hopefully.

On her way up to the house Susie passed Alison stretched out under an olive tree in the garden.

'That you Keith?' she said, without opening her eyes.

'No.' Susie stopped and turned back.

'He went to get me a cold drink.'

Susie sat down beside her. 'Are you all right, Alison?'

'Mmm. Just hot.'

'It's better up here. It's like an oven by the pool unless you're actually in the water.'

'I suppose so.' Alison still didn't open her eyes.

Susie took her hand. 'I can get you something if you like.'

'Oh, Keith will come back.' Alison smiled to herself. 'He always does in the end.' She pressed Susie's hand in return. 'I'm glad you came to the villa.'

'What's it been like?'

'I don't really know. I've been sleeping a lot.'

Susie looked down at her with a surge of pity. She hadn't realized how much Alison had aged in the past couple of years. She remembered the slim, energetic Alison of her childhood. Now the slender body was little more than a bundle of bones, the long brown hair greying and dull and her face, with little flesh to fill it out, was drawn and lined.

'At least the food is good here,' she said and then, abruptly, 'Are you eating?'

'A bit,' Alison said. 'Don't worry about me, Susie.'

'I can't help it.'

'Save it for those deprived families you work with, love.'

'They don't let me loose on their problems much, not yet. I spend most of my time cleaning up the incontinent. Gillian, of course, thinks social work is the absolute pits.'

'Gillian likes to pull the strings.'

'I know. She didn't want me to do children's nursing, but she made a terrible fuss when I gave it up.'

'She's not exactly over-sensitive, Susie.'

Susie shrugged. 'She likes things tidy.'

'You and I must be a great trial to her, then.' Alison opened her eyes and laughed.

'She says it was stupid to start again from scratch, that it will take years to qualify. Maybe she's right.'

'You know she isn't. Did you manage to do any studying in Denmark?'

'A bit. It was very peaceful.'

Alison's moment of liveliness seemed to have passed. 'I imagine it was,' she murmured.

'I would have stayed, only Jenny's sister was coming with her baby and I didn't want—'

'A baby. Oh Susie.' Alison's voice was full of distress.

They fell silent and were still sitting there, holding hands, when Keith arrived ten minutes later with a jug of orange juice and ice-filled glasses.

Lunch passed without incident and the villa settled down to a somnolent afternoon. Pino had not returned but Giulio had come back from the port in a more cheerful frame of mind. Maria-Grazia had made *fettuccini*, her anger dispersing as her hands worked the dough. Making pasta had the same effect as another woman might have got from taking tranquillizers.

Rose went to the library. Tom was there looking at a book of maps of the area and he nodded briefly as she came in and then closed the book and put it down.

He picked up a new novel, still pristine in its dust cover. 'Think I'll try this.'

Rose was about to comment on it when he gave her a dismissive smile. She remembered she was the hired help, suppressed a smile of her own and began to browse along the shelves. Why should she bother to explain that she had been given the run of the library by Mrs Venables-Brown?

He was still watching her and, after a moment he said, 'Are you expecting any more guests at the villa?'

She turned back to him. 'Not that I'm aware.'

'Ah.' He stood irresolutely by the fiction shelves and then went out, leaving the book he had chosen behind.

Rose went back to her room and began a letter to Arthur.

I've settled down here, she wrote. *It's a beautiful place and I get on very well with the Italian couple.* But she'd said that in her first letter. She certainly wasn't going to tell him about the missing money. She stared out of the window and then began to write again. *I've met an old friend, Laura Grenbelli's mother. Do you remember Laura? She had dinner with us some years ago before she went off to Peru?*

She filled half a page with the doings of Laura's children, then looked around for more inspiration and began to describe her room. She could tell Arthur more about the clash of personalities in the villa another time. When she went back to England, perhaps. She grinned to herself. What he didn't know. . . . *You mustn't worry about me,* she added, *things have calmed down,* then looked down at the words thinking that this was the absolute opposite of the truth.

Her perspiring fingers slid along the pen as she added a few more comforting platitudes but eventually heat and lassitude overtook her and she lay down and closed her eyes.

She slept for longer than she intended and woke with a dry mouth. She

80   *Maureen Donegan*

splashed cold water over her face, changed quickly into fresh clothes then hurried across the courtyard to help with the preparations for dinner. Maria-Grazia had slept too and was almost her old self. Dinner passed quietly although Johnny Langdon Smythe arrived late and appeared to be irritated by the sight of Dom and Elizabeth carrying on a lively conversation and laughing at what were evidently private jokes. Alison seemed to be more awake and was behaving nicely to Keith. Only Susie was silent, watching Gillian who had her head close to Mike's and was listening with rapt attention to some story he was telling. But there was also some general conversation and, as Rose moved back and forth to the table, she felt that the atmosphere was much calmer. With any other group of people she would have said it was normal.

It wasn't very late when they finished clearing up. Rose rinsed out the last tea towel and went to the terrace to see if she had overlooked any glasses. Dom was perched on the edge of the parapet.

'It's a wonderful night,' he was saying. 'Who's for a midnight swim?'

'Why not? Will you come, Mike?' Susie asked.

'Uh, uh. Too tired.' He was leaning back in his chair, eyes half closed, watching Gillian rocking gently on the swing. 'But you go.'

Susie sank back in her chair. 'No, I don't think so.'

'Nor me,' Tom said, and Keith and Alison shook their heads.

'I think I'd like to,' Elizabeth said.

'Such energy,' Gillian murmured.

Johnny watched until their figures had merged into shadows of the lower terrace and then went over to Peter who was staring out at the plain below. He put his hand gently on the younger man's shoulder. 'Come for a walk?'

'Dom and Elizabeth seem to hit it off well together,' Gillian was saying to no one in particular as Rose returned to the kitchen with her tray and breathed a sigh of relief that the day was over.

CHAPTER 7

'I'd like you to keep better control over what is being spent, that's all.' Gillian went out, closing the kitchen door with a sharp click.

'Now what?' Maria-Grazia demanded.

Rose sighed. 'La signora has finally taken an interest in the housekeeping,' she said.

Maria-Grazia's black eyes glittered. 'But what did she say?'

'She thought we could serve up the fish mousse again.'

'*Beh*, if it was still there it would walk to the table by itself, and everyone would end up in hospital.'

'I told her we'd eaten it, but according to her we should be buying our own food.' Rose held up her hand to prevent Maria-Grazia's inevitable explosion. 'I know, I know. I told her to read the rental agreement.'

'She thinks we are thieves,' Maria-Grazia said. 'Now do you see what I mean about tenants?'

'I'm beginning to,' Rose said. This was something else she would omit from her letter to Arthur. No point in anticipating the inevitable lecture.

But suddenly, Arthur and the problems of the housekeeping were totally forgotten as Giulio came flying across the courtyard, dust and gravel spraying behind him as he ran.

He burst into the kitchen and collapsed, grey-faced, on to a chair.

'Pino,' he gasped. 'Pino!'

'What is it?' Maria-Grazia shouted.

Rose went over to the sink and filled a tumbler with water.

81

82 *Maureen Donegan*

'Here,' she said quietly, 'drink this.'

He took the glass with shaking hands and drank in huge gulps and then looked up at them, his eyes wide and terrified.

'Dead,' he said, 'at the bottom of the ravine. Beyond the pool. I thought he was asleep but when I climbed down and touched him. . . .' He began to shake again, not just his hands, but his entire body and Maria-Grazia moved to the back of his chair and wrapped her arms around him, as though she could hold his bones together with her ample flesh.

'Shsh, shsh,' she said gently. And then she lifted her head and stared at Rose. 'What shall we do?' she asked.

Sergio Tavazzi asked Rose to come to the library. Later, everyone staying in the villa would have to go down to the local *carabinieri* station to make official statements but, in the meantime, he wanted to get a clear picture of the events leading up to the death. The *sostituto procuratore* had given verbal authority for the team from Central Office to proceed without his presence and the colonel had agreed that immediate questioning might produce more effective results but had sounded a warning note.

'Remember this is not Bedfordshire, Captain,' he said, 'and you are not in the middle of some English country-house detective story. An Italian citizen has in all probability been murdered and it may be that this ties in with your other investigations, That is the only reason I am putting you in charge of the case, giving you a free hand.' Sergio heard his expelled breath down the telephone wires. 'It is not the way that things were done in the old days and so it is even more important that you observe all the regulations scrupulously.'

Some free hand, Sergio thought. The colonel disliked his subordinate's English upbringing and the way Sergio had been sent into the area with no more than the most cursory nod at the usual chain of command.

The complex machinery of a homicide enquiry moved into action. A dark-blue Fiat van was parked in the drive together with half a dozen police cars; the grounds were full of armed *carabinieri* and the doctor and forensic squad were still at the bottom of the ravine with the body.

Sergio sighed and thought that the only compensation in this whole business was the Englishwoman now seated opposite him. He liked the way her thick dark hair sprang in an uncontrolled mass from her forehead, the coolness of her grey eyes, her slender figure and the decisive way she moved. He even liked her understated English clothes. But what was she doing here working as a maid? He could recognize class when he saw it. Was she perhaps writing a book and looking for local colour, or was there a more sinister reason, the smuggling racket, or something else underhand? He cleared his throat as her eyes met his, clear and calm. Surely, he told himself, it was ridiculous to imagine she could be involved in anything criminal.

'I'm talking to you first,' he said, 'because I feel you will be objective.' And calm, he thought, unlike the lady of the house who had retired to her room shouting that it wasn't fair, she was on holiday, that she should never have come to Italy. Sergio endorsed that. It would have saved them all a lot of trouble. Mrs Tenby was a nasty piece of work all round, according to the Mulettis, even given their prejudice against any tenant of the Villa Antonia.

Sergio took out a coin and passed it back and forth between his hands. He let it slip into his sleeve and then, aware of Rose's gaze, retrieved it and put it back in his pocket. Her eyes were the colour of English skies and he felt an unbearable stab of nostalgia. Would his life have been better if he'd stayed in Britain? If he'd married a woman like this, someone who was not smothered by her family, someone who might conceivably have had interests of her own? Interests that didn't include another man.

He dragged himself back to the business in hand with an effort. 'I'd like to go through the events of the past two days,' he said. 'When did you last see the dead man, for instance?'

'It must have been two days ago,' Rose said. 'In the morning. He was in the garden. I saw him in the distance, but we didn't speak.'

'And you didn't see him return to his room? Or hear anything?' he asked.

She frowned. 'I heard something that night, or rather the early morning. I thought at first it was Pino coming in, but it was wild boar.'

The young *carabiniere* who was taking notes at another table looked up, his pen poised in mid air and Sergio's eyebrows shot up. 'Wild boar?'

'Looking for food. Giulio says they come down from the mountain.'

'Ah yes.' He grinned suddenly. 'But it's unlikely that they killed Pino.'

84   *Maureen Donegan*

'Unlikely,' she agreed. She hesitated. 'Was he . . . I mean, could it have been an accident?'

'We don't know yet but we have to consider all the possibilities. In the meantime—'

'You have to ask a lot of questions.'

'Exactly,' he said. 'Now, let's move on to last night. Dinner was finished at. . . ?'

'About half past ten, quarter to eleven.'

'And after that you were still in the kitchen with the Mulettis?'

'We'd cleared up everything by eleven. I went out on to the terrace to collect glasses.'

'And who was there?'

'Everyone, I think. Then Dom Tenby and Miss Halliwell said they were going down for a swim and I think Mr Langdon Smythe and Mr Kinaid went for a walk. I assume everyone else went to bed.'

'As you did yourself?'

'Yes.'

'And you saw nothing, heard nothing unusual?'

'Nothing,' she said. 'It had been a difficult day and I was very tired. I think I went to sleep almost immediately.'

'Difficult, you say?'

Rose folded her hands on her lap. 'Some money was missing, and there was an atmosphere. Then the money was found, but unfortunately things had been said.'

'The Mulettis had been accused, in fact.'

'Oh. You heard about that.'

'Yes.'

'But surely. . . ?' Her eyes seemed to look through to his soul. He wished again he wasn't involved in a murder enquiry. 'Surely,' she went on, 'the missing money hasn't got anything to do with this?'

'Who do you think took the money?' he asked.

'Not the Mulettis,' she answered quickly.

'The dead man?'

'Perhaps. But then no one liked him much. He was taciturn, unfriendly,

TUSCAN SHADOWS

85

and so it was tempting to put the blame on him.'

'Hmm,' Sergio said. 'And now he can't defend himself.'

He was aware of a restlessness in the corner. 'There's no need to write that down, Pascucci,' he said mildly, and the *carabiniere* crossed out the last thing he'd written.

'So,' Sergio said, 'the dead man may have returned to his room but you didn't actually see him. You say he had been given a few days off.'

'Yes.'

'And yet he hung around.' He paused. 'And would you say his relationship with Mr . . . er . . . Langdon Smythe was cordial?'

'Yes, I would say so.'

'And with the other people in the villa.'

'You want my personal opinion?'

He nodded.

'He didn't talk much, but when he did he had a kind of arrogance.'

'Well, he was a Sard. No, don't write that down, Pascucci,' he said, irritably, and Rose suppressed a smile.

'He was arrogant with Mr Smythe?'

'Yes, but with everyone else too. A don't care attitude, I suppose. As though he was about to give notice. In fact, I didn't expect him to come back.'

'Did he say he wasn't coming back?'

'No, I don't think so. I was simply aware that he had been given time off.'

'Hmm. Is there anything else you can tell me about him?'

'Nothing that could be described as hard facts.'

'You weren't aware of any special friendship he might have had?'

'He appeared to get on better with Mr Kinaid than with anyone else.'

'Better than with Mr Smythe?'

'I would say so.'

Sergio leaned back in his chair and tapped his teeth with his pen. 'Then I think that's all for now,' he said. 'Will you make sure that everyone brings his or her passport when they come to make their statements.'

Rose got up to go. 'Yes, of course.'

'Just a minute.' He waved a detaining arm. 'Pascucci, go down and see if they've finished with the body.' When the young *carabiniere* had gone, he asked abruptly, 'Signorina Rose, off the record, what exactly do you think was going on between the owners of the boat and the Sard?'

'I think they are – were – all gay,' she said. 'And so I suppose they could have been a threesome.'

'Or a twosome and one left out.'

'It's possible.'

'And the twosome would be Kinaid and the Sard. Another twosome being Kinaid and Smythe.'

'That was my impression too.'

He smiled suddenly. 'Thank you. You've been very helpful. I'd heard this story elsewhere, but I wanted your opinion.'

'I see,' she said.

The business of taking the statements was long and drawn out. The local *maresciallo*, who was in charge of the station at the port, made three rooms and several desks available in his already cramped quarters, and non-commissioned officers from Central Office tackled the interviews, battering out the results, hunt and peck, on ancient manual typewriters. Reams of carbon paper were used to make endless copies. Two professional translators were called in and Rose was also pressed into service after some initial hesitation on Sergio's part.

It took most of the day, and it was very hot. At a certain point it was realized that Elizabeth had forgotten her passport and had to go back for it.

'Won't tomorrow do?' she demanded of Sergio.

'Unfortunately not,' he said, as patiently as he could. 'The details all have to be typed on the statement, name, place and date of birth etc. otherwise it isn't valid. And I'm afraid we must hold on to the passports until this is all cleared up.'

'What? You mean we can't leave?'

'Not at the moment, no.'

'Incredible,' she muttered, as she climbed back into the police car.

The results of the interviews were not very revealing.

Gillian was vague about whether or not she was alone in her room in the late evening. Alison was sleeping and didn't remember very much anyway. Johnny and Peter had walked down to the port, then separated, Johnny to collect something from the boat, Peter to have a drink. Mike and Susie were together in her room and Tom said he was sitting in the library reading but no one actually saw him. Rose, Maria-Grazia and Giulio had gone to bed after clearing up the dinner things.

The house and grounds were searched and so was Johnny Langdon Smythe's boat, but nothing incriminating was found. Death, according to the police surgeon, had taken place about ten or eleven hours previously. Probably after midnight and before four o'clock. Rigor mortis was well advanced but not complete and a more precise time would be available when the pathology results were known. Sergio wasn't too hopeful about this because no one knew exactly when Pino had last eaten. The victim's neck was broken and the body was full of contusions from the fall. Or the push. Or both. The most significant injury was a head wound in which fragments of wood had been found.

'It's murder then,' Sergio said to Massimo Pascucci as the last of the interviewees left the station, 'not that there was much doubt.'

'Yes sir.'

'A homosexual trio. Maybe a lovers' quarrel? Or a jealous fiancé? Miss Halliwell's a pretty cold fish, didn't you think? Or it could be something else, quite outside the doings of the villa. Hmm?'

Massimo stayed silent, guessing rightly that the capitain was thinking out loud.

'The something else being smuggling. In other words where we came in.' He paused again. 'They're all English,' he said eventually, 'except the Sard. Mr Tom Graham's an interesting one. Mrs Tenby didn't know him until a week ago. Seems to have met him on a plane. By chance. There seems to be a lot of chance involved in this. Not a premeditated crime, I think. Or at least not planned long in advance. Something happened to upset the status quo.'

He banged his hand on the library table. 'And when we finally get the chance to search the boat we find *cazzo!*'

*

88 *Maureen Donegan*

'I think,' Maria-Grazia, said, rolling pasta, 'that there was a fight. And he fell. And the others were too frightened to tell.'

'What others?' Giulio asked. 'The two Englishmen?'

'Yes, of course.' Maria-Grazia had dark shadows under her eyes after her ordeal at the station. 'You will see, it was nothing to do with any of us. Just the people on the boat.'

She had made her statement very reluctantly and the worst part, she told Giulio afterwards, was having to sign it with her mark. And in front of Sergio Tavazzi, too. 'Never in my life,' she had said, angrily, 'have I been so humiliated. And to be "invited" by the *carabinieri*. It was like being arrested.'

'You don't seem to understand, I can't just get on a plane,' Elizabeth Halliwell said on the telephone to her father. 'The police won't let us leave the area, never mind the country.'

His voice rumbled down the line. 'I'd better come out then.'

She made a face into the phone. 'Please don't.' She listened, shaking her head then smiled wanly at Dom as he passed through the hall.

'There's absolutely no need to do that, Daddy, no need at all,' she said, finally. 'I'll ring you again tomorrow. Yes. Yes, I promise.'

She hurried after Dom into the courtyard. It was still hot but an evening breeze from the sea had lightened the air.

'Everything all right?'

'Well, apart from a little matter of murder, and my father ranting and raving.'

His face twisted in sympathy. 'It's tough on everyone, until it's cleared up.'

'I don't see that happening very quickly,' she said, angrily. 'The police here seem to be more interested in bureaucracy than investigation.'

'It's a foreign country.'

'My father doesn't understand that.'

'Mine would have been the same. He didn't travel well.'

She managed to smile. 'All the same I think you were close to him.'

'I was, but I didn't realize it at the time. It was a terrible shock when he died.'

'What happened?'

'A car crash, but they think he had a heart attack.'

'How awful.'

'I suppose it made me grow up. One day from the next.' He made a wry face. 'They tell me I was a spoiled brat.'

'They say that about me too.' She smiled again then her expression changed and she said, 'I . . . wanted comfort from him tonight but all I got was shouting.' Her voice trembled. 'I feel homesick, but there isn't really any home. My father has this awful . . . person in Edinburgh. She's not the only one but she's by far the worst.'

'Your mother?' he asked.

'She was very gentle. I can just remember her. She died having another baby. The baby died too.'

'How old were you?'

'Six. I can just remember her scent when she put me to bed. And I remember her crying one night and my father shouting. I know he's more bark than bite but I wonder if she knew that. I think about it a lot.'

She fumbled for a handkerchief. Dom put his arm around her shoulders and led her away from the house and into the quiet garden.

'The police even asked my age,' Gillian said later. She was making up her face as Dom watched.

'Well it is on your passport, so why get upset?'

'You don't understand. I had to actually say it. With that young translator smirking.'

'I don't suppose she was, really.'

'I don't imagine things,' Gillian said. She leaned forward and peered at her reflection. 'At least I managed to get an hour's sleep this afternoon. I don't look so bad, do I, in spite of everything?'

'You've put on too much eyeshadow,' Dom said.

'Oh.' She wiped her eyelids with some cotton wool. 'That better?'

'A bit.'

'I told that smart-alecky captain that none of us could have had anything to do with Pino's death, that all the people staying here are old and dear friends.' She thought suddenly of Keith going off to America and leaving her behind all those years ago, and how much it had hurt. She had got him back though, eventually. She'd barely even clicked her fingers, but now he'd become a liability: possessive, depressive and almost as much a bore as Donald.

She'd lost count of how many times she'd told him to face up to the problem of his marriage. Alison needed treatment, not long gloomy conversations with Susie. And that was something else. Why didn't Susie move in with Mike? Get her life together, instead of just talking about it?

She might get a flat too, get rid of all that old furniture, have white walls and natural fabrics everywhere. She imagined Tom coming to visit. He'd told her he spent some time in England. But he wouldn't even get to see the bedroom and congratulate her on her designer skills because they'd make violent love on the floor the minute he arrived.

'And that's another thing,' she said to Dom. 'Captain What's-his-name had the cheek to point out that I'd just met Tom on the flight here. He more or less suggested that I'd picked him up. Anyway, it's obvious that Tom didn't kill Pino. He'd never met him before, or any of us.'

'Bit of a lack of logic there, Ma.'

'Well, you know what I mean. I must say you're not very sympathetic.'

'Sorry.'

'It looks as if it's . . . murder, doesn't it? It's absolutely horrible when you think about it.' She smoothed cream into the area below her eyes. 'What were you talking to Elizabeth about?'

'Mmm?'

'I said, what were you talking to Elizabeth Halliwell about?'

'My father.'

'Why on earth were you talking about him?'

He stared at her in the mirror. 'You know you've never told me how much the villa cost.'

She laughed but avoided his gaze. 'Now you even sound like your father.'

'You haven't forgotten your promise?'

'Of course not, darling. Don't worry. There'll be plenty of money from the house.'

'What?'

She dropped her eyes and inspected her nails. 'You're not the only one who has financial difficulties, darling. I was thinking of selling the house.'

'But Dad left you—'

'He had a cash flow problem too, at least that's how it was explained to me. He'd borrowed to cover it. He just . . . died at the wrong time.'

Dom's expression tightened in disbelief. 'Is that what's holding up probate?'

'I imagine so. Your father's finances were pretty complicated.' She leaned forward and removed an imaginary speck from her cheek. 'You and Susie got your shares in the company, but neither of you bothered to ask if I was all right.'

'I assumed . . . since you had the bulk of the estate.'

'What estate?'

'It couldn't be as bad as you say, the insurance policies alone—'

'He'd surrendered one and the other I, well, I needed it.'

'You mean you spent it on the villa. My God! How could you?'

She gave him a defiant look. 'We were all having a wonderful time and we will again just as soon as this Pino business is cleared up.'

'Oh, absolutely wonderful,' he said, 'you spend money we don't have to play let's pretend.'

'Let's pretend?' she said in a soft voice. 'What about your private little games?'

An uncontrollable twitch crossed Dom's features. 'We're mixed up in murder!' he shouted.

'Pino's death has nothing to do with us,' Gillian said.

'You can't just dismiss it, like that.' Dom's voice had gone up another decibel.

Gillian felt a surge of anger. 'Why don't you ask Susie for a loan? She has money.'

'That's not money; it's a small annuity Anyway she wouldn't give it to me.'

'Or ask your rich new friend, Elizabeth.'

'Don't be disgusting.'

'Why not? Isn't that what friends are for? Oh, come on, Dom. This isn't like you.' She put on a cajoling voice. 'Trust me, I'll sort something out.' She turned to him but he evaded her outstretched arms and strode out of the room, banging the door behind him.

She looked after him. Poor little Dom. He was so confused about things. Himself. Life. She resumed her study of her reflection. Yes, the sleep had smoothed out the signs of strain. She remembered that she had promised to go for a walk with Tom after dinner. She smiled. Afterwards she would invite him to her room. He was the best thing that had happened to her for a long time. She put her make-up into her handbag and patted its bulk automatically. Just as well she'd kept it with her all the time – it was obvious that the villa would be searched.

Dom shouldn't have tried to make her feel guilty about money because she was going to get her finances together as soon as she got back. Keith would help her. In fact, asking his advice might stop him from moaning about Alison. Of course, Alison didn't suspect anything about their relationship. Not really. She was too full of pills. She couldn't remember anything from one day to another. And hadn't she, Gillian, always included her in everything, even at school when Alison was such a dull swot? She'd tried then to get her to have more fun. This holiday was for everyone's benefit. They should jolly well enjoy it. Susie didn't have to be so possessive about Mike either. She ought to realize that it was, well, rather nice to have a younger man making a fuss of her. And that was all there was to it. Sometimes her stepdaughter had such a look of Donald that Gillian felt like screaming. But Dom had worried her tonight. Surely he wasn't going to turn out like his father, too?

'How long do we have to stay here?' Johnny demanded.

'Until the brave *carabinieri* say we can leave. It's a mess,' Peter said.

'They think it's murder.'

'Yeah.'

'He was a proper little whore, your Pino.'

Peter coiled and uncoiled the jib sheet. 'He wasn't "my" Pino.'

'No?' Johnny leaned against the cradle holding the boom and the boat swung on her moorings. His eyes were cold.

TUSCAN SHADOWS

Peter's gut tightened. He knew that Johnny could be violent. He had lashed out at Peter more than once but that had been in their early days when jealousy had sprung more from affection than wounded pride. Pino had also been another kind of threat. But murder was something else. And his death seemed to be bringing further disasters in its wake.

As if following his thoughts, Johnny said, 'Anyway, brave or not, the *carabinieri* didn't find anything. Not in the house and not on the boat. I suppose that's something.'

They exchanged uneasy smiles. 'They'll be back,' Peter said.

'Then we have to ride it out, don't we?' He didn't say that he had seen Sergio watching when he met Franco Nardi on the marina.

Alison, who had endured the hot, wearying day at the *carabinieri* station uncomplainingly, didn't go to lie down after she had made her statement, instead went for a swim. It was extraordinary, Keith thought, but the shock of a violent death appeared to have had a salutary effect on her.

But unpleasant as the situation was, it was in no way anything to do with them. Neither of them had even spoken to the paid hand. He was obviously the same kind as Smythe and Kinaid. Probably all had it off together. Or maybe Pino had picked up some rough trade at the port and brought him up to the villa. That seemed more likely. Keith didn't see either of the yachtsmen as a murderer.

He was on the roof and had a bird's eye view of Gillian emerging from the house on to the terrace. She looked stunning. Tom Graham, following her, obviously thought so too. If I were going to kill anyone, Keith thought, Tom Graham would be the first on the list.

He wished he could get Gillian out of his system. He remembered how warm and loving she used to be. And understanding. But that, he told himself bitterly was because she'd needed a break from Donald and he, Keith, had provided it.

Christ, oh, sweet Christ, he thought as he walked over to the other side of the roof. Dom and Elizabeth Halliwell were walking down the drive. He wondered if he cut the same pathetic figure, crawling after Gillian, as Elizabeth did in her efforts to hold on to Johnny Langdon Smythe.

94   *Maureen Donegan*

Although now she seemed to have asserted herself a bit and taken up with Dom. Or had Gillian pushed those two together? He sighed again. The trouble was that sooner or later his mind, and unfortunately not just his mind, returned like a boomerang to his obsession with Gillian.

'I should have stayed in Denmark,' Susie said gloomily. 'I'd have missed all this. Or is that terribly selfish?'

'It's very human,' Mike said, 'and I could have stayed in England. But since we're here, we have to make the best of it.'

'It's frightening,' Susie said. 'I mean these windows open all the time. Anyone could get in.' She put her arms around him and pulled him down on to her bed. 'I'm glad you're not in England. Will you stay with me tonight?'

'Yes, of course.'

'Just as well we were together last night.'

'Yes,' he said. He smoothed back her hair. 'But nobody could seriously suspect anyone in the house.'

There was a knock and Dom put his head in. 'Oh, sorry. Thought you were by yourself.'

'What is it?' Susie asked in an alarmed voice. 'Nothing else has happened, has it?'

CHAPTER 8

'I don't suppose the police will have any objection,' Gillian said.

'You could find out right now,' Dom said, 'the captain's in the kitchen.'

'It's like having mice,' Gillian said. She gave a nervous laugh. 'It's still all right with you, is it, Johnny?'

'Yes, of course.' Johnny was spreading some of Maria-Grazia's cherry jam on to his *cornetto*.

'You'll get fat,' Peter said.

'Now if anyone is inclined to pudginess . . .' Johnny said.

It was true, Gillian thought, there was a slight thickening around Peter's jawline that could easily become a jowl. It wouldn't be long before he lost his looks.

'Do you want me to ask?' Dom was saying.

'I feel as though I'm at school,' Gillian said, irritably, 'but yes, if you don't mind. And ask for a picnic too. Whenever I go into the kitchen the atmosphere's positively glacial. By the way did you know that woman can't read or write?'

'Who?' Dom demanded.

'The cook. Well, it explains a lot.'

'What does it explain?' Alison asked, coldly.

'How primitive they are.'

Alison snorted derisively.

95

96   *Maureen Donegan*

Gillian shot her a suspicious glance. 'People like that are different from us. They react at a very basic level.'

Dom intervened quickly. 'What time do you want this picnic for?'

'About eleven. You're coming, aren't you Tom?'

'Wouldn't miss it for the world,' he said.

Gillian gave him one of her brilliant smiles. Sometimes she noticed that Tom's wish to please had something mechanical about it. She pushed aside the thought that perhaps even his lovemaking was, well, a tiny bit practised.

'Is the funeral going to be here?' Rose was asking Sergio.

'We haven't been able to trace any family,' he said, as Maria-Grazia refilled his cup with coffee and hot milk. 'He never talked about them to you?'

'He never talked,' Maria-Grazia said.

'Except about the trip over. Said something about the rich being able to please themselves,' Giulio put in.

'You think the other two were wrapped up in themselves?'

'Maybe. He said he was bored.'

'He liked excitement then?'

Maria-Grazia sniffed. 'He found it, didn't he?'

'Yes, indeed he did.'

The door opened and Dom Tenby put his head in.

'Captain Tavazzi?'

'Yes?' Sergio stood up.

'We'd planned a short sail today. Is that all right?'

'I think so. All of you?'

'Mrs Drinkwater isn't too keen, but I think her husband will persuade her.'

'So long as you're not planning another exodus,' Sergio said. He half smiled. 'I need hardly remind you not to leave Italian waters.'

'No fear of that,' Dom said. 'Um . . . Rose?'

She looked up.

'My mother wondered if we could have a picnic.'

'Yes, of course. Giulio is going shopping now. Cold meats, cheese and fruit?'

'That's sounds great. Thanks.' He nodded at Sergio and then retreated, awkwardly. 'Thanks.'

Shortly after they'd all left for the port, Lena Grenbelli telephoned Rose. 'My dear, I believe you're involved in *un imbroglio* over there. It must be absolutely dreadful.' Her voice buzzed with excitement. 'A body in the swimming pool.'

'No. Not in the pool. In the ravine.'

'Ah, Carmina had it that it was in the pool.' There was a mumbled aside and then her voice came back on the line. 'I'm sure you're longing to get away from there. Why not come over?'

Rose had been planning to take her sketchbook up on to the cliffs to capture the old fort on paper and at the same time try to forget Pino's death, at least for a few hours.

'I'm not sure,' she began.

'Four o'clock. I'll look forward to seeing you then.'

Rose put down the receiver with a sigh.

'That was the *contessa!*' Maria-Grazia had taken the call. Surprisingly she smiled. '*Beh,* she is a busybody, but Giulio and me, we like her.'

Praise indeed, Rose thought, amused. She had already telephoned Mrs Venables-Brown in France and told her about the death and she wondered if there had been a call from France to ask Lena to keep an eye on the situation. Fortunately Mrs Venables-Brown had sounded quite calm, as though bodies fell into ravines at the villa every day. She had pointed out that it could well have been an accident and so she wouldn't inform her sister yet, but that Rose should keep in touch about any further developments.

'Because I'm sure it will all be cleared up quite soon,' she had added firmly.

On her way out, Rose bumped into Sergio Tavazzi walking across the courtyard to his police car. 'Can I give you a lift somewhere?' he asked.

'If you're going to the port, yes, thank you.'

He nodded. 'Maybe we could have a coffee together?'

'I'm sorry,' Rose said, 'but I've been invited out to tea.'

'Ah.' He opened the rear door of the car. 'Then we must do it another time.'

She smiled and got into the car.

'Where exactly do you need to go?'

'Oh, the Grenbellis. Beyond the port.'

He gave her a searching look then spoke to the driver and got in beside her. 'Forgive me if I'm being rude, but don't you find it difficult being a friend of the countess and yet working here?'

'No,' Rose said, 'why would I?'

He laughed. 'Not many people would be able to handle them together.'

'Maria-Grazia didn't understand it either, but she's come around, finally.'

The car took a fast corner on the winding unmetalled road and she was thrown against him.

'Take it easy, Massimo! We're not going to an armed robbery,' Sergio said. He steadied her, holding on to her arm for a moment. 'Are you OK?'

'Yes.'

He hesitated and she looked up at him. 'You know you could be very helpful to me,' he said, eventually.

'In what way?'

'By keeping your eyes open. I think you enjoy studying people. And you're in an ideal situation here. No one is going to relax with me, but they might with you.'

'It wasn't an accident then?'

'No. There was a very severe blow to the back of the head which wasn't at all consistent with the fall.'

She hesitated. 'I would feel horrible actually spying on people.'

'If it makes you feel any better, and this is just between you and me, it may have nothing to do with the guests at the villa. At least not directly. The dead man had a record of petty crime, smuggling cigarettes mainly, maybe a few drugs, but more recently we think he may have been involved in moving artefacts out of the country.'

She thought: who were more likely to be smuggling than the owners of a boat? So how could he say the villa wasn't involved? Johnny Langdon Smythe didn't look like a master criminal, though. Was there a big organization somewhere and had Pino run foul of them? Perhaps he'd tried a spot of blackmail, but that led straight back to Peter and Johnny.

'Does it worry you?' Sergio was saying.

'No. That is, yes. Of course it does. But if I can help. . . .'

'I've been keeping an eye on the Sardinian for quite some time,' Sergio said.

It was Rose's impression that he'd been keeping an eye on everyone. She reminded herself that he was first and foremost a detective.

'We could meet from time to time, socially,' he said blandly, 'as a cover.'

'All right,' she agreed. This was something else she wouldn't be confiding to Arthur, not even when she got back.

Peter had gone down ahead to get the boat ready. He washed dirty glasses and put out the cushions in the cockpit, filled the engine with diesel and reflected that without Pino he was now the unpaid and unappreciated dogsbody. Still, Johnny had been nice to him last night. Thank God. But Gillian had made it abundantly clear that she wasn't going to keep quiet about the smuggling if he didn't succeed in keeping Johnny at the villa for the next few weeks.

He knew he'd been stupid, stupid and boastful that weekend in Berkshire. He'd brought pot. 'Pot and a pot,' he'd said, handing Gillian a small glazed urn with a tiny plastic packet inside it.

'What a pretty bowl,' she said, but at least he didn't tell her he'd liberated it from the last trip they made. Let her think he owned it. She'd seemed fascinated by his life when they'd met at that party in London but he didn't think she'd believed what he called his adventures. And so he'd brought proof.

There was something about her that he wanted to get through to, a warmth that had been missing from his own life. And she was a great listener. He'd even pulled that old chestnut about being packed off to school at seven, the youngest of a family of brothers who were more or less grown up when he was born. Perhaps, he told Gillian, his unexpected arrival would have been more welcome if he'd been a girl. It was a poor-little-me story he often trotted out coupled with melting looks from under his lashes. He used it on men and women alike, seducing them for sex, for friendship, for hospitality, or whatever he might need at the time. What he hadn't realized was that he'd met his match when his blue eyes met those of Gillian and they embarked on that disastrous conversation. He'd meant just to hint at the smuggling, but Gillian asked a number of apparently artless questions and he told her far more than he had intended. And then she'd forced him to invite Johnny, whom she had met at that same party in London.

He hadn't intended to get in this deep with Johnny either. He'd been under the misapprehension that Johnny had family money. Now he realized that Johnny was almost as much of a remittance man as he was himself. If he'd thought things through he'd have known that Johnny was marrying Elizabeth not only for respectability but also for her money. That is if the wedding ever came off.

And now Gillian seemed to be doing her best to throw Dom and Elizabeth together. Well, he'd no objection to that. Elizabeth's presence was a constant thorn in his side. But what a pity Dom was straight. Very sexy, he was, with those sapphire eyes. There was something off key about him though, something Peter couldn't quite work out. In fact, he wished to God he'd never met either of them.

'There's quite a breeze,' Gillian said, nervously, as the boat heeled over smartly on the first tack.

Alison was enjoying her discomfort. It was clear that Gillian was almost as afraid of sailing as she herself was of flying.

'Let her off a bit, Peter,' Johnny said in a bored voice.

Peter eased the jib sheet and the boat steadied up and slowed somewhat.

Alison shivered and wished she'd brought a jacket. She'd forgotten that it was always cooler on the water.

Johnny caught her eye and nodded towards the cabin. 'You'll find some sweaters in the first locker on the bunk on the port side,' he said. 'That's the left side,' he added with a slight smile.

'Thanks.' She went below, surprised that he could be so thoughtful. He seemed a different person on the boat. She came back up and stood in the hatchway and watched him. She was impressed by the teamwork. Johnny's hand barely rested on the tiller but his eyes were never still, ranging over the water ahead of them and flickering back every now and then to his passengers. Peter, his long hair tied back, was perched on the gunnel, playing the jib sheet and occasionally glancing at Johnny to anticipate the next move. There was no doubt who was in charge.

Elizabeth was stretched out on the foredeck in the sun and, after a while, Dom and Susie and Mike went to join her.

'All the youngies up for'ard,' Johnny said, grinning, and Alison looked at Gillian to see how she would take this, but Gillian had her eyes half closed and was clinging on to the rail. She was holding on to Tom's arm with her other hand and she was very pale. You had to hand it to her, Alison thought. If she'd felt as Gillian did about sailing, wild horses wouldn't have dragged her on this trip. But Gillian would endure almost anything so that she could boast about 'sailing in the Med'.

'Ready about,' Johnny said, 'lee-oh,' and the boom swung over their heads. The boat shook herself, then plunged ahead on the other tack.

Gillian turned even paler.

'There's not much more of this,' Johnny said, reassuringly. 'We'll anchor along the coast for lunch and coming back should be a good calm run before.'

'What does that mean?' she asked in a tremulous voice.

'It means she won't heel over. We'll have the wind with us.'

'Oh.' She smiled at him faintly. 'Good.'

Alison was thoroughly chilled. She had tried to do without pills the day before and she was feeling the effects. The sea air would blow the cobwebs away, Keith had said, but as they cut through the blue and purple water she felt nothing more than a strong urge to throw herself in. Keith was watching Gillian huddled next to Tom. He turned suddenly on Alison. 'You're absolutely blue,' he said, angrily. 'Why don't you put something on?'

'I did,' she said.

'And get something for Gillian. She's freezing.'

'But Gillian said she'd lo. . .ove to go for a sail,' Alison said softly, imitating Gillian's voice.

'Don't be such a bitch!'

'I may be a bitch but I'm not a bitch on heat,' she said.

'I don't know what you mean,' he said, turning away.

'You just can't stand to watch her flinging herself at Tom, that's all. You'd rather she came to you for comfort.'

'For God's sake, Alison, not here,' he muttered.

'Why not here? It's not exactly a secret, is it?' She raised her voice over the wind. 'The way you go sniffing around her. And where were you the other night? You were with her, weren't you?' She glared at him. 'I was awake you know. Not unconscious. Awake.'

His eyes blazed back at her. 'Be quiet,' he hissed.

The others had begun a discussion about where to anchor. Gillian had lifted up her head and looked slightly better. Tom smiled and pulled her closer and Keith gave them one agonized look and then turned back to Alison.

'Haven't you had your Valium? Is that it?'

She backed down the companionway so that he wouldn't see her tears. The one time, she thought shakily, the one time I'm making an effort, he has to throw it back in my face. Her heart was pounding. Why the hell had she left her pills in the villa?

There was sudden activity above her head and the sound of the anchor chain running. After a moment Susie's head peered down at her.

'We've arrived,' she said. 'Come on up, Alison.'

'Yes, all right, I'm coming,' Alison said. Sharp points of light began to overlay her vision. The boat was riding gently at anchor and Peter was making a rope fast around a winch. There were a few other boats in the bay, but no one on the small sandy beach.

'No access from the shore,' Johnny said, following her gaze.

The colour was coming back into Gillian's face. 'It's absolutely super,' she said, standing up rather unsteadily, 'just as I always imagined it.'

In spite of herself, Alison felt a reluctant admiration. It took courage to continue to summon up charm in the face of real fear.

'Put the ladder down, Peter, if anyone wants a swim.' Johnny was making fast the tiller.

Alison accepted a glass of wine from Johnny and swallowed it quickly. She stripped down to her swimsuit and dived in, hitting the water hard. The wine had induced a feeling of well-being and the water was cool and silent.

What a pleasure it would be to leave everything behind, to stay under, to let it all go. Would Keith be sad, sorry? He'd be free to marry Gillian then. Except that he wasn't rich enough. Why not let Gillian have him if she wanted him? Sometimes Alison wasn't even sure about this. But she was sure that Keith wanted Gillian.

The water tugged her seductively downwards and Alison's thoughts drifted back to her wedding day. Even the sight of Gillian giving Keith a more than congratulatory kiss hadn't spoiled the day. After all Keith had apparently got over Gillian, had chosen her, Alison, and they were going to be happy forever and a day. They'd thought three children would be a good number, maybe even four. How naive she'd been but, all the same, the months that followed the wedding were total joy. Even afterwards, when the children hadn't come, they'd been contented. Until they moved house and found the Tenbys living nearby. Now she marvelled at the way she'd let Gillian take over without so much as a murmur.

Fight, she told herself suddenly. Fight. She began to struggle, gasping as she swallowed water. She kicked wildly, not sure if she had the strength to get back to the boat and then found herself on the surface, choking and coughing. She swam infinitely slowly back to the ladder, her limbs shaking and uncoordinated. Peter helped her back into the cockpit. Keith didn't appear to notice how long she had been in the water. He handed her a towel without a word and then went down into the cabin where Elizabeth and Gillian were organizing the food.

She watched the line of his back as he descended the companionway, carefully, as he did everything else. She loved him. And that was the bitter and insoluble heart of the problem.

Sergio Tavazzi sat at a desk in the *carabinieri* station rereading the statements in an attempt to reconstruct the Sardinian's last two days.

Pino had gone to get a new pump for the boat and after that had taken a couple of days off. Langdon Smythe said this was quite usual after a long trip. In any case, they were staying at the villa and didn't really need him. On the subject of the money, Langdon Smythe said that it was possible that Pino had taken it but he, personally, had never found the Sard dishonest.

Kinaid's contribution to this possibly well rehearsed account was that he didn't know whether the Sard was coming back or not. He denied knowledge of any disagreement. Blackmail, perhaps? But if Pino had been blackmailing them, then he wouldn't have stolen the money.

There was also the incident with the car. Was it an accident? Could someone have had it in for Gillian Tenby? Giulio had said he had a spanner missing but he could have been lying about that. On the other hand he was also the most likely person to have driven the car after it had been tampered with. Only who on earth would want to kill Giulio? And why?

Sergio returned to the Sard. Pino had taken time off, enough to go away from the area, but he had stayed in the vicinity at least one night. Had he slept in his room? Rose had heard something. What? Had Pino stayed on the boat? He could even have stayed in the town and come back to the villa late on the day he died. Rose had seen him in the garden, wandering around and then going towards the thick copse beyond the annexe but that was the day before he died. That is if what she said was true. His training, unlike his instinct, told him he shouldn't dismiss her from the list of suspects. He frowned, and glared at the telephone, then took out Rose's statement and asked Massimo to get a London number. She would have had to give references for the job, he could check those.

The line was engaged, Massimo told him. Sergio groaned and went back to the statements. Why did Pino come back to the villa? To meet someone? To deliver a message to someone? To give Langdon Smythe and Kinaid some kind of ultimatum? If only they had found something on the boat the case could be cleared up in no time. But if there had been artefacts on board when they came into port, they were already on their way through well-established routes to northern Europe. Or had they been delivered in Sardinia, rather than picked up there? Was he at the wrong end of the line?

These *maledetti* loose ends were worse than his *nonna*'s knitting. The trouble was that there was no clear motive. It wasn't as though Pino had tried to seduce Maria-Grazia and been killed by a jealous Giulio; this thought made him smile and he decided to go for a walk before even more far-fetched theories presented themselves.

The murderer could have been a woman, Sergio thought, as he walked along the street to his local bar. He took out a coin and tossed it absently from back and forth between his hands. Pino had been hit with a blunt instrument, a piece of wood, but the weapon hadn't been found. He tried to imagine a figure creeping up on the Sard as he stood at the end of the pool. Doing what? Admiring the moon? Hardly. Pino must have been there by appointment. There had been no sign of a struggle, nothing under the victim's nails and, apart from the blow on his head, all his injuries could have been caused by the fall.

The murder could have taken place soon after Elizabeth Halliwell and Dom Tenby came up from their midnight swim. They might have killed him together. But what possible motive could they have had? Perhaps Dom returned to the pool. Suppose he had seen the Sard take the money and threatened to call the police if he didn't get a cut. But it was his mother's money, not some stranger's. And in any case the money had been found.

The bar was quiet. He ordered a coffee, added three spoons of sugar and swallowed it in one gulp, then went back to the office and shouted to Massimo to try the London number again but when he got through he was told that Mrs Venables-Brown was in France. He took down the new number then pushed it on one side. Why was he wasting time like this? It was obvious that Rose wasn't involved in Pino's death.

'I've seen the "couple" around the port,' Lena Grenbelli said. She was doing most of the talking, fluttering from subject to subject like a frail butterfly. 'I knew Johnny Langdon Smythe's mother slightly, in England. Nice family. I think Johnny was always a worry. But I don't know this Tenby woman. Bunny Martin got the usual reference of course, but you can never tell, can you?' She poured another cup of Earl Grey for Rose. 'And are you going to stay on after this?'

'I don't have any choice,' Rose said, 'the police won't allow us to leave.'

'I believe Sergio Tavazzi is in charge. Local boy makes good, if you like, but very capable. Attractive in a severe kind of way. Women seem to like him very much, but he's not a pipe and slippers man.'

'No,' Rose agreed, 'he isn't.'

'I think he had a little whirl with the Greek girl they had at the villa last

106   *Maureen Donegan*

year, although Maria-Grazia told my Carmina she was no better than she should be.'

So that was the source of most of Lena's information.

'He's a womanizer, then?' Rose felt her heart sink, but she forced a conspiratorial smile at the older woman. She also resolved to keep her future dealings with Sergio Tavazzi purely on a business level.

Lena sniffed. 'Like most men, my dear. In any case, I suspect he's rather isolated, and his job doesn't make it any easier. He has a sister here, but she's kept busy with her own family. Tell me, have you told your young man about the murder?'

'My young. . . ? Oh, you mean Arthur?'

'Is that his name? I knew an Arthur once when Papa was posted to London.' A smile crossed Lena's face. 'He was tremendous fun. I hope your Arthur makes you laugh. It's important.'

'Yes, he's amusing,' Rose lied. She wondered why she wanted to present Arthur in a good light because whatever else his qualities might be, being amusing wasn't at the top of the list. 'But I haven't told him about Pino's death. He would have a fit.'

'Of course, he must worry about you. It's natural.'

Rose nodded and felt guilty. How could she explain to Lena that Arthur's solicitude often irritated her because it smacked of possessiveness.

Lena cocked her head to one side like a shy bird. 'Where did you meet him?'

Rose laughed. 'It was sheer chance – a skiing holiday in the Dolomites. I only went to please a girlfriend. I'm a total rabbit and Arthur is an expert skier.'

'He's an outdoor man?'

'Yes, but not just that. He's also a stimulating companion, someone I can say anything to, or just be quiet and reflective with. He organizes his life well, too. He has that gift of making his surroundings warm . . . mmm . . . and welcoming.' Rose remembered only too well the miserable conditions she had endured during her brief marriage. 'He's even a a good cook.'

Then she remembered Stefan and the night of the nettle soup.

'And so you've known him for years?' Lena said.

'Yes.' She paused. 'On and off.'

Lena appeared eager for more information but Rose wasn't going to tell her about Stefan. She was still ashamed of the way she'd behaved.

Arthur had been sitting at the head of his table during a meal in honour of his former student, Stefan, a Hungarian Canadian, who had come to Britain on a sabbatical. Arthur had been describing, no pontificating, in excruciating detail how he'd made the soup, from the moment he'd donned heavy gloves and picked the nettles in his mother's garden to the final addition of eggs and cream. Perhaps it was the way Arthur had pulled in his mouth as he'd admonished his captive audience to beware of it curdling, not to let it boil if it had to be reheated, and only to make it in the spring when the nettles were young. He hadn't noticed that his guests' level of interest had been flagging for some time. He went on to boast how full of iron it was. Duly appreciative murmurs ran around the table and the guests were finally allowed to pick up their spoons. Rose felt deep embarrassment for Arthur. And for herself for being with him. As they all tucked into Arthur's *magnum opus* she became aware of Stefan's leg against her thigh.

'I like to grasp the nettle, not put it through the food processor,' he whispered.

Rose stared at him as he removed his spoon from his mouth and ran his tongue over its contours. He watched her reaction.

She glanced down the table and suddenly saw Arthur through Stefan's eyes. Boring. Pompous. She'd offered Stefan a lift back to his hotel but they'd ended up at her flat.

Her behaviour was all the more reprehensible because Arthur was proud of his former student and fond of him too, no doubt. On a whim she'd destroyed a friendship.

She'd had a whirlwind affair with Stefan, knowing it was madness, knowing there was no future in it, knowing that she was hurting Arthur. Stefan went back to Canada promising to write. He hadn't, of course, nor had she wanted him to. She couldn't face Arthur. She broke off her relationship with him and they didn't see each other for a year but, eventually, he had worn down her resistance with patient letters and phone calls. Now they were back to where they had been before. Well, almost.

'That man who died,' Lena Grenbelli said, breaking into her thoughts, 'was he a homosexual?'

'Mmm. I think so.'

'I imagine he was bi, my dear. Carmina says he's been seen around the bars with different girls, tourists mainly.'

Rose couldn't hide her surprise.

'It's a small place,' Lena said, smiling. 'Don't ever forget that.'

'I wanted to talk to you,' Gillian Tenby said, 'because something rather awkward happened on the boat today.'

Sergio sat opposite her on the terrace, a coffee table between them. 'And you wish to change your statement.'

'Not change it exactly. Just add to it.'

Her dark hair had been newly washed. It followed the contours of her head in a smooth line, leaving wisps escaping around her face. She was wearing a transparent, multi-coloured loose jacket over a short, turquoise dress; a scarf of the same transparent material was tied through the handle of a large, soft handbag next to her on the floor. Sergio didn't know much about women's clothing, but he thought he recognized an expensive outfit. He saw that she was made-up, but the effect was natural. She managed to look younger than her age and, although she wasn't beautiful, her eyes were outstanding. He felt a brief stab of lust in spite of himself. This was a very sensual, very assured and self-confident woman and he remembered Maria-Grazia's gossip; it seemed that La Tenby put it about quite a lot.

She tapped the typed statement with an immaculate red nail and gave a light girlish laugh.

'The thing is, Inspector—'

'Captain.'

'Captain. The thing is that I wasn't alone in my room the night poor Pino died. Mr Drinkwater passed by with a book for me and we stayed chatting for a while.'

'For how long, Mrs Tenby?'

'Oh, a couple of hours perhaps. You know how it is with old friends?' She

TUSCAN SHADOWS

produced a guileless look.

'And that was . . . from what time?'

'From about midnight, I think.'

'And why didn't you tell us this before?'

'Well,' – the laugh tinkled again – 'Alison, Mrs Drinkwater, can be a wee bit difficult sometimes. She has . . . some problems . . . and I didn't want her to think. . . .'

'What kind of problems, Mrs Tenby?'

'She's rather neurotic, wrapped up in, well, what can only be called imaginary problems. She gets the wrong idea sometimes.'

'In that case, why did you change your mind?'

'I . . . er . . . overheard her accusing Keith, that's Mr Drinkwater, of being missing from their bedroom on the night that Pino died, so I thought I'd better put the record straight.'

'Very well. You'll have to come down to the station and amend your statement.'

She pouted. 'Not now, surely?'

'Tomorrow morning will do,' he said, brusquely.

'But can't you just add what I've just said?'

'I'm afraid not.' He stood up and quoted his colonel, 'We have to go through the proper procedures. Is there anything else you wish to change?'

'No, I don't think so.'

'You still have no idea who took your money?'

She spread her hands dramatically. 'It could have been anyone. We're very informal here, anyone could have gone into my room.'

'So you tell me,' Sergio said.

Her smile hardened. 'What I mean, Captain, is that we don't go around locking doors.'

'It might have been better if you had, Mrs Tenby. Tomorrow morning then? In the meantime, please think carefully about the rest of your statement.'

As he turned to leave, he thought he saw a figure in the trees below the veranda. Above, from the roof terrace, he could hear voices. The villa was not exactly the most private place to have an official conversation.

Johnny Langdon Smythe caught him up in the hall. 'Captain, could I have a word?'

'Yes?'

'I . . . that is . . . we were wondering when it would be possible to leave?'

'When I've found your employee's murderer, Mr Langdon Smythe.'

'Ah. You're no nearer?'

'We've made some progress,' he said, carefully.

'I see.'

'In fact, you may be able to help. Did you by any chance hear a conversation between Mrs Drinkwater and her husband on the boat today?'

Johnny looked puzzled. 'They didn't talk to each other much.' He paused. 'They did have an argument, but I couldn't catch the words.'

'Thank you.'

'Is that all?'

'No not quite. Did Pino have a girlfriend?'

'Not that I know of.'

'Does it seem likely that he would have?'

'Anything is possible,' Johnny said. 'I'm not in the habit of discussing personal matters with my paid hand.'

Rose was arranging glasses on a tray as Sergio came into the kitchen.

'How was your tea party?' he asked.

'Fine,' she said, coolly.

'Did the countess have anything relevant to say about the case?'

'Only that Pino was seen around with various girls.'

She began to move away and he put out a gentle hand to restrain her. 'And that was all?'

'That was all.' She eased her arm away.

'Look, we can't talk here. Can I pick you up after dinner?'

'I don't think so,' Rose said, 'we usually finish very late.'

'I don't mind waiting.'

She shook her head. 'Better not. We also have an early start in the morning.'

'Tomorrow afternoon, then?'

'I was planning to go to the beach.'

'We could go together.'

'Surely you have to work?'

'This is work,' he said.

The glasses tinkled as she picked up the tray. 'Look, I must do the table. Sorry.' And she was gone.

The warmth she had shown earlier, in the car, had disappeared completely and he felt confused, humiliated even.

Massimo Pascucci was leaning against the porch, smoking. He jumped and ground out his cigarette as Sergio strode across the courtyard.

'I thought you were supposed to be on duty!' Sergio snapped. 'This isn't a holiday camp!' He got into the back of the car and banged the door. The lock caught but it didn't close properly. He struggled with the handle, aware of having offended Massimo, who hurried around to the driver's seat. 'Bloody hell!' Sergio said, between his teeth. The rest of the journey was conducted in silence.

'Oh, come on, Johnny,' Peter said, 'what's the harm in it?'

'The harm, Peterkins, is that we have the *carabinieri* around. Nosy, suspicious and dangerous.'

They were in Johnny's room, their voices muted, but angry.

'So what did he say, for God's sake?'

'It was more an implied threat than an accusation. Said Pino had girlfriends.'

'So what?'

'Pino had a little cottage industry going, selling grass. Hard stuff too, for all we know. It's a miracle he didn't lead the police straight to us. I reckon we should keep a low profile.'

'I promised Gillian—'

'I don't give a fuck about Gillian!'

'But she—'

Maureen Donegan

Johnny grabbed him roughly by the shoulders. 'She knows, doesn't she?'

Peter opened his blue eyes very wide. 'Knows what?'

'That's the hold she has over you, isn't it?'

Peter was silent for a few minutes, burrowing against Johnny's warmth like a small child nuzzling his mother. He remembered how good it was on the trip from Sardinia. Moments like this made him wonder why he was so easily tempted to stray. 'What makes you think the *carabinieri* suspect?' he asked after a while.

'The captain was like a cat playing a mouse.'

'They found nothing. They're grasping at straws.'

'Suppose Gillian talks?'

'About what?'

'Don't take me for a total fool. She's made cracks, she'll start dropping hints to Elizabeth next.'

'Oh, Elizabeth!' Peter said. He took Johnny's hand and brought it up to his face. 'Gillian hasn't talked to anybody.'

Johnny pushed him away violently. 'So she does know.'

'She might have guessed.'

'Guessed! You fucking idiot! Never learned to keep your mouth shut, did you?' Peter jumped back, his hands raised defensively as the older man lurched towards him, knuckles bunched. Johnny stopped, then his rigid body relaxed and he sank on to the bed, head in hands. 'Oh, what's the use? You know she's going to see the captain again tomorrow.'

'Only to give Drinkwater an alibi.'

'Let's hope that's all it is,' Johnny said.

Dom found Rose alone in the kitchen. 'Can we hold dinner back a bit? Johnny and Peter had to go to the port.'

'How long?' she asked.

'Half an hour. An hour.'

'There's an Italian expression, *"un'oretta",*' she said with a smile. 'It means more or less an hour, but it's always more and never less.'

'I think that covers this situation,' he said, grinning.

'It'll be all right,' Rose said. 'I'll tell Maria-Grazia. She won't put the pasta on until the last minute anyway.'

He leaned against the counter and his eyes wandered around the room. 'You seem quite friendly with that policeman,' he said at last. 'Did he tell you anything?'

She shook her head. 'No.' Sergio wanted to be more than a friend, she thought, but Lena's account of Melina the Greek made Rose think about her foolishness with Stefan. She didn't want to be this year's summer girl.

Dom said, 'I think there's something up with that pair on the boat. Johnny was talking to Captain What'sit and then he got hold of Peter and they went rushing off.'

He opened a packet of bread sticks then belatedly offered her one.

She shook her head. 'Do you know where they've gone, or what they're worried about?' she asked cautiously.

'No idea.' He shrugged. 'Mum always gets involved with curious people, she collects them.'

CHAPTER 9

'Peter, that's enough!' Johnny said sharply. The younger man looked up from the joint he was rolling and giggled.

'We need it after all we've been through,' Gillian said, raising her eyes dramatically. Johnny was afraid, she thought, but he'd given in to Peter on this one. Well, he could go on giving in. Peter would jump when she said so. 'Why don't you make one for Keith, darling?' she said, taking the joint from Peter.

'No thanks,' Keith said.

'C'mon. Relax.' She giggled again.

Peter laughed. 'Is that what it does for you, Gillian?'

'It does all sorts for me,' she said, looking at Tom. She called over to Elizabeth. 'Don't you be a spoilsport too.'

Elizabeth shook her head. She was standing at the edge of the terrace looking down at the shadowy olive trees.

'Didn't the police leave a man in the grounds?' she said.

'Did they?' Gillian said, vaguely. 'One of the ones in the fancy uniforms. Well they won't come up here tonight.'

'Just as well, but they are very pretty,' Peter said in her ear.

She was inclined to agree. The severe but handsome captain for example dressed up well in scarlet and black and it would be even more enjoyable to remove his uniform, item by item. Tomorrow morning she would be very nice to him.

She looked around. 'Peter, do one for Tom.'

'Not for me. Did that road when I was young.'

'And you're not young any more?'

'Not very, no.'

She gave her silvery laugh but wondered at the same time if she was being snubbed. 'This stuff is wonderful,' she said. 'You're forgiven for making us wait for dinner, Peterkins, if this is what you went to the port for.'

'Hey,' he said, 'only Johnny is allowed to call me Peterkins.'

'Oops, sorry.' She raised her voice. 'Elizabeth, isn't that very sweet – Johnny giving Peter a pet name?'

The girl's head swung around and she flushed with anger. Dom went to stand beside her and put his hand on her arm.

Gillian smiled to herself as her eyes took in the rest of her guests. Keith was taking a glass from Alison's limp fingers. He looked up but she let her glance slide past him. She wanted Tom in her bed tonight, not Keith. There wasn't much time left. He would leave as soon as the police said he could. Johnny wanted to go too, but she could get at Peter to stop that. Pity Susie was such a drag. Otherwise it was a great group: three very attentive men, an Honourable and the Halliwell millions. And one could put up with Alison. She, Gillian, had been Keith's first love and it was hardly her fault if he found Alison less than attractive now.

'Why can't everyone just do as they like and enjoy life?' she asked out loud.

'Is that your philosophy?' Tom asked, grinning.

'Sometimes.' She wriggled coyly.

'Good on yer,' Peter said, in a mock Australian drawl and Gillian laughed again.

'All right, do one for me,' Keith said suddenly, in a harsh voice. Alison stirred and opened her eyes.

'Coming up.' Peter was squatting on the *cotto* tiles with a tobacco tin, a twist of grass and cigarette papers in front of him.

Keith took the proffered joint and drew on it. He'd smoked pot in college. God, over twenty-five years ago. He remembered Gillian, high as a kite, surrounded by a group of men, as now. And the sex, afterwards, or rather the out-of-the-world ecstasy. He couldn't remember one single detail, no, that wasn't true, he remembered creeping up the stairs, giggling and shushing, afraid of his landlady.

He looked across the terrace and Gillian shook her head. Not tonight, the message was loud and clear. Christ, it was like a bloody broken record. Not tonight, it's too risky. Not tonight, Alison will guess. She never worried about that. She must be having it off with Tom.

He began to count the people on the terrace, ticking them off slowly on his fingers: Gillian, Peter, Johnny Langdon Smythe . . . Alison, Susie, Mike, Tom, Elizabeth, Dom, himself . . . ten, no eleven with Rose moving around, but he had the curious sensation there were twelve, that Donald was here too. How he must be hating it. 'Poor bugger', Alison had called him. But he, Keith, had taken on the role of watcher now. Frustrated, jealous, impotent with rage. How had Donald managed to handle it all those years?

The smoke sent soothing messages to his tense muscles. Did Donald know about the secondhand car salesman she'd had a fling with? Gillian, or rather Donald, had paid over the odds for a 'one-old-lady-driver, only-twenty-thou-on-the-clock' job. Ninety thousand more like. The prick who'd sold it to her must have been laughing himself into a hernia. Wealthy, indulgent husband and a wife who was . . . avid, yes that was the word, avid for it.

Another scene from his student days flashed into his brain. He heard someone say, 'Stunning eyes', and Alison reply, 'Pity they're not quite straight.' But that couldn't be because Alison wasn't at any of the college's parties. They'd gone to different universities. Christ, he shouldn't have smoked . . . it was the kind of thing Alison might have said though.

Gillian appeared to be a long way away and yet he could see all the details of the intricate pattern of her skirt and the way her black halter top outlined her unsupported breasts. Under the cloth were enormous purple-brown nipples, he could taste them in his mouth now. His eyes travelled up to her face; it was as though he was seeing her through a telescope. Was there . . . Yes, there was a slight turn in her left eye. How extraordinary that he'd never noticed it before. He began to laugh and then the telescope swung around to Tom. His face was wearing an anticipatory grin. Keith stopped laughing. Suddenly he felt more like crying.

TUSCAN SHADOWS

His mind seemed to divide, one part taking in the candles on the table and the calculated effect of the soft light on Gillian's laughing face, while the other roamed sadly through the distant byways of his youth. What had gone wrong, all those years ago? What had stopped him taking Gillian to America? Or sending for her? It was pricks like Tom Graham, he told himself. There'd been plenty of them around. And how Gillian had made him pay for it since. He saw it quite clearly now. The seduction in her husband's kitchen, the subsequent now-you-have-me-now-you-don't. But she was made like that, born like that.

He leaned back in his chair and continued to watch her while more images from the past clicked through his mind like clips from an old and familiar movie.

'Peter!' Johnny called and Peter got up, giggling, and went over to him. Johnny took another joint and inhaled deeply. 'Peterkins.'

'Mmm?'

'You're a wicked boy,' Johnny said softly.

'Just helping everyone to enjoy themselves, that's all.'

'Foolish, foolish.' Johnny's hand circled Peter's neck and drew him into the shadows at the end of the terrace.

'You're enjoying it, too. Go on, admit it.'

'But I'd be better off without you, wouldn't I?'

'No!'

Johnny laughed. Peter's insecurity gave him a charge. His hand dug into the boy's shoulder. 'What exactly did you tell the Tenby bitch?'

'Only—'

'Names? Did you give her names? Nardi, for instance? Pulcini?'

'No . . . no! I said it was just . . . for kicks . . . I didn't make a big thing of it.'

'A hobby?' Johnny asked, with cold sarcasm. 'Is that what you called it?' He felt Peter squirm under his hand. 'I really should get rid of you, get rid of the whole fucking lot of you.'

Peter wriggled free and rubbed at his shoulder. 'Let's go down to the boat, Johnny,' he said, pleadingly.

118   *Maureen Donegan*

'Later.'

'Down to our room then?'

'You think that's the solution to everything, don't you?' Johnny said. His voice was not pleasant.

Gillian was smiling at Mike. 'Come over here and try mine.'

Mike heard Susie say, 'Don't, please,' and then felt his cotton sweater slip off his shoulders as he stood up.

Gillian laughed. 'You weren't quick enough,' she said to Susie, who was half standing, clutching the sweater in her hands.

Alison said quite clearly, 'Cradle snatching again', as Gillian pulled him down beside her and then Keith hissed a warning, 'Alison!'

Gillian was gripping Mike's arm. 'I'll bring one over,' he called to Susie. She shook her head. 'I don't want one.' She looked near to tears.

'Take it easy, Mike. You're your own man, surely?' Gillian murmured. She passed him her joint.

Tom was giving him a speculative look and Keith's expression was actually hostile. Mike drew on the joint and wished, not for the first time, that he hadn't come to Italy, that he had never accepted Keith and Alison's hospitality, not from day one, and above all that he had never become involved with any of the Tenbys, least of all Gillian.

But Susie needed him and he needed her. They were going to create their own family and then they'd be safe, secure. In a moment he would get up and go back over to Susie. In just another moment.

Alison filled a glass with water and wondered how long she'd been asleep. It felt like a century. Her eyes roamed around, slowly. They were all here, all except . . . except the two gays – they must have slipped away.

How like Gillian. How juvenile it was. Even Keith, oh God, even Keith was staring into space. She didn't know why she was surprised. Keith would walk on hot coals if Gillian snapped her fingers.

Mike was laughing at something Gillian had said and he seemed quite unaware of Susie slumped dejectedly in her chair, her hands knotting and

TUSCAN SHADOWS 119

unknotting the sleeves of his sweater. Gillian too, was giggling while the tips of her fingers played a tattoo on Mike's knee. Tom Graham was watching them. He didn't seem to be smoking; his stillness suggested barely controlled irritation.

They were more or less evenly divided, the smokers and the non-smokers. Dom had a joint. He was talking to Elizabeth Halliwell but her figure, like Tom's, was rigid with tension.

'Maybe a joint would help me,' Alison said to Susie. 'Maybe it would drive away the demons.'

'I don't think it would,' Susie said. She had let Mike's sweater fall on to her lap and was still watching him.

'I expect you're right. They'd probably come in droves then.'

'I meant it wouldn't mix with. . . .'

'I'm trying not to take anything, Susie.'

'Yes, I know.' Susie hand touched hers, comfortingly.

'And you?'

'Oh, I'm OK.' Susie turned her gaze reluctantly away from the scene across the terrace.

'It doesn't mean anything,' Alison said. 'It's a game with her.'

'Yes, I know.'

Alison tried to tell herself it was a game with Keith, too. A spasm of grief passed across his face and she felt it transfer, like a cold stone, into her own heart. 'Gillian has more . . . determined paths to follow,' she said.

As if in vindication of her words, Mike stood up and shook off Gillian's caressing fingers. He moved over to Susie, purposefully, dislodging a chair on his way.

Gillian's voice followed him. 'That's right, children, run along, time you were in bed.'

Susie got up to meet Mike and they walked slowly together towards the steps at the end of the terrace.

'Why don't you leave them alone, Gillian?' Alison said.

'Susie hasn't a clue how to handle a man,' Gillian said loudly and Alison saw Susie's step falter.

Oh Gillian, Alison thought, I hope someone makes you suffer some day.

120   *Maureen Donegan*

Rose had appeared with a tray and was collecting empty glasses and dirty ashtrays.

'Would anyone like a nightcap?' Gillian asked. 'Tom?'

'That would be nice,' he said.

'Elizabeth? And I'm sure Alison won't say no. Rose, would you mind bringing some brandy?'

Elizabeth turned from her contemplation of the dark sky. 'Not for me,' she said. Alison noticed her take a rapid glance to where Johnny and Peter had been standing.

'Don't go,' she heard Dom say, but Elizabeth picked up her bag from a chair and went into the house without answering.

Alison wondered why Elizabeth had managed to find herself in such an invidious position. Not that her own was any better. And she had been putting up with hers for far longer.

'Come over and talk to me,' she said to Dom, who was gazing disconsolately after Elizabeth.

Dom nodded and came to crouch down beside her.

'She's an attractive girl,' Alison said.

Dom sighed. 'But it's not easy to get close to her.'

She felt like saying that the only person who found closeness easy seemed to be Gillian. Instead she ruffled his hair, as she used to do when he was little.

'I think she got engaged to him to get away from her father. I can't think of anything else to explain it.'

'Perhaps,' Alison said, gently. She wondered if she would be able to sleep tonight. Would Keith even react if she called him over? She tried to remember how long it was since they had made love.

Dom stood up, abruptly. 'I'm going to bed. I'll see you in the morning,' he said and, like Elizabeth, went into the house via the French windows.

'Now what?' Maria-Grazia asked as Rose took out brandy glasses and arranged them on a tray.

'Another drink,' Rose said. 'Why don't you go to bed, Maria-Grazia? You're always up before me in the morning.'

But at that moment the kitchen door opened and Mike came in.

'Any hope of getting some hot milk? Susie's having trouble sleeping.'

'Yes, of course,' Rose said. She wondered if they had had another row. 'Sorry, Maria-Grazia, but he wants hot milk.'

Mike smiled at her encouragingly. 'Maybe I'll have one too. Hot milk,' he enunciated slowly, '*per favore.*'

'*Subito, subito,*' Maria-Grazia said, taking out an enamel saucepan. 'You see, it never finishes,' she muttered to Rose.

Mike seemed to find it necessary to make conversation. 'This is a wonderful kitchen. The food is superb.'

'He likes your cooking,' Rose said to Maria-Grazia, who smiled briefly.

'You know, I didn't want to come on this holiday, nor did Susie, but Gillian persuaded us and I'm glad. She's a wonderful person, Gillian. It's fantastic the way she organizes it all. She loves getting everyone together.'

'I'm glad you're enjoying yourself,' Rose said.

'I am. Very much, despite the bit of trouble.'

Trust the English to describe a dead body as 'a bit of trouble', Rose thought. She nodded politely.

'Susie was a bit tense when she arrived, all that travelling, but she'll settle down.'

'Yes, of course,' Rose said. Maria-Grazia filled two glasses with hot milk and handed them to Mike.

'*Grazie,*' he said, 'and well, goodnight then.'

When he'd gone Maria-Grazia said, 'He's not so bad, that one.'

'Mmm. Maria-Grazia, did you know some of them were smoking pot out there?'

Maria-Grazia grunted. 'And then brandy. You know what is the best recipe for a good night's sleep? Hard work and a clear conscience.'

Rose laughed. 'You're right.'

'And you. I know what you need, Rosa.'

'What?'

'Babies. It is not too late. What are you doing, a girl like you, waiting on those *pezzi-grossi?* They are not worth that.' She snapped her finger.

'First, one needs a man,' Rose said.

'*Beh*, that would not be difficult. Who is that *inglese* who telephones you?'

Rose half laughed. 'You sound like Lena Grenbelli. It has to be the right man, Maria-Grazia.'

'*Questo non è facile*,' Maria-Grazia agreed. She put away the milk pan with a clatter. 'Sergio Tavazzi is a good man.' she said, her back to Rose.

'Is he?'

'And he likes you.' Maria-Grazia straightened up and faced her.

Rose shrugged. 'He was involved with the girl who was here last year. It would be the same thing.'

'*Beh*, that was just to pass the time. She was a *puttana* and, well, he is a man.'

'Yes,' Rose said.

'But with you, it's different.'

Perhaps, Rose thought, but Sergio Tavazzi wanted to make use of her in another way, to be his spy in fact. She found herself hovering between temptation and annoyance. It would be very satisfying to find Pino's killer and to be one step ahead of Captain Tavazzi, very satisfying.

'You think too much,' Maria-Grazia said. 'I can see it in your face.'

Rose gave her a hug. 'Maybe . . . maybe you're right.'

'Of course I am right,' the Italian woman said.

Giulio came into the kitchen and Maria-Grazia started to tell him about the marijuana.

'How do you know?' he demanded.

'The smell. A sweet sort of smell, Rose says.'

'That must be what I could smell in Pino's room,' Giulio said.

'I got it too, when I went in there to clean,' Maria-Grazia said. 'This year is the worst, the very worst we've ever had,' she went on dramatically. 'Death and drugs and a thief. Nothing could be worse.'

'At least another day is over,' Giulio said.

Later they walked across to the annexe together and stood for a moment in the scented moonlight.

Rose sighed. 'It's a wonderful night.'

'A night for *amore*, Rosa,' Maria-Grazia said. 'Remember what I told you.'

Giulio, picking up the word *amore*, put his arm around his wife and Maria-Grazia pushed him away half-heartedly.

'If you were as tired as I am, Giulio Muletti.'

'*Beh*,' he said, 'no one is ever too tired for that.'

Rose grinned and said goodnight.

'*Buona notte, cara*,' Maria-Grazia called. 'Don't forget what I said.'

'I won't,' she called back. She heard Giulio asking what she meant and Maria-Grazia whispering back. How lucky they are, she thought.

CHAPTER 10

As usual the night was breathlessly hot. Rose slept badly until the temperature fell just before dawn and still felt hot and sticky as she unwound herself from her crumpled sheets. She decided on a quick dip in the pool before the household stirred.

She rinsed her face with cold water, collected her swimming things and went down the steps very quietly so as not to wake the Mulettis. As she rounded the end of the main house and glanced across, she saw Tom, a towel over his arm, emerging from Gillian's terrace door. He stood for a moment at the top of the path before going down to the pool.

She sighed and turned back and went instead to sit in the garden, remembering childhood injunctions from her grandmother's League of Health and Beauty days to let fresh air wash around her body. But it wasn't as good as a swim. She could see the castle from where she sat, clear and golden in the morning light and wished she had brought down her drawing things. So far she had barely put pencil to paper. Laziness, she told herself. She watched Tom, swimming strongly far below, following what looked like an established discipline of one length after another despite the smallness of the pool.

She wondered what his business was, whether he was really what he appeared. He said so little, keeping himself rather distant from the rest of the party but Rose felt that he was watching all the time. Watching and listening.

TUSCAN SHADOWS

'She did not leave a menu last night,' Maria-Grazia announced during an interminable breakfast session as one latecomer after another came demanding fresh coffee or tea, 'and she is not up yet. If Giulio does not go soon he will not be able to park and there will be queues everywhere. I'll have to prepare lunch in a hurry and suppose she wants something which takes a long time?'

Rose glanced at the clock. It was almost ten. 'Then we do pasta and *prosciutto crudo.*'

'But now she is poking her nose into my kitchen, she will say it is too expensive and *mortadella* she does not like.'

Just then an official car drew up in the courtyard and a young *carabiniere* came to the open kitchen door.

'Car for La Signora Tenby,' he said.

'Now we have to wake her,' Maria-Grazia said, triumphantly. 'Come in, come in. You're Captain Sergio's driver, no?'

He clicked his heels. '*Si*. Massimo Pascucci.'

Maria-Grazia sat him at the kitchen table and gave him some coffee. 'You will have a good wait, if I know La Signora Tenby.'

He laughed and eyed a plate of *cornetti* hopefully.

'Eat,' Maria-Grazia said, 'no one else wants them.'

'I'll go and call her,' Rose said, hastily.

'And ask her what we are to eat today,' Maria-Grazia called after her.

Rose made her way down the stairs to the bedroom corridor and knocked on Gillian's door. There was no reply. She knocked again, more loudly. After a few moments she opened the door and went in. The shutter doors were slightly ajar and a wedge of light cut the darkness of the room. Gillian seemed asleep, her face in shadow. Rose touched her on the shoulder but she didn't move. She called Gillian's name and went over and opened the shutters flooding the room with morning sunlight.

Rose gasped. Gillian's enormous eyes were wide open, a look of surprise frozen on her face. When she felt Gillian's pulse her fingers met chill flesh.

Rose hurried back to the kitchen and called Massimo Pascucci and he returned to the bedroom with her, a startled Maria-Grazia bringing up the rear. The young *carabiniere* took one look and asked if she had touched anything.

126   *Maureen Donegan*

Rose shook her head. 'I wanted to close her eyes, but. . . .'

He nodded approval. 'Where is there another telephone?'

Behind them Maria-Grazia was making a low keening noise. 'It's not true!' she repeated over and over. She threw her apron up to her face and backed out of the room.

Massimo took the key from inside the door with a large white handkerchief and was locking it from the outside when Dom appeared.

'What is it?' he asked, white-faced and tried to push past the *carabiniere*.

'Your mother,' Rose said. She hesitated. 'It seems she was taken ill in the night.'

'I want to see her!'

Massimo Pascucci ignored him and spoke to Rose. 'Please go to the terrace and stop anyone from going in that way.'

Dom was pulling at his arm and shouting and other doors opened along the corridor.

'You can't go in there, *signore*,' Massimo said. He looked absurdly young, but his face was grim and determined.

'I'm afraid your mother is dead,' Rose said gently. Dom was shaking so violently that she was afraid he was going to collapse. 'Maria-Grazia, can you take Mr Tenby into the kitchen and give him some strong tea with a lot of sugar,' she said.

Giulio had joined his wife and now he put his hands on her shoulders. 'Come,' he said, 'do what Rosa says. The poor young man. . . .'

Dom was completely silent. He slumped against the wall. Giulio took his arm and drew him gently up the stairs. Maria-Grazia, still whimpering quietly, followed them.

Keith had come out of his room and was facing Massimo Pascucci with an angry face.

'What's going on, here?'

'I'm very sorry but Mrs Tenby has . . . has . . . died,' Rose said, 'and we have to wait for the *carabinieri*.'

Keith turned grey. 'I want to see for myself,' he said. He tried to put his hand on the door but Massimo spread out his arms and hustled him back to where Susie and Mike stood staring in the doorway of Susie's room. Their voices chorused together.

'Dead?' Susie said, in a tone of disbelief.

'She couldn't be,' Mike said.

Susie moved into the circle of his arm and put her face against his shoulder. Rose looked around at the horrified faces.

'Please everyone, come to the terrace. I'll bring fresh coffee,' she said. Massimo Pascucci was already hurrying towards the hall telephone. She followed with Mike and Susie and left them on the terrace with Elizabeth, Peter and Johnny who had arrived a short time before.

She heard Mike telling them the news as she went down to stand guard on the bedroom terrace. Gillian's red bikini hung over a chair outside her door and somehow this more than anything else brought home the fact of her death. Rose held on to the chair for support then sat down quickly before her legs gave way.

Pino's death had also been sudden and shocking but there was still the faint hope that he had been killed by an outsider. Now with the discovery of Gillian's body, it was difficult to reason like that. And it was this thought as well as the memory of Gillian's terrible staring eyes, that was frightening her now. Gillian did not look as though she had died peacefully in her sleep. Was a cold-blooded killer loose in the villa? Someone who perhaps even now might be waiting for a comforting cup of tea or coffee?

Rose remembered the previous evening, Gillian taunting the three women on the terrace. But bitchiness was hardly a motive for murder and Alison and Susie were surely used to her by now. Elizabeth, too, struck Rose as someone who could take good care of herself. She wondered why the Halliwell heiress had taken up with Dom Tenby. Perhaps he was the only possible ally in this incongruous group. Could the killer have been Keith or Tom, vying for Gillian's favours? Did Mike come into this category, too? If Sergio Tavazzi's theory was correct the pair on the boat were smugglers. Could Gillian have also been involved in something illegal? It was odd that she had all that cash with her. Was the villa just a cover-up? But Sergio had said he found nothing incriminating, either on the boat or in the house, and Rose could not see either the laconic Johnny Langdon Smythe or his posturing friend as a murderer. In any case they must have spent the night on the

128   *Maureen Donegan*

boat. She'd seen them walking up the avenue earlier. She didn't remember them leaving the night before only a realization at one point, when she was clearing the terrace of glasses, that they were no longer there.

The sun slanted across her face and she put her hand up to shade her eyes and then moved her chair into the shade, wondering as she did so if she was interfering with evidence. And then Maria-Grazia was beside her with a cup of tea.

'With much sugar, also for you,' the Italian woman said firmly, but the hand that held the cup was trembling. 'Me, I have had some hot milk, and now dozens of *carabinieri* have come, vans and cars and lamps and doctors. And I do not know what La Signora Martin is going to say when she hears about all this.'

'You did well,' Sergio Tavazzi said to Massimo Pascucci as they stood looking down at Gillian's body. Permission had once again been given by the *sostituto procuratore* to begin the investigation in his absence. Sergio's colonel had been and gone, muttering that the death was very unfortunate and should have been prevented. Someone had been making telephone calls. Sergio doubted if Johnny Langdon Smythe was sufficiently close to his family to get them to influence the Italian establishment. Money, however, equated power and Sergio suspected that it was Elizabeth Halliwell's father's angry and paternal concern that had buzzed across several frontiers. The end result, of course, was the colonel's tirade against Sergio.

'I want this cleared up quickly,' he said, as a parting shot, 'and please don't think that you have all the time in the world.' He had stopped shouting by then and the last words were delivered in a tone of deadly civility.

'You would think,' Sergio said to Massimo when his superior had departed, 'that I'd killed her myself just to inconvenience him.'

The preliminary opinion from the police surgeon was that Gillian appeared to have had a heart attack.

'Drugs?' Sergio asked sharply.

The older man shrugged. 'There are a couple of puncture marks on her arm and I have my own ideas about that, but she wasn't a junkie.'

TUSCAN SHADOWS

'I gather there was a pot and brandy party last night, but the evidence has disappeared, of course.'

The doctor nodded impassively: he had seen it all during a long career. 'I can tell you more after the post-mortem.'

'That's what you always say,' Sergio complained.

'Well, let's say it doesn't look like natural causes, OK?'

'OK.'

'Do we know anything about her medical history?'

'The son says she was in good health as far as he knew.'

'Hmm.' The doctor packed up his bag. He glanced down again at the bed. 'Fine looking woman. I hate to see a life wasted.'

But Sergio wondered who would really mourn Gillian Tenby. He was afraid that if he didn't find out quickly who killed her he would be taken off the case. When the telephone wires began to hum in high places anything could happen. The whole affair would very likely be hushed up and he would lose the trail to the big boys, if indeed they had not already closed up shop in the area. None of it would do his career any good at all. And these days his career was just about all he had.

He felt a small gnawing pain in his gut. It drew him down to the kitchen where he found Maria-Grazia making pasta. Her face was devoid of colour and she was handling the dough with grim determination.

'Any chance of a coffee?' he asked.

'For you, yes.' She wiped her hands on her apron. 'All morning coffee, tea, tears and shouts. The telephone, the cars, men tramping through the house. . . .'

'They'll soon be gone,' he promised.

'But what is left behind?' she asked, as she cut him a slice of almond cake.

What indeed? he wondered. Outside on the terrace came the intermittent murmur of voices. The ten members of the house party were all there, clinging together, perhaps for mutual comfort. Or out of fear.

'Giulio?' he asked.

'Has gone to the market.' She made a wry face. 'We still must eat.'

'And La Signorina Rosa?

'Is telephoning Signora Martin's sister in *Francia*.'

130   *Maureen Donegan*

'Ah.' He ate the cake and felt his grateful stomach begin to settle.

'Will you tell her I'd like to see her.'

She nodded. He swallowed the rest of the cake and picked up his cup. 'If I am not in Signora Tenby's room, I'll be in the library.'

'I will tell her,' Maria-Grazia said.

'I will get in touch with my sister immediately,' Mrs Venables-Brown said. She gave a small uncertain laugh. 'We've never lost a tenant before. Oh dear, I must be hysterical and there must be all kinds of practical details to sort out but I can't think—'

'I'll ring you again,' Rose said, soothingly, 'when you've had time to take it in.'

'Take it in. That's right. And you, are you coping?'

'Well, yes. Everyone has to stay here, of course, during the investigation. There is a captain who speaks very good English, that makes it a bit easier.'

'Ah, that would be Sergio Tavazzi, I imagine.'

Did everyone know him? Rose wondered. 'Yes.'

'Very decent person. But what a dreadful thing to have happened. Poor woman, dead. And on holiday. Are some of her family there?'

'A son and stepdaughter. The rest are . . . um, friends, I guess you could say.'

Massimo Pascucci came into the library. In his gloved hand he was holding a woman's handbag which had a delicate multi-coloured scarf tied to it. Sergio, who had seen that combination before, raised his eyebrows. 'Mrs Tenby's?'

'It was in her room, yes.'

Sergio also put on gloves and held out his hand for the bag. He opened it carefully and drew out a small object wrapped in another silk scarf. 'And what was she doing with this?' he asked, as he touched a small glazed urn with the tip of his finger. Then he went through the rest of the contents, a bill and envelope with her name and address on it, make-up, hairbrush, tissues, pen, keys, a purse with some Italian small change and a wallet bursting with English notes. The money that had found its way down the side of a chair, no doubt.

TUSCAN SHADOWS 131

*

Maria-Grazia added a little more flour to the dough and began to work it in. Those people on the terrace would not care what they ate today, but good nourishing meals were needed in times of shock.

In the south, friends and neighbours brought home-cooked food to the house of the bereaved to help them to get through the difficult days surrounding the funeral. She remembered the deaths in her childhood, the pathetic little sisters and brothers who had scarcely known life, the black clothes and sad resignation in the faces of her parents.

That poor boy had lost his mother. He was the only one she really felt sorry for. The others, *beh*, they were cold the English, but Dom, he had something of the Mediterranean in him. She had seen him weeping. The sister too had wept but she had her *fidanzato*. The son did not seem to have anyone. He had loved La Tenby, perhaps too much, and in a way which Maria-Grazia sensed was not quite a boy's love for his mother. She saw their faces, the way their bodies moved. She felt that Dom and La Tenby were creatures apart, animal-like. They hunted and caught, groomed each other, sought mates, but found comfort only when they were together.

Beh, she was being fanciful. She, Maria-Grazia, was not sorry La Tenby was dead. She was in a class with the *marchesa* of three summers ago. And if it had not been for Rosa she did not know what they would have done when they were accused of taking the money. She had never seen Giulio so angry. She shivered at the memory. He moved slowly, her Giulio, but when he was aroused. . . .

But Rosa had advised caution and *grazie a Dio*, he had listened to her. Otherwise they would have been out of a job without a place to live. She had conveniently forgotten that she had been the one who wanted to hand in her notice, no, to throw it in the face of La Tenby.

Now, she thought with satisfaction, these people would soon go and it would be too late to find another tenant. She smiled to herself. She would make *fettucine funghi porcini* this evening and then perhaps a *frittata di zucchini*. Dinner would be on time too. There would be no trips to the port,

132   *Maureen Donegan*

no party on the terrace. And it would also be an early night because shock and unhappiness made people very tired.

'We'll take the statements this afternoon,' Sergio Tavazzi said, 'and I'm afraid I'm going to have to rope you in again to translate. If you don't mind?'

Rose gave him a slight smile. 'I'd be happy to help.'

'In the meantime, could you tell me a little more about last night? Was everyone here?'

She nodded. 'Eventually. Dinner was late because Mr Langdon Smythe and Mr Kinaid went out beforehand. We had to keep the food warm and Maria-Grazia was annoyed.'

He tapped a coin on the table then absently circled it with his thumb and first finger.

'That I understand. And then?'

'The meal went smoothly enough,' Rose said slowly. Her eyes were following the movement of the coin between his hands. He dropped it on the table and half laughed.

'What is it?' she asked curiously.

'My lucky piece. Not that I'm having much luck with this case.' He passed it over to her. 'It's a Roman sesterce.'

She turned it in her hand. It was worn thin and shiny, the markings almost obliterated. 'I thought they were silver,' she said.

'It's a kind of brass, *orichalcum*. Debased in the time of Nero. Devaluation is nothing new, you see. Sometimes I do tricks for my nephews, but I don't do them very well. Or maybe they're too big now.'

She nodded and her smile was warmer as he took the coin back.

He sighed slightly. 'So, tell me what happened after the meal?'

'I think Mrs Tenby was smoking marijuana.'

'Do you know where it came from?'

She hesitated. 'I've no proof, but I think Peter Kinaid had brought it.'

He nodded. 'Go on.'

'There was some bickering. Mr Langdon Smythe seemed worried and annoyed.'

'Annoyed about the pot?'

TUSCAN SHADOWS

'Yes, I think so.'

'OK, we can follow that up. And the others? Were they smoking?'

Rose described the glimpses she had had of the scene on the terrace. 'Mrs Tenby was in a strange mood. No, perhaps not strange: it was an exaggeration of her usual behaviour. She was making innuendoes, niggling away at everyone, except perhaps at Tom Graham.' She stopped suddenly.

'What is it?'

'I got the impression they were going to spend the night together and this morning I saw him leaving her room. Then he went down to the pool and swam.'

It sounded so unlikely that Sergio almost laughed. Even if Gillian Tenby had died of natural causes her bedmate must surely have noticed.

'And last night he was the only one she was nice to.'

'How did the others react? The ones she wasn't being nice to?'

'Alison woke up and suddenly she didn't seem out of it any more.' Rose related the snatches of conversation she had overheard. 'Elizabeth was very cold, and Susie was resentful. It was . . . normal, only not quite. Gillian Tenby was often like that. She seemed as though she wanted to have everything everyone else had. Only more.'

'It sounds as though you were not an admirer?'

'She was my employer. Whether I admired her or not is irrelevant.'

'But none of this . . . nastiness you describe is a motive for murder,' he said.

'I agree, ' Rose said, 'I've been thinking about it a lot.'

Sergio gave her a sharp look. 'And the English do not go in for crimes of passion?' he asked drily.

'Not often,' Rose said.

He half grinned. 'We'll see what the statements reveal.' He tilted his chair back and rubbed his head. 'I appreciate your help very much,' he said, after a moment.

'It's in everyone's interest to find out what happened,' Rose said. 'I spoke to Mrs Martin's sister, Mrs Venables-Brown, and she was also very anxious to have it all cleared up.'

He hoped it didn't mean that she would be leaving the job. He didn't want her to go. He was also afraid to admit to himself that the case might never be solved, if those busy wires didn't stop buzzing. The situation was as unclear as the rest of the muddled relationships in this house. But her cool manner had thawed slightly, although he was not sure why. He resisted the temptation to lean across the table and take her hand.

'Have you seen this before?' he asked abruptly. He flicked aside the silk scarf which he had left covering the small urn.

Rose shook her head. 'No, is it. . . ?'

'Etruscan,' he said. 'It was in Mrs Tenby's room. In her handbag, as a matter of fact. She must have been carrying it around with her all the time.'

'Yes, I saw her with her bag. I thought it was because of the money.'

'She evidently used it as an all-purpose safe.'

'But . . . something like that. It's extraordinary,' Rose said.

'Indeed it is. Tell me, what time did the party break up last night?'

'About eleven, I think. I didn't look at the clock, but it wasn't very late.'

'And how did they all pair off?' he said, his thoughts lingering on the idea of warm, satisfying sex.

'Gillian Tenby and Tom,' she said, ticking them off on her fingers. 'Johnny Langdon Smythe and Peter.'

'Not with his *fidanzata*?'

'I don't think so. Susie and her boyfriend went off together and I saw them coming out of her room this morning. Dom Tenby was with Elizabeth Halliwell most of the evening, but I don't think they spent the night together. Keith Drinkwater was giving Gillian hopeful looks but his wife pulled herself together just before they all went off to bed and I doubt if he would have been able to get away from her.'

Sergio let the legs of his chair fall back on to the floor again. 'Did I say the English were cold?'

CHAPTER 11

The written statements took hours to process and added very little to the information already taken verbally by Sergio and his staff in a fraction of the time.

Dom, pale and at first inarticulate, said that he had gone to Elizabeth's room around midnight, but she was tired and he did not stay for more than a few minutes. He had heard nothing from his mother's room, did not see anyone go in there. He didn't know of any reason why anyone should want to kill her.

'She was so full of life,' he said, slowly.

He didn't know anything about marijuana. He didn't take drugs, nor did his mother.

'Did she take sleeping pills?' Sergio asked. There had been traces of sleeping pills in the glass of brandy beside the bed.

'Always,' Dom said in the same toneless voice. 'She was' – he paused as though finally acknowledging a disturbing fact – 'she was very insecure. That easy manner was a cover up. She needed reassurance. People around her.' His face suddenly crumpled. 'I didn't say goodnight to her!' He burst into anguished tears, his thin body shaking uncontrollably.

'I realize how distressing this must be for you,' Sergio said, when Dom had got himself under control again. The grief appeared real. If Dom was crying for effect he was a brilliant actor.

'She'd said something to Elizabeth,' Dom said, in a more normal voice. 'It was nothing, something about Johnny, his pet name for Peter. Elizabeth

135

was annoyed and I wanted to explain that my mother didn't mean anything. It was the kind of thing she said, that's all. She liked to tease.'

'Miss Halliwell and her fiancé were not on close terms, I gather?'

'He's gay,' Dom burst out. 'He only wants a wife to keep up appearances.'

'I see. And have you ever seen this before?' the captain asked, unwrapping a small piece of pottery.

Dom stared at it. 'No, never.'

'In your mother's room, perhaps?'

'No.'

'She never spoke to you about acquiring ancient artefacts?'

'Of course not. She didn't have the money.'

The captain indicated that he could go and Dom left the station and walked down to the marina. He felt despairing and confused, remembering with a sick feeling how angry he had been with Gillian about the money, how he had shouted at her. The memory gave him a sharp, nauseous pain. He had been angry again last night. Normally he understood the reason for the way she behaved because he had the same instincts, the same needs. But Gillian's wisecrack had stung Elizabeth. She must be in love with that bastard, he thought, staring out at *L'Alba* bobbing gently against the walkway. It was incredible.

But what was even more incredible was that what had started as Gillian's – and his, too – bit of mischief making had turned into something quite different. Now he understood that Gillian had had half an eye on the Halliwell money. His mother was in a financial mess, the extent of which he neither knew nor wished to think about.

And he had come to like Elizabeth. He liked her very much. Of course he wasn't in love with her; he felt sorry for her rather. And he would like to have someone like her in his life. Especially – he threw a small pebble into the slightly oily water – especially now. Elizabeth had suffered in the past too. Had lost her mother. Her father was obviously a difficult man. He tried to imagine Halliwell père, bluff and blustering, thinking money could buy everything. Domineering too, he imagined. And a womanizer. Elizabeth was very straightforward and this was something else he liked. Gillian had not seen this because she was a poor judge of character. She liked the wrong kind of people. She had despised his father. This thought, long submerged, came drifting to the surface like a bloated corpse.

His throat tightened again as he tried to imagine life without his mother. She had been his best friend, his confidante, but he had quarrelled with her and now he was alone.

And what was all that about the piece of pottery? It couldn't have been Gillian's. She didn't go for stuff like that. She must have found it somewhere, in the villa probably.

Elizabeth denied that she had found anything offensive in Gillian's conversation.

'She was always rather . . . ironic,' she said. 'One of those shallow but amusing women,' she added, as she recounted her version of the evening's events. No, she wasn't aware of any undercurrents. It was her fiancé who had originally invited her to join the house party. She gave Sergio a half smile. 'He likes me to be with him, naturally.'

'Naturally,' Sergio said, and translated so that the *carabinere*, crouched over his typewriter in the corner, could take down her reply.

Of her relationship with Peter Kinaid, she said she had known him for a long time and was fond of him.

Fond, Sergio thought, one of those bland English words that depended so much on tone.

Elizabeth Halliwell's voice was without inflection when she spoke about her fiancé's friend. 'I don't do much sailing,' she went on, 'and Peter is a splendid hand in a boat. Quite invaluable to Johnny.'

Pressed, Elizabeth finally admitted that she had overheard Gillian say quietly to Keith, 'No, not tonight, later.'

'She liked to play the field, I think,' Elizabeth said, without emotion. 'I feel rather sorry for his wife.'

'Play the field? By that you mean she had a lot of men friends?'

'It was a game with her, I think. There are women like that.'

She made it sound like a harmless pastime, like knitting, Sergio thought. He said smoothly, 'Then I imagine she tried it on with your fiancé and Mr Kinaid too?'

'Without much success,' Elizabeth said, straightfaced, but her clasped hands tightened. 'Peter and she used to tease each other a lot, that's all.'

'No doubt he was "fond" of her too,' Sergio said, drily.

She considered this and then said, surprisingly. 'I think he was afraid of her.'

'Why was that?'

'I don't know why,' she said. 'I only saw the effect. The way he looked at her when he thought she wasn't aware of him. That sort of thing. The way she was able to persuade him to do things.'

Sergio listened to the measured words and wondered just how much she hated Peter Kinaid. 'Like procuring marijuana?' he suggested.

Elizabeth's expression became even more detached.

'I hardly think he'd do anything like that,' she said. 'After all he was Johnny's friend too, and I don't think Johnny—'

'We have reason to believe that marijuana joints were being passed around last night,' he said.

Her pale eyes opened a little wider. 'Not to my knowledge.'

Nor, apparently did she recognize the little Etruscan urn, merely said, 'Is it the real thing?' when Sergio showed it to her.

'We believe so,' Sergio said. He waited but Elizabeth made no further comment.

'Do you remember anything else of significance?'

She shook her head, her fair hair swinging against the soft blue of her blouse.

'Mr Tenby said you were upset by something his mother said.'

She made a soft dismissive sound. 'Dom is . . . was . . . very close to his mother. He tended to overreact.'

'Perhaps it was you who overreacted, Miss Halliwell?'

She went slightly pink. 'It was an excuse.'

'Your reaction?'

'No, no. Dom came to my room to . . . to talk about the evening, but really he had quite another intention.' She waved her hand dismissively. 'I got rid of him after about five minutes.'

Sergio felt a twinge of sympathy for the young man. That was, of course, assuming he was innocent. This girl who blushed so charmingly was in reality, he suspected, a very cool customer.

Sergio sighed and went through the statements yet again in order to summarize their contents for the report to his colonel and the procurator. He had already filled several sheets of paper and his writing had deteriorated to the scribble which was the bane of Carabinere Pascucci's life.

Neither Keith Drinkwater nor his wife had seen the Etruscan pot before although Sergio was not quite convinced by Keith's denial. When pressed he said Gillian had shown it to him when he commented on how heavy her bag was but he'd almost forgotten. 'Said she'd found it in a market,' he said.
'You didn't think it was valuable?'
Keith shrugged. 'Don't you see that sort of tourist stuff everywhere?'
He denied any tentative or postponed assignation with Gillian but admitted that a few sharp words had passed between himself and his wife. He had gone to his room with Alison in order to calm her down. She suffered from nervous troubles, he explained, and no, he had not left their room at all, nor had his wife.
Alison, who had appeared rather shaky in the *carabinieri* station, Sergio remembered, had nevertheless confirmed this and said that Gillian was 'always like that'.
'Your husband was an admirer of Mrs Tenby?' Sergio had asked her.
'They practically grew up together,' Alison said. 'You know how it is.'
Indeed everyone in the villa must have known how it was between Gillian and Keith, but none of them, apart from Elizabeth, seemed prepared to spell it out.

Mike and Susie were both pale and subdued and each said they had gone to Susie's room together and stayed there the whole night, nor had they ever laid eyes on the Etruscan urn.
Mike said Gillian was a super person and he couldn't imagine anyone wanting to kill her.
'And your relationship with her was that of a son-in-law to be?'

140   *Maureen Donegan*

'Yes, of course, only she was more like a big sister than a mother-in-law.'

Susie said it had been a terrible shock coming so closely after the death of her father. Her eyes were swollen with dark shadows beneath them and new tears began to form again as she spoke. These too, Sergio felt, were genuine. He offered his condolences and then asked if she was on good terms with her stepmother.

'I hardly remember my own mother,' Susie said, 'and of course it can't ever be the same as having . . . but she was good to us, to all of us.'

'And there was no question of her, shall we say, flirting with your fiancé?'

Susie's laugh was both unexpected and carefree. 'Oh, that. She liked attention. Usually I didn't take any notice.'

'Meaning that sometimes you did?'

'I couldn't really take it seriously, could I? Anyway I think she'd become fond of Tom Graham.'

That word again. Did the English never feel passion? He searched back through literature and found reassurance in Shakespeare, although one had to remember that Romeo and Juliet were Italian. And the race did continue after all. Something other than mere duty must occasionally happen between the polyester sheets of the English.

Johnny Langdon Smythe and Peter Kinaid provided flawless alibis for each other. They had left the villa early and spent the night on the boat, anxious about their expensive radio and radar equipment. However, Rose had confirmed that all the guests had keys to the villa and either or both of the yachtsmen could have returned during the night.

'You find radar necessary on a pleasure boat?' Sergio asked.

'Safety is always a prime consideration,' Langdon Smythe drawled. 'And now without Pino one can never be completely at ease.' He gave Sergio a level look. 'There is so much crime in Italy, after all.' The implication appeared to be that Sergio should be doing something about it, rather than asking inane questions about marijuana.

'Isn't that all a bit sixties-ish,' he had said in response to questions about the brandy and joints. '*Démodé?*'

'Not entirely,' Sergio had said. He produced his silk-wrapped parcel and

Langdon Smythe appeared to stiffen as it was opened, but said he had never seen it before. 'It's rather charming though,' he added, laconically.

Peter Kinaid denied all knowledge of any pot. No, he had no contacts in the bars and, if Pino had indulged, he wasn't aware of it. He'd opened his blue eyes very wide and Sergio was reminded of one of his nephews a few years ago, denying any knowledge of missing jam, the tell-tale red smears still around his mouth.

How stupid, but how arrogant the two *inglesi* were, bringing even soft drugs into a house where police were actively investigating a murder and when they themselves, he was convinced, were involved in smuggling other items. Sergio wondered whose idea it had been. Rose thought Gillian had provoked Peter into bringing the marijuana. Had she got the urn from him too?

'Right. Thank you for your help.' He waited until Peter reached the door then called him back. 'I'd like you to look at this,' he said, and watched Kinaid's expression freeze as the silk fell away from the Etruscan pot. 'It was in Mrs Tenby's handbag,' he added pleasantly.

'I've never seen it before,' Peter said, the words falling over each other, 'and if anyone says I did they're lying.'

'It occurs to us that Mrs Tenby could be deeply involved with smuggling,' Sergio said.

'Mrs Tenby?' Peter repeated.

'With the help of accomplices, of course.'

Peter stared at him and wiped his hands down the side of his cotton trousers.

'Yes, accomplices,' Sergio said. 'That's all then, Mr Kinaid.'

The door swung back violently as Kinaid rushed out. Rattled, certainly. Sergio smiled to himself as he wound the silk around the urn again.

He wished fervently that Gillian was still alive. She may have been the one person he needed to break the dealers' chain. It was like a series of cells, each linked only by the most limited knowledge of the next. Johnny Langdon Smythe, Peter Kinaid, Franco Nardi, Gillian Tenby. He had wanted to put a round-the-clock watch on Nardi weeks ago but the colonel had

142 *Maureen Donegan*

overruled him, saying they were overstretched as it was. So far all the evidence against Nardi's involvement in smuggling had been circumstantial but no matter how Sergio repeated that the two Englishmen were obviously in touch with the Italian, and that there was now the physical presence of an illegal treasure on the premises, plus the obvious fact of Langdon Smythe making the villa his headquarters, his boss remained adamant.

Somehow Sergio doubted that Gillian was involved directly but there had been something between herself and the two yachtsmen that was certainly not simple friendship. And by the *madonna*, he was going to find out what it was.

When he was told he had been seen coming from Gillian's room, Tom Graham said, 'I thought she was asleep and I didn't want to wake her.'

'Did you touch her?' Sergio had asked.

Tom shook his head.

'You spoke her name?'

The other man hesitated. 'No, that is, I may have done. But quietly.'

Sergio switched tack. 'Had you spent the night there?'

'No! Of course not. Otherwise I would have known—'

'She was dead. Yes, quite. But I'm suggesting you did know.'

'And stayed there beside her all night?' Tom asked.

'But you don't deny she invited you to her room?'

'Who said . . ?' Graham began angrily, then stopped. He was silent for a moment. 'All right. She did . . . um . . . indicate. . . .'

'And it wasn't the first time?'

'No, but I didn't go!' A look of embarrassment came over his tanned face. 'I went to my room and had a shower and then I lay on my bed for a while, until the house had settled down and I must have fallen asleep. When I woke up it was the middle of the night and far too late to. . . .' He gave Sergio a man-to-man look. 'You can understand that, I'm sure.'

Sergio did understand; life was full of such absurdities. But Graham might well have gone to her room late into the night, crept into her bed and provoked a row. A row which led to . . . to what? Blows? But there had been no violence of that kind. This had all the hallmark of a coldly premeditated act. One perhaps which had benefited by a sudden opportunity, but certainly one which had been thought out in advance. It had required preparation.

'What time was it exactly, when you woke?'

'Three. Five past.'

'You put on the light. Looked at your watch?'

'Yes. I was feeling bad about it. You can imagine. I needed to know how late it was.'

'And this morning? You didn't begin to explain what had happened?'

'How could I when she was . . .' – Tom hesitated fractionally – 'when I thought she was asleep.'

'I put it to you that you did touch her, did speak to her. Perhaps you had an argument then about your broken appointment?'

But she was already dead, Sergio knew, and had been for some hours. It was a useless line to follow.

'I went to invite her for a swim,' Tom said, sullenly, 'that's all.'

Hot passion plunged into a chilly pool, Sergio thought disbelievingly. There had still been no reply to official enquiries about Graham's business connections. Suppose, just suppose that he was the missing link in the smuggling chain. And Gillian who had undoubtedly been intimate with him, had somehow found out. The meeting on the plane might well have been fortuitous but nevertheless he could have decided to take advantage of it. And far-fetched as this seemed, it was the most promising theory he had so far.

And then, at that point, Tom Graham looked down at his loosely clasped hands and said that, well, perhaps he should come clean.

Old-fashioned slang, Sergio registered. Maybe it's some time since he lived permanently in England.

'I did realize she was dead,' Tom said. 'I . . . I stroked her hair first, then her face and . . . I couldn't believe it. I . . . well, I must have panicked. I went down the garden, down to the pool and just swam, blindly.'

That wasn't exactly the way his movements had been described by Rose. They had sounded very much unlike a man in a panic.

'Did you move anything, touch anything, other than the body?' Sergio asked brusquely.

'The . . . body. No, no I didn't. I was shocked, startled. My only thought was to get out of there.'

'Had you perhaps given her this?' Sergio showed him the urn.

Tom Graham shook his head. He looked bemused. 'No. What is it?'

The necessary changes were made painstakingly to his statement and after he had signed it Sergio indicated that he could go.

'But I shall need to talk to you again,' he warned. He sighed. He would need to talk to them all again when the results of the post-mortem were known.

Finally, Maria-Grazia and Giulio vouched for each other. They had, when Sergio extracted the brief facts from a flurry of protestations, gone immediately to bed at the end of the day's work, pausing only to look at the moon, in the company of Rose in the courtyard. They too did not appear to have seen the Etruscan urn before.

Rose confirmed that she had walked to the annexe with them and added that although she was probably one of the few to do so, she had spent the night alone. Sergio smiled to himself and wondered if she had intended her remark to be as provocative as it sounded. His spirits lifted slightly.

CHAPTER 12

Although Rose was writing another letter to Arthur, she was not sure if she would post it. But describing the events of the past few days helped to clear her mind.

In an unconscious imitation of Sergio's report but without the formal language required by the Procurator of the Republic, she outlined the events of the past few days, leaving out all mention of smuggled artefacts, instead concentrating on the relationships of the temporary occupants of the Villa Antonia.

I think Gillian saw herself as a femme fatale and put a lot of effort into maintaining that role. She had a kind of soft, silvery voice and she would whisper, well, sweet nothings I suppose, to the man she was nearest to, but at the same time she used her enormous blue eyes to great effect.

It might well have been an accident of genes that gave her eyes unusual prominence, but this could well have resulted from thyroid trouble. She reread the last bit and decided it was the kind of thing Alison might say. Funny how Alison had woken up that night. It was almost as if she had only been pretending to be asleep on the terrace.

Gillian Tenby had a stepdaughter, Susie. I don't think it could have been easy for either of them living together but perhaps the barbs Gillian directed at Susie were intended to prod her into some improvement of her life. Gillian was frivolous, and a flirt and even tried it on Susie's boyfriend, but I think that was to provoke Tom – he's someone Gillian picked up on the plane – to make a move, or maybe even just a flexing of her talents to seduce.

146 *Maureen Donegan*

It sounded like a soap opera, Rose thought. She wondered if Arthur would be able to sort out who was who and, more specifically, who was doing what to whom at the villa.

Gillian, she went on, *seemed to see life in black and white, 'I want' being the driving force behind most of her actions. 'I want to be the centre of attention; I want to be forever young." And she certainly succeeded in the last wish. She will never have to face her mirror with a lined, dissatisfied face now.*

She continued in this vein for some time because she thought it would give Arthur something to get his teeth into. All the same he was going to say, 'When are you getting out of there?' and 'I knew something like this would happen some day. How could you get involved in murder, Rose?'

I am perfectly all right, she added at the bottom of the last page, *so please don't worry about me. There is an excellent captain of the carabinieri in charge of the case and I have every confidence that. . . .'* She stopped, pen in mid air, reflecting that this was more or less what she had said to Mrs Venables-Brown. A sudden mental picture of Sergio making coins disappear for his nephews swam into her mind. He'd had a touching air of vulnerability for a few moments. What else had Lena Grenbelli said, something about a sister but that he was rather isolated? Perhaps he wasn't as tough as he liked to appear.

Gillian had been drugged with a sleeping pill and then her bloodstream injected with a massive amount of air. The resulting gaseous embolism had caused a heart attack; had it reached the brain first it would have caused a stroke.

'At one time,' the police surgeon said, with a certain amount of pride, 'such a method was virtually undetectable but nowadays thanks to improved methods of—'

'So it is murder,' Sergio said, interrupting.

The doctor looked annoyed. Perhaps was waiting for congratulations.

'And any ordinary syringe would have done it?'

'It would have to have been a pretty large one, 25ccs at least.'

'So we're looking for a horse doctor?' Sergio said. He saw the police surgeon's expression. 'I was joking.'

TUSCAN SHADOWS 147

'That is your concern,' the doctor said, stiffly, 'but medical knowledge is hardly necessary in this case. Anyone who reads detective stories, and I understand that the English are particularly addicted to them, would have heard of this particular method of killing. Indeed, I suspect that many apparently natural deaths in the past could well have been induced in this way. I would say, *Capitano*, that lack of knowledge is indicated, since obviously the murderer expected the death would be accepted as a heart attack.'

'Then I have even more reason to be grateful to you, *Dottore*,' Sergio said to the Sicilian, who was pompous and bristling with pride. No one bothered to massage his, Sergio Tavazzi's, ego. All he got from his colonel was a crack of the whip and instructions to jump.

'And the time of death, *Dottore*?'

'I would say sometime between midnight and four a.m.'

'I see. You've done a great job. I didn't expect to have the results so quickly,' he lied and the small, green-eyed doctor looked mollified.

Norman blood, Sergio registered and this reminded him of Gillian Tenby's surprised blue eyes. A phrase from his boyhood came to him: 'a good thing'. That's what the dead woman had been, a good thing. A good thing in illegal possession of an ancient artefact. The urn had been identified as coming from a tomb at Nauro. It had been among a collection of treasures which had disappeared last year. He would have to interview all the suspects again and go over their movements and their relationships with a fine tooth comb, to say nothing of initiating a search for the syringe and another, no doubt futile one, for the rest of the Etruscan pottery and ornaments. It occurred to him that if Peter Kinaid had wanted to give Gillian a present a necklace would have been much more appropriate, but perhaps he thought jewellery was more easily traced; he hadn't taken into account the meticulousness of archaeologists.

'It was premeditated then,' he said, dragging himself back to the present.

The doctor nodded in agreement. 'The average killer acts on impulse. He pushes his victim down the stairs or grabs what's at hand. In the Sard's case it was evidently a piece of wood since there were splinters in the head wound.'

Sergio wondered, not for the first time, if the two deaths were connected

148   *Maureen Donegan*

at all. They were so dissimilar. Could coincidence have thrown up two dead bodies on the same property within days of each other? Two dead bodies and a robbery? Real coincidences were rare. One murder must have triggered another. Cause and effect. But the trail leading from Pino's death was as cold as a winter in Bedfordshire and Gillian Tenby, it seemed, must have been a better detective than he was because it seemed more than likely that she'd discovered or guessed something that had got her killed and that something had to be smuggling. He found it hard to believe though that she'd been running a racket herself; the little urn was probably to encourage her to keep her mouth shut. Kinaid, but not Langdon Smythe, could have been stupid enough to believe that it would. But didn't Gillian Tenby know what an accessory was? At least two people, then, who lived in fantasy land.

'Let's have a coffee later,' he said to the doctor. They shook hands warmly and the man went off smiling, a dour but irritatingly self-satisfied smile. The doctor's work was done and the lucky sod was probably going home to a loving wife and a steaming plate of pasta.

His mind flew back suddenly to his own marriage and the passionate nights of the early years. The trouble with this case, he thought bitterly, was there was too much of that sort of thing and he, personally wasn't getting any of it. He wasn't even getting any hot pasta.

Keith Drinkwater had finally fallen into a deep sleep about four in the morning after tossing and turning for the better part of the night. In his half-waking moments, he had been remembering Gillian as a young girl and then, more recently, as an available widow. But less available, for some reason, to him. It had once been quite different. He could see her quite clearly that day in the kitchen as she sat at the table and told him how unhappy she was. From there it had not been very far, nor had it taken very long, to move from the kitchen to the bedroom. He was trembling, he remembered, as he trembled now at her loss.

That afternoon didn't come entirely out of the blue, of course. Thighs had been pressed against thighs under the respective Tenby and Drinkwater dining-tables. And they had danced together whenever they could. Gillian was clever at organizing a social life. She used to gaze up at him with those brilliant eyes and then move her body softly towards him, a sweet reminder of when they were young together. Young and yet, even then, not innocent. Thinking of those days now, he realized that the dancing had slowly but inexorably raised the emotional temperature until it culminated in that frantic, slippery, noisy afternoon in the Tenbys' spare bedroom when she had torn the buttons off his shirt and dug her fingernails into his buttocks, drawing blood.

Afterwards they crawled naked around the carpet, searching for the buttons and he took her again from behind. She shrieked so loudly that he put his hand roughly over her mouth and pulled her head back sharply as he drove into her.

'Did I hurt you?' he had asked, as they got back into bed to recover. And he would never forget the way her eyes gleamed as she said, 'It was like rape.'

After that her conscience prevented them from seeing each other very often, seeing each other alone that is. But it was a long time before he began to think that she might, just possibly, be playing games with him. There had been that Scottish guy staying at the house, someone she had met on holiday with Donald, and invited to stay. With hindsight he could see the parallel with Tom Graham all too clearly. Another time it had been an Austrian hitchhiker in the guest room. Then she had taken up with that pompous prick from the dramatic society and there was the man who'd sold her a car. . . . He preferred not to think about the rest. *De mortuis nil nisi bonum*, he told himself firmly, *nil nisi bonum*.

He had woken, hot and parched into another anxious day. Beside him, Alison was in a deep but troubled sleep if her restless movements were anything to go by. Once she made a sound, an alarmed cry, then turned on her side and curled herself up into a foetal, defensive ball.

In Keith's dream it had been Gillian not Pino who lay bloodied and dead at the bottom of the ravine. And someone, a shadowy someone, leaned over the parapet looking down at the body. He got out of bed and went to the open window to get some air, then shivered as the sweat dried on his body. One step at a time, he thought, turning to look at the still unconscious Alison, one step at a time we go down the primrose path until suddenly it becomes a steep and dangerous precipice.

Today he would have to work out a careful version of events for that clever bugger of a captain.

Susie knew that somehow she and Dom must attend to the practical details of their mother's death, but Dom was still in a daze and she herself felt very little better. Eventually it was Mike who made the calls to the travel insurance company, the British Embassy and Gillian's solicitor. Gillian had not specified provisions for her interment, perhaps because she had never seriously envisaged her own death.

Using similar words to those used by the consular officer, Mike suggested, gently and tactfully, that in view of the necessary delay and the, er, season, it might be best for the funeral to be held here, in Italy, as soon as the authorities released the . . . released Gillian's body.

Susie was aware of Dom looking at her for guidance and she nodded mutely. She could not bear the thought of shipping the body, of prolonged funeral rites, the endless regulations.

Finally she spoke. 'We could have a memorial service at St Gregory's afterwards.' Dom nodded, silent.

'I was going to suggest that,' Mike said. He looked relieved.

Sergio Tavazzi had also been on the telephone. Mr Harvey of Price and Harvey, Gillian's solicitors, after some preliminary skirmishing, had informed him, reluctantly, that Gillian had left her house and the rest of her property to Dom.

'Cutting out Susie Tenby?' Sergio asked.

There was a silence down the line.

'Mr Tenby set up a trust fund for his daughter when she was a child. Her grandmother also made provision for Susie in her will,' the solicitor said eventually.

'And in Mrs Tenby's case what kind of money are we talking about?'

'I'm not in a position to say.'

'Mrs Tenby has been murdered, Mr Harvey, and I'm looking for a motive and a killer.'

'Shall we say, er, that there wasn't very much involved,' the voice at the other end said slowly.

'Oh? I understood that she was a very wealthy woman.'

'The house is worth quite a lot, but with the present state of the market. . . .'

'But her late husband left a great deal of money?'

'Not a "great deal", Captain. The, er, late Mr Tenby made some unwise investments and he suffered considerable losses a few years ago when the stock market crashed. In fact it was Mrs Tenby's intention to put the house on the market.'

'I see,' Sergio said. Had the dead woman been having a final fling with what was left of her husband's money, perhaps to find another rich husband in Italy? Or was she simply set on a course of reckless self indulgence? Whatever it was, someone had put a stop to it.

He thanked Mr Harvey whose dry voice assured Sergio that he was glad to have been of assistance.

Sergio sat for a moment, his hand still on the receiver, then he called Massimo Pascucci to go and get *caffè e cornetti* from the bar.

So the rich woman wasn't rich. She must have been either very stupid or very unhappy with her life to spend so much on a holiday. But her financial situation did explain why she was so concerned about the food bills. Poor Maria-Grazia never had much luck with the tenants, he thought wryly.

In any case it was clear that Gillian hadn't been murdered for her money unless (a) her son had expected to inherit a fortune, or (b) the stepdaughter hadn't known that she wasn't in the will, or (c) Gillian had been killed to stop her throwing away the little money that was left. And both her children could be in the last category.

The coffee arrived and Sergio bit appreciatively into his *cornetto*. 'Get the car,' he said, his mouth half full, 'we're going back to the villa.'

'I want you,' Sergio said to Keith Drinkwater, 'to tell me what you can about Mrs Tenby's life.' As opposed to her death, he thought. 'Could she, for example, have been involved in smuggling?'

'What?' Drinkwater's incredulous voice seemed entirely genuine, but his

152   *Maureen Donegan*

face was strained and he had shaved badly, missing patches of stubble under his chin.

'The piece of pottery I showed you had come from an Etruscan tomb.'

'It couldn't have!'

'I assure you that it did.'

'Then she must have bought it here.'

'But not, I think, from a market stall.' Sergio paused. 'All right, let's go back to your relationship with her.'

Keith shifted slightly on his chair. 'I've known her for a long time,' he said, in an over-loud voice, 'since we were children, in fact. We lived in the same town, went to the same school.'

'Was she a happy person?'

Keith looked surprised. 'I suppose so. I never thought about it.'

Too anxious to get into her knickers, no doubt.

'Was she, for example, happily married? You knew her husband?'

'Yes, yes, of course, I knew old Donald. They got on very well together.'

'Was there an age difference?'

'Not really. He was only a few years ahead of us but that always seems a lot at school.'

'But you said, "old Donald".'

'He was a bit . . . set in his ways, that's all. I was surprised—'

'When was that, Mr Drinkwater?'

'I beg your—?'

'When were you surprised?'

'I'd, er . . . gone to America, after I qualified. And we'd sort of lost touch, well, not exactly, but I didn't know. . . . She wrote to me, said she'd met my mother in the street and that she'd introduced her to the man she was with, Donald that is. I took it from that, that we were to go our own way.' He stopped and half raised his hand as though to wipe the sweat from his face, then let his arm drop again. 'When I came back from the States we bumped into each other. We went for a drink and . . . caught up with all the news.'

'She was married then?'

'Yes.'

'You'd had a relationship with her. Were you upset?'

TUSCAN SHADOWS 153

'No, it was over. I told you. And it was only boy and girl. Nothing really.'

'You'd made no promises to each other?'

'No! Nothing like that. Anyway Gillian was always a bit of a butterfly, no harm in it of course.'

Sergio wondered if the man opposite realized how absymally naive he sounded.

'You didn't expect her to marry so soon though?'

Keith appeared to consider that. 'Perhaps she needed, you know, security.' His voice was nervous. 'Her own father died young.'

'Leaving the family badly off?'

Keith moved uneasily on his chair. 'I believe so.'

The words hung in the air, together with the unspoken implication that Gillian had married for money.

'But they were happy, Donald and Gillian,' Keith said. 'She had Dom and Donald was thrilled.'

'So after you came back from America and bumped into Mrs Tenby, you kept in touch.'

'Yes, we'd always known each other, I told you.'

'And you subsequently married your wife?'

'Yes.'

'Soon afterwards?'

'What?'

'When did you get married, Mr Drinkwater?' Sergio asked patiently.

'About ... a few months later, I suppose. I'd known Alison for a long time.'

'You were all part of a group?'

Keith cleared his throat. 'In a way.'

'So Gillian and your wife were friends?'

'They knew each other. You know how it is.'

Sergio was becoming tired of being told that he knew how it was. 'No, Mr Drinkwater, I don't. I'm asking you to tell me.'

There was a silence and then Keith had further trouble with his larynx. He coughed and cleared his throat again.

'Well, I wouldn't have thought motherhood was her style, but she took

154   *Maureen Donegan*

to it like a duck to water. Looked after Susie really well and then when Dom came along, she didn't let the baby tie them down. Always well organized, babysitters and so on.'

'I gather you saw them regularly.'

'Yes. Donald was more of a home bird, but she said it was good for him to get out.'

'You make her sound bossy,' Sergio said.

'No! She was . . . enthusiastic about, about everything almost. She loves – loved – meeting new people.'

'As on this holiday?'

'What?'

'I understand Mr Graham is a very recent acquaintance.'

'Oh. Oh, yes.' Keith managed a thin smile. 'Met him on the plane. She tended to pick up waifs and strays.'

Tom Graham hadn't struck Sergio as being in either of those categories but he let it go for the time being.

'And how did Mrs Tenby get on with her stepdaughter? When she was young, I mean?'

'As I told you, very well. Of course, the baby was the centre of the universe and Susie's nose was a bit out of joint on that account. Only to be expected.'

'Not an easy situation for a young child, I imagine. What happened to her mother? Was Donald Tenby a widower?'

Keith shook his head. He appeared slightly less harassed now that the conversation had moved away from his own past.

'She went off. Did a flit with some chap. Think she's in Canada. She left the baby, Susie that is, with a neighbour for a couple of hours and never came back. Donald got the police . . . missing person . . . found her car at the airport.'

'And she was never traced?'

'Oh yes. She wrote after, oh, I don't know, a month or so and Donald eventually got a divorce.' Keith gave his unhappy smile. 'I think Gillian felt sorry for him. He used to do the martyr a bit, before he met her I mean. But she did wonders for him. Brought him out of himself.'

'One of her waifs and strays?' Sergio suggested.

'Er . . . yes, in a way.'

'It wasn't exactly a love match then?'

There was a silence then Keith said, 'I wouldn't have said that, they were very—'

Sergio tapped his forefinger on the library table. 'Fond of each other?' he suggested.

Keith stared at the wall of books behind Sergio's head. 'Yes, of course.'

'I see,' Sergio said. 'Thank you for your help, Mr Drinkwater.'

'Is that all?' The other man sounded relieved.

'For the moment. Perhaps you'd ask you wife to come in next?'

'She's not . . . well this morning. I left her asleep, in fact.'

'In that case I'll see her later. Please let me know when she's recovered.'

Keith heaved himself up with an effort, his shoulders hunched as if against a blow. Sergio watched as he left the room and then leaned back in his chair thinking not so much of the cool English countryside but rather of his own interior landscape and the misty hills and valleys of the past.

Keith Drinkwater had bungled his life, marrying a woman on the rebound and continuing to hang around his former girlfriend. But had he, Sergio, done much better? He had married out of a need that had little to do with love and quite a lot to do with lust. Also, since he'd chosen to live in Italy, marrying a girl from a very traditional Italian family had reinforced his feeling of belonging. Perhaps it was only now that he thought like this. Bargains of that sort are seldom spelled out, even in the mind.

If he'd stayed in England, would his life have been better? It would certainly have been different. Would he have longed for Italian sun, for the warmth and confusion of Mediterranean life? Would he always feel, wherever he was, to be standing on the sidelines, looking on? He knew that this objectivity helped him in his work, but it didn't do much for his sense of isolation, especially in the dead hours of the night.

CHAPTER 13

'I don't really see that I can help you further.' Johnny Langdon Smythe gave Sergio a disarming look.

'Perhaps you'd let me be the judge of that,' Sergio said. 'Shall we start with how you met Mrs Tenby.'

'I thought I'd already told you. She was someone Peter met. At a party. He's a bit like an eager puppy is Peter. Brings one the odd bone.'

'Do I take it you didn't care for the deceased?'

'You can take it any way you wish, Captain. Peter certainly liked her. Think she got him in a corner and let him blab about his unhappy childhood. He goes for that sort of thing, rather.'

'So you hadn't met Mrs Tenby before you came here?'

'I'd met her once. Peter brought her to a party one night and afterwards we went to a restaurant.'

'Just the three of you?'

'There were several of us, I believe.'

'And on that slight acquaintance she invited you to the Villa Antonia?'

'Oh, Peter knew her. He'd been to her place. In Berkshire, I believe.'

'But you hadn't been there.'

'No.'

'Were you invited?'

'I may have been. I forget. In any case one doesn't have much spare time in England. Flying visits usually.'

156

'Business trips?'

Langdon Smythe shook his head. 'My family are there. Mother is quite frail and I like to spend as much time as possible with her.'

His mother must be as old as God. An incongruous picture of Johnny's sleek, bleached head bent in filial solicitude at the bedside of an ancient dowager flashed through Sergio's mind.

'And of course your fiancé lives in England.'

'Indeed she does.'

'But she hadn't met Mrs Tenby before either?'

'England is relatively large, Captain.'

Two could play at this. Sergio's voice sharpened. 'Mr Langdon Smythe, can you think of any reason why anyone should want to kill your paid hand?'

Johnny looked momentarily disconcerted. 'I thought we were discussing Mrs Tenby.'

'There have been two deaths, one following hard on the footsteps of the other.'

'Heels. Hard on the heels. Idiomatic speech. But otherwise your English is surprisingly good.'

The 'surprisingly' almost made Sergio punch the well-preserved bony face in front of him. 'You're very kind,' he said, coldly, aware of Massimo Pascucci shifting uneasily in the corner no doubt glad he wasn't in the firing line. Sergio rearranged the papers on the table in front of him.

'The deaths are almost certainly connected,' Sergio went on, regaining control.

'Oh, do you think so? I rather thought Pino might have been done in by a jealous husband. He probably had a girl in every port.' Johnny Langdon Smythe's manner was still mild but his eyes had taken on a wary look.

'I doubt if you really believe that.'

'But isn't that what they say about sailors?'

'Not all sailors, no. Surely it could hardly have escaped your notice that he was a homosexual.'

'Then it couldn't have been a jealous husband, could it? But are you sure about that? I, personally, am very surprised to hear it. He was constantly chatting up girls. I've seen him myself.'

He leaned back and crossed his legs, contemplating his dark-blue *espadrilles*.

'What is your relationship with Mr Kinaid?'

'Goodness, I thought you were going to ask me what my relationship with my paid hand was.'

'As you wish. We can deal with that first.'

'All right. Pino was an employee. That's all. Reasonably efficient. Frequently surly, but decent enough. I'm sorry that he came to such an unfortunate end.' Johnny uncrossed his legs again and looked straight at Sergio. 'And Mr Kinaid is my crew master. He's also an old friend. Great on a boat, very helpful, good company . . . and quite incapable of killing anyone.'

'And totally trustworthy.'

'Yes.'

'To the extent of keeping his mouth shut?'

'I don't quite follow.'

'I suggest to you that Pino was a blackmailer.'

Langdon Smythe allowed a look of polite disbelief to cross his face. 'Blackmailing whom? And why?'

'That is what I'm asking you.'

'I'm afraid I've no idea, Captain.'

'He could have discovered some crime.'

'If he did, he certainly didn't take me into his confidence.'

'No? Perhaps Mr Kinaid talked to Pino about your association with Franco Nardi.'

Langdon Smythe raised his eyebrows. 'I'm afraid I haven't had the pleasure.'

'Perhaps I could refresh your memory.' Sergio knew it was a mistake to persist but he had an overwhelming desire to get some kind of reaction from this man. 'He's about your own age. Thickset, but not tall. In business; business of a diverse and rather mysterious nature, Mr Langdon Smythe. Wears a lot of jewellery. Has a boat on the marina.'

'You could be describing almost anyone, any Italian that is.'

Don't let him draw you out. 'Where were you before you came to Villa Antonia, Mr Langdon Smythe?'

'Sailing around, a bit of racing.'

'In Italian waters?'

'Mostly, yes.'

'Where exactly?'

'Portofino, Porto Cervo. . . .'

'Any other part of Sardinia?'

'We took a trip to the south. One likes to get away from it all, occasionally.'

'That's where Pino comes from?'

'Is it? He didn't say.'

'Did he say he had a record?' Sergio hadn't intended to reveal this, admittedly pitiful, piece of information and, as he might have expected, got very little response.

'No, he certainly did not,' Johnny Langdon Smythe said.

Sergio waited for him to ask what Pino had gone down for, but if Langdon Smythe was waiting for further enlightenment he did not allow it to show. His expression portrayed total boredom.

'Did you give Mrs Tenby the piece of Etruscan pottery I showed you before?'

There was a sudden flicker in Langdon Smythe's eyes, gone almost as soon as it appeared.

'Indeed I did not. Had I been fortunate enough to own it, I should certainly have hung on to it myself.'

'That's all,' Sergio said abruptly, and the other man unfolded his body from his chair.

'Send Mr Kinaid in, please.'

'I'm afraid he's gone down to the boat,' Langdon Smythe said. 'He'll be back in about an hour.'

Giving you time to check your stories. Sergio bit back an expletive and nodded. 'When he comes back, then.'

Rose looked up as Sergio came into the kitchen. His face was tight with anger.

'Maria-Grazia?' he asked.

'She went to pick some flowers.'

'Flowers? At a time like this?'

'For the house. She likes to do it. And I think it's important to her to keep to her routine.'

'Oh.' He walked over to the window and stood with his back to her. 'Yes, I suppose it is.'

'What did you want? Can I help?'

'I wondered,' he said, without turning around, 'if she'd made a cake?'

'Instead of picking flowers, you mean?' Rose controlled a strong desire to laugh.

'I have this great need for something sweet.'

She smiled and went over to the fridge. 'Apricot *crostata*?'

'Wonderful.' He came over and sat at the table as she cut him a piece. 'I shall get fat on this case.'

'I think you've a long way to go before that.'

He sighed. 'And a long way to go before it's finished.'

'Coffee?'

'I'm drinking too much coffee as well. But yes.' He held out perfectly steady hands. 'Look, the shakes.'

'I can't see anything.'

'No? Feel them.'

She laid her hand briefly on one of his. 'They feel all right to me.'

He sighed again. 'It must be your calming effect.'

He was practised with women, Rose thought. Well, she knew that all along. But he was beginning to have a disturbing effect on her.

'I gave up smoking last year, too,' he said. He licked a finger and stabbed up the last crumbs from the plate.

'Does it still bother you?'

'Mmm.' He gave her a sideways look and let a little silence fall between them. 'Particularly on days like this,' he added.

She spooned coffee into a small *macchinetta*.

'How are they all behaving?' he asked, abruptly.

'It's very quiet,' she said. She lit the gas under the coffee. 'I think they're all in shock.'

'Murder is shocking,' he said. 'But the Brits are cool customers. Langdon Smythe, for instance. He makes *me* feel like committing murder.'

She got out cups and saucers. 'Milk?'

'No thanks. Black.' He rubbed his face. 'It smells wonderful. I didn't know the English could make coffee.' He smiled, for the first time.

'We can do all kinds of things,' Rose said.

'Yes, I'm sure you can.'

He added three spoons of sugar to his cup and drank the coffee in one gulp.

'Oh, that's better.' He stood up. 'If I pick you up after lunch, we could go for a drive and talk about it all.'

She hesitated for a moment then said, 'Yes, all right.'

'Good.' He suddenly had a very boyish look. 'I'll look forward to that.'

She poured herself another coffee after he'd left and wondered what Johnny Langdon Smythe had said to annoy him so much. She found the Englishman's laid back air false. He ignored her, of course. He took it for granted that she was part of the villa's equipment. Which was fair enough. But it was hard to tell if he was the shallow playboy he portrayed, or if the shell was not hollow after all, if it contained a shrewd and calculating mind. Of the two, Peter Kinaid seemed the more harmless.

There was no doubt, too, but that the party had fallen apart since Gillian's death. However much she may have been disliked by some of them, she had been the lynch pin which held them together and, without her, the group was wandering listlessly around the house and garden. Occasionally someone used the pool, but even the splashes seemed subdued.

Johnny found Elizabeth on the roof terrace. She spent most of her time in this vantage point, as though waiting for some gallant rescuers to come galloping up the avenue. Dom was the only one she talked to now but he, too, had gone into himself.

'Fancy a walk,' Johnny said, 'or are you determined on getting a tan?'

Hadn't he noticed that she was in the shade? He must be rattled.

'All right,' she said, slowly. She began to gather up her book and writing materials. 'Give me ten minutes.'

162   *Maureen Donegan*

'Can't you leave your things here?' he asked irritably.

'I'd rather not.' She pulled a T-shirt over her swim suit. 'Five minutes then. I'll meet you in the hall.'

'Who are you writing to?' he asked.

'Daddy.'

'Ah. In the hall then.'

She went down to her room and changed into shorts and a loose shirt. She brushed her hair and looked at her serious face in the mirror, added lipstick and sprayed on scent but wondered why she was bothering. Johnny never sought her out unless he wanted something.

He glanced impatiently at his watch as she came up the stairs.

'Where are we going?' she asked, ignoring the gesture.

'The cliff walk?'

She made a face. 'It's very hot.'

'There'll be a breeze up there.'

The air was completely still and the heat seemed to simmer around her head. 'I doubt it.'

'Oh, come on. I just have to get out of this place.'

'We could go down to the boat,' she suggested.

'Peter's down there,' he said abruptly.

Even more curious. Had they quarrelled?

There was very little conversation as they plodded up the unmetalled road. The sun burned their shoulders and Johnny occasionally wiped his forehead with a handkerchief.

'You should wear a hat,' Elizabeth said at one point.

He grunted. 'I expect you're right.'

They stopped eventually beside a fragment of old stone wall. Johnny pulled Elizabeth down beside him and put his hand out towards her.

'It's peaceful up here,' she said.

'Mmm. There're eyes everywhere down there. Bloody woman, getting herself bumped off.'

'Who do you think—'

'I have no idea,' he said, loudly. 'I just want to get away from here.'

'So do I.' She looked down at his long fingers as they stroked her arm.

TUSCAN SHADOWS 163

'We never seem to get a moment alone together,' he said.

'No.'

'I'm sorry, Elizabeth. I shouldn't have brought you here. It's a mess.'

'Yes.'

'It just seemed like a good way of having a few weeks together.'

'I could have stayed in a hotel somewhere.' Anywhere but here, was what she thought.

'But that's so impersonal.'

He had used these arguments before but she still didn't know why he had been so keen on the Villa Antonia and the awful Tenby woman.

'This has become rather too personal, don't you think? We're trapped here with people we hardly know and I for one certainly don't like.' She felt his mouth on her neck. 'I'm really sorry, sweetie.'

'I'm sorry too.' But she let herself be drawn into his arms.

'When this is all over we should go away somewhere, just the two of us.'

'Yes. . . .'

'Give me your hand. Here . . . yes, like that. . . .'

'Why can't we. . . ?'

'Don't you like this?'

'Yes, but. . . .'

I'm being manipulated, a little voice told her, and not only physically. Was this the only way he could bear . . . or did he really, in his own way love her, need her, as he was now vowing repeatedly with a low, intense whisper into her ear. Or was this something they both had to do, something repugnant to both of them, in order to seal their bargain?

She had told him, once, something of her fear of sex. The father of one of her school friends had seduced her when she was sixteen, had crept into her room while she was staying with them for the holidays. Where was her own father then? Off with one of his women, no doubt. It had begun with soft sighs, and stroking and she had been lulled into a sense of warm but false security. He said she'd given him sexy looks over dinner. And yes, she remembered his own twinkling eyes and his jokes and how she had wished her own father could act the host with such aplomb. But the sighs turned to grunts and the stroking to an intense pain. His hand splayed across her

164 *Maureen Donegan*

mouth and pushed her head into the pillow to stop her screams. She remembered him shuddering. Shuddering as Johnny was now.

Afterwards there had been more soft words, talk of love even. He had come to her room every night. She had never really enjoyed his lovemaking, only the warmth, the sense of being wanted. She'd been terrified that Sandy or her mother would find out, but they didn't seem suspicious. And then, back at school in the autumn, someone had asked about her holiday, sniggered and told her that Sandy's father was a randy old goat and hoped she hadn't fallen foul of him. 'He tries it on with everyone; housemaids,' the girl had said, sniggering again, 'girls in the village, sheep even. Everyone in the county knows about him.'

She'd thought it was love. She'd really thought that. It was yet more proof of her stupidity and ineptness. She remembered her humiliation, how she'd locked herself in the loo and vomited until her stomach reacted with only dry retching. Afterwards she cried and cried. And then the worry for the next few weeks until she got the curse. But he'd used something. There'd been some fumbling, a rubbery smell. He must have had ten hands, she thought bitterly. After that she had only loved at a distance – no, not loved, had crushes – and she had always retreated long before the man really noticed her. Until Johnny.

'Tissue?'

'I have some.' She sat up, aware of a reddening patch on her thigh where the grass had raised a rash. She must have been lying on a stone too, if the pain in her back was anything to go by. Luxury villa in Tuscany, she thought. With one's loved one. She'd wanted to be Lady Stennington but, for the first time, she wondered if life without Johnny might not be preferable after all. There had to be more to life than these few crumbs.

Johnny lit a cigarette. 'You said you were writing to your father?'

'Yes.'

'I suppose you've been on the phone to him too.'

'Yes, of course. Why?'

'I wondered if there was anything he could do.'

'In what way?'

'To get us out of here. The police can't keep us for ever.'

So that was it.

'Doesn't he trot around the corridors of power a bit?' Johnny's voice was languid, but his eyes had a hard, penetrating glitter.

Was that really the only reason why he'd brought her up here? To get her to put pressure on her father? She turned her head away so that he wouldn't see the sudden tears.

'I'll see what I can do at my end as well,' Johnny said briskly, and helped her to her feet.

Alison didn't remember if she had taken off her make-up the night before. She creamed her face and wiped it with a cotton pad but the dark shadows remained. Not mascara then.

'Pull yourself together,' Keith had said, unhelpfully.

Yes, well. But right now dark glasses would have to serve. 'And try not to say too much about Gillian,' he'd added. 'I know how you feel but it will only make matters worse.' But he didn't know how she felt, would never know, not in a million years. If she'd had a child perhaps. She peered at herself once more in the mirror and then began to dress slowly and carefully.

'Ah, Mrs Drinkwater,' the captain said, 'I understood you were not feeling well?'

She looked at him cautiously. 'I had a bad night, that's all.' She lowered herself into the chair opposite. 'Do we have to do all this twice?'

'I'm sorry?'

'Do we have to do a tedious re-run down at the police station?'

'At present,' Sergio said, 'I'm gathering impressions. Should any significant facts emerge then, yes, certainly, they would have to be incorporated into your statement.'

Alison took off her sunglasses, wiped them and put them on again. 'Ah.'

'I'm trying to build up a picture of Mrs Tenby,' he said pleasantly. 'What made her tick, what brought her to Italy, that sort of thing.'

'I understand.'

'You've known her a long time, I believe.'

'We were at school together.'

'So you've always been close friends.'

166   *Maureen Donegan*

'Not close, exactly. We were in different streams.'

'Streams?'

'At school.'

'Ah, yes.'

'I did history and English.' Let's hope all this bores him to death and he'll leave it alone. 'That's right, history and English and Gillian did commercial subjects.'

Gillian used to say, 'You're so clever', in that special voice she used to cut people down to size. Alison could still feel the same shrinking inside when she thought of Gillian's sycophantic groupies. Because that's what they were.

'And did you see much of her after you left school?'

'Not a great deal.'

'You didn't like her very much then?'

'We didn't have much in common, that is, at school.'

'But you and your husband were in her, er, circle later on?'

'Yes.'

'Do I take it that wasn't of your making?'

She'd genuinely thought Gillian had changed. And that she, Alison, had grown out of her childhood feeling of inadequacy. She had, let's face it, positively glowed in the barrage of Gillian's charm, had felt at first flattered but cautious and then indispensable when the grown-up Gillian had come calling. Again and again.

'Keith and Gillian always got on well and I rather liked Donald; I knew him vaguely at school,' she said, carefully. 'So we saw each other fairly often, I suppose.'

'Did Mrs Tenby initiate these meetings?'

She hesitated. 'Usually.'

'She liked to socialize?'

'Yes.'

'And despite the fact that you disliked her at school—'

'I didn't say I disliked her.'

'Let me put it this way, she wasn't a great friend when you were young, but you subsequently spent a lot of time in her company. Had she changed?'

He's clever, Alison thought. She remembered Gillian with tickets for the theatre, just for the two of them, a night on their own without their boring menfolk, she'd said; Gillian lending her a favourite blouse, bringing Alison to her own hairdresser, encouraging her to do yoga. It all seemed well meant as it should be between best friends. That's how Gillian had referred to them – best friends. It was only later, when Gillian got what she wanted, that she started seriously carving away at Alison's self-esteem. 'No, sweetie, of course I can't see any grey hairs. It's more a sort of . . . fading. All over.'

'I found her pleasant company,' she said to Sergio.

'You knew that she was once your husband's girlfriend?'

Alison rather liked the 'once'. She managed a wry smile. 'They were very young. It wasn't important.'

'So you were quite happy to come here on holiday, and stay with her?'

'I like Italy.'

'Tell me about Mrs Tenby's husband.'

'What do you want to know?'

'Anything you can tell me.'

'They weren't very compatible,' Alison said. 'He wanted a quiet life but Gillian was more extrovert.'

'Was she faithful to him?'

She hadn't expected such a blunt question. The Italian's voice was quiet and his manner mild, but the brown eyes which regarded her so steadily were sharp. And they were waiting for an answer.

The captain went on in his calm voice, 'It's simply that since your husband was in America at the time the Tenbys got married, you are probably in a better position to tell me about it.'

Alison gripped the arms of her chair. 'Gillian was pregnant, at least I think so.' No harm in telling him that. 'Donald was cautious, it might have been the only way she . . . could. . . .'

'It was his child?' the same even voice asked.

'Yes, of course it was!' she said and then, before she could stop herself, 'It couldn't have been Keith's! He went to America a long time before Gillian and Donald got married.'

She remembered the rumours that had gone around, the heads bent over

168   *Maureen Donegan*

the pram. 'Dom is like Donald in many ways. You couldn't mistake it. He has Gillian's features but his build and colouring are exactly like his father's.' Her head was pounding.

He was making notes in Italian on a pad in front of her. He had nice hands, long and artistic. She wondered why he had wanted to be a policeman and then if there was something going on between Rose and himself. He spent an enormous amount of time in the kitchen.

'You were about to say something, Mrs Drinkwater?'

'Er . . . no.'

'How did Mrs Tenby get on with her stepdaughter?'

'Quite well,' Alison said. 'Susie was jealous of Dom at first, but that was only natural.'

Natural. It was what Alison used to say to the little girl when she came for comfort. It's natural your Daddy loves the baby, but he loves you. Of course he does.

'But it was better when Susie went away to school,' she said. It had been, too.

'And more recently?' the captain said, making another indecipherable mark on his pad.

'More recently?'

It was no use pretending that all was sweetness and light around Gillian, whatever Keith said. 'They got on reasonably well. Gillian tended to have a go at Susie occasionally. I suppose there was a bit of jealously on both sides. Susie adored her father. But Gillian encouraged Susie to do things. She was very positive that way.'

'But there were no really bad feelings between them?'

'No.' Alison felt overwhelming relief that the questions about Keith had stopped. Her shirt was sticking to her shoulder blades and she could feel drops of moisture running down inside her sun glasses. 'I saw a lot of Susie when she was young, I would have known if she was really unhappy.'

'Do you know anything about Mrs Tenby being involved in smuggling?'

Alison tried to suppress a bubble of hysterical laughter. 'Smuggling? Gillian?'

'Yes, ancient artefacts.'

TUSCAN SHADOWS 169

The bubble threatened to burst. 'Gillian was . . . well, all the things I've told you, but she wasn't into . . . You can't be serious?'

'Mrs Tenby was murdered and there has to be a reason. She could have been taking stolen goods out of Italy.'

'But she'd only been to Italy once before, with Donald on her honeymoon. And she's always lived in England. It's not possible that she—'

'She hadn't changed her habits, her routine lately?'

'No, she was the same bitch she'd always been,' and then the laughter erupted, uncontrollably. She was having trouble stopping, though. She scrabbled for a tissue to dry her eyes and finally subsided into gulps that were more like sobs.

The captain waited patiently. When she had stopped snuffling, he asked, 'Are you all right, Mrs Drinkwater?'

'Yes, yes, I am.'

'That's all then. For now. Unless you have anything to add?'

She shook her head.

Alison felt somewhat better as she left the room. She was embarrassed by her laughter but it had been a release and presenting Gillian in a relatively reasonable light had shifted her own view of the past. Keith's obsession with Gillian when he was young, the way he went on loving her while he was in America and still loved her, somehow it had all become easier to bear. Only a crazy woman, Alison thought, would have allowed herself to be manipulated the way Gillian had manipulated her. But she wasn't crazy. It was the captain who was off his rocker if he thought . . . smuggling indeed. She giggled again.

Her head had cleared and now she had a sharp, sane picture of how it might have been. But Gillian's shade still hovered between them, smiling her lop-sided smile, waving her flashing red nails. Perhaps she would always be there.

If only I'd had a child, if only . . . but Keith had said she wasn't capable of looking after one. Gillian had made him say that.

CHAPTER 14

'Did you walk into a door, Mr Kinaid?

Peter's hand went to his face. 'Oh, that. Tripped over a rope.'

It was a pity, Peter thought, that the brave capitain was straight. He was an archetypal Mediterranean man, dark and sinewy, but taller than Pino who would have turned into one of those desiccated, sun-dried little men who sat around the *piazze* in Sardinia. This man would age well, like good wine. Like Johnny.

'Quite nasty. You should put something on it.' But the captain was looking down at the papers on the table between them as he said this. Peter followed his gaze.

'Your statement,' the captain said. 'You were on the boat the night Mrs Tenby died.'

'Yes, with Johnny.'

'With Mr Langdon Smythe, yes. And neither of you left the boat.'

'Correct.'

'Tell me, what brought you both to the Villa Antonia?'

'We were invited.'

The captain nodded. 'I understand Mrs Tenby was your friend, not Mr Langdon Smythe's?'

Johnny had warned Peter to avoid talking about Nardi, about Pino, about Gillian and about Sardinia. That was when he'd calmed down a bit after their fight. Not that it had been exactly a fight, but this time Peter hadn't been able to avoid Johnny's fists.

TUSCAN SHADOWS

171

'I met her last winter, with other friends, and we started talking about Italy and it turned out she was coming here.'

'Just like that, Mr Kinaid?'

'No, not exactly like that. I saw her a number of times. We were friends.'

'You went to her house, I believe?'

Johnny had already told them that. 'Yes.'

'She saw you coming,' Johnny had said in disgust, 'thought you'd improve her social life.' He'd laughed but without much amusement. 'Didn't know we were the ragamuffins of the Med.'

'So you arranged to meet Mrs Tenby in Italy in the summer?'

'Correct.'

'How long were you in England last winter, Mr Kinaid?'

'Um, ten days or so.'

'In ten days' time you became close friends with Mrs Tenby?'

'We wrote to each other, kept in touch.' He shivered as he remembered Gillian's exclamation marks on the notes which arrived regular as clockwork, and tried to forget the Etruscan urn which she had assured him was sitting in a cupboard in Berkshire. How in the name of God had she got it through Customs? And why? But he knew the answer to that. She'd brought it to the villa to keep him in line.

'Penpals?' Sergio said, raising his eyebrows.

Peter managed a small laugh. 'If you like.'

The captain leaned back in his chair. 'There are a number of . . . incongruities about this case, Mr Kinaid, and a curious mixture of people. Mrs Tenby being in possession of a bit of Etruscan antiquity is one anomaly. Do you know what that suggests to me?'

Peter's mouth was dry. 'No.'

'It suggests blackmail. Did you give her this object?'

'No, of course not. Where would I have got it?'

'Where indeed? I can quite see that Mrs Tenby might want an international yachtsman in her party, but I fail to understand why he would have accepted the invitation since it's clear neither he nor his fiancé liked the dead woman. And so we come to you. The fulcrum, Mr Kinaid. So what was the lever?'

172   *Maureen Donegan*

The captain waited, but Peter had suddenly remembered Johnny's instructions to say as little as possible.

'Did she also perhaps put pressure on you because of your sexual preferences?'

Peter was too relieved at the shift in the conversation to be angry. 'Consenting adults,' he said, and smirked at the olive-skinned face in front of him. And then he remembered Gillian's slightly parted red lips and her hand pouring brandy and began to feel less sure of himself.

At first he had felt completely safe with Gillian, as he often did with middle-aged women. It had been like settling into a warm nest, but his downfall had been that he had wanted to show her what a clever boy he was.

'Tell me why you stay with him,' she'd said, in a soft voice, 'if you're so upset about him getting married. Why do you put up with it?'

And so he'd told her, not that he was infatuated with Johnny, she knew that, but the other thing. Her eyes had glittered with excitement. 'Modern-day pirates, how romantic.'

He'd realized his stupidity very quickly and come to dread seeing the envelopes with her large aggressive handwriting which arrived so regularly but when they met again at the villa he found himself once more under her spell.

The joints were a terrible mistake though. 'They're all so dull,' Gillian had said, giggling, 'Let's shake them all up.' Stirring up trouble while she checked for an escape route appeared to be one of her specialities. But someone had finally closed that route. He controlled a shiver.

'Mr Kinaid?'

'Yes?'

'You were about to tell me the real reason you brought Mr Langdon Smythe and his fiancé to Villa Antonia.'

'It suited them,' Peter said. 'Elizabeth doesn't like racing. She doesn't even like staying on the boat.'

The captain's expression was not very encouraging but Peter ploughed on. 'We were racing in Porto Cervo and she said she'd like to come out after that. It all rather slotted into place.'

The captain wrote several lines on a scribble pad. 'That is more or less what Mr Langdon Smythe told me.' He looked up. 'Almost word for word, in fact.'

Sergio was playing with him. Just like Gillian had played with him. The relief he'd felt at her death hardened into a feeling of pleasure. Pleasure which could easily be multiplied were Captain Tavazzi to be murdered, too.

It would be wonderful if he could just move on but he could never leave Johnny, not voluntarily. And now Gillian was reaching out from the grave, taunting him, holding him back. Had she, could she have told the police something?

'Signor Franco Nardi,' the captain was saying.

'I've never heard of him,' Peter said, quickly.

This time the captain wrote in English on his pad. 'Never heard of him.' Peter could read the letters upside down. 'Never heard of him,' Sergio repeated.

'Correct.'

'That's rather strange. His boat is near yours on the marina and I believe he frequents the same bar. Doesn't the yachting fraternity stick together rather?'

Improvise, Peter told himself. He'd got through most of his life doing just that. 'We may have met him, I'm not sure.'

The captain added, 'May have met him', to his notes. 'Tall, rather fair for an Italian?' he murmured.

'Ah no. That's not the person I was thinking of,' Peter said. 'This man was dark.'

'And so you've had no business dealings with either a tall, fair or a dark, Franco Nardi?'

'Of course not.'

'Where did you get the marijuana, Mr Kinaid?' the captain asked suddenly.

'What marijuana?'

'That you were smoking the night Mrs Tenby died.'

Johnny had told him to deny any knowledge of it. Between blows.

'I thought pot was legal in Italy,' he said sulkily, 'for your own personal use.'

174 *Maureen Donegan*

'Many years ago that might have been the case,' the captain said, 'but I can assure you it certainly isn't now.'

'If anyone was smoking, it wasn't either of us,' Peter said, emphatically. 'Maybe Gillian got hold of some. It was her style.'

Sergio leaned forward and looked at him intently. 'Some smuggling goes on in this area, quite a lot in fact.' He took a coin from his pocket and passed it from his left hand to his right, and back again, slowly at first then more quickly. Peter seemed mesmerized by the movements.

He was still watching the coin as Sergio said, 'So if, as you say, Mrs Tenby procured the marijuana, perhaps she was also involved in something more serious. Had you thought of that?'

Peter started. 'I know nothing about drugs,' he said. It was practically true, he thought.

Sergio Tavazzi nodded and put the coin back into his pocket. He wrote on his pad, 'Knows nothing about drugs.'

'Or any other kind of illegal traffic?' he asked.

'Or any other kind of illegal traffic,' Peter repeated firmly. He felt this was not a moment for improvisation. 'And neither does Johnny.'

Sergio added this disclaimer to his notes and drew a line beneath it, but the smile he gave Peter was disturbing.

'Right. I'll have this typed up and get a translator organized and we can get you to sign it at the station tomorrow.'

'I thought this was just a chat,' Peter said, alarmed. 'Johnny said it wasn't an official statement.'

'You discussed it with Mr Langdon Smythe?'

'Yes, of course I did,' Peter said. His leg which had been twitching uneasily under the table, suddenly jerked uncontrollably.

'Until tomorrow then, Mr Kinaid. And thank you for your co-operation.'

'I think the family have been through enough,' Mike said. 'Why can't you let us all go home?'

The captain opened his arms in a Latin gesture. 'My hands are tied, unfortunately, and I do appreciate the patience you've all shown.'

Smarmy bastard, Mike thought. But underneath the charm he sensed cold determination.

'You are engaged to Ms Tenby, I believe?' the captain went on.

'Yes. And I'm concerned that she shouldn't be upset any more than necessary.'

'Is there some particular reason why you say this?'

'Damn it all, man, she lost her father not long ago. Had a bad time. It coincided with some career problems too.'

'Career problems?'

'Not problems exactly. She decided to give up children's nursing. She realized she prefers working with old people.'

'And this was after how long?'

'How long? Oh – she'd done a couple of years, I think.'

'Quite a break then.'

'Well yes, but I think it was a good decision.'

'Have you known her a long time?'

'Keith, Mr Drinkwater, introduced us about eighteen months ago. We're in the same computer company. He's my boss.'

'Ah. Tell me about the Drinkwaters, Mr Harding.'

'There's nothing much to tell. I got on well with Keith at work and we became friends. My own family are all dead and so I've seen a lot of them. They've been very kind.'

'Mrs Drinkwater too?'

'Yes, of course.'

'One has the impression that she is ill.'

'She's had . . . some nervous problems.'

'A breakdown?'

'Well, something like that.'

'And do you know the cause?'

Mike swallowed. 'She wanted children and it just didn't happen. Look, I don't see the point of all this . . . this delving into people's lives.'

'I assure you, Mr Harding, that I am just as anxious to bring this affair to a quick conclusion as you are. And I'm afraid that delving into people's lives, as you put it, is part of my job.'

176   *Maureen Donegan*

Mike took a deep breath. 'Yes. Sorry.'

'Let's go back to Mrs Tenby. You can recall no other threat to her life? No hint of violence in the family?'

Had the captain heard about the row Dom had had with Gillian?

'You're hesitating Mr Harding. Was there something? If you can remember anything, anything at all that might have any bearing on the case I'd like to hear it.'

Mike shook his head.

'Then it seems likely that the events which led up to Mrs Tenby's death were connected with Italy.'

That was a really brilliant piece of deduction. 'And no doubt the fact that the sailor was killed first.'

The captain's face tightened. 'I'm well aware of that, Mr Harding. So, you know the family well. Did Mrs Tenby get on with her husband?'

'Yes, of course.' What was he getting at?

'He died in a car crash, I believe?'

'Yes. It was tragic. He was a really nice man.'

'Good but rather dull?' The captain gave him a conspiratorial smile.

'No, not at all.'

'That is not the impression I have been given. It also seems Mrs Tenby was rather bored, rather restless in the marriage.'

'I can assure you it wasn't like that,' Mike said, quickly. God, but it was hot. His mind went to the pool and Gillian's breasts bobbing in the cool water. He wiped his hands on his shorts and caught Sergio watching him thoughtfully.

Mike wondered, angrily, who had been talking; Alison probably.

'Gillian liked to flirt a bit,' he said, after a considerable pause. 'It was harmless.'

But it hadn't been so harmless that day in their garden, the day she'd persuaded him to come to Italy. He'd pushed her against the wall of the conservatory and stopped her slightly mocking laugh with his tongue. She'd responded with enthusiasm and drawn him towards the house, tilting her head and giving him her lop-sided smile and he was lost. When he finally left she'd strolled down to open the gate for him and stood blocking it, jumping away at the last moment, laughing. He'd almost run into the gatepost, he remembered.

It had only been that one time and afterwards he had managed to keep his impulses in check although the emotional temperature continued to simmer between them. Had her flirtation, he tried not to give it a cruder word, with Tom been to punish him?

But Gillian's life, he thought, hadn't been very happy. She'd told him she had fallen in love with someone when she was young, but it didn't work out and she'd married Donald on the rebound. Mike was fairly sure that the someone was Keith. Susie said he was always around while she was growing up. But, whatever Alison might think, Keith seemed to be out of the running now.

Alison hadn't put up much of a fight for him, poor cow. But Mike saw Keith more as a patient spaniel than an active lover. And it wasn't as if Gillian was promiscuous. She needed comfort, affection. He'd always admired the way she put a good face on things. She'd once confessed that she'd never really loved Donald. He was a workaholic, only interested in the business and she'd spent a lot of time alone. She'd felt sorry for him. Her easily aroused sympathy often led her into unfortunate situations, she'd told Mike ruefully. But marriage was for life, and she was stuck with it.

Sergio Tavazzi coughed. 'Mrs Tenby flirted, as you put it with Mr Drinkwater, I believe.'

'He was an old friend.'

'And Mr Graham?'

'That was absolutely harmless.'

'And with you, Mr Harding.' It was said in a flat voice, a statement of fact.

'She needed someone to talk to. I think she found it easy to talk to a man; she preferred men's company.'

Sergio coughed again. 'Yes, that does seem to be the case. And was your fiancé aware of Mrs Tenby's interest in you? As a confidante, that is?'

'There was nothing to be aware of.' That was almost true. 'It was all quite innocent.' Yes, innocent. Only the once, he told himself again. 'Susie didn't take any notice when Gillian . . . well, when she talked to me. She was used

178   *Maureen Donegan*

to her. Anyway, I've told you, it meant nothing. She just needed to have, well, to have a bit of attention.'

But life was easier without Gillian around, he had to admit. Because he loved Susie and he would have hated her to be hurt.

'Do you know anything about the Tenbys' finances, Mr Harding?' the captain asked, suddenly.

'Donald had a successful engineering company. I don't think there was any problem there.'

'I've been informed otherwise. It seems that the late Mr Tenby had made some risky investments.'

This was more tricky ground. 'Er ... Susie said her father had been worried about something just before he died, but I think he worried too much about money. Business was his only real, well, passion.'

'And Dom Tenby? Did he inherit the business?'

'No. He was never interested. He's involved in his own property company.'

'Would you say that Dom Tenby had financial problems?'

He must have heard about the row with Dom, then.

'I think he's doing OK,' he said quickly. 'Probably has his father's head for business. I don't think he really needed help from Gillian. He gets excited about things sometimes, that's all.'

'Excited?'

'Well, loses his rag about once a year ... but it doesn't mean anything.'

'And did he lose his rag, as you put it, recently?'

'There was a slight argument the other night.' God, how had he got into this?

'Between Dom Tenby and his mother?'

'It wasn't even an argument. Dom just happened to mention to us, to Susie and me, something about Gillian selling the house. He was a bit fed up about it.'

'Then you are aware that Mrs Tenby was very short of money?'

'But how could that be?' Mike waved a bewildered arm to indicate the villa. 'Otherwise she wouldn't have come here, spent all this money?'

'Quite.' The captain leaned back and tapped his teeth with his pen. 'And

Ms Tenby, does she have financial worries?'

'I don't think so. She doesn't have much spare cash. Well, we all have cash flow problems, but her grandmother left her some kind of legacy and her father set up a trust fund when she was young.'

'All right, Mr Harding. That's all. For now.'

Mike hurried away and found Susie in the garden. She was sitting above the vine terrace, her arms around her knees, gazing out beyond the pool at the hazy plain below. A slight movement in the air lifted her hair back from her face. He bent to drop a kiss on her forehead.

'OK?' she asked.

'I suppose so.' He crouched down beside her. 'Only. . . .'

She looked up, sharply. 'Only what?'

'He asked me about Dom.'

'What about Dom?'

'His business affairs mostly. I got the impression he knew about the row he had with Gillian and I, well, I rather put my foot in it.'

'Oh, Mike.' She put her hand on his. 'What exactly did you say?'

'Only that Dom didn't want her to sell the house.'

She let out her breath. 'Nothing else?'

He shook his head and Susie gave him a reassuring smile. 'If that's all, you could have told him I didn't want her to sell it either. There's too much of my father there.'

'I know. But you have to let go of the past, Susie.'

'Yes. It will probably be sold anyway now. And we have the flat . . . you do still want us to live together, don't you?'

Mike was watching Elizabeth emerge from the changing-room at the pool. 'What? Oh, yes, yes of course.'

'Are you sure?'

Mike put his arm around Susie and hugged her. 'I'm sure,' he said. 'Mmm, do you think there's anything between Elizabeth and Dom?'

Susie followed his gaze. She shrugged. 'Holiday romance, maybe.'

'It's odd, isn't it?'

'It is rather.'

'Do you think we should warn him?'

'About Elizabeth?'

Mike half laughed. 'About Captain What'sit.'

'Oh.' Susie leaned against him and took his hand. 'I think we should leave well alone. It isn't as if Dom could have had anything to do with Gillian's death. He adored her.'

Maria-Grazia had steeled herself to clean Gillian's room. The *carabinieri* had finally finished with it and returned the key to her.

And she wasn't afraid of the dead. They couldn't do any harm, but there was something else in the villa, something evil, something that could well be concentrated in Gillian Tenby's room.

'One of them did it,' Giulio had said. He was *nervoso*. He kept forgetting things, the coffee yesterday and fruit today. She had shouted at him and was immediately sorry when she saw his face. She'd put her arms around him and felt him shake.

'I wish we could leave this place,' he said, against her shoulder.

'They'll all go, and then it will be all right.'

'I don't think it will ever be all right,' Giulio said. 'She's left something behind.'

He was spending more and more time in the storeroom, crouched among the tools and garden equipment, and his gardening activities had been reduced to a sketchy maintenance of the pool. And when she asked him to help to move the furniture in Gillian's room, he refused point blank.

'You should keep out of there,' he said. 'It will touch you, somehow.'

'Nonsense,' she said, more bravely than she felt. She would let in some fresh air and drive out the dust. She would have the satisfaction of beating the rugs and spreading them out in the sun. Whatever spirits were in the house would be swept out with her brushes and mop. It was always the women who had to be strong, she thought, as she made Giulio a *camomilla* to calm him down.

She went to get the key which Massimo Pascucci had given her and found the hook empty. She shrugged. Perhaps Rosa had already gone down to air the room. They had talked about it at breakfast.

She collected her cleaning things and went down the steps to the bedroom corridor. The dead woman's room was still closed and Maria-Grazia put down her things and tried the door. It swung open and she bent down to pick up her bucket, then dropped it with a clatter and shrieked.

Rose was setting the table in the dining room when she heard the scream. She dropped the cutlery she was polishing and ran down the steps from the hall.

Maria-Grazia was leaning against the wall outside Gillian's bedroom, clutching her ample bosom and making terrified moans. Her face was ashen. Water had spilled on to the floor and Rose almost slipped as she ran to comfort her.

'What is it?' Rose put her arms around her.

'She's still in there.' The Italian woman pointed to the half-open door.

'No, she's not. She's dead, Maria-Grazia. The *carabinieri* took her away, don't you remember?'

'Not her body,' Maria-Grazia whispered. 'Her. Moving about.' Rose released her gently and went towards the door.

'Don't go in there, Rosa!'

'No, don't.' Sergio Tavazzi's voice came from the top of the stairs. 'Let me.' Behind him were Massimo Pascucci, Mike Harding and Peter Kinaid.

Rose stood back obediently. She was not at all anxious to go into the room. The image of Gillian's still figure, head pillowed away from her, was still vividly imprinted on her mind.

Sergio hurried past her and into the room. The door to the terrace was wide open, spilling light into the room and something white was caught on the handle of a still swinging shutter. The wardrobe door was also open and several of Gillian's dresses were thrown across the bed. Otherwise the room was empty.

Sergio came back in from the terrace. 'Whoever was here has gone,' he said. 'Massimo, go around the other way and see if you can see anyone. And check where the rest of them are,' he called after him.

'It couldn't have been a ghost,' Rose told Maria-Grazia. 'They don't exist.' The other woman was sobbing but more quietly, and her face had regained some colour.

'No, it certainly wasn't a ghost,' Sergio said. He surveyed the room.

'Someone was looking for something and Maria-Grazia disturbed him. Or her.' He picked up a transparent *pareo* with the tips of his fingers and dropped it back on to the bed.

By now the group in the doorway had been joined by Elizabeth and Johnny Langdon Smythe.

'Nothing to be alarmed about,' Sergio said.

'But I saw her!' Maria-Grazia said. 'She was wearing that thing.' She pointed at the *pareo*. 'She was by the mirror. I saw her!' Her voice began to rise again, dangerously.

Johnny Langdon Smythe shrugged. 'Over-active imagination,' he said. But Rose noticed that Elizabeth lingered, her eyes flickering briefly around the room before Johnny drew her away.

Rose led Maria-Grazia back to the kitchen.

'My turn for *camomilla*,' Maria-Grazia said a little later, cradling a hot cup in her hand. 'And I thought Giulio was foolish.' She had stopped shaking and her voice was calmer. 'But I did see something.'

'Yes, I'm sure you did,' Rose said, soothingly.

Sergio joined them. 'Everyone accounted for, but none of them together,' he said, in disgust. 'Mr and Mrs Drinkwater were in different parts of the garden. Young Tenby was by the pool. Tom Graham was on the roof. And Giulio' – he glanced at Maria-Grazia – 'was in the pump room.' She gave him a dark look and he went on quickly, 'It could have been any one one of them. Even someone who appeared in the corridor. There was time for them to run around from the terrace.'

He slumped down at the kitchen table. 'But we've been over that room with a toothcomb. I don't know what anyone would want in there.'

CHAPTER 15

'Where are we going?' Rose asked, as she got into the car. 'Out of here.' He drove down the avenue and turned not left down to the port, but right towards the mountain.

'I've left Massimo Pascucci in charge of ghost-hunting and baby-sitting. There is no way I can interview anyone else until I've had a breath of air.' He sighed. 'I've a meeting with the procurator and my boss tomorrow. They're expecting me to come up with a quick miracle.'

'Miracles are difficult.'

'You're telling me.' He slapped his hand hard on the steering wheel and took a corner too fast. 'Sorry,' he said, glancing at her. 'I'm driving like Pascucci.'

She made a reassuring sound and he slowed down. He was frowning; there were deep lines along the side of his mouth and a matching crease between his eyes.

'How's Maria-Grazia?'

'She's making pasta.'

'Ah. That says everything.'

Rose laughed. 'You know her well.'

'Yes.'

She hesitated. 'You don't think Giulio had anything to do with it?'

'I have to check up on everyone.' He half turned towards her.

'Yes, I know that. But Maria-Grazia was offended.'

'This is a murder enquiry, Rose.'

'Yes, I know,' she said quietly.

183

He drove more carefully into a hairpin bend and she looked down at the glittering sea, far below. 'I must be under suspicion too, then?'

The car jerked suddenly. 'I thought we were getting away from the Affair at the Villa Antonia,' he said. He gave her an embarrassed smile.

'So you don't think I'm going to push you over a cliff?' she said, half laughing.

'My instincts,' he said, after a moment, 'have ruled that out as unlikely.'

'And your instincts are usually sound?'

'In some things,' he said. His hand brushed her knee, so swiftly that she wondered if she had imagined it.

The road had become less steep as it wound through a high wooded valley. 'It's beautiful,' she exclaimed.

'It's the best place on earth,' he said. 'It's where I was born.'

'Here on the mountain?'

'Over there.' He waved his hand vaguely.

'You were very lucky.'

'In some things, yes.'

He stopped the car at the head of the valley and she could see the water again. Toy-like boats floated in the harbour and in the far distance were specks that could have been islands.

He leaned over and opened her door. 'Let's get out,' he said. He drew her into a hollow with a view of the multi-shaded turquoise sea. Beyond the marinas stretched endless white beaches lapped by creamy surf and backed by sand dunes and groves of pine trees. Further inland were gentle, olive-covered hills.

'It's difficult to think of violence here,' he said.

'Yes.' They smiled at each other. His face was slightly flushed and she felt suddenly embarrassed.

'When did you go to England?' she asked, quickly.

'I didn't go; I was taken. I was nine. We had relatives there and because my father couldn't find work here we went to stay with them. It was going to be temporary. After a while, of course, I had to go to school. I didn't know a word of English and they put me in the bottom class. Thought I was backward.'

'It must have been terrible.'

He shrugged. 'It wasn't so good. It's a wonder I can add two and two.'

'I think you can do rather more than that,' Rose said. She tried to imagine what it had been like. A little Italian boy alone in a playground, probably having to fight and not knowing what he was fighting about.

'Maybe I was lucky. There was one teacher who knew some Italian, and he helped. But otherwise. . . .' He shrugged again.

He took her hand and for a moment she thought he was going to take her in his arms.

'Come on,' he said. 'We're going to be late.'

'You still haven't told me—'

He led her back to the car. 'Shsh. We have to be quiet up here. It's dangerous.'

'Is it?' God, was she flirting with him?

'Mmm. It's a magic place. The old gods come out and cast spells. But you have to be very still. Otherwise they'll stay away.'

He fastened her seat belt around her, touching, but not quite touching her.

'Which gods?' she asked.

'Don't you think Diana might have hunted here?'

'It's possible.'

'I think it's very likely.'

'Then I'm sure you're right.'

'And Venus is somewhere around too, and Daphne turning into a tree.'

'Was she a goddess?'

He grinned. 'She became immortal, running away from Apollo.'

'They're all women, your gods then?'

'Up here they are, yes.'

They drove around the mountain, still climbing. 'There's something, oh, I don't know, clean about high places,' he said, after a while, 'even if Jove and Mars are hanging about.'

She laughed. 'Yes.'

'My job isn't clean, though.'

'But it must be satisfying.'

'Sometimes I hate it. This is not England. There's a lot of bureaucracy, and even more politics.' He looked straight ahead. 'I see people at their worst. All the deadly sins and a thousand variations of them.'

186 *Maureen Donegan*

'Not a romantic job.'

'Romantic! God, no. I work on people's weaknesses, humiliate them, lay open their secrets for all the world to see. And even when I don't like them, I understand the pain it causes.'

'But you wouldn't like to do anything else.'

'No.' He braked suddenly to avoid hitting a dog. 'And you?' he said, turning his head slightly. 'Why do you want to humiliate yourself?'

'What?'

'Working for these awful people. You do admit they're awful?'

She wouldn't have taken this from Arthur, but Sergio's directness took her unawares.

'They're not very nice,' she said, slowly.

'Then why? What are you running away from?'

'I'm not—'

'Are you running away from yourself?'

'No!'

'I think you are.'

For a moment she couldn't speak. A number of strong and conflicting emotions surged through her body and settled in her throat. 'I . . . don't like doing ordinary jobs,' she said, eventually. 'This way I can travel, observe human nature.' It was the standard answer, the one she gave Arthur.

'And take a lot of shit in the process.'

Her blood was pounding in her head. How dare he? How dare he!

He was beating time on the steering wheel. 'You run up and down after these people, feed them, clean up after them, ally yourself with two *contadini*.'

'Maria-Grazia and Giulio are decent people,' she began.

'I know they are, but they're peasants.' He hesitated, fixing his eyes on the road ahead. 'But then, I'm a peasant too.' He seemed to gather in his breath. 'But you are not!' he shouted. 'You're throwing away all your talents!'

Into the ensuing silence she said quietly, 'That's just it: I don't have any talents.' Her anger had become something else. She was frightened of this man. He seemed to want to cut her open, dissect her. And it had been a long time since she had let anyone even attempt that.

'Of course you have. You could teach, you draw.' The voice went on inexorably. 'You have the right background, education, influential friends probably. Are you running away from some man? Like Daphne? Is that it?' The car lurched over a fall of small stones, punctuating his words. 'You're drifting around like some eccentric . . . oh, I don't know . . . is this your version of going into a convent? Or are you slumming, laughing at us all behind our backs?'

'No!' But what he said about the convent was so near the bone that she felt a physical pain, like a knife. She tried to speak calmly. 'I don't. . . .' She clasped her hands together, and looked unseeingly at the landscape. 'All right. I'm a poseur. A nothing. Because I don't draw well. I thought I was a genius but I left art school after a year. A mediocre talent, they called it.'

'Rose,' he said, 'I didn't mean. . . .'

'It's not a big tragedy,' she said. She tried, ineffectually, to dry her eyes. 'But I do know how you felt at the bottom of the class.'

'*Cristo*, I can't stop here,' he said, 'the road . . . I . . . Rose I didn't want to—'

'It's all right. It's all right.' She crumpled up a tissue and found another one. 'I'm sorry. I hate . . . I hate making a fool of myself.'

She hadn't allowed herself to think about college for years. It wasn't a big tragedy, as she'd said. It was a little one. And its insignificance was something she'd found even harder to take.

'I used to think I was something special, that's all. And then I found out that I wasn't going to be another Gwen John or Georgia O'Keefe or even Grandma Moses.' Her voice was rising. 'And I'm glad you don't think I'm guilty, because if you did, I'd have to confess straightaway. You're very good at interrogation.'

'Rose.' His voice was stricken. 'You're not one of those people down there, and I had no right to . . . your life is none of my business.'

She didn't answer.

'It isn't any of my business,' he said again. They were descending the far side of the mountain and there was a clear stretch of road. He drew up in the shade of a rocky overhang.

He put his arm around her shoulders. 'I'm truly sorry, Rose.' His other arm was across her lap, heavy and warm. She let herself lean against him. He began to kiss her, soft fluttery kisses on her neck and tear-stained cheeks.

'I spent the whole day playing cat and mouse with *gli inglesi*,' he said in a subdued voice. 'They're driving me crazy, but I shouldn't have taken it out on you.'

'It's all right.' She didn't think it was in any way all right.

'No, don't say that. Don't go back to being the cool Englishwoman. Shout at me again. Hit me.'

His mouth found hers and she felt even more terrified. She was sliding down a slippery path into unknown territory.

'Melina,' she said, when she got her breath.

'*Scusa?*'

'Last year. Maria-Grazia said—'

'I was lonely. She was lonely, that's all. Why do you always have to put yourself in some kind of role?'

'I don't.'

'Yes, you do. *Stai zitta.*'

'It's too hot for this.'

'Mmm. You don't mean that.'

'Too hot and too public.'

His face moved back just enough for her to see his eyes. They were moist and he was trembling almost as much as she was.

A car accelerated past them with a cloud of exhaust smoke.

Sergio swallowed. '*Carabinieri* captain arrested for indecency,' he muttered.

She began to laugh. The indistinct landscape was taking on a less hostile shape. Perhaps it would not be so frightening as she'd thought.

'Won't it keep?' she heard herself saying.

'I doubt it.' He nuzzled her throat. 'But I think it will have to.'

He looked at his watch, stroked her face and settled himself back into the driving seat.

'You haven't told me—'

'Where we're going,' he finished for her. He patted her leg. 'We're going to having coffee with my sister.'

He began to whistle softly as he started the car and continued on down the road.

*

The low, red-roofed house nestled in a fold at the end of a stony track. Olive trees sheltered it from the north and below were terraces of vines and then the sea. Rose sat among earthenware pots of herbs and flowers with the smell of coffee drifting out from the kitchen behind her.

She was pondering on the nature of love. It's just an interlude, she warned herself. A bit of light relief for him, an adventure for her. But it didn't feel like that. She shivered slightly although the early evening air was still very hot.

Sergio had disappeared into the vines with his brother-in-law, Marco. His sister, Silvana, emerged from the house with coffee and a bottle and glasses on a tray.

'Where are they?' she asked, in mock irritation. 'Just like them, as soon as it's ready they disappear.' She laughed, displaying beautiful white teeth. She was very much like Sergio, only younger and without his guarded expression. 'Sergio likes to talk vines and crops. I think he finds it restful, but he would never have made a farmer.'

'No,' Rose agreed. Silvana had expressed no surprise at their visit. Rose presumed Sergio had telephoned her. She wondered what he'd said: I'm bringing one of the people in the murder case, or I'm bringing you a woman to inspect, or I'm bringing you an eccentric Englishwoman or. . . . Her thoughts were interrupted by the reappearance of the men. And in any case, deep down, she believed and hoped he'd brought her because he wanted to be with her. The euphoria would wear off of course but, in the meantime, she was almost drowning in it.

'Sugar?' Silvana said.

'Please.'

Sergio sat down opposite her, his eyes warm. He picked up the bottle on the tray. 'Cherry?'

'Give some to Rosa,' Marco urged. 'It's good.'

It was. The liqueur slid down her throat, sweet and sharp at the same time. 'It's wonderful,' she said.

Marco smiled. He was a burly man with thick, greying hair and an open, weathered face. 'All the best things are in Italy,' he said. He patted his wife's bottom. 'Even though this one grew up in England.'

190   *Maureen Donegan*

'But you came back,' Rose said to Silvana.

'I was born there, but I was always Italian. In here.' She struck her breast. 'Sergio, he was born here, but he is half and half, I think.'

'The search for justice,' Marco said. 'That is very English, no?'

Sergio was leaning back, listening to them and half smiling. Rose remembered something Lena Grenbelli once told her, 'It is a great privilege to be invited to an Italian house. It means much more than in England.'

'How is Maria-Grazia?' Silvana asked. 'Do you get on well with her?'

'She's fine. She grumbles a bit, but. . . .'

'Ha, always in the summer,' Silvana said. She laughed.

'I like her very much,' Rose said.

'How could you not? She has a heart of gold, that one. And her life has not been easy.'

'It is still not very easy.'

Silvana gave her a penetrating glance and looked for a moment exactly like her brother. Was she too wondering what Rose was doing at the Villa Antonia, frittering her life away, as Sergio had implied?

The moment passed and the conversation moved to the tourists in the port and the number of cars on the roads. A cousin, Rose gathered, had a *pensione* and another a bar.

'I'm the only one who came back to the land,' Silvana said. 'This was my father's house. Marco's father bought it when the family went to England. He already had the vineyard beside it.'

'So I got the house and the girl,' Marco said, smiling.

'*Sei furbo,*' Silvana said, affectionately, but Rose was sure that he was the exact opposite of cunning.

I could stay here forever, she thought, basking in the warmth of their contentment. But she knew that wasn't possible. She was having a glimpse only, and a privileged one at that.

Two young boys rattled around the side of the house and dropped their bicycles against the wall.

'Zio Sergio!' they cried and rushed to kiss him. Then they shook hands shyly with Rose, as Sergio made the introductions.

These must be the boys he did the tricks for. They had their mother's lean frame topped by Marco's broad, open face. Rose felt a pang. She knew she would never have this. Although it was not, as Maria-Grazia had pointed out, too late. You're crazy, she told herself. He probably brought Melina here, and a hundred others.

Silvana was pressing them to stay to dinner. 'There's rabbit,' she said, 'with herbs and oil.'

'It sounds wonderful,' Rose said, 'but I have to go back.'

'We'll come another night,' Sergio said firmly. 'OK, Rose?'

'OK,' she said.

'Your parents?' she asked, as they drove back.

'My father died in England and my mother brought Silvana back. She died last year.'

'And you stayed in England.'

'For a while. I got a scholarship to university. I wanted to be an English barrister, but you need money and connections for that.' He smiled grimly. 'In that respect most countries are alike. And I needed money just to eat. So I came back and became a private in the *carabinieri* until I finally won a *concorso* to the Academy. And eventually became a *sottotenente*.'

Rose saw again the young boy with his back to the playground railings, thin and leggy like his nephews, and then a gangly youth wanting to take on the British establishment.

'You did well,' she said, quietly.

'Perhaps.'

'You know you did.' She leaned back and thought about perseverance and willpower.

Sergio was taking a more direct route back and she could already see the port. The group at the Villa Antonia edged themselves back into her consciousness and she shivered slightly as she remembered that the determination Sergio had displayed in pursuing his career was also concentrated on finding a killer.

'I was thinking about Alison,' she said, slowly.

'Not now,' he said, taking her hand.

CHAPTER 16

'And,' the colonel said, pushing a pile of statements dismissively to one side, 'you've also been indiscreet.'

'I'm afraid I don't follow,' Sergio said.

The Procurator of the Republic, who looked as if he'd much rather be at home making an inventory of his stamp collection, coughed uncomfortably.

'Thinking with your *cazzo*,' the colonel said, pointing an accusing finger. 'Running around with a key witness.'

The course of pure justice would be better served, Sergio thought, if the investigators weren't constantly under a microscope themselves. He wondered who'd been talking out of turn; not Pascucci surely? He forced himself not to react. Discipline from above irked him and the colonel knew it.

'Ms Childs could be involved in the smuggling,' his superior went on silkily. 'Anyone could have put the Etruscan artefact in Mrs Tenby's room.'

Sergio realized he would have to make those phone calls about Rose but he was even more reluctant to do so after the time they had just spent together, nor could he imagine what she would think of him if she found out.

'All I needed was an objective opinion away from the atmosphere of the villa, away from eavesdroppers, that's all,' he said, as calmly as he could.

'Are you suggesting the house is bugged?' the colonel asked. He inspected his nails.

'No, I'm not suggesting that,' Sergio said, wearily. His mood had not been improved by sexual tension and the knowledge that he had only himself to blame for its arousal. Rose had disappeared into the maw of the kitchen and the preparation of dinner while he had come back to the station to put together yet another empty report.

'We have two deaths,' the colonel said, ticking them off on his fingers. His nails had evidently passed muster. 'Two completely disparate types: a sailor, a drifter, and a *signora per bene*. The only thing you can come up with is a lot of psychological stuff about their sex lives. You haven't even made it clear whether you believe Mrs Tenby was the intended victim all along. You are off on half-a-dozen tangents at once, Capitain, and we're getting no nearer to finding a motive for the paid hand's death.'

'There have been several tombs robbed recently, the one at Nauro and others near Tarquinia,' Sergio said irritably. He'd been over all this ground before. 'Smuggling has to be the motive. Artefacts are being moved, Etruscan and others. Valuable items continue to disappear from the dig at Turbi. They're getting out of the country somehow.'

'But have you come up with one iota of proof? Are we any nearer an arrest?'

'We're still waiting for some forensic reports,' Sergio said, stalling. 'We know how both victims were killed—'

'But not why. And there's no sign of either murder weapon.'

'I've initiated another search. It will also have the effect of putting pressure on the people in the villa.'

'I do not want innocent people intimidated. I thought I'd made that clear.' The colonel gave Sergio a fox-like smile. 'It has always been my opinion that if a murderer isn't found in the first twenty four hours, the likelihood of solving the case decreases in direct proportion to the days that go by.'

'I agree with that,' the procurator said, hurriedly, 'and in the circumstances—'

'Which circumstances are we talking about?' Sergio asked, coldly.

'In the circumstances, I don't think we can detain these people much longer,' the procurator went on as though Sergio hadn't spoken. 'I'm under a lot of pressure, too.'

'From whom?' Sergio didn't really expect a reply and in fact the procurator blinked rapidly and hid himself behind the reports.

'Perhaps we should just go through these once more,' he said.

When they had gone, with further injunctions to wrap up the case as soon as possible, Sergio sat at his desk staring into space. He could kill for a cigarette. Both the colonel and the procurator had been smoking and the smell of stale tobacco hung heavily in the air. He could smell it on his clothes, it was probably in his hair, too. Massimo Pascucci put his head in a couple of times and looked at him enquiringly. He wanted to go home, poor sod, better let him.

The telephone rang and he answered it himself, half hoping it would be Rose.

'Sorry to bother you at this hour, Captain, but I expect you're always on duty,' the voice at the other end said.

'You could say that, Mr Langdon Smythe,' Sergio said, masking a mixture of disappointment and irritation as well as he could. The sound of the others man's drawl always set his teeth on edge. 'Do you have some information for me?'

'Not really. It's rather that I hope you could help me. I've just heard that my mother has had a serious attack. She's had a bad heart for some time and, of course, I would very much like to go to see her.'

Sergio raised his eyebrows at Massimo Pascucci. 'I'm sorry, Mr Langdon Smythe,' he said, 'I do sympathize but until this case is cleared up. . . .'

The languid drawl sharpened. 'You do realize that this could be a matter of life and death?'

'I appreciate that and, as I've said, I am very sorry, but I'm dealing with a life-and-death situation here too, as I'm sure you are aware.'

'And if I'm not able to see my mother before she dies – are you prepared to take that responsibility?'

'I sincerely hope your mother won't die,' Sergio said, wondering how much of all this was a fabrication, 'but I'm afraid I can't agree to you leaving until—'

'Yes, yes, until the case is cleared up. But when will that be?'

Sergio thought he heard him mutter, 'Total incompetence!' before he slammed down the phone. Langdon Smythe was rattled too. That was something, he supposed.

'Let's call it a night, Massimo, shall we?' He stood up and stretched wearily, then tidied the papers together on his desk. They were going out of the door when the telephone rang again.

'Leave it,' Sergio said, and then changed his mind. This time it might really be Rose. He nodded. 'OK, get it.'

Massimo picked up the receiver. '*Si. Si, un attimo.*' He turned to Sergio. 'Commissario Pavesi, from Milan, sir.'

'Enrico.' Sergio's face lit up as he took the phone. '*Ciao*, good to hear from you. *Come stai?*'

'*Bene, benone, tu?*'

'Not bad, apart from two unsolved murders.'

'Working late, huh? I tried you at home.'

'Working all hours, but not getting anywhere.'

'You off the smuggling?'

'No, no. It looked as if it all tied in, but now I'm not so sure. How are things there and when are you going to get down here for a couple of days?'

'Ugh, I'm up to my neck in it, but we'll catch up with each other soon. Meanwhile I might have something for you.'

'Yes?'

'We have Franco Nardi under house arrest.'

'What?'

Massimo Pascucci looked up startled at Sergio's tone.

'He's being investigated by the magistrates, bribery, tax evasion, the usual stuff. One of the many, but I remembered you said his transport business might be a front for the scam down there.'

Sergio let out his breath. 'Has he talked?'

'Not a whole lot,' the other man said dryly. 'They're going through his books with a fine toothcomb, but he's a cute boy. If we come up with something, I'll let you know straightaway.'

'Just a minute, where is he? His boat's down here, and I saw him the other day.'

'Yes, I know. He was being watched to make sure he didn't make a run for

196   *Maureen Donegan*

North Africa. He was arrested down there, in Capanula.'

'On my patch?'

'You know how it is; I've only just heard about it, as a matter of fact.'

Sergio knew all too well how it was. The police seldom told the *carabinieri* what they were doing, or vice versa.

'He was escorted to his villa in Como.'

Sergio grinned at Massimo. The information swirled around his brain as he listened, and finally settled into a knot of certainty. 'Any chance of talking to him?' he asked.

'You'd have to speak to the magistrate.'

Sergio grabbed a pen. 'Who is it? Santi? OK.' He scribbled down the number. 'And if I can't get hold of him, do you have access?'

'I could have,' Enrico said, cautiously, 'but it would be your responsibility.'

'You owe me one, don't forget.'

The voice at the other end was mild. 'I thought this call was the one I owed you.'

The previous year, Sergio's contacts had helped Enrico track down a contract killer who'd gone into hiding in the mountainous hinterland behind the port.

Sergio took out his sesterce and tossed it in the air. 'Twenty minutes would be enough. It's the first real break I've had.' He wondered if the colonel knew about the surveillance on Nardi, but doubted it. However he wasn't going to risk asking him. He would go to Como first and answer any awkward questions afterwards.

'Twenty years wouldn't break down that bastard,' Enrico Pavesi said, 'but if you think it's worth a try.' He paused. 'How's Silvana?'

Enrico was from a village near Capulana and Sergio had known him almost all his life.

'She's fine.'

'The boys?'

'Growing like trees.'

There was a faint sigh down the phone. Enrico had wanted to marry Silvana, when they were both very young, but he'd been posted to the south and spent several years there, first in Bari, then Cosenza, before his present job in Milan. And Marco had been in Capulana all the time, solid and dependable, offering Silvana not only a stable life, but also the chance of living and bringing up their children on what had been her family's land. Enrico couldn't begin to compete with that.

'Who'd be a *poliziotto*?' Enrico said.

'Who indeed?' But when Sergio finally put down the phone, he felt a surge of optimism that had been lacking from his professional life for some time.

'I'm going to Como,' he told Pascucci.

'When?'

'Tomorrow. You can drive me to Florence. But first book me on the *pendolino* to Milan.' The *pendolino* was the first-class, super fast train with many of the features of an aeroplane; there were reclining seats, food was served by a hostess and newspapers were also available. It was also almost as expensive as flying but it would look slightly less self-indulgent on his expenses. 'Do it now,' Sergio said, 'or I won't get a reservation. And then you can go. I have to stay and make some phone calls.'

The telephone rang in the villa during dinner.

Elizabeth's head jerked up. 'It's probably for me. Daddy said he'd ring.' She half rose and Johnny gave her a meaningful look.

Tom also moved back in his chair expectantly as Giulio appeared in the doorway.

'Rose,' he said, 'for you.'

Rose was serving Maria-Grazia's *fettucine*. She put down the dish on the side table. Sergio, she thought, her heart skipping a beat. He'd finished his meeting, he would come to collect her.

She hurried out to the hall but the man's voice at the other end was not Italian.

'Rose?' Arthur said. 'Are you all right? Why haven't you written?'

'I'm fine,' Rose said, more heartily that she felt. 'And I did write, twice. She didn't say that she hadn't sent them both. 'The post can be very slow from here.' Her breathing settled into a more normal rhythm. Perhaps Sergio would ring later. He had made no promises. 'Didn't you get them?'

198   *Maureen Donegan*

'I got one.' Arthur's voice sounded querulous, old-womanish, even.

'I've been very busy,' she said. 'There's been,' she almost said, some little local difficulty, but stopped herself in time. 'That is, Mrs Tenby died.'

'Who's Mrs Tenby?' Arthur demanded.

'The tenant.'

'Oh. But wasn't she quite young? I hope it wasn't the result of the car cash you told me about.'

'Arthur. . . .'

'So you can come home now.'

'What?'

He spoke slowly, as if to a retarded child. 'If the person you were working for is dead, she can hardly require your services any longer, can she?'

'I'm afraid I can't leave yet. The police—'

'But you said it was an accident.'

'No, the accident was something else. She died afterwards. It looked like a heart attack, but—'

'Hmm. I suppose there has to be an autopsy in that case. I remember an aunt of mine. She must have had a weak heart without knowing.'

'Arthur—'

'So as soon as the inquest is over you'll be back, then?'

'Will you please listen, Arthur. Mrs Tenby was murdered and . . . and there was another death before that, the paid hand on the boat.'

There was a hollow silence down the wires.

'Boat,' Arthur said, in a puzzled voice and then, 'Murder! Rose, what are you talking about?'

'I've written a long letter.' she said. 'I'll post it tomorrow.'

'I'm coming to Italy,' he said.

'No!'

'Then you must come home.'

'I've told you Sergio Tavazzi won't let me.'

'Who's Sergio whateverhisnameis?'

'He's the police. The *carabinieri*, I mean. He's in charge of the case. He speaks very good English.'

'I don't care if he speaks Hindustani,' Arthur said in a loud voice. 'What sort of a mess have you got yourself into? I told you not to go out there.'

'You have no right to tell me to do or not do anything,' she said, sharply.

'I told you I had a feeling about all this,' Arthur went on, 'right from the beginning, I had a feeling.'

'Wait for my letter,' she said, 'please Arthur. If you came out it would only complicate things.' But she could hardly explain just how complicated it would be. 'I've written you a kind of . . . travel report,' she tried to keep her voice light, 'and I'll ring you as soon as everything's sorted out.'

There was a snort from the other end. 'I hope you are not trying to "sort things out" yourself as you put it.'

'Of course not, Arthur,' she said, soothingly. 'Look, I'll talk to you soon.'

She had always placated him in the past, afraid of losing him, but it was only now, in this moment, that she realized she'd strung Arthur along because she wanted someone manageable in her life.

She shivered slightly. Whatever Gillian Tenby had or had not done in her life, the reverberations following her death were reaching out even to her. She herself must have become slightly crazy because, on the strength of a kiss and a cup of coffee, she'd begun to imagine exchanging Arthur for the insubstantial support of a hard-headed Italian who had, let's face it, plenty of problems of his own, not least a murder case on his hands. The idea was as frightening as contemplating stepping off the edge of a cliff. And, if Maria-Grazia was to be believed, there was a semi-detached wife somewhere in the background. It was something Sergio hadn't spoken about so far. Something else that had to be faced. She could find herself completely alone. But that was a kind of freedom, too. Something she hadn't wished for before now. Not that Arthur was going to be shaken off that easily. Unfortunately.

She went back to clear away the pasta plates and saw Elizabeth, who was sitting next to Dom, put her hand on his arm.

'Let's go shopping together again tomorrow,' she was saying, 'to take our mind off all this.'

He jerked away from her. 'We have to think about my mother's funeral,' he said, 'as soon as . . . had you forgotten?' His eyes filled with tears and Susie went over to put her hand on his shoulder.

200   Maureen Donegan

Elizabeth reddened. 'Sorry,' she muttered. 'I hadn't really forgotten. It's just that—'

'Everyone's under stress,' Mike said, soothingly, and Tom got up and went to look out over the dark countryside from the edge of the terrace.

Rose went out to the kitchen, but not before she heard Alison, who seemed a little brighter than usual say, 'I haven't anything black. How could any of us have known. . . ?'

But someone knew, Rose thought. Someone had come to Villa Antonia planning murder.

And she could think of far more reasons why Gillian was the intended victim, rather than Pino. The paid hand must have got in the way. Unless Gillian had found out something about his death. But then there was the car accident. That was actually the first thing that happened. She tried to remember who had already arrived then: Johnny, Peter, Elizabeth and Dom. Mike and Tom came the same day and Susie a couple of days later. So if it wasn't an accident, three people could be ruled out. Maria-Grazia and Giulio were there, of course, and Giulio had seemed very agitated at the time. Rose felt that he knew something and was afraid to speak. Alison, too, seemed to be hiding something. All that sleeping could be escapism.

Enrico Pavesi picked up Sergio at Milan's central station in an official police car. He was slight and not very tall. His head was slightly pointed and his hair fell soft and straight over one eye. A wide monkey-like smile lit his face now. He looked completely harmless, someone who might well be the life and soul of a party, but was otherwise physically and intellectually light-weight. It was a useful front and Sergio knew that the lop-sided, casual grin disguised a sharp intelligence and that Enrico also held a black belt in karate.

The two friends embraced. 'How goes it?' Enrico asked.

Sergio flexed his hands, then stretched. '*Beh*, could be worse.'

'The journey?'

'Not bad, not bad at all. I could get used to the fat-cat life.'

Enrico laughed. 'Did you get in touch with Magistrato Santi?'

Sergio shrugged. 'Couldn't get hold of him. Kept on ringing until midnight, and this morning it was too early. It doesn't really make any difference, does it?'

Enrico grinned again. 'Not to me,' he said.

'I'll get in touch with him in due course,' Sergio said vaguely as they got into the car. 'So, fill me in.'

'Nardi has been putting on every appearance of being on holiday in Capulana, but there seemed to be some slightly odd activity the other night, the fifteenth.'

'The night Gillian Tenby died,' Sergio said.

'Someone left Nardi's boat that night, the officer couldn't identify him, but by the size we don't think it was Nardi. It was a man, though. He went along the marina and on to a boat nearby.'

'What boat?' Sergio asked, sharply.

'*L'Alba*, English registered.'

'I wonder if Nardi was sending a warning of some kind.'

'To one of your villa people?'

'Exactly. So, what happened then?'

'Well, whoever it was returned to Nardi's boat. Does this fit in with any of your theories?'

Sergio sighed. 'I don't have any real theories, only a lot of disconnected facts and a selection of possible motives. Did Nardi have any inkling that he was going to be investigated?'

'Seems so. A lot of money was moved out to Switzerland recently. That's what triggered the arrest. We think there's been a fair amount of hurried laundering.'

'Langdon Smythe's denied all knowledge of Nardi, of course, but I'm convinced that if he isn't the actual brains behind the Etruscan thefts, he is involved in some way. The murders couldn't have been more inconvenient for the smugglers, even if they didn't have anything to do with them, but their paid hand was the first person killed and I don't believe in coincidences. He could have been blackmailing them. I've also got a strong feeling that the other victim could have been blackmailing them. It would be nice and neat if I could get Nardi to implicate them both.'

Enrico shook his head. 'To do that he'd have to implicate himself.'

'It's worth a try,' Sergio said, as they headed out of the city as quickly as the dense traffic allowed. 'My boss says I'm grasping at straws. He could be right.'

Franco Nardi's villa was situated in an isolated position with a superb view of the glittering blue-black waters of Lago di Como. As the police car slowed in front of two enormous gilt-tipped iron gates, two German shepherd dogs rushed forward barking menacingly and a thin, balding man watched nervously from the doorway of a small lodge just inside the entrance.

Enrico showed his ID to the *portiere*, who spoke briefly into a portable phone before pressing a switch to open the gates. A Roman sarcophagus filled with begonias sat just inside the *portone* and marble urns of petunias and geraniums lined a curving avenue which led to a large, tightly shuttered villa. Stone balconies decorated with pillars and domes were empty of flowers but, above the mock battlements, they glimpsed the rich foliage of a shaded roof garden.

The main door had a solidity which suggested steel reinforcement. To the right, a double, or perhaps treble garage, also had tightly closed doors. The dogs were quieter now; the porter had shouted them into submission and they had flopped down behind the gates, ears alert, hair bristling, uttering occasional rumbling growls of warning. The overall impression was not only of an absent owner but also of a fortress that had been buttressed efficiently against the outside world.

A maid in a pale-blue and white striped uniform opened the door and looked disdainfully at Enrico's ID.

'Wait here, please,' she said. She went down a wide hall and into a door on the left.

Enrico exchanged a glance with Sergio and then they heard an irritable voice saying, '*Falli entrare.*'

The woman reappeared and nodded at them to go in.

Franco Nardi was sitting in a long, elegantly furnished salon. One end of the room was in shadow. Swagged white linen curtains and the closed shutters behind them kept out the sun, but an open French door at the other end lit that part of the room, revealing thick oriental carpets on a gleaming parquet floor and the dark patina of antique furniture. The walls were covered with paintings, Dutch interiors, the rich colours of the Venetian school, English water-colours and others that appeared to have more than a nodding acquaintance with Van Gogh's Provence. Sergio wondered how many were genuine, and suspected that many were.

Nardi had his back to the French door. Behind him was a large terrace and to the right of it a stretch of lawn; below the garden was the lake. Sergio assumed there was a landing stage, out of sight, under the drop of the land. No point in being filthy rich and living on a lake, without a boat to hand. A small steamer was making its leisurely way across the water, its funnel puffing smoke. It looked for all the world like a toy. Around it, motor boats darted about and the faint sound of music drifted up to them. The sun, high in the midday sky, reflected back an intense glare from the lake but, up here, sprinklers sent a cool haze into the air, softening the brightness of the immaculate flower borders and drawing an other-worldly veil over the garden. It could be Eden, Sergio thought, but Nardi was a prisoner in it, his life as circumscribed as Adam's once had been.

They were waved to two comfortable chairs, but Nardi didn't get up.

'*Signori*,' he said, impassively.

'Captain Sergio Tavazzi.' Sergio clicked his heels and sat down. He wasn't going to be intimidated by this particular fat cat. His eye was caught by three small icons above the massive stone fireplace.

Nardi followed his gaze. 'Albanian,' he said. 'You'll notice the absence of red. Lovely, aren't they?'

'Yes,' Sergio said. 'Very nice.' He wondered what their provenance was. But that would be a futile trail to follow. 'I believe you have a boat in Capulana, Signor Nardi?'

'I do, yes.' Nardi appeared to have accepted his presence, but now he turned his head to Enrico. 'Surely the police told you that?'

Sergio inclined his head slightly. 'And that you were on board her until very recently?'

'Until I was um . . . invited to return home, yes.'

It was hard to see his expression. His eyes were concealed by very dark glasses and, with the light behind him, the rest of his face was in shadow.

'The boat is moored on the new marina.'

'That is correct, yes.' Nardi spread his hands. 'But I fail to see what this has to do with present investigations. The details of the purchase of the boat, and indeed of all my property, have been made available to the magistrates.'

'Quite. And I believe some friends of yours were moored quite near you in Capulana.'

'A number of friends, certainly. It's one of the reasons I go there.'

'I was thinking of Johnny Langdon Smythe.'

'Ah. Not someone I know. English, I imagine.'

'And Peter Kinaid, his crew master? Young. Langdon Smythe is much older.'

Nardi shook his head.

It reminded Sergio of his interrogation of Johnny Langdon Smythe, but he continued doggedly. 'They do some racing.'

'Unfortunately I don't these days,' Nardi said. 'Lazy, I suppose, but mine is more a family boat.'

And which family supports it? Sergio wondered.

'Someone on your boat was seen visiting *L'Alba*, the Englishman's boat, the night of the fifteenth at about eleven-thirty.'

'Someone from my boat?' Nardi shifted the balance of his sunglasses slightly with his middle finger.

'Yes. Can you tell me anything about that?'

'I'm afraid I can't. If' – there was a slight emphasis on the word – 'if what you say is correct it could have been one of the crew.'

'Delivering a message?' Sergio suggested.

Nardi shook his head, disbelievingly, but didn't answer.

'Perhaps you could tell me who was on board that night?'

There was a short silence and then Nardi said, 'I fail to see the point of these questions, Captain. It was a private family holiday.'

'Nevertheless I would be grateful if you could give me this information. It might well clarify another case which I'm working on.'

'Naturally I am more than willing to co-operate with the authorities but I would like to know exactly what this is all about,' Nardi said, smoothly.

Sergio had wanted to avoid telling him, but there didn't appear to be a choice. He looked beyond the heavy man half blocking the French door and imagined what it would be like lying in the shade of one of the sweeping willows in the garden, the droplets of water from the sprinklers shot with rainbow hues around him. Instead, there was this enervating, luxurious room, and the prospect of another long journey at the end of the day.

'There has been a constant drain of art treasures from the country,' he said, eventually. 'In particular, artefacts from the Etruscan tombs at Turbi. We have reason to believe that they're leaving through Capanula. By boat.'

'Then, when I am allowed to resume my holiday, I will certainly keep my eyes open for you, Captain. I find it quite shocking that Italy should lose even a part of her heritage.' He waved his hand around the room. 'As you see I'm an amateur collector myself.'

Sergio let his eyes flicker over a cabinet where several colourful bowls and drinking vessels were displayed among some earthenware shards.

'Minoan,' Nardi said. 'My father was at Knossos as a very young man, before the war. He worked with Arthur Evans for a while and well, at that time, there weren't the same controls.' He smiled, wolfishly. 'Very reprehensible, I'm afraid.'

Sergio inclined his head slightly. 'To go back to the night of the fifteenth. You were about to tell me who was on your boat.'

'Ah.' Nardi appeared to be trying to remember. 'My daughters, my son-in-law, my grandson. Certainly none of us visited any other boat that evening.'

'And the crew?'

'Mmm. The captain was . . . no . . . he wasn't on duty. His mate was on watch, and there was the man who cooks for us, and two other helpers, I think. Any one of them might have left briefly, to buy cigarettes, or meet some girl, I really can't speak for them.' He gave Sergio another of his dangerous smiles. 'And frankly, Captain, I really don't wish to discuss this any further. In fact I can't imagine why Magistrato Santi has asked you to pursue this line of questioning. It seems to me to be quite irrelevant to the present enquiry.'

Enrico Pavesi shifted slightly on his chair.

'We're talking about organized crime, Signor Nardi, and there's nothing

206 *Maureen Donegan*

irrelevant about that.' Sergio paused. 'You have a transport company, finance and insurance businesses. You also deal in high class furniture and antiques.' Sergio let his eyes sweep slowly around the room. 'That must give you a great deal of' – he paused again – 'flexibility. Perhaps even a cover for a thriving smuggling racket.'

Nardi seemed to swell in his chair. 'I find your tone offensive, Captain. Are you actually suggesting that someone is using my business, abusing my trust?'

He was good, Sergio thought. Money, or perhaps simply the ruthlessness that must have accompanied the making of an enormous fortune, had also given Nardi a tremendous presence.

'I'm suggesting that someone is also organizing art thefts. We're talking about an extremely efficient network.'

Nardi laughed softly. 'You have an extraordinary imagination, Capitain, but I can assure you that if there is anything in this . . . this fairytale, I certainly know nothing about it.'

'I would have thought,' Sergio said, trying to penetrate the smoky darkness of the other man's glasses, 'that such an astute businessman as yourself would be able to put your finger on everything they goes on in your empire.'

Nardi laughed again, but sounded less amused. 'I'm flattered by your confidence in my ability, but we are all fallible. I'm sure that you, in your dealings with the . . . ah . . . less pleasant side of our society must be even more aware of this than I am.'

Nardi must have pressed a bell somewhere, because the maid came in and stood looking at her employer enquiringly. Nardi stood up, his bulk blocking even more of the light.

'I don't have to answer these allegations,' he said, in a quiet voice. 'I thought perhaps you had come about some minor technical questions, otherwise I would have had my lawyer here. The gentlemen are just leaving, Bianca,' he said. He took off his glasses finally. There were grey-black stains below his deep-set eyes and his expensively acquired tan sat uneasily on flesh which appeared to have lost some of its elasticity. He did not look like the same man, Sergio thought, who had strode so confidently along the quayside in Capulana such a short time before.

Sergio and Enrico also stood up. All three of them knew the Milanese's rights. House arrest didn't include bullying and there was every chance that Nardi would emerge from the *tangente* enquiry smelling of roses. In any case, as he had so rightly implied, he didn't have to talk to an officer of the *carabinieri*, whose brief was flimsy and authority undefined. In fact, Enrico's expression indicated that they should get out while the going was good.

Nevertheless Sergio persisted. 'Peter Kinaid was probably being black-mailed,' he said, 'because of his involvement in the smuggling. And now the blackmailer is dead. Murdered. *L'Alba*'s paid hand has also been killed.'

'*Arrivederci, signori,*' Franco Nardi said, with studied formality.

They left, silently, following the maid through the hall to the heavy main door. As she closed it behind them with a dull thud, the dogs leaped towards them and then, teeth bared, then positioned themselves strategically to bar their path.

The *portiere* appeared. '*Basta, basta,*' he shouted. Sergio dropped the arm which he'd flung up to protect his head and he and Enrico edged their way carefully past the angrily growling animals.

'A somewhat ignominious departure,' Sergio muttered as the gates swung to behind them.

'Did you really expect anything else?'

'I wanted to face him. I wanted him to know that someone has been killed, that two people have been killed, and it's not just a question of *tangenti* and tax fiddles. That he's in the *merde*. Deep in it.'

'But can you prove anything?'

'I can prove *cazzo*,' Sergio said, gloomily. 'Have you got a copy of the report about the surveillance on *L'Alba* that night?'

'In the office.' Enrico put his hand on Sergio's arm. 'But first lunch, huh?'

After *risotto alla milanese* – 'What else could you possibly eat?' Enrico had demanded – and roast veal, washed down with a bottle of barbera Sergio felt a little more human.

'Is this where you eat every day?' he asked, grinning. His arm embraced the crisply laundered tablecloths and attentive waiters.

'*Certo,*' Enrico said, straight-faced. 'Dinner too.'

'Mmm. Always thought you did yourself well. But what you need is a wife. Then you wouldn't have to suffer like this.'

Enrico grinned. 'You mean I could suffer at home.' His expression became more serious. '*Beh*, it's a little late for that.'

'You should come with me to see Silvana, the next time you're down.' Sergio was also suddenly serious. 'See her with her family. Face up to it, get it out of your system. No use going on year after year.'

Enrico shrugged. 'I'd find that rather difficult.'

'I'm sorry,' Sergio said, abruptly. 'It's none of my business.'

'It's your sister. And you are right, I am foolish. Ridiculous even.'

'But you must meet other women?'

'From time to time, yes, but I'm getting set in my ways. I expect that's it. And you?'

'Me?'

Enrico smiled slyly. 'Are you in a position to criticize?'

'No,' Sergio said. A curious expression crossed his face.

'What is it?' Enrico asked.

'Nothing,' Sergio said quickly. 'I'm probably getting past it too.'

During the morning Rose took a call to say that the body of Signora Tenby was now being released and would she kindly convey this information to the family. She wondered why Sergio hadn't rung himself, then consoled herself with the thought that the message must have come from a different section of the *carabinieri*.

She went in search of Dom and Susie and found them with Keith on the terrace.

Dom was lying on the swing, his eyes closed and a cup of coffee balanced precariously on his chest. Susie and Keith were at the table, among the detritus of the breakfast things.

'In the autumn I'm doing a two-month block of study and after that I'll be working directly on cases, supervised of course,' Susie was saying, as Rose approached.

'You'll like that,' Keith said.

'Oh, yes,' Susie said. She smiled and Rose thought how much more together she was than her brother. Susie turned to Rose. 'Did you want to clear? Sorry, we can make ourselves scarce. I think everyone else has finished.'

'In a moment, yes,' Rose said. She hesitated. 'There's a message for you, from the *carabinieri*. They've rung to say that the funeral can take place now.'

'Oh.' Susie's face changed and Keith put his hand over hers.

'They've . . . finished then?'

'Apparently.'

Susie glanced across at Dom, who was struggling to sit up. His cup slipped and shattered noisily on the tiled floor.

'Do you know if they . . . if they found out who . . . no, that's a stupid thing to say, of course they wouldn't,' he said, in an unsteady voice.

'No,' Rose said. 'They didn't say anything else.'

Susie had gone over to put her arms around Dom. 'What happens now?' she asked Rose, who was picking up the broken pieces of china.

Rose straightened up. 'Would you like me to find an undertaker?'

'Oh, yes. That would be. . . .'

'It's horrible,' Dom said.

'It brings it all home,' Keith said. His eyes glistened suspiciously. 'Why did it have to happen? She was so. . . .' He lifted his head and shook himself slightly. 'Yes, we'd all be very grateful if you could help us, Rose,' he said.

On the drive back to Milan, Sergio went over the events leading up to Gillian Tenby's death.

'Let's suppose Nardi did know he was going to be investigated,' he said, 'and that he sent someone to warn Langdon Smythe, telling him to leave, to disappear for a while. But Johnny couldn't leave. He was trapped because Pino had been killed. That's what set off the whole train of events. Pino could have threatened to reveal their involvement with the smuggling. And La Tenby could have been putting pressure on him. I'm convinced she knew about their activities. Suppose Langdon Smythe killed Pino to keep him quiet, then panicked when Nardi told him he was in the *merde* with the magistrates. Langdon with or without Kinaid went back to the villa and

210   *Maureen Donegan*

killed Gillian Tenby to reduce at least one of the dangers. If he'd killed once, he wouldn't have hesitated to kill again.'

'If,' Enrico said, slowly. He swerved to avoid a suicidal boy on a *motorino*. 'Wouldn't Langdon Smythe be more likely to want to remove Nardi? Wasn't he a bigger threat?'

Sergio shook his head. 'Nardi's a worried man, but as you've said yourself, he's tough. Having seen him in action this morning, I'd put my money on him sitting this out. Johnny Langdon Smyth knows him even better. He'll have come to the same conclusion.'

'Yes, I see that.'

'So who's the greater threat, who's the unknown quantity? La Tenby. It's obvious. But it's still all supposition and what my boss calls a half-baked theory. I haven't a shred of proof about any of it.'

Enrico pulled into the parking area behind the building which housed the police.

'What else did the police report say about that night?' Sergio demanded, as they went into the building.

'I only skimmed through it. It was when I saw Capanula mentioned and Nardi's boat that I rang you. But I've got a copy for you.'

Enrico shared an office with a tall, hawk-like man who nodded at them pleasantly.

'Going for a coffee,' he said, 'Can I get you one?'

'No thanks,' Enrico said. He waited until his colleague had gone then took the photocopy of the report from a locked drawer in his desk.

Sergio looked through it quickly and then went back and began to read it more slowly. Nardi, his daughters, son-in-law and grandson had returned to the marina at eleven in the evening.

Sergio looked up. 'This gives the movements of some of the other people around. Two men – they have to be Langdon Smythe and Kinaid – boarded *L'Alba* at eleven-forty and . . .' – his eyes moved down the page – 'someone left Nardi's boat a few minutes later, went over to *L'Alba*, stayed ten minutes, then returned to Nardi's boat . . . and after that. . . .' His voice trailed off, then resumed very quietly, 'after that the surveillance continued on both boats and no one else left or visited either boat. *Cristo!*' He could have done the surveillance himself had he had enough men.

'What is it?' Enrico asked.

'I'll tell you what it is,' Sergio said bitterly, 'Gillian Tenby was killed some-time between midnight and four o'clock on the night of the fifteenth and the police, your colleagues, have managed to provide a perfect alibi for our two *finocchi*. They couldn't have done it. They were tucked up in their bunks or bunk more likely, as secure as if they were under lock and key in a cell at the station.'

CHAPTER 17

Rose had only spoken to Lena Grenbelli once in the confused days which followed Gillian Tenby's death, and then only briefly to acknowledge Lena's offer of help. Now she badly needed that assistance.

'My dear,' Lena said, 'of course. I suggest Castello's firm. They're very reliable. Would you like me to ring them? I know them quite well.' There was a moment of silence. 'So many of one's old friends have gone . . . and when Giorgio died. . . .'

'I know,' Rose said, gently. There was another silence down the line then a sigh. 'Yes, Castellos,' Lena said in a firmer voice, 'they're excellent.'

'I'd be very grateful if you would get in touch with them,' Rose said. 'There's also the problem of a service. Mrs Tenby was Church of England, her daughter tells me.' Dom had been too distraught to enter much into the discussion of what had to be done.

'I think I know of an Anglican clergyman,' Lena said. 'Just leave it with me. But what about you, my dear, how are you coping?'

'Well, all right, I think. There hasn't been one spare moment between interviews and statements and a certain amount of hysteria. Of course the house doesn't run itself either during all this.'

'I don't imagine it does. And how is Maria-Grazia bearing up?'

'Wonderfully, considering. Although she thought she saw a ghost yesterday but it seemed that it was somebody or something more solid.'

'Good gracious,' Lena said. 'I can't imagine what it must be like to be in such a situation. I wish you could get away from it.'

'Well, I suppose I will, as soon as it's all cleared up. But in the meantime. . . .'

'Yes, I do understand. And I suppose the police are there all the time?'

'More or less,' Rose said.

'My Carmina thought she saw you driving over the mountain with Sergio Tavazzi. . . .'

'Ah,' Rose said.

'. . . but I told her she was imagining things. If Ms Childs was going anywhere with him, I said, it would be to the *carabinieri* station to help out with translating the statements. It just goes to show how people's imagination runs riot at a time like this, doesn't it?'

For a brief moment Rose was tempted to tell her about visiting Silvana to see if Lena had anything more to say about Sergio or his family, but she suppressed the urge. At the moment, the fewer who knew about their more personal contacts the better.

But as the day wore on, interrupted by calls back and forth to Lena, the undertaker and Mr Perry, the Anglican minister, she wondered why she hadn't heard from Sergio, if he were already regretting the impulse to take her to see his sister, because perhaps that was all it was, an impulse. Each time the telephone rang she jumped, and hurried to answer it, and each time was disappointed.

The funeral was arranged, with the help of Lena's contacts, for the following day.

'It's always done quickly here,' Lena told Rose, when she expressed surprise.

Keith Drinkwater and Mike had taken over responsibility for the arrangements. Dom appeared to be incapable of making a decision and Susie looked almost as exhausted as her half-brother. And it was certainly easier, Rose thought, to deal with the two men, who although involved, were not actually members of the family. By the end of the day, she, too, was extremely tired and the vaguely nagging worry about Sergio's silence, suppressed to a certain extent during the endless telephone calls and discussions of the day, re-emerged with a far from vague intensity when she finally got to bed.

How stupid she was, she told herself as she tossed and turned and sweated through the night, how stupid she was to have allowed herself to want him so much, to let herself be so vulnerable. It was to protect herself from this kind of suffering that she had stayed so long with Arthur. Running away from life, as Sergio had put it so succinctly.

Sergio was at the Central Office early the following morning in response to a summons from the colonel, who kept him waiting for twenty minutes. He used the time to make the phone calls which he had been putting off for days.

First he rang the French number and Mrs Venables-Brown, told why he was ringing, assured him that she considered Rose an excellent person and that she had certainly supplied references. Sergio took a note of the names then rang one of the English numbers.

After Sergio had introduced himself and begun to explain the reason for his call, the professor said that Ms Childs had already told him about the deaths. He sounded calm and pompous but his voice went up a couple of octaves when he was asked to verify Rose's credentials.

'Of course she is who she says she is,' he said, angrily. 'I have known her for years and told her time and time again that these kind of jobs are totally inappropriate, if not positively dangerous, and now I've been proved to be absolutely right.'

'I do not think Ms Childs is in any danger,' Sergio said, surprised to find himself on the defensive. He began to wonder exactly what Rose's relationship with this man was.

'You must be Sergio Tavazzi,' Arthur said.

'Er. Yes. You must understand that I am merely following procedure. Ms Childs is not under suspicion.'

'I should think not indeed,' the professor said. 'You may tell her that I'll be out to collect her as soon as I can.'

'The . . . er . . . guests at the villa are not free to leave at the moment,' Sergio said, 'but we hope it will not be long before—'

'Then I will be there to offer Ms Childs support until such time as she can leave.'

'As you wish,' Sergio said, and the conversation terminated abruptly.

He put out his hand to make another call, this one more difficult and had only just finished when the door of the colonel's room opened and his superior shouted at him to come in.

'I understand that you had a busy day, yesterday,' he said, silkily.

'Yes, I—'

'And may one ask the reason why you went to Como?'

'In pursuit of enquiries connected with the present case,' Sergio said. He had a headache, the combined result of insomnia, severe disappointment and the previous long and tiring day. Going up had been all right, buoyed up as he was by the certainty that he was going to crack both the murder and the smuggling cases. But for the journey back there was no *pendolino*; he had to change trains twice, there was a delay on the line and an endless wait for a taxi at the end of his journey had put the finishing touches to his mounting depression.

The colonel made a minute adjustment to the alignment of the pristine blotter on his desk.

'You went to see Franco Nardi, in fact.'

'Yes.' Enrico had told him Nardi wasn't allowed to make telephone calls, except to his mother who was in very poor health, but he had evidently managed to complain to someone.

'It didn't occur to you to ask for my. . . .' The colonel evidently managed to stop himself from saying permission and substituted 'approval', instead.

'It came up rather suddenly,' Sergio said.

'In other words, you just took off without considering the consequences.'

Sergio wondered if an expression of outraged innocence from a big crime boss was one of the consequences the colonel had in mind but he didn't say so.

His superior sighed. 'I'm tired of reminding you about observing the correct procedures. You didn't obtain Magistrato Santi's permission, nor did you have the courtesy to inform me.' He paused, waiting to see if Sergio was going to reply, then went on, 'Suppose the papers get hold of it? Had you thought of that?'

'I think it's very unlikely,' Sergio said.

'Do you?' The older man pushed his face forward, glaring. 'Franco Nardi is a powerful man and is not a suspect in this case.'

216   *Maureen Donegan*

'Which case are we talking about, sir?'

'The Tenby murder.'

'I'm convinced he's involved in the smuggling. He could also be a material witness.'

'Could he? Could he? Then you'd better tell me what you found out.'

Sergio laid the report carefully on the desk. He'd written it during the sleepless early hours of the morning. 'Langdon Smythe and Kinaid appear to be eliminated from the murder suspects.'

'They are?' There was a rustling noise as the colonel began to glance through the report. 'Hmm. This is definite?'

'Yes. The police were watching Nardi and also the Englishman's boat on the marina in Capanula the night Mrs Tenby was killed.'

The colonel turned an interesting shade of puce. 'Without telling us?'

Sergio kept his face expressionless. 'It appears so, sir, unless you. . . ?'

'No! This is the very first I've heard of it. Why can't the police co-operate with us at times like this? Do you know, Captain?'

'I've no idea, sir,' Sergio said. Privately he thought that if the two forces got together they might form a powerful and dangerous junta and that it was in the interest of a number of highly placed individuals in the country to avoid precisely that. However, this didn't seem to be the moment to indulge in political speculation.

In any case the colonel's anger had been diverted. 'After all, we're pursuing the same things, law and order, justice,' he said in an aggrieved voice. 'As a matter of fact' – he paused and coughed – 'when Magistrato Santi spoke to me, although he didn't exactly ... er ... put it into words, it seems they're having trouble making the financial irregularities stick.' He coughed again. 'They may have to release him.'

'Yes, sir.'

'Hmm. Very well. I'll read this and we'll talk later.'

'Yes, sir.'

'You do realize that I'm still under pressure from, ah, other quarters, to wind up this murder enquiry.' He went on without waiting for a reply, but his voice was more conciliatory. 'You're not a fool, Sergio, you know what we're up against. Be realistic.'

'What exactly are you asking me to do?'

'To get this case tied up, one way or another.'

'How long do I have?'

'Twenty-four hours.'

Sergio took a deep breath. 'Seventy-two,' he countered.

'Forty eight,' the colonel said, with the appearance of relief. No doubt that was the deadline he had secreted in his new pigskin briefcase. 'And then they get their passports back.' He gave a wintry smile. 'After that you will be free to pursue this smuggling business.'

'Yes sir.'

The colonel's voice stopped him at the door. 'And, Captain Tavazzi, I don't ever want a repetition of this kind of thing. We're under enough pressure as it is.' He passed a spotless linen handkerchief over his face and resumed his plaintive voice. 'You know I sometimes wish the telephone had never been invented.'

'Yes, sir,' Sergio said again. He took out a tissue and wiped his own face, but waited until he was out in the corridor and the door of the colonel's door was closed behind him before he did so.

The telephone rang as Rose was emptying the dishwasher.

'Rose? Is that you? Are you still at the villa?' Arthur asked in a strangled voice.

'Yes, it's me and of course I'm at the villa. Isn't that where you're ringing?'

'The police have been on to me!' Arthur was almost shouting.

'What do you mean the police?'

'The er . . . *carabinieri*, that captain fellow you told me about. Checking up on you.'

'What?' She thought of Sergio's mouth on hers, the way he'd looked at her. How could he have done this?

'Said it was routine, but I think it's pretty damned cheeky all the same. I was very short with him, I can tell you. Told him I'd be out to look after you myself.'

'No. Arthur, no, please.'

'Are you actually being detained? You haven't explained yourself very

218   *Maureen Donegan*

well, Rose. Now, I can get Hammond to take over my summer school. I could probably leave tomorrow, or the day after at the very latest.' She held the receiver away from her ear. 'Surely you're not under suspicion? Have you been in touch with your solicitor? I could ring him for you.'

'No, Arthur. There is absolutely no need. In any case I'm perfectly capable—'

'I don't think you're capable of looking after yourself at all.'

'Arthur, they have to check up on everybody and we have to stay, everyone has to stay while they make their enquiries. It's obvious.'

'Oh, I'm sure it is,' he said, sarcastically.

'I am perfectly all right,' she said, again. 'There is no need for you to do anything.' She emphasized each word. 'I can handle this by myself.'

'Yes, that's what you always say.'

'Why do you always want to interfere in my life Arthur?'

The words fell into a hurt silence, and then he said, 'I don't consider wanting to help a friend who is in trouble exactly interfering with their life.' He waited for her to speak and when she didn't, went on, 'I shall ring again tomorrow. You're obviously under a lot of pressure. You have a very stubborn streak, Rose, I've always said so, and I've always been afraid it would land you in a mess like this.'

'It must be very comforting to be always right.' She wondered who she was more angry with, Arthur or Sergio as she banged down the phone.

Lena Grenbelli was looking at the English mourners who appeared bewildered by the votive lamps and pictures of the dead.

'So sad, my dear,' she whispered to Rose, 'to die so far from home, and in such circumstances. Is that all her family?'

'There's the son and daughter,' Rose whispered back, 'the others are friends.'

'I see.' Lena paused. 'By the way I had a call from Sergio Tavazzi, he was checking your references.'

Rose looked at her in horror. 'Not you, too.'

'He said he was just doing his job, that he hated doing it but he was under orders.'

'Oh.'

'In fact, I rather got the impression he wanted me to tell you that. About being under orders, I mean. His boss is frightfully old-womanish; we play bridge sometimes, never bids up, *senza coglioni* as my dear Giorgio used to say.'

Rose's lips twitched despite herself. 'Lena!'

Lena gave her a disarming smile. 'It's true. Certainly he never had any children.'

Rose said, 'Sergio rang my friend Arthur. He was another reference.'

'And do you think he would have done that if he wasn't interested in you?'

'I don't know. I don't know what to think.'

Lena was still smiling. 'And what did your friend Arthur say?'

'Oh . . . went crazy. Threatened to come out; I said no.'

'But how nice to have two ardent admirers, my dear.'

Alison came up to them before Rose could reply. 'It's all so strange,' she said, waving at the small, drawer-like marble caskets lining the cemetery. She'd solved her sartorial problem by wearing a dark-blue linen dress and her face was pale but less sleepy looking under her straw hat.

'The bodies are put into a vault first,' Lena Grenbelli explained, 'then after enough time has elapsed and there are only the bones left, they are put into their permanent tomb.' She pronounced it to rhyme with bone, sounding the final 'b'.

Alison shuddered and turned away. 'How absolutely horrible.'

'No, it is not horrible, it is comforting to the family. There is a little ceremony when the bones are reinterred. At one time the relatives, the mother or the wife would wash the bones. It is always the women, of course, who have to cope, with death as well as life.'

'Gillian always liked the exotic,' Alison said, in a faint voice, 'but she'd have drawn the line at this.'

'You must be one of her friends,' Lena Grenbelli said.

'Sorry,' Rose said. 'Lena, this is Mrs Drinkwater.'

'Lena Grenbelli,' Lena said, holding out her hand.

Dom and Susie stood close together, flanked by Elizabeth and Mike.

Dom put his arm around his sister as the minister, Mr Perry, beckoned them over to the coffin which had been placed near the open door of a vault.

A flight of metal steps led down into a neon-lit chamber. It too was marble-lined and appeared to be quite empty. The flowers on the coffin were already wilting in the hot sun and one of the men from the funeral firm lifted them off and pushed them to one side.

The mourners gathered around, nervously, as the clergyman began the familiar words, 'I am the Resurrection and the Life saith the Lord. Whosover believeth in me, though he should die, yet shall he live. . . .'

'It's bizarre,' Alison said, in Rose's ear.

They stood bunched together, sweating in the heat.

'Man that is born of woman hath but little time to live. . . .'

Susie's knees buckled and Mike caught her before she fell. A little eddy of wind stirred a flurry of sand beside the open vault and the small group stirred as though Gillian's ghost had passed among them, then they were still again.

'In the midst of life we are in death; of whom may we seek succour but of thee, Oh, Lord, who for our sins art justly displeased?'

Who indeed? Rose thought. She glanced around. Dom was openly weeping. Keith, who was sweating profusely, also had tears in his eyes. But, perhaps aware of Alison's scrutiny, he succeeded in holding them back. Johnny's face was expressionless and Peter looked, if anything, merely embarrassed. Tom Graham was standing back a little. His manner was composed and his eyes lowered, as if in prayer. Maria-Grazia was the only one in black. She stood, clutching Giulio's arm, each dry-eyed and solemn.

Rose suddenly caught a glimpse of Sergio in the background. She didn't know whether she was furious or comforted at the sight of him. She gave herself a little shake and reminded herself that this was a murder enquiry and that he wasn't the kind of man to put his personal life before his work. Perhaps Lena was right and he had put it before his work briefly, only then he must have panicked and backtracked. And quite apart from that, where on earth had he been for the past twenty-four hours? He nodded at her, unsmilingly. He was very still, only his eyes moving, watching the mourners and she was reminded forcibly that one of these people around the coffin had probably killed the body that lay inside it.

Two men stepped forward and, with the aid of ropes, began to slide the coffin down the metal steps. A third man, who was holding a shovel, indicated they should follow the coffin into the vault. They all stood back. looking at each other uncertainly. The minister spoke to Susie and she gave a beseeching glance at Mike before moving forward reluctantly.

The air that came up from the vault was dry and slightly dusty; it had the faint but not unpleasant odour of dead leaves. Rose felt a primeval fear that she was sure the others shared as their shoes rattled on the metal steps. A large marble slab had evidently been lifted very recently to reveal a waiting hole. Beside it was the coffin and a small pile of sand.

The clergyman placed his hand on the coffin. He cleared his throat slightly. 'I did not know the deceased but I am certain that Our Heavenly Father has taken his daughter Gillian to his bosom and' – he made another sound in his throat – 'that her soul has flown free, just as her mortal remains are now at rest in this peaceful place. In this foreign field,' he misquoted, 'forever a little corner of England.'

The men slipped the ropes and the coffin sank down. The slab was lifted with the aid of more ropes and dropped efficiently into place. Keith moved quickly to support Dom who had burst into sudden shaking sobs.

A man Rose had not previously noticed, approached one of the workmen. He took off the silk jacket of his suit and exchanged it for one of the men's shovels. Carefully he smoothed the last of the sand into the cracks around the slab, then handed the shovel back and retrieved his jacket. He shook hands with the clergyman who took him over to Susie and then Dom and he shook hands with them too before going off up the steps. They all followed him and emerged blinking into the white glare of sunlight.

'That was Fernando Castello,' Lena Grenbelli whispered. 'His family have been undertakers here for generations. A nice touch, I thought.'

Rose thought that Gillian would have appreciated the very last rites being performed by a man in a silk suit. Because there was unlikely to be a second ceremony. Gillian's bones would be moved without any further ritual, and the few people who cared about her would be far away.

'Can I give you a lift?' Sergio had come up behind her, silently.

222   *Maureen Donegan*

You have to sort it out with him, she told herself, no point in getting in a raging temper but it was difficult to smile calmly and say, 'Please.' She went over to tell Maria-Grazia she wouldn't be travelling with them.

'Take your time,' Maria-Grazia said. 'Everything is prepared for the lunch.'

'I couldn't ring you,' Sergio said, as she got into his car. He was driving himself and she wondered where Massimo Pascucci was.

'It doesn't matter,' she said.

He passed his hand over his face. 'I was in Milan yesterday.'

'Milan?'

'Mmm. And Como. Complications. But it came to nothing. Or almost nothing. It was too late to call when I got back and then this morning I had a meeting.' He fell silent, then said, 'There is something I have to tell you.'

'About the phone calls?'

'Oh, you know.'

'Yes. Arthur rang me. And then Lena. . . .'

'I had no choice,' he said. 'I'd eliminated you in my mind from the very beginning, well, it was obvious that. . . .' His voice trailed off. 'I told you I have a rotten job.'

'It's all right,' she said, in a low voice, 'it's just that I've been . . . confused.'

The cemetery was high on the hill over the port and he took the winding road slowly. 'Don't be. Try to take me on trust. I know I didn't seem to trust you, but that's what my life is about.' He took his hand off the wheel for a moment to touch her face. 'My wife never accepted the job,' he said. 'She hated it, said I was always missing when she wanted me.' He skirted the centre of town and drove out past the marina.

'You're not together?'

'Not for years,' he said. 'She lives with someone else, but there never seemed any urgency about getting a divorce.' She waited for him to say, 'until now', but he didn't.

Don't anticipate, she told herself. Let it happen if it's going to happen. The complications can be dealt with later. Because she was sure that more lives than theirs would be touched. God, she was doing it again, trying to

TUSCAN SHADOWS

223

solve problems that hadn't yet presented themselves. It would probably be simpler to try to find the murderer. Or murderess.

He turned and smiled, as though he knew what she was thinking. 'I don't always have a lot of time for the niceties, Rose.'

'You do all right,' she said, returning his smile.

'And now tell me who this man Arthur is?'

'He's part of my past. Someone I should have said goodbye to a long time ago.' She felt a stab of guilt as she said it, remembering Arthur's over anxiety to please. Sergio pulled up outside a bar, but didn't get out of the car.

'And now?'

'I told him Sergio Tavazzi wouldn't let me leave Italy,' she said.

He grinned. 'I gathered that from our conversation.' The car keys jangled in his hand. 'But I'm going to have to let you all go soon.'

'What happened? Have you found. . . ?'

'I've found very little. Except that the two on the boat have an unbreakable alibi. I was convinced that Gillian Tenby was blackmailing one or other of them, if not why did she have that Etruscan urn? Maybe Langdon Smythe considered silencing her, but then it looks as if someone else did it for him and now everyone's sitting tight and saying nothing.' He began to tell her what had happened in Milan.

'So they are involved in smuggling,' Rose said, when he'd finished.

'They've always been conveniently around when artefacts have gone missing, but we've never been able to catch them with the stuff. But they're certainly involved with Nardi and this business proves it.' He grimaced. 'Only in a way that doesn't help me at all.'

'Yes, I see that,' Rose said. They made their way to the bar. 'Shall we sit outside?' she asked.

He shook his head and went into the dark interior and she thought he said, 'Too public.'

They sat at a small table and he ordered two *cappuccini*.

'And Tom Graham seems genuine,' he said gloomily. The coffee arrived and he put in three spoons of sugar. He sighed. 'I'm sorry. I'm using you as a sounding board, but I had this appalling session with my boss this morning.'

'It's all right,' she said, gently.

'Sorry, did you want a *cornetto?*'

'No thanks.'

'I think I will.' She watched as he went over to the counter and thought how tired he looked. He came back biting into the cake and the cream filling spilled down his chin.

'*Cazzo,*' he said. 'Sorry, but this isn't my day.'

Rose smiled and handed him a paper napkin. 'Tell me about Tom Graham.'

'He works in pharmaceuticals. I had a fax from the UK this morning.'

'That doesn't mean that he didn't kill Gillian.'

'No. I'd thought perhaps she'd found out something about his background or his job, something he couldn't afford to have known, and that she was blackmailing him, perhaps not even for money, just to make him stay with her. She seemed to be obsessed about keeping her party together. She could have discovered something by chance.'

'She had this very intense way with her,' Rose said thoughtfully. 'Well, with men, she had. A kind of "tell me everything about yourself" intimacy.'

'Exactly. But it seems Tom Graham is more or less what he said. I imagine he thought saying he was a businessman sounded better than a salesman. Aspirin and condoms probably. And I suppose that when he met Gillian he jumped at the idea of a little dalliance in Tuscany, but didn't except to get involved in murder, and that it was as simple as that.'

Sergio bent back one of his fingers, as though ticking off another suspect.

'Apparently Dom Tenby had an argument or a row, I'm not sure which, with his mother the day before she died. About her selling her house and presumably spending money she didn't have on the Villa Antonia.'

'It's not a very strong motive,' Rose ventured.

'No. Motive is the big stumbling block all around. The other big problem is trying to link the two deaths.'

'But why are you letting everyone go?' she asked.

'Orders from above. I've got two days.'

'Can they do that?'

'They can do anything they want,' he said, wearily. He took her hand. 'What time do you finish tonight?'

'About ten-thirty.'

'Would you like a visitor?'

'I'd love one.' It occurred to her that this was the best bit, the world narrowed down to just the two of them and a physical awareness so heightened that contact when they finally made love, might almost be an anticlimax.

'Because,' he hesitated, 'don't misunderstand if I say. . . .'

'What?' she asked in a gentle voice.

'It's something I want to get out of the way.' He stroked the inside of her wrist. 'I know we should get to know one another better, away from all this, but I am not sophisticated in matters of the heart. I should take you to Capri or Venice.'

He said heart, she thought, her own racing. 'Isn't that rather a long way to go?'

'Much too far.'

'And since it's become so urgent. . . .'

'For you too?'

'For me too.'

He passed his hand over his face again in an endearingly half embarrassed gesture, then smiled at her, ruefully. 'I think you'd better give me your impressions of the funeral,' he said.

'The funeral, yes.' She forced herself to concentrate, dragging her mind from the contemplation of his long, thin hands lingering on her body.

'They all behaved pretty much as I expected. The children were distressed, Dom more than Susie, but that's to be expected. He was her son and if he'd quarrelled with her he must have been feeling even worse. Keith was trying not to break down. The others were politely respectful, except Alison who made her usual cracks.'

'I think she hated Gillian,' Sergio said. 'She's had her around her neck all her life, when she was young, then later when she found herself in a foursome with the Tenbys. She could have tampered with Gillian's car. She was here.'

'Yes, I've been thinking that too. But Pino?'

'Perhaps he saw her.'

226   *Maureen Donegan*

'There are too many loose ends, the missing money, for example. Otherwise I'd say it was a straightforward *crimine passionale*. Then there's the business of someone searching Gillian's room.' He sighed. 'I've initiated another search this morning, but I don't expect to find anything. In a way I'll be quite glad to let the two yachtsmen go. I'm convinced that sooner or later they'll make a mistake, but in the meantime I have two murders to solve.'

'I think Alison might hold the key,' Rose said, slowly, 'at least to some of it.'

'Or her husband,' Sergio said. 'He must have been very jealous of Gillian Tenby's other men friends.'

'I got the impression he was resigned to the situation,' Rose said.

'Everyone has a breaking point. Her affair with Tom Graham might just have been the final straw.'

'Would you like me to try to talk to Alison?'

'You're not to do anything dangerous,' he said, alarmed.

'I won't,' she said.

'I shall have a man on duty,' Sergio said, 'and if anything happens, get him to contact me. But don't find yourself alone with any of them. Promise me.'

She nodded, thinking it would be difficult to extract anything out of Alison without getting her on her own.

'Promise me,' Sergio said, insistently.

'I promise,' she said. She released her hand and pushed it into her pocket. And crossed her fingers.

Elizabeth found Dom in the little grove at the top of the garden. He was half crouched on the grass, his head in his hands. He looked up at her approach and she saw that he had been crying.

'I didn't really believe she was dead before,' he said, 'until they put her in that place.'

She squatted down beside him and put her hand on his shoulder. 'My mother died when I was six and they wouldn't let me go to the funeral, so I kept on waiting and waiting for her to come back.'

'She used to sit here and I thought if I stayed very quiet I might . . . feel nearer to her. Does that sound stupid?'

'No.'

'Susie always said I was a Mummy's boy. But she was my very best friend, until. . . .'

'Until what?'

Dom was twisting his hands together, his face drawn and anxious, a skewed mirror image of Gillian.

'Until what?' she asked again.

'She was going to pay off. . . . She was going to help me . . . but there wasn't anything left. She'd spent it.' His voice rose. 'How could that be? All Dad's money.' He was silent for a moment then went on in a more conversational voice. 'We used to do everything together. We were like two halves of the same . . . person.' He stopped suddenly. 'Except about the money.' He rocked back and forth on his ankles. 'About the most important thing of all, she betrayed me.'

'When did you find out?'

He looked at her slyly. 'Find out what?'

'About the money. Was it before she died?'

'I asked her to help me. And she laughed. Laughed.'

'When?' Elizabeth said. She glanced around anxiously.

'She laughed. She thought it was a fantastic joke. She'd already mortgaged the house. She was going to sell it, but there would have been practically nothing. I was so angry I went away without saying goodnight.' He paused for a long moment. 'I didn't say goodbye to her.'

'You went to her room, that last night?'

'No,' he said quickly. 'The night before. I came to your room that night, but you wouldn't let me stay, remember?' He gave her a crooked smile and grabbed her hand. 'We will see each other in England, won't we, Elizabeth? You're not going to marry Johnny, are you?'

'No,' Elizabeth said. 'No, I'm not going to marry him.'

She wasn't sure what had brought her to this decision. Once before she had been tempted to break off her engagement, to spite her father more than for any other reason. He wanted her to have a title very badly. Well, so

228   *Maureen Donegan*

had she. At least she'd wanted the freedom and independence she thought
it would bring. Perhaps it was being at close quarters with these people:
Alison hanging on to a man who didn't love her, Susie bitter and unsure of
herself; and Peter . . . however much she had resented him, she'd always
known he loved Johnny. Johnny could be completely ruthless, though. He
would get rid of Peter too, if it suited him, even if it meant cutting out part
of his heart. She shivered.

'You could come to stay,' Dom was saying. 'We could travel back
together.'

'I'm going home to my father,' Elizabeth said. She tried to release her
hand, but Dom's grip was like iron. She looked around again. The oleander
grove was entirely hidden from the house and she doubted if anyone was in
earshot. But there was something else she had to know.

'It was you in your mother's room yesterday, when Maria-Grazia
screamed, wasn't it?'

He gave a wild, uncontrolled laugh. 'You saw me? You know then?'

'Yes,' Elizabeth said sadly, 'I know.'

Rose brought a tray of coffee out to the terrace. Keith and Alison were
sitting with Susie and Mike in a subdued group.

'It was a most unnerving experience,' Keith said. His hand shook as he
took a cup and helped himself to sugar. 'There was nothing comforting at
all.'

'Death isn't supposed to be comforting,' Alison said.

Keith gave her a look. 'But leaving her here, in that place. Wouldn't it
have been better to take her home?'

'We've been through all that,' Mike said wearily. Susie leaned against
him and took his hand.

'You did the best you could,' she said, gently.

'Yes, yes of course,' Keith said. 'It's just that. . . .' He took out a handkerchief and blew his nose. 'I just don't think I'll ever forget today.'

Alison drew in her breath and there was a long silence.

Rose went quietly over to the far end of the terrace and began to plump
up the cushions on the swing.

'Where's Dom?' Mike asked suddenly. 'Do you think he's all right?'

'Of course he's all right,' Susie said. 'Anyway, he has to begin standing on his own feet.'

'Isn't that a bit harsh?' Mike said.

'Why does no one ever think of me?' Susie said, edgily.

'Of course we do.' Mike wrapped his arm around her and she leaned against him, her eyes half closed.

'Dom went off up the garden,' Keith said, soothingly. 'Maybe it's best to leave him alone.'

Alison put down her cup. 'He isn't alone. I saw Elizabeth going after him.'

Susie gave an unexpected snort of laughter. 'They do rather deserve each other, don't they?'

'Shsh darling. He's your brother and after all he's lost his whole family, too.'

Susie jerked up her head and turned very red. 'What about me?' she asked loudly. 'And my parents? Nobody every cared about that, did they? I have no family either, remember, no father, no mother, no child.' She pushed aside Mike's restraining arm and rushed off down the steps, brushing past Rose.

'Oh dear,' Keith said. He half rose.

'Leave her alone,' Alison said, in a sharp voice. 'Can't you see she doesn't want anyone.' There was a reflective expression on her face. 'Poor Susie,' she said, almost to herself.

Rose picked up her tray and collected empty cups and full ashtrays and, unable to think of a further excuse to linger, took them to the kitchen.

'Who was that shouting?' Maria-Grazia asked.

'Susie.'

'She's upset. *Nervosa*. It's natural.'

'Yes, but it seems more than that. She seems almost on the edge of a breakdown.'

'*Poverina*. I didn't think the English could be so emotional.'

Rose frowned. 'She said something about having no family. No child, even.'

'She has time for that. Time and a strong young man.'

'Yes,' Rose said, slowly.

'I never told you this.' Maria-Grazia pleated her apron. 'But I was *incinta* many times. And each time it was as if I lost a live child. Like my poor mother, one after another. I couldn't stop thinking of it at the funeral today.'

'Oh, Maria-Grazia,' Rose said. She pulled a chair over and put an arm around the older woman.

Giulio was sitting by the window, staring out at the courtyard. He'd looked around as Maria-Grazia spoke and then put his hands together as though to stop them twitching.

'All funerals are very melancholy,' Rose said.

'You are right. There would have been no one at Pino's.' Giulio's voice came as if from far away. 'Only for me. Not even the two Englishmen. There was no priest, no prayers. They just put him in the ground.'

'You were there?' Rose asked, in total surprise.

'He was a human being.'

Surely, Rose thought, with a sinking feeling, it wasn't guilt that had driven him to the unceremonious despatch of the paid hand. She tried to imagine the scene. It must have been a hundred times more depressing than Gillian Tenby's obsequies.

'I'm going out for some air,' she said abruptly. The whole house was under a cloud of desolation today, but it was not only sorrow that hung around. Rather it was a reminder of mortality. And in one case it must also be the fear of discovery.

'Can I pick some cherries, Giulio?' she asked.

'Pick whatever you like,' he said, in a toneless voice.

As she passed through the hall the telephone rang and she answered it. A female voice asked in English for Mr Graham.

'Hold on please,' she said. She put her head into the kitchen and Maria-Grazia shouted that she thought Tom Graham was on the roof terrace. Rose went back to the phone and said she would look for him.

'Never mind,' the girl said, 'just ask him to ring the office. He'll know.'

Rose hung up and then went up to the roof. She found Tom Graham sitting on a striped chair, looking down the avenue towards the port.

Rose gave him the message and saw a look of relief cross his face.

'Thank goodness for that. I can't wait to leave this place.'

'Today was very distressing,' Rose said.

'Horrible,' he agreed. 'And our rooms have been searched again. Very tasteless, on a day like this, in my opinion. Do you know when your policeman friend is going to give us our passports back?'

She shook her head, wondering how he knew she was a friend of Sergio. Perhaps he'd been up here, standing back and observing with that same slightly sardonic smile on his face, when she'd gone off in Sergio's car. There was a harshness about his mouth, she thought, that she hadn't noticed before and his eyes were cold.

'I've learned one thing from all this, Rose.'

'Really?'

'The next time I find myself sitting next to an attractive woman on a plane, I'll pretend to be asleep. It's not the first time, mind you. I once met a girl going to Athens who turned out to be the girlfriend of a big time racketeer.'

Rose nodded. She wondered if he was already marshalling his version of Gillian's death, polishing the details. It would be produced at various dinner tables as an alternative to the racketeer story and delivered with Tom's rather spurious charm. 'Invited me to her place in Tuscany with all these offbeat characters and got herself bumped off while I was there. Yes, really, I'm not making it up. She was murdered. Murdered. And so was this gay sailor. Yes, I know it sounds far-fetched, but it really happened. What? Who did it? Ah, well. . . .' Rose found herself unable to complete this imaginary monologue. The frightening reality of the situation and the huge question mark that hung over all of them made that impossible.

'Funny things, families,' Tom said, unexpectedly. 'Gillian used to talk about that a lot. I don't think it was easy for her, taking on one ready made. She took a lot on her shoulders . . . with her friends too.'

Rose made a small sound.

'I mean how could Alison have looked after a baby, the state she's in? Good job Gillian had the common sense to see it. But I doubt if she would have been allowed to adopt. They go into the background pretty carefully, don't they?'

232   *Maureen Donegan*

Alison had wanted to adopt a child? But what had Gillian had to do with it, unless by her influence on Keith? One thing was clear: Tom was quoting Gillian. Rose could almost hear her voice. She moved one of the chairs a fraction, in a pretence of tidying and waited to see if he had anything else to say about Alison, but instead he unfolded himself from his chair and stood up.

'I'd better ring HQ then,' he said. 'Let's hope the *carabinieri* will let me go.'

Out of the corner of her eye she saw Elizabeth running breathlessly towards the house with Dom some little distance behind. His gait was unsteady and his body lurched from side to side as he stumbled after her. Elizabeth reached the front door and Rose heard it slam as she disappeared from view. Dom was brought up short. He stood, swaying and rubbing his eyes before forcing himself forward again towards the closed door. Rose felt a throb of unease.

'Bird's-eye view up here.' Tom's voice came from behind her. 'That boy's unstable too, if you ask me.'

Tom Graham had certainly been shaken out of his monolithic silence, she thought. He indicated Alison and Susie who were sitting on the steps leading down to the pool. Alison had her arm around the younger woman. 'I felt sorry for Gillian. Nearly everyone in her orbit was a bit strange.'

He sounded as though he had dismissed the Tenbys and relegated their problems to an unsatisfactory but finished episode. Perhaps he was even more of a hollow man than she had imagined. Or more ruthless.

She remembered she'd been on her way out and she went back to retrieve her basket. If she skirted the far edge of the cultivated terraces, she thought, she might well find herself within earshot of the two women.

'You have to put the past behind you,' Alison urged.

Susie picked a stalk of lavender and rubbed it between her fingers.

'It's not easy,' she said, sullenly.

'Don't you think I've had to?' Alison said. 'I've been stupid, I know. Gillian and Keith . . . well, he's weak. But not as weak as I've been.'

'So is Mike,' Susie said. 'And so was my father.'

'Men are notoriously unable to cope with life. They're easy prey to a woman like Gillian. But your father was a good man and she brought him out of himself. I remember you always said that.'

'I had to say something,' Susie said.

She goes through life like me, all her raw edges exposed, Alison thought, it's a sisterhood.

'She used to torment him,' Susie said. 'She used to say Dom couldn't be his because he was so lively. So like her, she meant. It was her idea of a joke.'

'I'm sure she didn't mean—'

'Oh, yes she did. She got a kick out of it. The colour used to come up in his face, first pink then bright red, almost purple. Because he always tried to control himself. He never wanted to give her the satisfaction of—'

'Susie, don't. . . .'

'And she did it when I had . . . after I was. . . .'

'When you had your abortion,' Alison said, gently.

Susie turned her dull eyes towards her. 'Why wouldn't Gillian let me tell Dad before? He was heartbroken. He would have helped me. He wanted grandchildren. And I don't suppose Dom will ever. . . .' Her voice trailed off. 'I don't think she expected Dad to react like that. Or maybe she did. She certainly didn't want any competition from a child.' Susie choked on the last word and began to cry quietly.

'She was jealous of everyone,' Alison said quietly, putting her arms around her. 'She wanted everything for herself. But she wasn't happy. She wanted security and found it boring. Anyone else would have worked that out in advance.'

'She got worse when Dad died,' Susie said. She blew her nose violently. 'Look at her so-called friends. Johnny and Peter are about the best of a bad bunch. It serves her right if one of them killed her.'

'Perhaps,' Alison said, staring down at the glittering blue water.

'Dom wanted her money,' Susie said. 'He doesn't really care about anyone. He was afraid she'd spend it all before he got his hands on it.' She laughed, rather hysterically. 'And I think she did. It was lucky for me that my grandmother left me something.'

'I think Gillian hated me,' Alison said.

'People always hate the ones they injure,' Susie said in a flat voice. 'Didn't you know that?'

A twig snapped and she looked around suddenly.

'What is it?' Alison asked.

Susie nodded in the direction of the terrace above, where Rose was pulling down the branch of a tree.

'Susie,' Alison said, 'I wanted to . . .' but Susie was already on her feet. She shook her head soundlessly and ran off, back up the steps to the house.

Franco Nardi was fairly certain he was being watched as he stepped out of a large black Mercedes on to the quay in Capulana and stood for a moment staring at *L'Alba*. The cover was on the mainsail and the boat appeared deserted, then he saw a man emerging from the hatch with a bucket in his hand. Nardi smiled to himself. At least some things were falling into place. His driver had already carried his bag on board his own boat and he followed him briefly only to find that his own family were missing too. He changed into more casual clothes then went on foot into the town.

Johnny Langdon Smythe and Peter Kinaid were sitting outside their usual bar but Nardi walked past them without apparently seeing them. He stood at the bar and drank down a *grappa* quickly. After he left Johnny went inside and spoke briefly to the barman.

Rose brought the cherries back to the kitchen and Maria-Grazia inspected them. 'Not enough for jam,' she said. 'I'll make a *crostata*. Tomorrow.' She gave Giulio a look, 'Perhaps he'll pick some more, before it's too late.'

'A *crostata* would be very nice,' Rose said, although the last thing on her mind was food. She badly wanted to telephone Sergio, but didn't want to use any of the extensions in the house. She wondered if Susie really believed that either Langdon Smythe or Peter Kinaid had killed Gillian. Sergio had said they had an unbreakable alibi but, on the other hand, he'd been convinced that the smuggling and the murders were connected from the very beginning. She could understand how frustrated he was. The news from Milan had brought him up against a blank wall but there had to be a crack, a chink, somewhere. The trouble was that everyone had a motive of some kind. They all either disliked Gillian, or were leching after her. She didn't seem to have inspired any milk-and-water emotions.

She heard a violent knocking in the nether regions of the house and went to the top of the bedroom corridor to listen.

'Elizabeth!' Dom's voice said, loudly and urgently. 'Please let me in.'

There was a muffled 'no' from Elizabeth and after a moment the knocking resumed. Then, when there was no further response, Rose heard Dom's footsteps retreating and the sound of a door closing and she assumed he had gone to his own room. She wondered where Johnny and Peter were and reflected how easy it was for them to disappear. Everyone would assume they were doing something to the boat, but they could be anywhere, somewhere in the grounds, even. For a moment she was tempted to go back into the garden and walk through the copse which led down to the ravine where Pino had been found. Murderers, she thought, often returned to the scene of the crime. But then she remembered Sergio's words of warning and decided against it.

Instead she went into the library and, very much to her surprise, found Alison there.

CHAPTER 18

'I should have looked around in here before,' Alison said, pushing back a stray lock of hair. 'I hadn't realized what a good selection there was.'

'It's wonderful,' Rose said. 'I brought a lot of books, paid excess baggage in fact, not knowing what riches there were here.'

'It must be a pretty dreary job, all the same,' Alison said, looking at her as though she had seen her for the first time.

'It's . . . all right, doing jobs like this I get a lot of variety.'

'I'm sure you do. And Maria-Grazia seems quite a character.'

'Yes, but she's lovely,' Rose said, remembering with amusement her misgivings at the interview with Mrs Venables-Brown.

'I imagine she is. Without the language . . . I don't really . . . but it must be. . . .' her voice ran on, in a vague way. 'It's so . . . awful all these horrible things should have happened.'

'Yes, really horrible. I realize everyone is very upset.'

Alison shivered. 'But you're on the outside.'

'In a way.'

'And you're in the annexe, aren't you? You couldn't have seen anything.' Her voice was sharper now but was she asking or telling? It was hard to decide.

Rose waited for a moment, then said, 'I think someone did.'

Alison walked away from her, running her fingers along the spines of the books. 'I'd like to get a job of some kind, but it's difficult. I once worked for

236

TUSCAN SHADOWS 237

a publisher. I have a degree, believe it or not. But I've lost all contact with that world.' She took Jung Chang's *Wild Swans* from the shelf and flicked through the pages. 'Have you read this?'

'Yes, it's wonderful. It's about the China none of us really know, but it's also about stoicism. And courage – the kind of courage women have to have,' Rose said, carefully.

'Yes women need to be. . . .' Alison paused. 'I suppose I've been finding it hard to concentrate lately. I've been involved with . . . domestic matters.'

She still had dark shadows under her eyes, but her face was more alert than it had been and Rose could see a glimmer of the pretty girl she must once have been.

'Gillian always made me feel inadequate,' Alison said. 'When I talked about going back to work she said, "You?" in that sort of voice. Keith said I should take no notice, but that was easy for him to say.' She put down the book and then put out a hand and touched it lightly.

'Gillian had a certain kind of charisma,' Rose said, 'but sometimes I imagine rather too much of it.'

'Ye. . .es. Men liked her. But even they found out what she was really like in the end.'

'What was she like?'

'She was . . . she made people do things, or not do things.'

'What things?'

Rose half expected Alison to tell her to mind her own business but instead Alison stared at her for a long moment and then said, 'She ignored everyone else's pain . . . moved us all around like chess pieces.' She laughed, harshly. 'But everyone had to love her. Gillian was the centre of the universe.'

Rose hesitated, then said, 'Did she make you do something?'

'No,' Alison said, harshly, 'she made me not do something.'

'I don't understand.'

'Nor do I,' Alison said. 'I don't understand how I could have agreed, how I could have been so weak.'

'What was it?' Rose said, no longer afraid of exceeding her position in the house. She was convinced that Alison was either involved in Gillian's death or knew who was. 'If you know something,' Rose said urgently, 'anything at all, you should tell the police.'

Alison sighed. 'There's been enough trouble and, in any case, I'm not sure that I do know anything. I've been having bad dreams . . . very confused dreams, that's all.'

Rose felt her heart beating faster. 'And was there anything in one of these dreams, anything to point to—?'

'No!' Alison said. She banged her hand violently on the shelf. 'They were just dreams.'

A shadow moved outside the open window which gave on to the terrace. Alison looked alarmed and Rose rushed over but there was no one in sight. Then Alison gave a small sound and when Rose turned round she saw Keith standing in the doorway.

'What's the matter, darling?'

'Nothing,' Alison said. 'I just thought I saw someone at the window. It broke my dream.' Her voice stumbled over the words. 'You know, when you remember last night's dream because of something that happens during the day.'

He stepped into the room and nodded at Rose. 'You should be out in the fresh air instead of brooding in here. Why not come and sit in the garden?'

'All right,' Alison said. Her face had resumed its habitual expression of weariness. She picked up *Wild Swans* and put it down again. 'Another time,' she said.

Did she mean the book or that she would talk to Rose later? Rose waited, hoping that Keith would go, but instead he took his wife by the arm and led her away.

'Nardi wants us to do what?' Peter said. They were walking back to *L'Alba*.

'Do the whole thing. Says he can't because his own people are being watched.'

'Don't you think we are?'

'I doubt it,' Johnny said, thoughtfully. 'The brave captain has the look of a man up against it. In any case they can't go on holding us here forever. I reckon if they close the murder enquiry he'll be sent elsewhere. Maybe

Sicily.' He appeared cheered by the thought. 'And when that happens, we move.'

Peter grinned but only briefly. 'It sounds too risky to me.'

'There's a lot more money in it,' Johnny said. 'Nardi will provide the transport, we won't have any extra expenses.' He looked sideways at Peter. 'But I think we'll rearrange the plan a little. We're not going to leave from here. We'll take the boat south a few miles and anchor off Rassone, drive to Turbi at night, pick up the cargo and go directly to *L'Alba*, and from there to Ventotene to deliver to Pulcini instead.'

'And screw Nardi?' Peter said, incredulously.

'Nardi's finished,' Johnny went on urgently. 'They're going to get him on some charge or other. He won't be able to touch us. Look, this way instead of getting a miserable cut, we clean up. We can go to England afterwards, or Greece, or Australia if you're so scared.'

This was improvisation on a scale Peter had never dreamed of. 'What about Elizabeth?' It was the only thing he could think of saying.

'Do you think we could have just one conversation without dragging her name into it?' Johnny asked angrily and, when Peter didn't answer, said more calmly, 'You can please yourself about Turbi. I'll find someone else if you're not interested.'

'And *L'Alba*?' Peter persisted.

'We can sell her, ditch her, send someone out for her.'

Boat burning then, but why was Johnny so desperate? He was looking tired, despite this sudden enthusiasm, tired and older. Maybe it was time to move on but if things weren't going well with Elizabeth. . . .

'It's madness, total madness,' Peter said slowly, 'but I do rather fancy Australia.' He thought for a moment. 'We'd need a third man for the driving.'

'The new hand.'

'But how can we trust him?'

'OK, we can send him with the boat to Rassone instead and when we sail we leave him behind. I've already contacted Pulcini. He'll be delighted to do business with us again.'

*

240   *Maureen Donegan*

'I buried my mother today!' Dom said. He jumped to his feet as Sergio and Massimo Pascucci came into the room. 'Can't you leave us alone?'

Sergio had sent a car for Dom and the younger man had been waiting for some time in an unused office in the *carabinieri* station. Official notices, yellowing with age, curled against grey walls which were more than ready for a coat of paint. The furniture consisted of two hardback chairs, a metal desk and a small table with a typewriter. Beside this, on the floor, sat a cardboard box. A mosquito screen covered the single window, leaving the room coloured with a dull yellow light. The effect was extremely dreary but Dom seemed oblivious to his surroundings.

'Please sit down, Mr Tenby. I'll try to make this as brief as possible.'

Dom subsided on one of the hard chairs as Sergio switched on a harsh neon light and then walked around the desk to face the younger man. 'I'm sorry to have kept you waiting, but something came up.'

In fact he had been going through the statements again, looking for some discrepancy in the morass of detail. And it would have done no harm to let Dom Tenby cool his heels for a while.

He nodded at Pascucci, who rolled a sheet of paper into his machine. Sergio opened a dull green folder and rifled through it.

'I believe you quarrelled with your mother?' he said, abruptly.

'No, no I didn't!' Dom's voice was alarmed.

'Something to do with money, I believe?'

'No!'

'You were concerned about her extravagance, I believe?'

'That's not true—'

'Because you're in financial difficulties yourself.'

'No!'

'We've been given to understand otherwise,' Sergio went on. 'It appears that your mother had promised to help you, but hadn't the wherewithal to do so. She was even obliged to put her house on the market to finance her spending.'

The typewriter clattered as Sergio repeated what had been said in Italian. Dom kept his head down. He appeared to be examining the square brown linoleum tile between his feet.

'Well, Mr Tenby?'

'We. . . .' Dom swallowed. 'We discussed it. It wasn't a quarrel.'

'But you must have been furious when you realized she'd spent a great deal of money on a holiday, when she was in financial difficulties too.'

'She said. . . .'

'Yes?'

'She said she'd sort it out.'

'And how was she going to do that?'

Dom raised a haggard face. 'I don't know.'

'I suggest, Mr Tenby, that you were made so angry by this situation that you decided to put a stop to her spending once and for all.'

Dom said, in a quiet voice, 'I loved my mother. I would never have hurt her.'

In any case the theory was as full of holes as the mosquito screen, Sergio reflected. Dom might, on the spur of the moment, have struck his mother, but he couldn't really see him planning her death in advance. And it was true that he seemed to have had real affection for Gillian.

'The night of her death you say you went to visit Ms Halliwell for a short time and then returned to your room?'

'Yes.'

'And you didn't see anything? You didn't leave your room again?'

'No. I slept . . . heavily. We'd been. . . .'

'Smoking pot?'

Dom returned to his examination of the linoleum.

'In your statement you said that you didn't say goodnight to your mother. I suggest that you went back to her room after you'd seen Ms Halliwell.'

Dom's head jerked up. 'Don't you think I wish I had?'

'And why would that be?'

'Because then I might have stopped who . . . whoever did it.'

'And do you have any idea who that might have been?'

'No.' He seemed to be recovering slightly. 'Why would I or anyone else want to kill her for money if she hadn't got any?'

'And you can think of no other reason?'

'She hadn't any enemies,' Dom said flatly.

242   *Maureen Donegan*

'I see.' Sergio tilted back his chair and a long silence filled the room.

'I don't know why she . . . why anyone would want to kill her,' Dom said, eventually. 'And there isn't anything else I can tell you.'

'I think there is,' Sergio said. 'Pascucci, pass over that box, will you?'

Dinner was a sombre meal. It was obvious to Rose that Sergio hadn't told them that they would soon be free to go and the conversation, such as it was, ranged backwards and forwards in speculation. Although Gillian's lease on the villa was not up for another two weeks, everyone had apparently discovered urgent reasons why they should go home.

Keith had a report to prepare and was annoyed that he hadn't brought his laptop.

'Why didn't you bring it?' Alison asked.

'I didn't think I'd have the time,' he said.

Alison's face settled into even more unhappy lines. 'I see. And now you have?'

'It's extremely urgent that I go to England as soon as possible,' Johnny Langdon Smythe said. 'My mother's condition. . . .'

Elizabeth glanced at him. 'Yes,' she said, 'I must say I'm more than ready to leave, too.'

Mike nodded in agreement. 'This has become a kind of limbo.' he said.

'You mean the acolytes have lost their goddess?' Susie said.

Mike put a restraining hand on her arm. 'That's not a very nice thing to say.'

'But it's true that we're all being kept here against our will,' Tom Graham exploded. 'Our belongings have been searched over and over. Even while we were at the funeral. There's no privacy here, only suspicion. Because one of us is a murderer.'

'Take it easy,' Peter Kinaid said.

'No, I'll have my say. We're all pussyfooting around, pretending we're on a holiday when in reality we're practically under house arrest. And these fancy-dress policemen who don't know their arse from their elbow are doing fuck all about it.'

Rose, a dish of lemon chicken in her hands, froze with indignation.

'I thought our things had been disturbed,' Alison said, slowly.

'But surely, if anyone had anything to hide, they would have got rid of it long ago?' Johnny said. 'Over the cliff or into the sea, it wouldn't be difficult.'

'Unless we're all being followed,' Dom said.

'As far as I can see there's only one man on duty,' Tom said, 'except, presumably, while we were all out today. They probably moved in in droves then.'

Rose wondered if anything had been found. As Johnny said, it would have been easy to get rid of the murder weapon. But the killer could be carrying it around, with the idea of using it again. It was not a comforting thought.

'I didn't expect to see you two tonight,' Elizabeth said to Johnny. 'Is it a mark of respect to the dead?' Johnny, who was sitting beside her and had been giving her his undivided attention, looked annoyed.

'You don't want our company?'

'You didn't answer my question,' she said.

'I felt,' Johnny said, in a controlled voice, 'that since we're all, well, implicated in this, we should stick together.'

'Keep an eye on each other, you mean?'

'No, that's not what I meant. And the reason why I'm free to come up here is because I've taken on another paid hand, so the boat should be secure.'

'Oh,' Elizabeth said. 'You've replaced Pino.'

'I need someone while we're here, but he has a family, so I'll pay him off when we leave.'

'Really? A married man?' Elizabeth raised her eyebrows. 'Anyway, Daddy thinks we should all be able to leave soon.'

Johnny took her hand and squeezed it but the skin of his face was tight with irritation. 'That's my girl,' he said.

So Sergio was right, Rose thought, the Halliwells must have put some kind of pressure on the Italian authorities.

Elizabeth withdrew her hand and dissected a piece of chicken, without answering. Dom, from the other end of the table, gave Elizabeth a mourn-

244   *Maureen Donegan*

ful look, but she avoided his eye. He was only playing with his food, Rose noticed, as was Susie.

'The sooner we're able to get away, the sooner we'll forget all this unhappiness,' Mike said.

'You may forget it easily,' Keith said, belligerently, 'but I certainly won't.'

Alison's chair scraped back and she got to her feet somewhat unsteadily. 'She's still here, isn't she? Like bloody Rebecca at Manderley. Whoever did it only did half a job, because we'll never get rid of her, never!'

'Alison. . . .' Keith dropped his fork with a clatter. But Alison was already at the french windows and she had disappeared into the house by the time he had got to his feet.

'She didn't mean that,' he said. 'She's overwrought.'

'Alison is not entirely wrong,' Elizabeth said, when he was out of earshot. Her eyes wandered around the table, lingering for a moment on Dom. 'Gillian had a very strong character. Her influence is bound to hang around.'

The french window slammed in a sudden breeze and the candles flickered as though to underline her words.

'She's dead,' Susie said, in a high voice. 'Dead. Can't we let it rest?'

'We've all been unnerved by the funeral,' Mike said. 'It's natural that we should be thinking of her.'

Rose wondered if Gillian really was present, perhaps sitting on the balustrade in her yellow silk dress, swinging her legs and listening.

Johnny coughed into the sudden silence. 'Mike is quite right,' he said. 'It's been a . . . difficult day. For everyone.'

Later, Rose walked in the garden with Sergio and described the scene at dinner. His hand was clasped around hers, warm and firm.

'I'm not very popular, then,' he said. 'But they're rattled, all of them, and that's good.'

'You're not popular at all,' she said.

'Does that include you?'

'No.'

'Good,' he said.

The moon was almost full, the trees silver and the sky clear and bright as though an exotic scene in a film had been inexplicably printed in black and white. A time of magic, of madness even.

'They know all about the search,' Rose said. She felt she had to keep talking. 'Did you find anything?'

'We found some women's clothes in Dom's room. Dresses, silk underwear. They were pushed into an overnight bag under his bed.'

'Do you think they were his mother's?'

'He's admitted as much. He's evidently a boy who never grew out of dressing up. Some of the clothes had semen stains.'

'Poor boy,' she said quietly.

Sergio grunted. 'Yes, well. . . .' He paused. 'But it's not a capital offence.'

They stopped and he kissed her, lingeringly. 'You've lost your *noli me tangere* air tonight.'

She laughed, gently. 'And so have you.'

He kissed her again. 'Do I have one?'

'A bit, yes.'

'Ah. But we're breaking down the barriers?'

'They seem to have more or less crumbled,' she said, softly.

'I was beginning to think that too . . . oh, Rose! I don't feel like going inside, do you?'

She remembered the grove. 'There's a place over there among the oleanders . . . only. . . .'

'Only what?'

'It's where Gillian used to go.'

'To do this?'

'I think so.'

'Does it matter?'

'No.'

'Come on then.'

So Gillian was still with them, Rose thought, but this time in a good way. She must have been happy here, if only briefly. It was a place where she had perhaps been more herself than anywhere else.

'I was wrong about something,' she said, a few moments later.

'About what?'

246   *Maureen Donegan*

'I thought . . . well, they say that anticipation is the best part, but. . . .'

'But?'

'It's not.'

'I'm very glad to hear it,' Sergio said.

What she did not say was that love and lust and passion and tenderness all rolled up into one comprised nothing short of paradise. But talking seemed redundant. There was a brief moment when she registered that the dew had fallen and that there might be insects, or even snakes, but then there was nothing but the frantic need to get rid of their clothes, and the urgency of their bodies.

'Sorry, sorry,' he muttered.

'For what?'

'For the romantic honeymoon. I've been waiting too long, that's all. Give me . . . a . . . little time and—'

'Sh . . . sh.' She held him.

'*Sei tutta bagnata*,' he murmured and then, 'this time for you. . . .'

She could hear herself moaning, saying his name over and over again.

'Wait for me,' he said, urgently. 'Are you. . . ?'

'Yes, oh yes. . . .'

He entered her again and moved with her, lifting her, holding her off the ground, plunging and rolling with her until they both came, gasping and shuddering and clinging to each other.

'It was . . .' she said, when she could speak.

He stroked her face and she could see him smiling in the moonlight.

'What?'

'Wonderful.'

'Mmm. I didn't think I. . . .' He half laughed. 'I haven't been so active for years.' He put his shirt around her. 'Are you cold?'

'Uh, uh.'

'But we should get dressed.'

'All right. Will you come back with me?'

'I don't think I should.'

She felt something tighten around her heart. 'You're afraid someone will see us.'

TUSCAN SHADOWS 247

'Shall I say it's not wise.'

'Will it ever be?' she asked, before she could stop herself.

'I hope so,' he said, 'but I have to tie this case up.'

He must have sensed her tension because he drew her into his arms again. 'Accept it, Rose. It's the only way. I have to accept it.'

She lay against him, trying to control her rapid breathing. She could feel him still trembling too. After a while he said, 'Tell me what happened when you left art college.'

'Oh.' She paused. 'I got married.'

'But I thought you'd never—'

'It didn't last very long. I made the mistake of thinking if I married an artist I would always be in that world.'

'And?' he asked gently.

She plucked at the damp grass under her fingers. 'He was a student, in the same college. Very talented. And I think ... I think he married me because he believed I would never give him any competition. That sounds terrible, put like that,' she laughed, a little bitterly. 'But artists can be very ruthless. He needed to feel superior, you see, in order to paint and he's become rather famous so perhaps I did help.'

'How long were you together?'

'Less than a year. He was very single-minded about his work, which didn't leave much time for being a husband. Immoral, amoral ... it was just as much my fault because I married him for the wrong reasons. At the time I wanted to ... to rebel, I think. My family were very upset at the time of the wedding – they're very conventional. They were delighted when we got divorced.'

'And then?'

And then she'd met Arthur. 'Then I vowed I was never going to get hurt again.'

'Hence the air of *noli me tangere*?'

'Yes, I suppose so.'

'É *la vita*. And I married ... like most young men of my generation, because we believed we could have regular sex. Of course we romanticized it. I thought I was in love, went through all the rituals. Italian girls were very

248   *Maureen Donegan*

protected then.' He sighed. 'But I found it wasn't as simple as that. It led to years of mutual misunderstanding and misery. I think what she wanted was simply stability, material things. Or perhaps she came to want only those things. There was . . . an emptiness that was impossible to fill.'

She made a small sound and moved closer against him.

'I think we've both been missing a lot,' he said, in such a low voice that she had to strain to hear him. Gillian, never far from her thoughts, seemed to drift in a mist of yellow silk through the grove.

'She didn't have a half life,' Rose said.

'Who?'

'Gillian Tenby.'

'I think she did,' Sergio said. 'Didn't she marry for the wrong reasons, too?'

'I wonder if she knew?'

'About us invading her hideaway?'

She laughed. 'No, I didn't mean that, although perhaps she does. I meant about Dom cross-dressing.'

'I think she knew a lot about all of them. But she'd hardly have been blackmailing her own son.'

'She could have put pressure on him to stop.'

'She could have. She held the purse strings, such as they were. But that's hardly likely to have made him kill her. And I thought he was genuinely upset by her death.'

'Yes,' Rose said, remembering the funeral.

'What I need is to establish some other link between one of them and Pino. That would be the key. But I don't want to talk about it now. I want to just sit here quietly. With you. And forget everything.'

'Can we?'

'We can try.'

Not only Sergio's job, but life itself could be a horror, she thought. At a moment when so much joy had come into her life someone was walking around with a lethal syringe, and two people had died violently.

The moon had disappeared briefly behind a little scudding cloud. Faintly, through the now black trees, she could see the loom of the port. Down there, she knew, were coloured lights, people eating fish and drinking wine. Boats would be swinging gently against their moorings and Johnny's new man would be on watch.

'But why Pino?' she persisted. 'That's something I can't understand, unless. . . .'

'Unless what?' Sergio said, quietly.

'If it was one of the people close to Gillian, if you've ruled out Johnny and Peter?'

He sighed. 'I was so sure one of them had done it. I'll check it out again but. . . .'

'What about Alison?' She told him about the half overheard conversation in the garden. 'She'd wanted to adopt a baby and couldn't. And she told me that Gillian had stopped her from doing something. It was probably that.'

'Well, it would account for her depression, but for my money she doesn't seem capable of planning this. She seems half dead most of the time. Did she say anything else?'

'Susie said Dom wanted his mother's money.'

'But then she didn't have any.' He groaned. 'None of these so called leads go anywhere.'

'I was wondering if . . . oh, it sounds stupid, but suppose they didn't all arrive when they said they did? That day when Gillian had her crash she was on the way to the station, but she never got there, so we don't know if either Tom or Mike were actually on the train. Tom had been in Italy a few days remember, and we only have Mike's word for it that he arrived in Rome that morning. They don't stamp EU passports now, do they?'

'No, but I can have the passenger lists checked.'

'And Susie . . . although she didn't come by plane, but that was a couple of days later anyway.'

'I can try to get in touch with the people she was staying with. The problem is time. Something I haven't got. I keep going over it all again and again. I've got my men rechecking the port, trying to find this famous missing link.'

'What if,' Rose said slowly, 'Tom came to this area earlier and Gillian had

250 *Maureen Donegan*

seen him, by accident. Or even by arrangement. Why did she insist on going to meet the train herself? Perhaps she'd arranged to pick one of them up somewhere else. Or. . . .' She stopped.

'Or what?' Sergio said. He sounded interested now.

'No, I thought maybe one of them had an accomplice who tampered with the car, but that could only be—'

'Giulio,' Sergio said, heavily. 'It could have happened like that. There was a spanner missing, but that proves nothing. The toolshed wasn't locked and anyone could have taken it, but then so could Giulio himself.'

'It's not possible,' Rose said.

Sergio sighed. 'Anything is possible.'

'I didn't like Gillian,' Rose said, suddenly, 'but she had a certain appetite for life. And no one had the right to take that away.'

'Killers play God,' Sergio said, 'and after you've seen some of their handiwork, you wonder if He exists, or has ever existed.'

CHAPTER 19

The last person Rose thought of before she went to sleep was not, strangely enough, Sergio, although she had thought about him a great deal when she returned to her room, but Arthur.

She had never experienced anything with him to compare with the hour she had just spent with Sergio and this made her very sad. It was not that there was anything wrong with Arthur's lovemaking, the fault had been with her. She had felt affection, and need, but not intemperate passion. She smiled to herself slightly. One couldn't apply the word intemperate to Arthur, although passion there had been. She had been afraid of love, afraid of vulnerability. And Arthur had provided just the kind of safety that she needed. Or thought she had needed. Better to be the one who was kissed, better to stand on the sidelines. And in a way it had been better.

Her euphoric mood had gone. She couldn't even remember the expression on Sergio's face, although she could still feel the weight and imprint of his body. He had said she put up barriers. Had he been afraid of rejection? And why hadn't he wanted them to be seen together?

You are indulging in stupid agonizing, she told herself. Stupid because the situation was as it was. She was entrusting her emotional life to him and she would have to wait for him to resolve the situation. This thought, intended to bolster up her spirit, terrified her.

She groaned out loud and drew her knees up into a foetal position. I wasn't fair to you, Arthur, not once, not from the very beginning.

251

252   *Maureen Donegan*

*

Alison woke to sounds she couldn't identify. There was a sliding noise, a rattle, a faint thud, then Keith's voice swearing.

She opened her eyes with difficulty. She had made up her mind not to take any pills, thinking it was perhaps these which were causing the nightmares. As a result she had slept fitfully, lying awake until far into the night, thinking of the twists and turns of the past. Finally, in the coolness just before dawn she had dreamed of death again. Now she was heavy with sleep and reluctant to face the day.

The sounds in the room increased and Keith swore again.

'Why don't you put things away properly?' he demanded.

She pushed a pillow behind her head and propped herself up groggily. Keith was hanging up one of her dresses and she registered that it was very creased.

'All these things in the bottom of the wardrobe. . . .' He rummaged through T-shirts and sandals and finally threw a tennis shoe into the room.

'What are you looking for?'

'The other one of these. Tom's booked a court and now I'm late.'

'Tom?' she asked in a startled voice.

'We're going to play tennis, aren't you listening?'

'Just the two of you?'

'Yes,' he said in an exasperated voice, 'did you want to come? We could get Susie or Elizabeth if they're awake.'

'Of course I don't want to! You know I don't like—'

'All right, but at least you could. . . .'

Keith pulled out a travel bag and then his back went rigid.

'Alison?' There was a note in his voice she had never heard before.

'Have you found it?'

'No. I've found this.'

He turned around and she gave a stifled scream. There was a large syringe in his hand and he advanced to the bed, the needle pointing towards her.

She shrank back. 'Take it away from me!'

'Alison,' he said again. 'I'm not going to . . . I found it there . . . Alison!'

He put the syringe down and came to sit on the bed. She pushed him away. Confused images jostled together in her mind.

'I will take it away,' Keith said, his face looked old, 'but I want you to tell me.'

'It's like my dream,' she said slowly, 'only not like.'

'This isn't a dream,' Keith said. 'You're awake Alison, and I want to know how this got into the wardrobe.'

'I want to know that, too,' she said, her voice trembling. They stared at each other and then the mists in her head cleared a little. 'The police . . . someone said they searched again. Yesterday, that's right. Yesterday. They were talking about it at dinner last night.'

'The police didn't put it there,' Keith said.

'I know that. Then. . . .'

'Then someone else did.'

'Keith, you've got to believe me, it wasn't me.' She grasped his hands.

He disengaged himself and began to pace the room. 'If someone wanted to incriminate us why didn't they put it here before the search?'

'I don't know,' she said. She got up unsteadily and went into the bathroom to splash her face with water.

'Because they didn't know there was going to be a search, of course,' he called after her.

She buried her face in a towel and thought that perhaps the person didn't want to incriminate them as much as frighten them. Or frighten her. Perhaps some of her dreams had not been dreams after all. Perhaps she was losing her mind, doing things she didn't remember. It was like a big black abyss, this fear, this half knowledge.

Keith came and took the towel away from her. 'I know how you felt about her,' he said, but his voice was gentle.

His face began to dissolve and she wondered if she was going to faint.

'I didn't . . . at least . . . I wouldn't have hurt her, I only wanted . . . I only wanted you.' She shuddered. 'It was such a horrible dream, the last one.'

He helped her back to the bed. 'What was it about?' His voice sounded kind. His face swam back into focus and that looked kind, too. Kind and

254   *Maureen Donegan*

pitying. 'She's dead now, Alison, and we have to go on living. Tell me about the dream.'

'Someone is trying to kill me. Trying to smother me. It's all . . . distorted, the colours are dark, the room is dark, blue and black and grey. There's a man. I can't see the face, but I think . . .' – she began to cry – 'I think it's you. He comes over to the bed and I can't move. And then there's a pillow over my face and my arms are thrashing about but he keeps pressing and pressing.'

He put an arm around her shoulders. 'It's the heat,' he said, in a helpless voice. 'I've had strange dreams, too. I was young again, we were all young. I didn't go to America; I stayed here and it was all different. It was better.'

'Because you married her,' Alison said.

'No.' He drew her closer. 'No, I didn't marry her. Either in my dream or in real life.'

She could feel her tears dampening his white shirt. Had there been a child in his dream? And what did he mean, he didn't marry Gillian in real life? Their affair had been the nearest thing to a marriage. Gillian had ensnared him, had ruined their own marriage, their lives.

'The syringe isn't a dream,' she said, eventually.

'No. And whoever put it in the wardrobe must hate us very much.'

'Yes,' Alison said in a muffled voice. She had hidden her face in the towel again and was thinking about hatred.

'Have you seen Mr Drinkwater?' Tom asked Rose, as she brought coffee out to the terrace. He was wearing whites with a blue cotton sweater knotted around his neck. A racquet in a leather case lay on the swing. 'We've got a court down at the Minerva for nine o'clock.' He glanced impatiently at his watch. 'We're going to lose it if he doesn't hurry up.'

But at that moment Keith appeared. He too had a racquet and also a small sports bag. He looked pale and drawn and his hand shook as he accepted a cup of coffee.

'Sorry, bit late. Alison isn't too well.'

'It's OK,' Tom said, but he looked at his watch again.

Keith shook his head as Rose brought over a cornetto from the heated trolley. 'I wonder, could you look in on my wife, Rose? She had a bad night and I'm a bit worried about leaving her.'

'Yes, of course,' Rose said. 'Shall I take her some coffee?'

'Tea, I think, if you wouldn't mind.'

'We're not going to be very long,' Tom said impatiently, 'an hour and a half at most.'

'OK, let's go,' Keith drained his cup. He stood up, searching for his car keys as he headed for the french windows.

'Hey, you've forgotten this,' Tom said, picking up the bag Keith had placed carefully on the floor beside him.

Keith snatched it from him. 'I'll take that!' He turned back to Rose. 'You will see that she's all right?'

'I will. Don't worry.'

Something has happened, Rose thought, but whatever it was, it had given her the chance to see Alison alone.

She prepared a tray and made some toast and put a vase with three small marguerites beside the plate.

Maria-Grazia nodded approvingly. 'It should always be an odd number to bring good luck and she needs it that one. She is *nervosa*. Giulio, he is also *nervoso*. Me, too.'

'We all are.' Rose subdued a flicker of fear. She was about to ask if Maria-Grazia had ever seen Alison driving. It would indicate a familiarity with cars, but she bit back the question. Maria-Grazia was also *nervosa* and although it could be simply part of the tension in the house, it could also be fear for Giulio. None of them would emerge unscathed from the past few weeks.

'Yes, Captain?' The Sicilian pathologist sounded irritated by the interruption.

Sergio glared at the telephone, irritated in turn. He tried to keep his voice placatory. 'Just a couple of points about the time of death of La Signora Tenby, *Dottore*.'

'It's all in my report.'

'Yes, of course. It's very detailed. Very helpful.'

'*Allora*? Is there some problem?'

256   *Maureen Donegan*

'You've pinpointed the time at midnight.'

'Not pinpointed,' the doctor said, edgily. 'I've indicated a time span of roughly four hours from midnight to four o'clock.'

'Roughly you say.'

'One can never be precise to the minute. Unless, of course, a bullet shatters the wristwatch, but I imagine even that can be arranged by a clever killer.' He gave a fussy little laugh.

'But we're not talking about a shot.'

'No, indeed.'

Sergio spun his sesterce and missed it as it fell. '*Cazzo*,' he muttered under his breath.

'Did you say something, Captain?'

Sergio coughed. 'I was wondering if there was some leeway in the time?'

'Hmm.' There was a tapping sound, like a woodpecker. Sergio wondered if he was tapping his teeth or the desk.

'Hmm,' the pathologist said again. 'Of course there is always some flexibility, half an hour, perhaps a little more. My report gave you the most likely time of death, given the meal that the dead woman had eaten and so on.'

'So she could have died earlier?'

'It's possible.' There was more tapping down the phone. 'Or later,' he added.

'But she did die instantaneously?'

'That is my considered opinion.'

Pompous bastard, why couldn't he just say yes? But Sergio was smiling as he gave the expected polite rejoinder. 'Thank you, *Dottore*, you've been very helpful.'

'*Prego, Capitano.*'

'As always.' No harm in laying it on.

'I am always glad to be of service.'

'It's very much appreciated.' They could go on like this all day, Sergio thought. He brought the conversation to an end with, '*Grazie ancora*,' and retrieved his sesterce from the corner where it had rolled. So, if Gillian Tenby had died a bit earlier, Johnny Langdon Smythe could have done it and got down to the marina by 11.40. Just. Or Kinaid could have done it for him. The important thing was opportunity. No one had noticed when they had left the terrace. No one had noticed anything very much, that was the trouble, but Langdon Smythe could have put a sleeping pill in La Tenby's drink and hung around the villa until she went to her room. In any case she would have been relaxed from the pot she'd smoked and unsuspecting. Her door would have been unlocked as she waited for Tom Graham.

Another thought struck him. If the same flexibility applied to both ends of the night and she had actually died later than four a.m. Tom Graham couldn't be ruled out either. What time had Rose seen him going to Gillian's room?

There was only the faintest reply to her knock.

'It's Rose,' she called, 'I've brought you some tea.'

After a few moments she heard the sound of a key being turned and the door opened and Alison stood there in a nightdress. She backed away and then slid back into bed. 'You're very kind.'

'Your husband's idea.'

'Oh.' Her voice was so faint that Rose could hardly hear her. 'It was such a horrible night. I couldn't get to sleep and I didn't want to put the light on in case I woke Keith.'

'Perhaps you could go back to sleep now.'

Alison plucked the sheet. 'I don't think so.'

Rose put the tray on the bedside table. The room was hot and airless and she went to open the window.

'No!' Alison said, more loudly. 'People can get in that way from the terrace.'

Rose came back over to her and poured the tea. 'I think most people are still in bed.'

'Yes, but. . . .'

'Would you like me to stay with you?'

'No, that is, I'm sure you have a lot to do. I can lock the door again until Keith gets back.'

Alison took the cup with shaking hands. She was clearly very frightened.

'Who do you think would try to get in?' Rose asked, carefully.

258 *Maureen Donegan*

'I expect I sound a bit . . . hysterical,' Alison said. The cup rattled in the saucer. 'It's because of the dreams. I usually take . . . something to help me to sleep, but now I don't want to.'

'What kind of dreams?' Rose asked.

'Shadows, dark figures, a door opening, someone trying. . . .'

Rose waited, afraid to interrupt her.

'Someone . . . smothering me. I've never experienced anything . . . I've always had . . . I used to dream about Gillian, now someone else is. . . .'

'Someone else is what?'

Alison broke off a piece of toast and crumbled it in her fingers. She laughed unexpectedly but it wasn't an amused sound. 'I wondered if they weren't all dreams. Insomnia is awful, it distorts everything. You feel you're the only person awake in the whole world. You doze for a few moments then there's a sound, something, and it's impossible to. . . . I get up sometimes and walk around in the dark . . . and I don't think they were all dreams . . . not all of them.' Rose moved around the room as unobtrusively as she could, picking up various articles of clothing.

'No!' Alison shouted suddenly.

Rose stopped, her hand on the wardrobe door.

'Leave it,' Alison said, more quietly. 'Please. I'll tidy up myself later.'

'All right, if you're sure.'

'Quite sure.' Alison leaned back against the pillows, her eyes dark and confused. 'I'm sorry,' she said. 'I really can't eat anything, but the tea was very nice.'

Rose took the cup and put it on the tray, then sat down on a chair at the side of the bed. 'What are you afraid of?' she asked.

Alison turned her head away and there was a long silence. Eventually she said, 'My thoughts . . . things that happened.'

'To do with Mrs Tenby's death?'

'I don't know. I have to do some more . . . thinking.' There was another silence. Alison coughed and fumbled for a tissue with a shaking hand. 'Sometimes,' she said in a whisper, 'sometimes you think you know something. And then you find out you really don't know anything at all.' She began to cry in great gulping sobs.

Rose moved over and put her arms around her. 'Tell me, Alison, please. Please. What sort of something?'

Alison shook her head and made a choking sound. Rose rocked her back and forth. 'You could be in danger, you know that.'

It seemed an eternity until the sobbing subsided. 'Tell me,' Rose said again, very gently. 'What did you mean yesterday when you said Gillian stopped people doing things?'

Alison's body tensed and when she spoke her voice was barely audible. 'She said it wouldn't be fair to . . . she said I was too old and . . . and that I wasn't fit to be. . . .'

'To adopt a baby?'

'How did you know?' she whispered. She eased herself away slightly. Rose was afraid she'd pushed her too far but after a moment Alison said, 'She told Keith it would tip me over the edge. He didn't tell me that but I heard her.' Her voice began to rise. 'She said I wasn't strong, that it was too big a commitment. She'd told him he would end up looking after the baby, that his job would suffer. She sounded so bloody reasonable. They didn't know I was listening. Sometimes . . . sometimes . . . they talked as if I wasn't there, but I wasn't always asleep, sometimes I pretended.'

'Oh, Alison, I'm so sorry.'

Alison gave her a look from under her lashes. 'Are you? Most people think I'm mad.'

'No.'

'Or at least disturbed.'

'I just think you're very unhappy.'

'That, too,' Alison said in a defeated voice. As she turned her head away, Rose saw the tendons standing out on her neck like brittle twists of string.

'I'm all right now,' Alison said, but she didn't sound all right. 'I just need to be by myself.'

Sharp anxiety tugged at Rose. Alison certainly had a motive to kill Gillian. The pain and disappointment of what she must have seen as Keith's further betrayal must surely have been more than she could bear. And although Gillian might have interfered for Alison's own good, Alison would hardly have seen it like that. Rose didn't see it like that either. At the very least Alison had been used and psychologically abused by her husband and his lover. They must have chipped away at her self esteem over a long period. It was no wonder she was emotionally damaged.

Rose didn't want to leave her. She also felt, illogically, that the conversation had moved away from what was really bothering Alison, but Rose wasn't sure if the danger she sensed was in the room, or if she should barricade herself in with Alison to protect her from someone outside it.

'I'll stay with you until your husband gets back,' she said, firmly, remembering once again Sergio telling her not to be alone with any of them and just as quickly suppressing the memory.

'No,' Alison said. She shrank back. 'I shouldn't have told you. He'll be . . . angry. He says I have to forget those things.'

'What other things do you have to forget?' Rose persisted.

'Nothing.' Alison stared at the shuttered window. 'Nothing,' she repeated.

'Alison, please tell me. I want to help you.'

'No one can help me,' Her voice was so low that Rose could hardly hear her.

She took Alison's hands. They were cold despite the stuffiness of the room. 'Who are you afraid of? Is it your husband?'

After a long drawn out silence Alison finally said, 'I don't know. I don't know anything any more.' She stared at the window again, as though mesmerized by the thin bands of light fragmented by the slats of the shutters. Then she shook her head slightly as though emerging from a trance.

'I hate to see you so upset,' Rose said.

'I'm not any more . . . upset than I. . . .' She shook her head, again. 'That is, I'm used to my situation, you see. I've had years to get used to it.' She gave a twisted smile. 'You know Gillian used to talk to me about her other men friends. I think she thought she'd put me off the scent like that. She always had someone in tow. She'd find out secrets . . . and then somehow they couldn't get away from her. I used to wonder if. . . .' Her voice trailed off.

This certainly confirmed Sergio's theory about Gillian being a blackmailer. He'd been thinking of Tom Graham but Gillian could have had some hold over Keith. Was that what Alison was trying to say, or rather not to say? Was she protecting Keith, laying a false trail? Alison's phrase, 'tip me over the edge' had given her another chill of fear.

Something must have triggered the killings. Or at least the killing of Gillian. Had some chance remark or action panicked the murderer? Like Sergio, Rose couldn't see any connection with Pino, unless he'd seen something to incriminate one of the people in the villa. But what could he have seen in advance of Gillian's murder? That was the most puzzling thing.

'What kind of secrets?' she asked urgently.

It must have been one question too many, or perhaps one that touched a raw nerve because Alison suddenly sat up straight and said, 'You've been very kind, but I mustn't take up any more of your time. Really.' Her voice was still strained but for the first time there was some spirit in it. She pushed the tray slightly towards Rose, as though redefining their roles and, although she didn't shout 'Go! Get out!' her body language was saying exactly that. Her face, too, had settled into an expression which hinted at a remnant of determined will, something Rose hadn't thought she possessed.

'Will you promise me you'll ring if . . . if there's anything you need? Anything at all,' she said, in a final effort to get through the barrier.

'Yes. Yes, of course I will. I'm better now, really.' Alison took a deep breath. Of relief? She even managed a faint smile. 'And Keith will be back soon.'

'Are you sure?'

'Quite sure,' Alison said. 'And thank you again for the tea. It was very nice.' She gave another unmistakably dismissive look and Rose had no choice but to pick up the tray and leave. She stood in the corridor for a moment and then heard the key turn in the lock behind her once again.

She wondered where Sergio's man was. Alison may or may not have killed Gillian but, if not, she was showing all the signs of being a stubborn but terrified witness. All that talk about dreams. Had she seen something when she was wandering around the house in the dark? Of course, Alison might simply be suffering from guilt and remorse. She didn't seem like a murderer but she had no shortage of hard feelings about Gillian. And murderers came in all shapes and sizes, according to Sergio.

Rose went to the telephone in the hall and tried to call the *carabinieri* station, but was told Sergio was unavailable. Would she like to leave a message? But there didn't seem to be anything definite she could say.

'I'll ring again later,' she said, then went into the kitchen and partly filled a bucket with water.

'What are you doing?' Maria-Grazia asked.

'I'm going to wash the floor in the corridor,' Rose said.

'But I did it already this morning.'

'Then it will be the cleanest floor in Tuscany,' Rose said, going to collect a mop.

Maria-Grazia tapped her head significantly. '*É una casa pazza,*' she said.

'The funeral is over,' the colonel said. He opened his pigskin briefcase and took out a bundle of passports with a criss-crossed rubber band around them. He threw them on to the table.

Sergio eyed them. 'The forty-eight hours are not up yet.'

'They will be by the end of the day,' his superior said. 'Do you have something for me? Did your men find anything at the villa?'

'Nothing.'

'And now I gather you're searching the whole port?' the colonel said sarcastically. 'Turning up the paving stones, no doubt?'

'I'm looking for a connection,' Sergio said, stubbornly.

'Keep on looking, by all means.'

'Of course I'll keep on looking, but if the villa party leaves we haven't a pig's chance in hell of finding the killer.'

The colonel looked annoyed. 'I told you that this wasn't an English detective story. This is reality. And the reality is that the plug has been pulled.' He paused and added in a slightly friendlier voice, 'It will reflect on me too, Captain.'

It was an admission and, as such, Sergio acknowledged it.

'I suggest you concentrate on the smuggling angle. After all, that was what you were brought in to do at the beginning. Get your two Englishmen. And if not. . . .' His voice trailed off, but the threat was there.

'I intend to,' Sergio said.

The colonel raised his eyebrows. 'But not for the murders, surely? You said they were in the clear.'

Sergio made a non-committal sound.

TUSCAN SHADOWS

'If you have some further evidence?'

Evidence was the one thing Sergio didn't have. He shook his head.

'It seems to me that Langdon Smythe and Kinaid had enough on their plates worrying about Nardi's little problems,' the colonel said, 'and if they were under police surveillance at the time of death, then, well.....' He spread his hands, expressively. 'You've had your chance to talk to Nardi, after all.' He refastened his briefcase and stood up.

'I shall hear from you tonight, then?'

'Yes,' Sergio said, heavily.

The door closed with a sharp click and Sergio went to the window and watched him get into his car. The old man was an expert in sitting on the fence and, had the murderer been found, the colonel would have taken most of the credit for a case successfully solved. *É la vita*, Sergio thought grimly and then he smiled as the memory of the previous evening flooded his mind, bringing with it a flush of arousal.

There were problems there too, of course, but he wasn't going to let her go. He tried to empty his mind of murder and corruption and think about his own life instead. But that was also a mess of loose ends. He'd done nothing about a divorce, nothing about building a house. He was living, if you could call it that, in a *casetta* on a piece of land he'd bought two years ago. Two rooms and a primitive bathroom. He would have to put it in some sort of order before he could even . . . perhaps some plants would make the place more lived in . . . he would ask Silvana's advice. She would laugh and give him a searching look, but he had sensed her approval of Rose.

There was a knock at the door and Massimo Pascucci came in with a slip of paper.

'Yes?'

'We've got a possible identification sir, down in the port.'

Sergio jumped up. 'We have?' The picture shifted suddenly in his mind. Who was the one person who had definitely been in Italy a day or two before his arrival at the villa? Who but the outsider, Tom Graham? Was his job just a cover for other activities after all? If Graham was some kind of government agent it would make sense of the political pressure, too. More sense than the Halliwell connection. Graham wouldn't have confided in Gillian, of course,

264   *Maureen Donegan*

but she could have found out and become a threat. They'd been in and out of each other's rooms all the time and she was inquisitive, dangerously so.

'Who've they identified?' he demanded.

Pascucci shook his head. 'Don't know, sir.'

'But where exactly?'

'A *pensione* in Via Vecchia Porta.'

The colonel's car was disappearing down the road. Well, too bad. Let him bite his nails and deflect phone calls from Rome for a bit longer.

'Let's go, then. Anything else?'

'Signorina Childs rang.'

Sergio hesitated. 'What did she say?'

'That she'd ring again.'

'All right. I'll try to get her from the car.' He picked up the passports. 'Let's see if anyone recognizes one of these photos.'

From the kitchen window Rose glimpsed Sergio's man cross the courtyard and head for the wooded part of the garden. She wondered if she should run after him, but she still had nothing concrete to tell him. It would be better to stick to her original plan and keep an eye on Alison and so she picked up the bucket and went down to the bedroom corridor.

All the doors were closed but there was the sound of a bath being run and then the rattle of shutters opening. Rose walked to the far end of the corridor pushing the wet mop in front of her, turned and made the return trip very slowly.

After a short time Dom came out of his room, nodded good morning and went upstairs. She could hear voices and doors opening and realized that some of the guests would leave their rooms via the terrace. How stupid not to have thought of that. The house was singularly unfitted for a solitary watcher. There were too many doors, too many levels. Nor was it possible for Sergio's man to adequately patrol the garden. Its size and the layout of winding paths and trees and fruit bushes screened many areas, not only from the house but also from each other.

She heard footsteps overhead and then Maria-Grazia's voice.

'Rose, are you still there?'

'Coming.' She gave a last look at Alison's door then picked up her cleaning equipment and went back to the kitchen.

'Sergio Tavazzi rang,' Maria-Grazia said.

'Oh, I didn't hear the phone! What did he say?'

'That he'd be coming up here later. That was all.'

'Didn't he say where he was?' Rose demanded.

Maria-Grazia didn't meet her eyes. 'I tried to. . . .' She pushed a scrap of paper across the table. On it four badly formed numbers were written. 'I didn't manage to . . . to hear him, properly.' She bit her lip. 'He said something about a car.'

'Never mind,' Rose said, quickly. 'If he's coming here, that's all right.' She patted Maria-Grazia's hand.

The older woman smiled, shamefacedly. '*Certo*, he will come here. He said so.'

They began to prepare the breakfasts. Dom, Peter and Johnny were already on the terrace and Elizabeth, Mike and Susie joined them soon afterwards. Rose heard Dom ask where the others were.

'Tennis,' Mike said, briefly.

'A threesome?'

'Of course not,' Susie snapped. 'Alison will still be in bed.' But there was no apparent reaction around the table to this. Rose went back to the kitchen and met Giulio coming in with the shopping.

'You're late,' Maria-Grazia told him. She started to put the food in the fridge. 'And you haven't cleaned the pool either. You'd better do it now.'

'I can't. I had a puncture,' Giulio said. He slumped into a chair and poured himself a cup of coffee. 'I have to go and collect the tyre. Anyway I cleaned the pool last night.'

'It's better to do it in the morning,' Maria-Grazia said, in an exasperated voice.

'It will be all right,' he said, defensively. 'A few leaves, that's all.'

Maria-Grazia straightened up. 'And you forgot the *parmigiano* and the *mozzarella*.'

'I'll get it when I go for the tyre,' he said.

'No, I will go with you,' Maria-Grazia said. 'You can drop me at the market. Otherwise you'll spend the whole day gossiping in the town.'

'I will not,' he said. 'I never have time to see my friends. It's, Giulio, clean this, Giulio, do that.'

'We are not on holiday, like them,' Maria-Grazia said, sharply. 'But I, too, would like to escape this place for an hour. You will be all right, Rose?'

'Yes, of course,' Rose said. Keith would be back soon, and she did not think that Alison would let him stray far from her side. Unless it was really Keith she was afraid of.

Maria-Grazia took off her apron. '*Allora?*' she said to Giulio.

He put down his cup wearily. 'I'm ready.'

As they drove off, Rose saw Tom walking up the drive alone and, a few moments later, he appeared on the terrace. She went out to ask if he wanted coffee.

'Please,' he said.

'And Mr Drinkwater?'

'He'll be back later. He wanted to do some shopping or something. I walked up.'

'Oh, I see.' Rose felt a further flicker of anxiety. Peter and Johnny had disappeared and Elizabeth was finishing her coffee. She looked up at the word shopping. 'I'd like to have one last look in that boutique beside the Bar Azzuro. Would you mind ringing for a taxi, Rose?'

'Can I come too?' Dom asked eagerly, but Elizabeth didn't seem to hear him.

Alison got up and dressed slowly. Her feeling of panic had subsided somewhat and had been replaced by anger. For one dangerous moment she had been tempted to confide in Rose. She had seemed genuinely sympathetic, she might even have understood, but she was too friendly with the *cara-binieri* captain. Perhaps she was even helping him. I'm surrounded by enemies, Alison thought, enemies who smiled; some even put their arms around her and made 'there there' noises. Even Keith, no especially Keith, did that. She felt a chill around her heart when she thought of him.

Now she could separate the reality from the nightmares and see the picture quite clearly. And then she thought that Keith would be back soon.

Would he have been able to get away from Tom? She sat down, exhausted and frightened. She re-ran her conversation with Keith that morning. She hadn't said anything . . . anything she shouldn't have said, had she?

Rose didn't know whether Dom had joined the shopping expedition or not because she hadn't seen the taxi go, but she had heard Susie call out to Elizabeth to wait for her so perhaps all three had gone to the port.

The house was very quiet. She went to clear the table on the terrace and leaned out over the parapet but there was no sign of Tom or Mike in the part of the garden that she could see. Perhaps they had gone for a walk, although it seemed unlikely. After tennis and his walk up from the town Tom had probably had enough exercise. It was even hotter than the day before. The heat was palpable and the air heavy with the threat of a storm.

It seemed strange, and rather eerie, without Maria-Grazia in the kitchen. Rose put down her tray and watched the courtyard hopefully for Sergio's car. There was a soft sound behind her and a hand touched her shoulder. She whirled around and found herself looking at Alison's troubled face.

'He hasn't come back,' she said.

'No.' Rose's thoughts were still on Sergio then she realized that, of course, Alison was talking about Keith.

'Tom Graham just came in and he said your husband wouldn't be long.'

'He said that? He's here?' Alison's eyes were glittering.

Rose nodded.

'And everyone else has gone, haven't they?'

'Not quite everyone,' Rose said, soothingly.

'There was something Keith had to do,' Alison said, in a faraway voice, 'but I didn't think it would take him so long.' She stared at Rose as though about to say something else, then put up her hand and lifted her heavy, greying hair from her neck. 'It's so hot,' she complained.

'Would you like some cold lemonade? On the terrace, perhaps?' That way she could continue to keep an eye on her.

'Yes. Yes, please.' Alison drifted towards the door. 'I would like that very much.'

But when Rose went out with a glass and jug on a tray she was gone.

The Pensione Perla was located over a sports shop in a narrow street not far from the open market. Sergio's men had checked all the hotel and guest house registers for the crucial period, beginning with the day of Gillian's car accident. It had involved a lot of leg work, but the number of foreigners in the area was not great. It was not on the tour circuit and most of the annual visitors were Italians.

A heavy woman, with an arrangement of excess flesh which would have delighted Fellini, leaned over the reception desk and fingered the passport Sergio had given her.

'Yes, that is the one,' she said, putting a plump finger on to the photograph. She produced the register and pointed to the corresponding entry. 'You see, my records are absolutely precise.'

'Very commendable,' Sergio said. 'And can you tell me how this particular guest passed the time?'

The woman shrugged her massive shoulders.

'Captain, we only provide breakfast, for the rest of the day I do not enquire, only if I am asked for advice or help.'

'And did this person ask for anything?'

'I do not think so.' She knitted her dark eyebrows. 'People come and go and it is hard to remember.'

'Try,' Sergio urged.

'If there was anything . . . it was perhaps because I thought, to myself, Perla, this is not an ordinary tourist. It was more what was missing, you understand, the beach things, the camera. Of course the English like to walk in the heat. Me, I stay behind the shutters. There is much work, Captain, and I have only an imbecile of a nephew.' She seemed set to embark on her life story. Sergio cut her short.

'What made you think of walking?'

She hesitated for a moment and then her eyes gleamed triumphantly in their folds of fat. 'There was a map, that was it, a map.'

It wasn't much, Sergio thought, as he strode quickly back to the car. Suspicious behaviour, circumstantial evidence, but with just a little

TUSCAN SHADOWS 269

more. . . . He glanced at his watch. The day which had started lethargically for him, in the pleasant aftermath of sex, but also with the inordinately heavy pressure of his chief's ultimatum, was accelerating far too rapidly towards the evening's deadline.

He had a vision of the killer leaving with a bag hastily packed the moment he announced that the people at the villa could go. And although he would then be free to pursue the smuggling angle the prospect of the murder enquiry being dropped because of political pressure both appalled and depressed him.

He wondered, not for the first time, why bother tracking down a criminal if the powers-that-be virtually turned a blind eye to the situation? And yet, and yet, things were changing. The prisons were full, no doubt about that. Corruption on a grand scale was no longer the norm, but money and the Old Boy network, in whatever country, would always influence events.

'But no point in philosophizing, either,' he said out loud.

'Sir?'

'Villa Antonia,' Sergio said, sharply, 'with your foot down.'

'And the siren?' Massimo Pascuccio asked hopefully.

'No siren. *Hai capito?*' Sergio closed the car door with a bang.

'I just thought. . . .' Massimo coughed into the silence. 'Villa Antonia, right.'

Alison made her way down to the pool by one of the shaded paths that skirted the cultivated areas. It was cooler there than on the open stone steps. But the real reason for her choice was that she didn't want to be seen because she had glimpsed the person she wanted to talk to.

Rose let her eyes range over the hot sleepy land below her, but could see no one. She put down the tray and ran down the steps to the bedroom terrace, but there was no sign of Alison there either and her door was closed. Rose knocked but there was no reply and the room looked empty when she pressed her face against the glass of the door.

She hurried back to the terrace and hung over the parapet. She thought she saw someone going into one of the changing rooms, someone wearing blue. What was Alison wearing? A dress? No, it was a flowered skirt and a black T-shirt. Mike was wearing a blue shirt at breakfast, wasn't he? And Tom Graham had something blue, too. She couldn't remember what the two yachtsmen were wearing. She wondered if they were still around. In any case what she could see now could just be a towel. Was Alison going for a swim to cool off after the stuffiness of her room?

Another figure appeared at the far side of the vegetable garden and made its way towards the pool. Rose recognized Alison from her walk and the way she put up her hand to push back her hair. Rose picked up her tray and headed for the stone steps.

The person Alison had glimpsed a short while ago was now sitting, legs stretched out, on a bench inside the retaining wall at the far end of the pool.

'I thought you'd gone shopping,' Alison said.

Susie half smiled. 'I changed my mind. Coming for a swim?'

'Not yet. I want to talk.'

'Are you all right?' Susie gave her a sharp look.

'Yes, I think I am now.' Alison walked over slowly and sat down beside her. 'I finally went back to sleep after Keith left and I had another dream.'

'Really?' Susie said. She widened her eyes as though anxious to hear every last detail of Alison's morning.

'You sounded like Gillian when you said that.'

'Bitchy, you mean? Well, if you're around someone long enough, they say you get like them.'

'I wonder.'

'People like Gillian get away with things,' Susie said. 'Too many things. Look at you and Keith.'

'I don't want to talk about Keith.'

'Then what do you want to talk about?'

'I don't sleep,' Alison said, deliberately. 'At least not without pills, lots of pills.'

'I know.'

'But I've been trying to give them up. And that means I'm often awake when everyone else is asleep.' A hornet buzzed around her head and she swatted it away nervously. 'Horrible things. They sting, don't they?'

'I believe so.' Susie was sitting quietly, her hands folded in her lap. 'You shouldn't antagonize it. You should leave dangerous things alone, Alison.'

There was a silence, then Alison said, 'Everyone thinks I'm half dotty with pills. But I'm not, and I don't want to leave things alone. Not any more.' She paused again. 'I walk around at night sometimes.'

'Do you?'

'At first I thought it was one of the dreams. I haven't really told you about them, have I?'

'Not in so many words, no.'

'Someone is trying to kill me, strangle me, smother me.' She half laughed. 'Keith says it's the heat.'

'It probably is,' Susie said, briskly.

'And when I saw you with something glinting in your hand I thought it was a gun and that it was another dream.'

'So you did see me,' Susie said. She didn't sound particularly surprised. 'I wasn't sure.'

'You were going into Gillian's room the night she died.'

'How can you remember which night it was when you've said yourself how muddled you are? Dreaming about murder, wandering around in the dark. Maybe you saw me going to say goodnight to Gillian another night.'

'Like a good daughter?'

Susie's face changed. 'All right. She'd annoyed me. More than annoyed me. I went to tell her to lay off.'

'With a syringe?'

Rose could see the two women sitting together. They appeared to be deep in conversation. She called Alison's name but the sound didn't carry. She was hampered by the tray and tempted to leave it behind but it was the best excuse she could think of to actually follow them down to the pool. She steadied the jug of lemonade, glanced around hoping to see the uniformed *carabiniere* and hurried on.

'I know she was difficult,' Alison said, 'but I still don't understand why you should want. . . .'

'She wasn't difficult,' Susie said, in a low, intense voice, 'she was evil. She hurt people. And . . . she killed Daddy.'

'No, Susie.'

'She sent me away to school, away from him. I lost my mother and then my father. She taunted him, drove him crazy. She used to tell him about her men friends. She did it the night he had the accident. Told him how they fancied her. Stupid bitch. She threw herself at them, didn't she? But she only told him things when it suited her. Like how she'd stopped me from having my baby, stopped you and Keith from adopting it.'

'Keith didn't want . . .' Alison said, falteringly.

'And who made him not want it?' Susie screamed. She grabbed Alison and her fingers dug into tender sunburned flesh. 'And then she tried to take Mike away from me. He was the only good thing that happened in my life but she had to tell him about my abortion and . . . breakdown. She told him I was unstable and he started to pity me instead of . . . and then I saw him in the garden one day. He was kissing her and then afterwards they went into the house. They didn't know I was there. . . .'

Alison tried to stand up, but Susie was still holding her. She half got to her feet but she felt herself being pushed to the edge of the retaining wall. Over Susie's shoulder, she saw a figure, not Maria-Grazia, it was too tall: it must be Rose. She was a long way above them, negotiating the steps with a tray in her hand. The wall scraped the small of her back and she began to struggle.

'You put the syringe in our room,' Alison gasped.

'I shouldn't have done that but they were suspicious of me you see,' Susie said, confidingly. 'I knew Keith would tell the police and they'd think you did it.'

But even if Keith believed she was guilty, he hadn't told the police. He tried to protect me, Alison thought, and she forgot her terror for a moment as a feeling of warmth flooded through her.

Susie must have sensed this because her expression changed. 'You could have stood up to her,' she screamed. Specks of spittle prayed from her mouth. 'You could have helped me.'

The figure on the steps put down the tray and began to run.

TUSCAN SHADOWS

273

'But I did, I did! Look, I won't say anything, Susie. I won't ever tell about that night.'

'You should have done something to her, too, feeble-minded cow! We could have done it together.'

Alison had a frightening glimpse of the bottom of the ravine. Susie was half straddling her and now she was hanging part way over the wall. But the edges of the puzzle had moved closer together. 'Pino,' she gasped. 'You were here with him.'

Susie gave a mad kind of laugh. 'Stupid man. He wanted more money. I hit him. It was easy.'

Keep her talking, Alison thought, but she knew Susie was much stronger physically. She tried to move her feet to lock one of them around the girl's ankle, but Susie retaliated by pushing her even further back. Her back hurt excruciatingly. Her blouse had ridden up and the rough stone of wall was cutting her skin. 'Why?' she managed to say. 'Why Pino?'

'He saw me, too. Like you. But not at night. He saw me fixing the car. I came back from Denmark early. I knew I'd find a way. The car would have been perfect, but it didn't quite work. So I had to try something else.' Susie's face was inches from her own, distorted, like a movie screen seen too close. Alison could no longer focus on the steps. She closed her eyes for a moment, then said, 'There's someone coming.'

'Don't be silly,' Susie said, her voice suddenly quite normal again. 'There's no one there and you're not going to mess it up for me now. I've removed the evil you see. Removed it forever. Aren't you happy she's dead, Alison?'

'Susie. . . .'

'They'll think you did it and then tried to kill me. I'll tell them I saw you go to her room, poor crazy Alison.'

Susie's hands let go her arms suddenly and went to her throat. Alison fought for breath as the fingers tightened, blocking the air. Susie was right, they would all believe she had done it, poor crazy Alison whose husband was having an affair. The memories were like a long tangled rope twisting backwards through a red mist of humiliation. Susie's face blurred. Her mouth was open, a red shouting maw, but Alison could no longer hear her. It was like the time under water, off Johnny's boat. It was easy, so very easy to give in, to let her body go limp, to let everything go. But something had made her fight back that day, what was it? Was it not allowing Gillian to win? But Gillian was dead. Gillian couldn't hurt her any more . . . couldn't hurt her any more. . . .

She slumped forward, Susie's hands still locked around her throat. With her last remaining strength she forced Susie's feet further apart. They both slipped and, in the struggle to regain her balance, Susie's hands relaxed their grip. Alison could hear someone shouting, but Susie seemed impervious to anything but their struggle. Her hands went down to Alison's shoulders and she gave her a tremendous push.

'Rose!' Alison screamed, as air rushed into her bruised throat. Only then did Susie look around. Alison twisted her foot away, slid sideways, still half under Susie's weight and almost took them both over the edge.

Another voice was added to the shouting and a uniformed figure was running towards them from the path she had taken around the terraces. Susie saw him too and her face registered a mixture of shock and fear. She released her grip on Alison who rolled away, bruising herself badly on the stone bench. Then someone leapt over Alison and she heard a long drawn-out scream.

The *carabiniere* reached Alison before Rose did. He said something to her in Italian, then took out his walkie-talkie, spoke even more rapidly into that, then made off down the steep path which led into the ravine.

She felt Rose's arms go around her and draw her away from the edge. She was shaking uncontrollably. 'She killed them,' she said, 'she told me . . . she killed them. And the worst thing, she tried to make them think it was me. Susie . . . my little Susie.'

'Hush,' Rose said, 'it's over. Come back up to the house with me.'

'Is she . . . dead?'

'I don't know.'

They went, infinitely slowly, up the stone steps, stopping every now and then for Alison to get her breath. 'I hope Keith is back,' she whispered.

CHAPTER 20

Susie wasn't dead. She was very seriously injured but still conscious as she was brought up on a stretcher to a waiting ambulance. Sergio arrived shortly after Rose and Alison reached the house and took over with brisk efficiency. But first he had clasped Rose's trembling hands and held them as if he would never let them go.

'It was very close. It could have been you.'

'It wasn't me,' she said, faintly.

She watched as he got into the ambulance. Mike had insisted on accompanying them and, since there had been no formal arrest, nor was one likely to be made, Sergio had silently concurred. It was, the police surgeon had told him, merely a matter of hours.

Rose went slowly into the house to help Maria-Grazia minister to Alison and to face the confusion and the questions.

'Susie,' Mike said urgently. She had been given something to kill the pain and her eyes were already glazing over.

Sergio sat on the opposite side of the ambulance. 'She'll be unconscious in a few minutes.' He had already told them quietly that the doctor had diagnosed multiple fractures and internal bleeding.

'Susie?' Mike said again.

She moved her head slightly in his direction. 'She . . . took you away from me,' she whispered.

'No,' he said. Her hand felt cold and he massaged it gently. He was find-

275

276   *Maureen Donegan*

ing it difficult to maintain a comforting expression. Alison had told him, in a very disjointed fashion, something of what had taken place between them and he was stricken not only by his memory of that day in Gillian's house and his guilty part in it, but also by the accusation that he had come to pity Susie. Because he knew it was true: he'd wanted out for a long time.

He turned his shoulders away from Sergio's impassive gaze and forced himself to smile at the figure on the stretcher. 'I love you,' he said and felt Susie's hand move in his.

'Safe enough saying that now,' she said, and her mouth also twitched into the semblance of a smile. 'I was clever, wasn't I?'

He nodded, numbly.

'I took the money to pay Pino, I didn't mean to hurt him but then he said he wanted more. He grabbed hold of me . . . pushed me down. His horrible face . . . horrible smell . . . threatening me. There was a piece of wood . . . hit him . . . hit him. . . .' There was a long silence and finally she said faintly, 'Then I didn't need . . . put it down the side of the chair.'

'Shsh.' He wanted desperately to stop the slow trickle of words. There was pain in every part of his body as though he too had fallen into a stony ravine. Gillian's smile swam into his mind. Her face was flushed and provocative. He closed his eyes but the image remained.

When Susie's mood had changed so dramatically after Gillian's death he had suppressed the tingling feeling of suspicion, had concentrated only on his relief that Susie had seemed to revert to the relaxed girl he'd first met two years before.

Nothing, he thought with anguish, had ever been what it seemed at the Tenbys'. The layers of pretence had lifted slowly revealing a great many things that he had preferred not to confront. And what Alison had said was true: he had come to pity Susie, but had lacked the courage to extricate himself. And at the centre of his dilemma had been the enigmatic attraction of Gillian. It was she, and not his original vision of a happy family that had kept him in the Tenbys' orbit. He realized with awful clarity that, had he known what they were all really like, he would still have stayed. Because of Gillian.

Susie made a small murmuring sound and he said, 'I love you,' once again. It came out automatically, as a mother might say it to a child, but this time there was no answering response from the limp hand that lay in his.

A hand fell on his shoulder. 'She's not suffering now,' Sergio said.

Mike stared down at the pale bruised face. A thin line of blood from her nose was drying on her skin. 'She never grew up,' he said, and wondered if he'd ever done so himself.

'She'd done nursing,' Rose said, suddenly. 'I remember something Gillian said about her doing night duty.'

'Yes. Mike Harding told me. It seems she knew enough about injecting air, but not enough to know that it would show up in an autopsy,' Sergio said. 'She planned it carefully in one way. At the same time she left an awful lot to chance.'

Rose shivered. 'She must have been incredibly unhappy.'

'Who was it who said, "All happy families resemble each other but each unhappy family is unhappy in its own way"?'

She shook her head. 'I can't remember.'

'Rose, don't be so sad. I was trying to impress you *modestamente*, with my knowledge of English literature. Russian, I should say.'

She managed a laugh. They were sitting in a restaurant beside the marina. Together in public, Rose realized.

'Not all unhappiness leads to murder, *cara*, one has to remember that and be thankful.'

'I know.' She paused. 'I suppose Pino was blackmailing her? It must have terrified the life out of her.'

'Yes. He must have seen her sneaking around the grounds a couple of days before she was supposed to be there.'

'Could he have seen her tinkering with the car?'

'He may have done. Or he could just have put two and two together. He was pretty *furbo*.'

'Too smart for his own good?'

'Exactly. I imagine he confronted her after she arrived the second time at the villa. He knew enough English, I imagine, from working for Langdon Smythe.'

'Yes, of course. And he'd have realized Susie was allegedly in Denmark just by sitting in the kitchen and listening to Maria-Grazia and Giulio gossiping. But she took incredible risks. Anyone could have seen her.'

'It was Pino's bad luck that he was the one,' Sergio said. 'I don't think she intended to kill him, but he would have been a permanent threat and she did intend to kill Gillian. Pino just got in the way. Killers are invariably arrogant. Some even imagine they are invisible. They're also very single-minded.'

'But was she . . . competent?'

'In her right mind, you mean? I'd say she'd have been able to stand trial, if it had come to that.'

'It was terrible that she'd been forced to have an abortion,' Rose said slowly. 'But letting Alison adopt her baby may not have been such a good idea, even if it was possible. Gillian was probably right about that. Don't adoptive parents have to be quite unknown to the mother?'

'I imagine so. But I doubt if either Susie or Alison were thinking straight then.'

'Susie also watched her stepmother take her lover.'

He reached for her hand across the table. 'I told you I had a horrible job, Rose.'

'Yes, you did.' She returned the pressure of his fingers. 'And none of this had anything to do with stolen artefacts?'

'Not directly. The Villa Antonia was a side issue, if you like, but I have a man watching the boat. In fact, we can see it from here.'

He took out his sesterce, thin and smooth after two millennia of wear, tossed it in the air, then palmed it.

She looked across the marina and saw Johnny Langdon Smythe sitting in the cockpit of *L'Alba.* smoking. 'Is that why you picked this restaurant?' she asked, grinning.

'Of course. Don't you know a policeman is never really off duty?'

'Never ever?'

'Well, occasionally in very special and private circumstances.' His eyes twinkled with amusement. He also appeared to have lost interest in his *fritto misto.*

TUSCAN SHADOWS   279

'Does that mean we could leave your man to look after things?'

'Right now?'

'Mmm?'

'I think it could be arranged.' He put the coin into his pocket, pushed his plate to one side and signalled for the bill.

The next day a chauffeur-driven car came to collect Elizabeth.

'Daddy wanted to come for me himself,' she told Johnny, 'but I managed to stop him.'

He regarded her warily. 'You can be very strong-minded.'

'About some things,' she said, 'and I'm learning about others.'

Dom was in the doorway. She hesitated then went over and shook his hand. 'I'll write,' she said. She knew that she would not.

She had been going to shake hands with Johnny, too, but on an impulse put her arms around him and kissed him on the cheek. 'I'll write to you too,' she said.

She was aware of Peter standing beside him, his eyes moving from her to Johnny. She hoped she would be strong enough to take this image away and remember it. She turned once as the car picked up speed down the avenue and saw Peter slide his arm through that of the older man. Behind them Dom was shading his eyes against the white glare of the morning and then the car turned a corner and they, and the villa, were out of sight.

Only Mike, Dom and Keith attended Susie's funeral. They returned with drawn faces, Mike and Dom to sit on the terrace with a bottle of wine, and Keith to closet himself in his room with Alison.

Johnny Langdon Smythe and Peter Kinaid had said goodbye and gone down to their boat but for some reason Tom wasn't leaving until the next day. A hitch about flights, he'd said. Over supper, the conversation dwelled exclusively on the various alternate routes the Drinkwaters could take to the channel ferry and whether Mike and Dom would travel back in the car or not. After they had eaten, Mike and Dom went for a walk, but Rose found Alison, Keith and Tom still sitting together when she went out to clear the last of the glasses. The air was by then heavy with silence.

280   *Maureen Donegan*

'It's a beautiful night,' Tom said suddenly. 'Wonderful moon.'

Alison raised her head and gave him a puzzled look.

'It's a lovely place after all,' Tom went on, easily. 'My little girls would have loved it.'

'I didn't know you had children,' Alison said.

'Thought I'd told you. They're eight and ten. I know I talked to Gillian about them.'

Alison looked at Keith and this time they both turned startled faces towards him. It was the first time Rose had seen them do anything so completely in harmony.

'I mean they'd have liked it in spite of . . . you know,' Tom ended lamely.

Keith eased himself out of the swing and went to look over the terrace. Lights twinkled here and there on the dark plain below. 'I don't think I ever want to set foot in Italy again,' he said.

Sergio was on his way to the villa to meet Rose after a dreary day of writing reports when his radio blared. *L'Alba* had slipped away with only their paid hand on board, he was told, and the two Englishmen were walking away from the marina past the bars and restaurants, each carrying a nylon holdall. He listened for a moment, braked and did a rapid three point turn as he issued instructions into the phone. He needed back-up and he wanted it *subito*. He also needed to know where the boat was heading. His colonel hadn't exactly congratulated him on solving the murders, but at least he might now be disposed to ask for the assistance of the *Guardia di Finanza* who patrolled the coastal waters.

The railway, he thought, trying to remember if there was a late fast train to the north. They might have decided to leave the country, although it seemed unlikely. Was it worth making a slight detour down the road to Capulana Scala? He screeched round the next right turn and cars scattered in his headlights. *Cazzo*, the *commune* had changed the one-way streets since yesterday. He made another violent right turn as Massimo Pascucci's voice crackled through again.

'Lavarini was the one on duty and he's just told us the *inglesi* have picked up a van in Via delle Chiese, just off the market square. They didn't have a key, the door was open so it must have been inside, or else they wired it. But it didn't look like that, Lavarini said.'

Why could Massimo never come to the point. '*Cristo*, just tell me which direction.'

'Inland, not the *autostrada*, but I was telling you, Captain, they were delayed by the key business so we had time to get a car to him.' Immediately afterwards another message came to say Lavarini was following the van and there was back-up on the way. 'Keep a safe distance,' Sergio said, 'I'll be behind you as soon as I can.'

He did another right turn and then a left but it took him a little while to get out of the maze of narrow streets. When he finally reached the old road north he put his foot down and felt his back pressing against his seat as the car leapt forward. He didn't remember Rose until he had caught up with the other *carabinieri* car and he could see the van a good way in front of it. He settled into a more leisurely pace, picked up his phone and punched in the number of the Villa Antonia but it was engaged.

Franco Nardi was sitting in the cockpit of his boat smoking a cigar when he saw *L'Alba* leaving. Francesca put her head up through the hatch as she heard him cursing. 'What is it, *Papi?*'

'Something that wasn't supposed to happen,' he said angrily. Bruno, *L'Alba*'s new hand, shouldn't have let the Englishmen out of his sight. He thought rapidly. The phones weren't safe; he couldn't move himself, or even send a man, but Francesca was keeping her sister's little boy, Stefano, company while his parents went to meet some friends. He had always believed that family life was sacred and normally avoided involving any of them in his business but he had to know what Langdon Smythe was up to. 'Is Stefano still awake?' he asked.

The *carabiniere* who was watching also understood that men of Nardi's persuasion kept their family well away from their less savoury activities and so he took little notice of the blonde young woman with the child who left the yacht. He had seen them coming and going every day after all and it

282   *Maureen Donegan*

wasn't unusual to see a small Italian child out late on such a warm evening. Sure enough when they came back a short time afterwards each was licking an ice cream.

'The sister of the *signora* will come next week,' Maria-Grazia said, 'but that will not be so much work. And then the season will be over.'

'And you can relax,' Rose said, smiling.

'Until next year,' Maria-Grazia said, gloomily. 'I said to Giulio I will not do another summer but he likes it here.'

'And so do you, really, Maria-Grazia.'

'*Beh*, it is better than the black clothes of Sicily, I suppose.'

Sergio and Carabiniere Lavarini were crouched in a hollow in a hill over-looking a neglected farmhouse. The small dark van was parked beside some outbuildings and a man stood next to it. A match flared and Sergio recog-nized Peter Kinaid. The tall figure of Johnny Langdon Smythe joined him and they put two bags into the van, then Langdon Smythe went back inside and came out with another bulky object. A third man padlocked the door of the barn as the two Englishmen finished loading up. The engine coughed into life and the van moved off with the sidelights on, lurching over the rough track which led back to the road.

Sergio spoke quietly into his radio. 'Let them go, but keep them in sight.' It would be easy to arrest them now but he wanted Nardi. He scrambled to his feet and nudged Lavarini to follow him. Their cars were in a lane higher up the hill but the back-up would pick up the *inglesi* when they reached the highway.

The telephone rang and Maria-Grazi went to answer it. '*Pronto?*' She listened for a moment, then handed it to Rose.

Arthur's voice poured out an excited story of his inability to get a flight. 'It's high season,' he said, 'I'm on the waiting list, but they didn't hold out much hope, not for another week.'

'I told you there was no need to come,' Rose said. 'It was very kind of you to think of it, but everything is all right now. The murderer has been found.'

'Thank God.' She could hear relief, and then hope in his voice. 'Then you're coming home?'

'Not yet,' she said. 'I . . . have a three-month ticket so there's no rush.'

She held the receiver away from her ear as he told her that she had been very lucky to escape serious danger and surely now was the time to call a halt to these stupid jobs and lead some kind of normal life.

'I have to go now, Arthur,' she said. 'Sorry.' This time she didn't add that she would write to him.

'I'm going to have a shower, Maria-Grazia,' she said. 'When Sergio comes tell him I won't be long.'

But Sergio didn't come, nor did he ring.

L'Alba lay at anchor off Rassone. The sky was still grey, but as the new paid hand, Bruno, came up on deck, he saw streaks of reddish gold behind the hills which ran in a long uneven ridge a few miles inland.

There'd been a message to say they were on their way and he knew exactly what had to be done. Nevertheless he looked anxiously at the lightening sky and muttered, 'Come on, come on,' under his breath. Then the dimmed lights of the van appeared at the top of a series of hairpin bends which led down to the cove.

Bruno lowered himself into the rubber punt and rowed towards the half-ruined jetty under the cliffs of Rassone. He knew better than to start the outboard. The van had cut its engine and it was cruising silently down the narrow road.

At the jetty, Bruno threw a rope and the older man caught it and made the punt secure.

'You're late,' Bruno said, but the Englishman barely nodded then muttered something to the younger one and they began to lower the first of their cargo gently into the dingy. It was almost fully light now and the risks were increasing enormously but there wasn't much Bruno could do about that.

The last of the canvas-wrapped objects were passed over to him and he jumped out to hold the dinghy as the others got in. The older one handed him a set of keys and a thick envelope.

'Your pay,' he said, in Italian, 'take the van back to Capulana.'

*

A *Guardia di Finanza* launch nudged its way around Rassone Head as Sergio's car reached the top of the road. He radioed instructions to the other cars and then had a quick look through his binoculars. Apart from the launch the sea appeared to be empty but, if he was right, Nardi would be protecting his investment somehow. He'd been told Nardi's boat had sailed from Capulana during the night but his colonel had refused to ask a second favour of the *Guardia di Finanza*.

'We can't send out an entire fleet, Captain,' he said, at his silkiest. Sergio knew that if he hadn't sorted out the murder at the villa his superior wouldn't even have requested the first favour. And even then he was reluctant.

So Nardi was untraceable unless the police were still watching him and the colonel was certainly not going to involve them. He wondered why Nardi had been released from house arrest. It wasn't necessarily because they wanted to give him enough rope. He could check with Enrico, but he doubted if a *commissario* would know why such a high level decision was made. And Nardi, Sergio reflected, had his tentacles everywhere. Over and over again he too had been deflected from going after the Mafia boss. A certain amount of it was bloody-mindedness on the part of the colonel, but not all. *Quis custodiet ipsos custodes?* Who shall guard the guards themselves? It was a question he often asked himself.

There was still no sign of another craft. His eyes turned back to the events on land. The Italian had jumped back into the dinghy and seemed to be trying to force the two Englishmen ashore. Something gleamed in a sudden ray of sunlight and the dinghy floated free. The paid hand made a futile attempt to start the outboard, then gave up and went for Langdon Smythe. The three men began to struggle.

By the time the *carabinieri* reached the cove one of the struggling men had jumped into the sea and was swimming away strongly. Sergio's *maresciallo* started shouting through a megaphone while another of his men stripped off his uniform and dived through the surf after the swimmer but the distance between them was too great and the *carabiniere* gave up after about fifty metres.

TUSCAN SHADOWS
285

When Sergio arrived at the jetty a few minutes later, Peter Kinaid was being dragged out of the water by a young *carabiniere* and Johnny Langdon Smythe, also soaking wet, was climbing up the steps of the jetty. He crouched beside Peter, whose jeans were covered with blood while Lavarini held them at gunpoint.

'Flesh wound,' the *carabiniere* said, laconically.

'And the other man?'

'Making for the far side of the cove. Tough bugger.'

Sergio could just see the dark head moving swiftly through the calm sea. The *Guardia di Finanza* launch had been requested to intercept *L'Alba* but the cove was too shallow for them to get in any closer to the man in the water.

'The dinghy?' Sergio asked.

'Bloody useless, must have slashed the airbags.'

Someone must be waiting to meet the Italian around the far point, expecting him to arrive with the dinghy and its precious cargo. Sergio sent a couple of his men to find a path around the rocks but he knew it was a waste of time. It was equally hopeless to send someone by car. If the swimmer made it, and it seemed likely he would, he would have been picked up by his friends before the *carabinieri* were halfway up the road, unless, of course, he'd been abandoned to his fate.

Johnny Langdon Smythe had taken off his jacket and put it under Peter's head. He'd been given a thick dressing which he was pressing against the younger man's thigh. His other hand was clasped tightly in Peter's.

'Needs a couple of stitches, that's all,' he whispered.

Peter gave a wan smile. 'Another couple of inches and I'd have been a boy soprano.'

Johnny raised his head. 'Peter jumped him,' he said in a shaky voice, 'saved my life. Didn't think he had it in him.'

'We'll look after him now. An ambulance is on the way,' Sergio said. He began the formalities of arrest.

Langdon Smythe wasn't listening. 'Bastard tried to kill us,' he said, angrily.

Sergio didn't bother to tell him they were lucky not to have been shot, the Italian must have been ordered not to use a gun.

286 *Maureen Donegan*

'So who was he working for?' he asked. 'Not you, evidently.'

'We thought. . . .' But Johnny stopped, no doubt more afraid of Nardi than of a prison cell. His statement, when he finally made it, in the *carabinieri* station in Rassone Scala, was quite specific. In return for the promise of possible leniency, he named a man called Pulcini and the delivery place as Ventotene, one of the islands in the Ponza group, west of Naples. Sergio knew Pulcini, he was relatively small fry, but Langdon Smythe was mistaken if he thought he was safe from him. He didn't operate on the same scale as Nardi but he, too, would have contacts in the prisons to deal with informers.

And the artefacts, sitting at the bottom of the sandy cove, were retrievable; Sergio supposed it was better than nothing.

'He must be working,' Maria-Grazia said, before she went to bed.

'Perhaps,' Rose said, dispiritedly.

She waited until midnight then went to bed herself and spent a restless night trying to hold on to what Sergio had said about his job interfering with his personal life, how his wife had hated it. I mustn't be like her, she told herself, over and over. He would surely get in touch in the morning. But as it started to get light she began to think of worse things than neglect. Something had happened to him, he could be in danger, injured even, or worse.

'He will ring,' Maria-Grazia said, over breakfast. But he did not.

At midday she rang the station in Capulana and was told that Captain Tavazzi was not available nor, the same anonymous voice said, could he tell her when it would be possible to speak to him.

The paperwork took most of the morning. Sergio had intended to ring Rose as soon as he was back in Capulana but when he got there he was called in to report personally to the colonel, who was for once in high good humour.

'You're going to Ventotene yourself, of course?' he said.

Sergio told him that Naples had been notified and he didn't think it was necessary.

'Better to tie up all the ends ourselves,' the colonel said blandly, 'draw in the net.'

TUSCAN SHADOWS 287

Sergio refrained from saying that one big fish had avoided the net completely and that he, personally, was shit sick of the whole business.

When he finally managed to ring Rose, Maria-Grazia told him she was in the annexe.

Sergio was trying to remember when he had last slept. 'Never mind,' he shouted. 'Just tell her I'm on the *autostrada* and I'll ring again. Ask her to meet me in Naples. We'll go on to Capri as soon as. . . .' A heavy lorry tried to change lanes in front of him and he swore under his breath. 'No tell her to go straight there. The Albergo Rosalina. Can you remember that?'

'*Si, si, ma quando?*' Maria-Grazie asked.

'Tell her to wait there. I'll join her as soon as I can.'

'Rosalina, Rosalina,' Maria-Grazia muttered to herself then, as Giulio came in, ordered him to write it down.

It was the blind assumption that she was ready to throw a toothbrush in a bag and jump on the next train and ferry that infuriated her.

'He's arrogant,' she said to Maria-Grazia.

The older woman shook her head. 'No, he's lonely.'

'But I'm not. . . .' A summer girl, was what she wanted to say, another Melina, but she knew it wasn't as simple as that. She was terrified that passion might not be enough and, if she followed him around like a gypsy, he would always be somehow just out of reach.

Her ticket was valid for a few more weeks but if she delayed her departure and it didn't work out well, going back would be even more painful than facing it now. There would also be lonely, frightening nights when he was away doing God knows what kind of dangerous things. It had come to her that she'd finally been cured of wanting to live with uncertainty and the edge of anxiety. In any case, how would she live?

'I could teach English in Capulana,' she said, out loud. Like Arthur, Sergio would feel easier if she had a proper job.

'*Si, si,*' Maria-Grazia said, eagerly, 'and then would come the babies.'

'Ten at least,' Rose said, drily.

Maria-Grazia laughed. 'Not ten, I think, but two or three.'

They talked, back and forth for hours, Maria-Grazia urging her have

288   *Maureen Donegan*

courage while Rose spelled out all the common-sense reasons why she should leave before it was too late. Giulio sat in his usual place in the corner of the kitchen and listened with a miserable expression on his face.

'Sergio loves you,' Maria-Grazia burst out, at one point, 'I know he does.'

Rose sighed. 'Perhaps.' Part of her knew she was playing the devil's advocate and that her logical arguments made the Italian couple's pleas seem without substance. But what did they really know about her, about her history? If she tried to explain she, too, would find herself in a welter of emotion.

In the end there seemed to be more reasons to go than to stay. But only just, she thought, sadly. Nor would she be going back to Arthur, although there were ends to tie up there.

She sighed and stood up. 'I'm going to pack,' she said and the image of their baffled faces went with her as she walked across to the annexe.

The next day she said a tearful farewell to Maria-Grazia. They hugged each other, then she hugged Giulio even though he was taking her to the station. Before she got into the car she clasped Maria-Grazia tightly again.

'I'll ring you,' she said, her face against the older woman's wet cheek.

Giulio seemed as upset as she was on the short journey. When they got to Capulana Scala, he told her gruffly to go into the station while he parked and brought in her luggage. She got out of the car and went slowly to the ticket window and hesitated in front of it, still unable to trust herself to speak.

'*Dica,*' the clerk said, irritated.

Giulio came up behind her, burdened with bags and her painting equipment. 'It's going in five minutes,' he said urgently, 'and you have to cross to the other side.'

Rose found her voice and pushed some money at the clerk. 'Does . . . does . . . the Rome train go on to Naples?' she asked, and then turned back to Giulio, 'I'm sorry, I've . . . look, could you take all this stuff back? I think I'll just bring the small case. For now.'